Lena Diaz was born in Kentucky and has also lived in California, Louisiana and Florida, where she now resides with her husband and two children. Before becoming a romantic suspense author, she was a computer programmer. A Romance Writers of America Golden Heart® Award finalist, she has also won the prestigious Daphne du Maurier Award for Excellence in Mystery/Suspense. To get the latest news about Lena, please visit her website, www.lenadiaz.com

Cindi Myers is the author of more than fifty novels. When she's not plotting new romance story lines, she enjoys skiing, gardening, cooking, crafting and daydreaming. A lover of small-town life, she lives with her husband and two spoiled dogs in the Colorado mountains.

Also by Lena Diaz

Cowboy Under Fire
Agent Under Siege
Killer Conspiracy
Deadly Double-Cross
Smoky Mountains Ranger
Smokies Special Agent
Conflicting Evidence
Undercover Rebel
Mountain Witness
Secret Stalker

Also by Cindi Myers

Disappearance at Dakota Ridge
Investigation in Black Canyon
Mountain of Evidence
Mountain Investigation
Presumed Deadly
Ice Cold Killer
Snowbound Suspicion
Cold Conspiracy
Snowblind Justice
Saved by the Sheriff

MURDER ON PRESCOTT MOUNTAIN

LENA DIAZ

CONSPIRACY IN THE ROCKIES

CINDI MYERS

MILLS & BOON

First Published in Great Britain 2022
by Mills & Boon, an imprint of HarperCollins*Publishers* Ltd
1 London Bridge Street, London, SE1 9GF

www.harpercollins.co.uk

HarperCollins*Publishers*
1st Floor, Watermarque Building,
Ringsend Road, Dublin 4, Ireland

ISBN: 978-0-263-30325-4

0122

MIX
Paper from
responsible sources
FSC™ C007454

This book is produced from independently certified FSC™ paper to ensure responsible forest management.

For more information visit: www.harpercollins.co.uk/green

Printed and Bound in Spain using 100% Renewable electricity at CPI Black Print, Barcelona

MURDER ON PRESCOTT MOUNTAIN

LENA DIAZ

This book, and series, is dedicated to the professionals who work tirelessly to solve cold cases and provide victims' families with the answers they need and the justice they deserve.

Chapter One

Grayson Prescott had been spoiling for a fight for over seven years. Tonight, he was going to get one. At least if his rusty instincts were right and the man he'd glimpsed moments earlier, skulking after a woman toward this back alley, had evil on his mind.

Not that it took much of an instinct to arrive at that conclusion.

The man was dressed in dark clothing, from the baseball cap obscuring his hair and face to the jeans and bulky hip-length jacket on a muggy night that didn't call for one. Even his dark-colored shoes helped him blend in with the shadows cast by the buildings one block back from Gatlinburg's tourist mecca, River Road.

But the most worrisome thing was that his right hand was buried deep in his pocket, possibly clutching a weapon as he slowly closed the distance between him and the oblivious woman engrossed in whatever was on her phone's screen.

Stop texting and pay attention to what's around you.

Hadn't she noticed the faded flyers still clinging to some of the community boards around town touting the four-year-old cold case, the unsolved disappearance of Erin Speck? The single mom had left her kids with her niece and went out for groceries, never to be seen again.

Equally alarming, nightly news reports warned of a potential serial rapist working this area.

He clutched his hands into fists, belatedly wishing he'd brought a gun on yet another of his useless pilgrimages downtown. It was only by chance that he'd finished another pointless meeting and had been heading toward his car when the suspicious-acting man had darted between two buildings where a woman had just gone.

Grayson had been concerned enough to follow. Once in the alley, he realized his fears were right. The man was definitely shadowing the petite curvy woman in a short skirt and high heels, probably no more than ten feet behind her. Unfortunately, Grayson was a good fifty feet behind both of them, struggling to catch up without making any noise.

If he'd been closer, he would have shouted a warning to the potential victim. But knowing human nature, he'd only startle her, make her pause, turn around. That would be all her pursuer needed to close the remaining gap between them. And Grayson would arrive seconds too late to save her from whatever mayhem was planned. Too risky. All he could do was work to close the distance as quickly and as quietly as possible. And pray.

If he even remembered how.

The woman's purse, carelessly slung over one shoulder, bounced and swayed along with her long brown hair like a beacon for the man following her. Wasn't she concerned about her safety? Maybe she was a tourist who hadn't heard about Speck's disappearance or the handful of unsolved rapes in the area. Or maybe she was a local, someone who knew Gatlinburg so well they'd grown complacent, thinking themselves immune to the dangers in their own backyard.

She must not realize the brutal lesson Grayson had

learned long ago, that the potential for evil lurked around every corner. One door accidentally left unlocked, one moment of inattention could become a death sentence. Life was so fragile, a precarious, precious gift. It could end in a second, dooming the surviving loved ones to a life of devastation, a void that could never be filled.

He clenched his fists again. He was much closer now, almost close enough to actually *do* something. *Almost.* And their ragtag trio was about to pass through a particularly dark section of the street, where most of the lights over the service doors at the backs of the businesses were burned out, or no one had bothered to turn them on in the first place. It was the perfect spot for an ambush. And from the way the other man was tensing, angling his body like a predator ready to strike, he agreed.

The woman hesitated, wobbling on her high heels as if finally sensing the danger. Grayson shouted and took off running, the need for stealth gone as the other man lunged toward his prey.

A shout echoed through the alley. Long hair twirled as the woman dodged to the side, narrowly avoiding the deadly arc of her attacker's arm. Weak moonlight glinted off metal as he raised the knife again.

Grayson made a desperate leap, arms outstretched. The woman shouted again, clawing at her purse as she fell back against the nearest building. Grayson's arms closed around the man's waist, jerking him to the side as his knife slashed toward the woman.

Hot fiery pain seared Grayson's arm, but he held on tight. The two of them fell to the ground in a flurry of flailing limbs and guttural yells. Metal flashed again. The knife bit into his other arm. Grayson swore and grabbed the man's wrist, giving it a vicious twist.

A sickening crack was followed by an agonized

scream. Metal clanged and scraped as the knife skittered across the pavement.

Shouts of alarm sounded down the alley, along with the rhythmic pounding of shoes on pavement.

"Freeze, don't move. Police!" a feminine voice shouted close behind Grayson.

He jerked around in surprise. The woman he'd been trying to protect was now holding a pistol, both hands wrapped around the grip, her no-longer wobbling legs spread in a fighter's stance. A good twenty yards behind her, two uniformed policemen were running toward her. Behind them, a heavyset man in a business suit struggled to keep up. All three were pointing guns.

White-hot pain slammed into Grayson's jaw. He stumbled back, his head cracking against the side of the building. Nausea roiled in his stomach. His vision blurred. Shoving to his feet, he whirled around to face the threat he'd foolishly ignored.

No one was there.

Or at least no one he could see since the whole world was rolling and pitching around him. Staggering, he shook his head, desperately trying to clear his vision and locate his attacker.

"Freeze," the woman yelled again.

The alley came into focus. He spotted the other man in the shadows, oddly hunched and cradling one arm. He was running away. He flew around the corner and was gone.

"Go, go, go," the woman yelled. "I've got this."

Grayson turned around, his world tilting and pitching again. He drew a steadying breath, shaking his head in disgust. He couldn't believe how many mistakes he'd just made, allowing himself to get distracted, letting the bad guy get away. Apparently, it wasn't just his instincts that were rusty. If his old team could see him now, they'd be ashamed of him.

The two uniformed policemen raced past him, presumably to catch the woman's attacker.

"Police," she yelled again. "On the ground. Hands and legs outstretched."

Was she talking to him? He glanced at her in surprise, fighting the urge to retch. Slamming his head against the building had done a number on him. His pulse rushed in his ears, a blooming headache throbbing with every beat of his heart.

Pathetic, Soldier. Inexcusable.

"On the ground," she said again, her pistol aimed squarely at his chest.

He stared at her in disbelief. "You're kidding me. I was trying to help—"

"Do it. Now." Her knuckles whitened around the grip of her gun.

The man in the business suit finally reached them, his lungs bellowing with his labored breaths as he too aimed a pistol at Grayson with deadly intent. "Get down, like the lady said, arms and legs out to the side, dirtbag," he rasped.

Grayson gritted his teeth and lowered himself to the ground.

Chapter Two

Detective Willow McCray adjusted her uncomfortably short skirt, then leaned against the wall, half inside the curtained doorway to the emergency room enclosure. Inside, a female nurse was stitching up the three-inch gash on the suspect's left forearm.

Willow itched to ask him questions, the most pressing being the name of his coconspirator. But other than a heaving sigh after proclaiming his innocence earlier, he'd gone silent. The pained look he'd sent her as she'd put him in handcuffs had somehow triggered a flash of guilt. Which was ridiculous, of course. She was just doing her job, while he and the man he'd been with had been stalking her, trying to make her their victim.

Hopefully, once the suspect was at the station in an interrogation room, Detective Wagner would get a full confession from him. Willow would have loved to conduct the interview herself, or at least sit in. But she wasn't even officially assigned to the serial rapist case. As a relatively new detective, she was a glorified gopher, doing whatever the other detectives needed until she was deemed worthy enough to take a lead role. The only reason she was involved tonight was because Wagner had put out the call for volunteers, half a dozen police women to act as bait on River Road.

"He's still not talking?"

She straightened, surprised to see her boss pushing back the curtain to join her in the opening. "Sergeant Jeffries. I didn't expect to see you at the hospital."

He arched a salt-and-pepper brow. "You made a collar in the River Road Rapist case and you didn't think I'd bother to show up?"

Her face heated. "I thought you'd wait until we brought him in." She motioned toward the two uniformed officers lounging against the nurses' station counter, waiting to take custody of their suspect.

Jeffries shoved his hands in his pants pockets and rocked back on his heels. Across the room, her prisoner spoke in low tones, answering whatever questions the nurse was asking. Both of his wrists were handcuffed to the bedrails so he couldn't hurt her. The nurse must have finished stitching the first cut because she moved to the other side of the bed to begin working on the gash on his right biceps.

Jeffries stiffened beside her. "*That's* the man you arrested?"

His incredulous tone put her on alert. "Is that a problem?"

"I thought you arrested the River Road Rapist."

"One of them, yes. Apparently, they're working in tandem together. The other one got away. But we've got uniforms canvassing the area, searching for his partner."

"His partner," he scoffed, motioning for her to move with him into the hallway. Then he faced her, hands on his hips. "Don't you realize who that guy is?" He kept his voice low so it wouldn't carry, but made no attempt to hide the censure in his tone.

Her face flamed hotter even though she had no idea what she'd done wrong, in his eyes at least. "I verified his name from his driver's license—Grayson Prescott. But I haven't been able to get any other information. He's exercising his right to remain silent. And since we arrived in the ER, they've been busy treating him. CT scan first because he bumped his head. Now the nurse is stitching his injuries."

"And how did he come by these…injuries?"

"He and his partner got in each other's way."

"Explain that statement, Detective McCray."

She cleared her throat, still not sure why he was upset. "They both tried to jump me at the same time and knocked into each other. Prescott hit his head against the side of the building. The other guy had his knife out and Prescott was cut when they both fell to the ground."

He stared at her a long moment. "Did it occur to you that maybe the other guy was trying to attack you, but *this* guy—" he jerked his thumb toward the enclosure "—was trying to help you? Maybe that's how he got hurt, jumping between you and the guy with a knife?"

She blinked, images of the scuffle in the alley flooding through her mind. "I, ah, I guess it's *possible*. Things happened so fast. I just—"

"Assumed he was a rapist too?"

She raised her chin, determined not to let him shake her confidence. She knew what she'd seen. He hadn't been there. "Sir, you didn't see what happened."

"And you did? Are you sure about that?"

She frowned. "Sir?"

He let out a slow deep breath. "I've no doubt you believe your version, that both men were trying to hurt you. But considering who the guy is that you've arrested, I'm inclined to think it might have been too dark, the attack too fast for your eyewitness account to be reliable. Especially—" he motioned again toward the room where her suspect was being treated "—since this man is Grayson Prescott."

He watched her, as if waiting for some kind of bell to ring, some spark of recognition. She looked at Prescott, who was silently watching both of them now. She scanned his admittedly handsome face, tanned golden from the sun, the sharp angles and hard lines softened by a barely-there beard and mustache. Even with the slight bruise forming along his jawline, he was uncommonly attractive. He was muscular, but not overly so. Trim, fit, average height, not quite six feet tall and wearing a navy blue suit that made him look more like a CEO than a criminal. But none of that mattered. She still had no idea what Jeffries expected her to notice.

"Figured out who he is yet?" Jeffries prodded.

She tore her gaze from Prescott and looked up at her boss. "Obviously, you recognize him and know more about him than I do. So far, I only know his name."

He sighed again as if disappointed in her.

I need this job. I need this job, she reminded herself as she struggled to maintain her respectful expression. Why was it that he always found fault with her? Was it because she was a woman? Or because she was the youngest to ever make the detective squad here in Gatlinburg and he was trying to prove she wasn't ready? Or did he resent her because his boss had made the decision to hire her against Jeffries's advice? Whatever the reason, it was no secret that he expected her to fail and found fault in nearly everything she did.

"Prescott is former Special Forces," he announced. "Army ranger. A decorated hero who didn't need to work for a living and yet he chose to risk his life doing one of the toughest jobs out there. Not exactly the poster boy for a typical criminal. You said you looked at his ID. Did you notice the address?"

A typical criminal? Was there really such a thing? How many people had her boss profiled over the years with his antiquated ways of approaching law enforcement?

She cleared her throat. "His address is local, if that's what you mean. I haven't looked it up on the internet to see exactly where, but based on the zip code, it's—"

"He lives on one of the highest peaks in the Smoky Mountain range, not far from Gatlinburg," he interrupted her again. "Unofficially, folks around here call it Prescott Mountain because his family owned the whole dang thing for generations. It's only recently that Grayson sold off a few parcels to other wealthy families. Like Mason Ford, the eccentric who runs that private investigation company he calls The Justice Seekers. He built his new house there. Prescott's just as nutty as Mason and his team. Maybe more so."

Somehow, she couldn't think of the man she'd arrested as *nutty*, whatever Jeffries meant by that. "I haven't heard of Prescott, but I've heard of Ford and his company. The local news did an in-depth story on them a while back. I thought they were well-respected, that they offered protection and investigative services to people in trouble who can't get justice through normal channels."

His eyes narrowed. "You sound as if you admire them."

"No, no," she hurried to assure him. "I'm not saying that. Just telling you what I saw on TV. I don't know anything about them besides what the reporter said. But the reason they did the story was because the Seekers were given some kind of award for saving the life of former

President Manning's daughter. That sounds admirable to me. Sir."

She struggled not to squirm beneath his scrutiny, already regretting the last part of her little speech. Hadn't she already learned not to poke the bear? Jeffries could, and frequently did, make her work life hell when provoked. But she couldn't keep her opinions bottled up 100 percent of the time, particularly when they were so often the exact opposite of his.

He crossed his arms, obviously not happy with her assessment. "The Justice Seekers are vigilantes, Detective McCray. There's no place for people like them in our justice system. They get in the way, make it more difficult for us to do our jobs."

"Yes, sir. Of course." She kept her tone carefully neutral. "Is Mr. Prescott one of them? A Justice Seeker?"

He stared at her, as if trying to decide whether she really agreed with him or whether she was trying to hide her true feelings.

She fought to keep her expression respectful. Jeffries wasn't one to abide by opinions that didn't support his own. He wasn't interested in alternate views or more modern ways of approaching investigations. She'd learned that the first week on the job when he'd listened to her enthusiastic ideas about steering the department toward relying more heavily on forensic techniques to help them solve cases. After he'd finished laughing, he told her she'd be much better served to focus on tried-and-true investigative tools, like fingerprints, fibers and, on rare occasions that warranted the cost, DNA. Everything else was pie in the sky, far too expensive to justify when a skilled investigator could solve a case without them.

She hadn't bothered to remind him about the growing

number of cold cases in their county and the surrounding ones, knowing that would only rile him up. From that day on, she'd been careful not to bring up any of her *pie-in-the-sky* ideas again. Instead, she was counting down until his retirement—eight months and three days from now. And she was praying that whoever replaced him would be more open-minded. She couldn't imagine anyone being worse.

Hoping to steer him back to the case, instead of his low opinion of her, she asked again, "Is Prescott a Justice Seeker?"

His neck puddled like an overfed pug as he shook his head no. "Did you not hear me say he was former Special Forces? That means he's a loner, used to working by himself. He wouldn't fit in with the team of Seekers working for Ford."

She didn't bother to correct his mistaken belief that Special Forces were lone wolves. They worked together as close-knit teams, something she knew about since her brother had been obsessed with becoming a navy SEAL when he was younger. He'd told her everything he'd researched about being in Special Forces, or at least being a SEAL. And he'd been beyond disappointed when he hadn't passed their rigorous training and was forced to choose a different path in the military.

Still, she couldn't let her boss's incorrect beliefs go *completely* unchallenged, not when they could directly impact this case. "*Maybe* Prescott isn't one to work on a team, but he *did* have a partner tonight."

To her surprise, his eyes brightened with amusement. "You're sticking with that theory, that he's tag-teaming with someone else? That he's a rapist?"

"I saw what I saw. Both he and the guy he was with tried to jump me."

"The man's swimming in money. Probably a billionaire, at the very least a millionaire. He owns a dozen highly successful companies. I swear his parents must have owned half of Tennessee. When they were killed in a car accident, their estate passed on to their two children. I imagine women jump at the chance to have sex with Grayson Prescott. He doesn't need to run on the backstreets, attacking anyone."

Eight months and three days, she reminded herself. And once again, she couldn't let his comments pass unchallenged, not when they were so blatantly offensive and completely wrong.

"Rape isn't about sex, sir. And being a rapist has everything to do with one's nature, not their wealth or status. Sexual assault is about violence and control. Maybe being wealthy gives Prescott a false sense of security, makes him think he's above the law and entitled to do anything he wants. He'd never expect the police to suspect him. Maybe that's the reason this case has dragged on so long. If his name came up in a tip in the investigation, it was probably tossed instead of being followed up."

He gave her an odd look. "I forget sometimes that you're new here."

She dug her nails into her palms. "I'm no rookie. I've been with Gatlinburg PD for six years. And I came to the team with a master's in criminology from FSU."

He chuckled.

Her nails dug deeper.

"I'm well aware of your résumé, McCray. But you only made detective a couple of months ago. And you were living in Florida when Grayson Prescott's family was in the news."

His announcement had her frowning. "The news? For what? Has he done something like this before?"

His teeth flashed in an amused grin. "You're quite the investigator. So many questions."

A chime sounded. He pulled his cell phone out of his pocket. After reading the text message on the screen, he typed his response. Once he put the phone away, he smiled again, his earlier annoyance seemingly evaporating after whatever information he'd just received.

"Detective McCray, I think this investigation might be better served if I don't say anything else about the suspect. After all, I wouldn't want to influence your opinions. I'll leave it to you to follow the leads and see what you conclude." He waved a hand in the air. "Fresh eyes and all that."

Since when had he ever cared about fresh eyes or not wanting to influence an investigation?

"I'd like you to take the lead with this particular suspect," he announced. "You can conduct the interview."

A kaleidoscope of butterflies seemed to take flight in her stomach. "You want me to be there when he's questioned?"

"Not just *be there*. Conduct the interview. You. Alone. Your first solo as a detective."

She stared at him in confusion. Either she'd lost her hearing or he'd lost his mind. This case was high profile, all over the media, the subject of daily status calls between the chief of police and the mayor. He couldn't really mean for his "rookie" detective to take the lead on the interrogation.

"Sir, isn't that Detective Wagner's call? I was only here tonight because he was recruiting female officers to act as decoys."

"I'm not saying I'm turning the whole shebang over to you, McCray. Wagner's still the lead investigator. But you're the one responsible for catching the suspect. You've earned this. Go ahead and find out what he has to say. Unless you don't want to question him?"

"No. I mean, yes. Of course, I want to question him. That is, if you're sure Wagner would be okay with it."

"You both work for me. I'll handle Wagner. As soon as Prescott's finished being treated, escort him to the station and take care of it. I'll expect a full report in the morning."

In the *morning*? Shouldn't he want the report *tonight* on a case this high profile?

Jeffries didn't wait for her response. He headed down the hall without a backward glance.

There had to be an angle here that she wasn't seeing, a reason that he wanted her to question Prescott. Was he punishing Wagner for some imagined slight? Did he want Wagner mad at her so Jeffries could use that as grounds to fire her? No, that didn't make sense. She was still in the probationary period for her job. He didn't even have to give a reason to let her go. He just had to explain it to *his* boss. Why then? What was he up to?

The nurse joined her in the hallway. "Detective, Mr. Prescott is ready. I'll get his discharge instructions for you."

"You have the CT Scan results on his head injury?"

"Just a really bad bump. Probably knocked him a little loopy for a bit. Understandable. But he's lucky. No concussion, no long-lasting effects aside from a bad headache. I gave him something for the pain, and he's just finished an antibiotic drip. As soon as I have the discharge papers, I'll take out the IV. Then he's all yours."

"Great, thank you."

"Yes, ma'am." She hurried past Willow to the nurses' station.

Willow motioned to the two uniformed officers, then headed into Prescott's room.

Chapter Three

Willow clutched her summarized copy of the case folder to her chest, outside the interview room where Grayson Prescott waited to be questioned. Being allowed to conduct this interview was monumental. It was what she'd been working toward for years. And she was having a hard time catching her breath, trying to hide her excitement. And her fears.

Fears that she wasn't good enough.

Fears that she'd make a mistake, that she'd somehow ruin the case.

She couldn't blame her nervousness, her doubts on her boss. Not really, even though he so often criticized her. No, the blame for her current state lay squarely with her. Because this, being a full-blown detective, was what she'd always wanted to do. She'd built it up in her mind until it had become her holy grail. And she was terrified that she wasn't worthy, that she'd do something that would destroy her life-long goals.

Even before her first day patrolling Gatlinburg's streets as a uniformed police officer, it had been her dream to become a detective. She'd wanted to solve puzzles, figure out mysteries, reunite loved ones or at least give survivors the closure that came from knowing what had happened. More than anything, she wanted to help families like those of Erin Speck.

The single mother had gone missing in broad daylight when Willow was still a patrol officer. She'd longed to work the investigation, but wasn't in a position to really do anything. Unfortunately, Erin Speck's case had gone cold long ago. But this new case—with women being beaten, some of them stabbed, all of them raped and in one instance killed—was active. It was happening right now. And Willow was finally able to do something to help, starting with her interview of one of the men she suspected of the crimes waiting in the room behind this door.

She grasped the knob, drew several more deep breaths, then pushed it open.

Prescott was still in handcuffs, attached by a length of chain to a metal loop in the center of the small table bolted to the floor. His dark gaze followed her as she pushed the door closed and then sat across from him.

She set the folder down and put her shaking hands in her lap. "Mr. Prescott, as you know, I'm Detective Willow McCray. I understand you've elected not to have a lawyer present. Is that true?"

He started to cross his arms but the chains pulled him up short. His brows formed a dark slash of annoyance as he rested his arms on the top of the table. "I prefer you call me Grayson."

"And I prefer you call me Detective McCray, Mr. Prescott."

He smiled. "Detective McCray, I'm aware of my rights. And no, I don't want a lawyer. Not yet. I want to know what's going on."

In a dark alley, diving at her, he'd been intimidating. Now he was even more so. Not physically, not really.

Those chains would keep him from hurting her if he was so inclined. What had her wanting to squirm in her seat like a child caught breaking some kind of rule was the force of his presence, his personality. He exuded confidence, power. Being the recipient of his laser-like focus was disconcerting, at best.

She tore her gaze from his and flipped through the folder as if searching for something. In reality, she was giving herself a few precious seconds to get her bearings again. Which had her wondering anew why Jeffries had suddenly done a one-eighty, trusting her to conduct this critically important interview.

Gatlinburg only had four detectives. In spite of its tourist population of well over a million in any given year, the permanent population barely topped four thousand. They didn't typically have enough major crimes to warrant keeping a larger staff of detectives. Getting a spot on the small elite team had only become possible because one of the senior detectives had retired. And her master's in criminology gave her the edge over the others who'd wanted this position—including Sergeant Mike Jeffries's own nephew, Brian Nelson.

Right place, right time—for her. But it hadn't exactly started her and the sergeant off on the right foot, since his boss made him hire her over Brian. She had to work twice as hard as everyone else to prove she was worthy. And that was exactly what she intended to do. She sat a little straighter, determined to work through her unwelcome case of nerves.

"For the recording," she motioned toward the camera hanging from one corner of the ceiling, "I'll advise you of your rights again." After reciting the Miranda warnings and adding the date and time, she said, "You've been arrested for assault. More charges will likely be levied, pending the outcome of this interview. We'll need a DNA sample, as well. If you refuse, we'll get a warrant."

He arched a brow. "Assault on whom? The guy who was trying to mug you?"

"Is that your defense? It was the other guy?"

"It *was* the other guy. I saw him following you and I was keeping an eye on him, catching up in case he tried anything, which he did. I didn't tackle *you*. I tackled *him*. Unfortunately, he was in the process of trying to stab you, so I can understand your confusion. Initially. But I'm quite certain your boss has informed you by now who I am, and that I'm the last person who'd hurt a woman. The assault charge is bogus. What other charges are you threatening me with? Why would you want my DNA?"

Without answering, she retrieved her carefully preselected pictures from the file, the ones that showed the most damage, the horrific trauma that had been wrought on each of the victims. One by one, she lined up the pictures taken of each woman when they were in the hospital. Bruises, cuts and haunted eyes stared back at the camera.

As she set each one down, she carefully studied his expression. His initial shock seemed to give way to empathy, then sorrow and anger as he took in the injuries inflicted on each woman. But as she placed the last picture down, the one taken in the morgue, his body stiffened and his head jerked up, as if everything had just snapped into place.

His jaw went rigid as he stared at her, his blue eyes the color of a violent storm. "I've seen her picture on TV. The River Road Rapist case? That's what this is about?" His voice was a deep rasp, dangerously soft. "You're accusing me of rape? And murder?"

"I am. Yes."

"You can't be serious."

"I wouldn't joke about something like that, Mr. Prescott."

His hands fisted on the table. A full minute passed as he seemed to struggle for control. When his gaze met hers again, the heat of anger had been replaced with the chill of contempt.

She forced herself to maintain eye contact when she really wanted to run from the room. Seeing that darkness peering out at her had goose bumps rising on her arms. Hopefully, he didn't notice.

"I saved you from being attacked in a back alley. I got punched, knocked silly and stabbed, twice. And you accuse me of this?" He swept a hand toward the pictures. When the chain rattled against the table, he swore beneath his breath.

"You didn't *save* me. I knew you were both following me, stalking me. My team warned me through the earpiece I was wearing. I was in that alley as a decoy. We had half a dozen female officers out tonight, trying to lure the man who's been attacking women for the past few months. What's the other guy's name?"

"Your team's timing sucked. You were almost killed." His voice vibrated with anger.

"I had to wait until the last minute to turn around. I had to make sure one or both of you was going to strike. Otherwise, we couldn't prove anything."

He shook his head in disgust. "You still can't prove anything. The man who attacked you got away."

"We'll find him. We locked the streets up tight when he took off. Half the force is going door-to-door."

"So a street criminal, who may or may not be the rapist you're after, is running free. And the man who was trying to help you sits in an interrogation room."

"What's his name?"

He frowned. "Who? The stranger I was trying to keep from killing you? Or the River Road Rapist? Either way, I can't help you, lady."

She pounced on his phrasing. "You say that as if you know the other guy isn't the rapist. Are you admitting *you're* the rapist? The guy on the run is, what, a mugger you stumbled across while trolling for your latest victim?"

He gave her a scathing glance but didn't answer.

She tried again. And again, using the information in the file, the pictures, asking the same questions in a dozen different ways. But he wouldn't break. He barely even spoke, except to occasionally swear or tell her again that he was only trying to protect her.

An hour into the interview, she was failing miserably. She had nothing to show for her efforts. She drew a deep breath, centering herself, trying to calm down. Then she started over from the beginning.

"Where were you when you supposedly saw the other man following me?"

"River Road. I told you that. I saw you cut between two buildings, then a moment later that guy followed you. He looked suspicious, so I went after him to see if he was up to something. My rusty instincts were right. He was definitely up to no good."

"Rusty instincts? Are you talking about your military career, in Special Forces?"

He sighed heavily.

"Why were you in town?" she tried, realizing she should have asked that from the start, instead of only covering the attack itself. "You live on Prescott Mountain, right?"

His gaze flitted back to hers. "I'm not a hermit. I do come down the mountain occasionally."

"It was late. Did you come to town for dinner? Don't you have a fancy chef in your mansion who could cook whatever you want?"

His brow arched. "Careful. Your class prejudices are showing."

Her face heated. "You don't have a cook? Or a mansion?"

"I didn't say that."

She smiled.

The side of his mouth crooked up reluctantly, seemingly acknowledging that she'd won that round. Then he straightened as if he'd suddenly come to some kind of realization. He watched her with that laser-like intensity again. "You're asking why I came to town tonight?"

"Yes."

"You really don't know?"

She frowned. "No. Why would I?"

"Wow." He shook his head, clearly bemused. "That explains a lot. I assumed, when I saw him at the hospital, that he'd told you everything. And I was baffled that he still allowed me to be brought here, and sent you to question me. I was curious what game he was playing, what game *you* were playing and what it had to do with me. Turns out, it's all about you. I'm just his pawn, for whatever reason."

"What are you talking about? You're not making sense."

"Only because he didn't tell you the truth. He sent you in here completely unprepared." He leaned toward her as far as the chains would allow. "Detective, in case you don't already know, your boss is an ass."

She hated that she was in complete agreement with a suspected rapist. "You know him, Sergeant Jeffries?"

He laughed without humor. "Know him? I've been meeting two or three times a year with him and the whole chain of command around here for seven years. You want to know why I was in town? Ask Jeffries. And while you're at it, get me a phone. I'm ready for my lawyer. We're done here."

She'd been about to demand that he explain what he meant about her boss, but the moment he said that hated word *lawyer* they really were done. The interview was over.

Her hands shook as she scooped the pictures back into the folder. "I'll get you that phone call. Give me a few minutes. Do you need to use the restroom or anything?"

He stared at her a long moment as if he wanted to say something else. But then he slowly shook his head. It was the pity in his gaze that nearly did her in. Her suspect knew more than she did about whatever was going on, about why Jeffries had sent her in here to interview him. Her boss had put her in an untenable position.

She calmly stepped from the room, shutting the door with a controlled click. After getting a uniformed officer to guard the door, she headed down the hallway toward her boss's office. The closer she got, the madder she became. As soon as she rounded the last corner and no one else was around, she took off running.

Chapter Four

Grayson let out a long slow breath and leaned back against the hard metal chair. He'd let his irritation and anger at this situation make him act like the ass he'd just accused Jeffries of being. He normally prided himself on treating people better, especially women. But after everything he'd gone through today—all for nothing, again—to have been arrested when trying to help someone had been the proverbial last straw.

And it had only gotten worse from there.

That ugly word—*rape*—had been thrown at him. After that, he'd been struggling not to shout and had barely managed that.

He was glad the detective left when she had. He'd needed the break to get himself under control, to remember what was important, his seven-year search for the truth. Being arrested was only a slight detour.

If he'd known upfront what they suspected him of, he could have put their suspicions to rest immediately. After all, he might technically live alone, but his *mansion*, as Detective McCray had called it, required a staff of people to keep it going. There were plenty who could vouch for his whereabouts on any given day.

Not to mention the security cameras around his property. After what had happened in the past, he'd been determined to make it safer for anyone working there, let alone him. All he'd have to do to prove he wasn't committing this series of attacks was pull the recordings. Proving where he was would be easy. But he'd been curious what kind of game the cops were playing.

He'd also hoped, foolishly so, to question McCray at some point and see if he could get more information from her about his seven-year quest, information the higher-ups weren't willing to share. But it hadn't taken long to realize how nervous she was and to begin wondering why Jeffries hadn't sent one of his seasoned veterans to question him. So he'd settled in to wait, more out of curiosity than anything else.

Now he just wanted out of here, to end this juvenile game, whatever it was.

An hour passed before a knock sounded on the door. As McCray stepped inside, her change in demeanor had him hesitating, instead of immediately demanding the promised phone call. Earlier, she'd been timid, unsure of herself. Now, her back was ramrod stiff, her movements confident, determined. She looked as if she were ready to do battle, or she'd just come from one.

She had a leather satchel with her, the kind people slung over their shoulders these days to replace the briefcases the older generations had used. She set it beside the chair, then sat with her hands clasped on the table, her shoulders rigid. "My apologies for keeping you waiting so long. But you'll be pleased to know that we're dropping all charges against you. And the DNA sample won't be necessary."

"Good to hear. I hope you'll explain why. When you walked out of here, you seemed far from convinced of my innocence."

"Yes, well, that was before I spoke to Jeffries. I've

confirmed you were here earlier tonight meeting with him and several others, including Police Chief Russo. The same meeting you have, as you mentioned, several times a year. I also found out that they all know quite a bit about you and are confident you're not involved in the spate of attacks in our town."

He leaned back in his chair. "Somehow, I doubt their opinions alone would be enough to sway you to drop the charges if you still believe I'm guilty. Unless you're not being given a choice?"

She crossed her arms on the table, leaning slightly forward. "Correct on both counts. I've been ordered to drop all charges. But I would have done so even without them telling me to, since I now know with absolute certainty that you were not involved in the other attacks and therefore were likely doing exactly what you claimed tonight, trying to help me because you thought I was in danger."

"I'm relieved you no longer think I'm a despicable rapist and murderer. But what exactly caused your change of heart?"

"Two things. The first being that we've caught the real perpetrator. Another female police officer decoy tonight was attacked. She's fine. Her backup was there immediately and they caught the guy. He's confessing like a nun to a priest, holding nothing back. We'll have to follow up with forensics, of course, but it looks promising that he's the River Road Rapist. And after hearing about your meetings here, I confirmed that one of them was during one of the rapes, providing you with an ironclad alibi. Since the same DNA has been found in all the attacks, obviously that rules you out."

"I'm so relieved," he said dryly, still aggravated that she'd suspected him in the first place.

She tapped her hands against the table. "We also

caught the guy who attacked me. As you suspected, he's a small-time criminal. He corroborated your story, had no clue who you were. And he's provided solid alibis for the other attacks. He couldn't have done them. He was in jail. So he's not part of some duo-rapist team."

"I get off by default. I feel so vindicated."

"Yes, well. For what it's worth, I *am* sorry that you were put through this."

"You said there were two things that changed your mind about me being involved. The first is that you found the real bad guy. What's the second?"

"Right and wrong, plain and simple. People in power shouldn't play with other people's lives."

He frowned. "I don't follow."

She flattened her palms on top of the table. "My boss knew, back in the emergency room, that we should have let you go. Not because of who you are, but because while he was speaking to me he got the text message about the rapist being caught. He *knew* you were innocent."

She looked up at the camera and spoke defiantly. "You never should have been put through any of this. Jeffries thought it was funny that I didn't know who you were. And since you were my first suspect interview, he let it go on when it never should have even begun. It's not right and I'm furious at him over this. Again, my sincere apologies."

He couldn't help admiring her courage in standing up to her boss if he happened to view the recording later. "Detective McCray—"

"Willow. We're way past the need for formalities now."

"I appreciate your outrage on my behalf, truly. But it's okay. I could have easily ended all of this at the hospital by calling my lawyer. You were right earlier, that I don't actually come to town all that often. It's likely my security footage at home can prove my whereabouts during most of the attacks. But, honestly, I wanted to see how this would play out too. Jeffries saw me, knew who I was. For him to not stop this, I knew something was up. First interview, huh? I'm guessing he thought I would be a good initiation for you, nothing to lose if you screwed it up since he knew I wasn't guilty."

Her face reddened. "Like you said. He's an ass."

He chuckled. "Well, don't worry about it. No big deal."

"It *is* a big deal. What Jeffries did to me is politics. It smarts, but I'll get over it. What he did to you was just wrong."

"Let it go. I'm not mad anymore." He rattled the chains on his wrists. "If you'll just—"

"Oh. Good grief. I should have taken those off immediately." She pulled the key out of her pocket and quickly unlocked the handcuffs.

He rubbed his wrists. "Thanks. That feels a whole lot better."

"I'm sure it does. Here, your keys and phone." She pulled them out of the satchel and handed them to him. "You'll need to sign for those, saying your property was returned. Just a sec." She retrieved a form from the satchel, along with a pen. "I'll be happy to drive you to your vehicle, wherever it's parked."

After signing the form, he stood, pocketing his phone and keys. "No need. It's a short walk from the station. I hope you can enjoy the rest of your evening. Good night."

She grabbed her satchel and intercepted him at the door. "Wait. Please." She glanced at the camera before continuing. "It will make me feel better about all this if you'll let me drive you to your car. A courtesy."

"Thanks, but it's really not far." He reached for the doorknob.

She put a hand on his arm. "Grayson." Her voice was

so low he could barely hear her. "Trust me. You *want* me to drive you to your car."

Puzzled by her insistence, he shrugged. It wasn't worth an argument. They didn't speak again until she pulled her aging Taurus into the parking lot off River Road where he'd parked his car to have dinner and then meet with the police.

"Thank you, Detective."

"Willow."

"Willow. Take care." He'd just slid behind the wheel of his car when the passenger door opened and the detective got in. He gave her a questioning look. "Was there something else? Another form to sign?"

Or was this something more personal? Was she hitting on him?

She glanced around the interior, hugging the satchel to her chest. "*Nice*. I've been in Audis before, but never a two-seater sports car like this. Bet it's a dream to drive with the top down, zooming along the mountain curves. What is it?"

So it was the car she liked, not him. Not that it mattered. Even as a long-time widower, he wore his wedding ring for a reason. He hadn't moved on, probably never would. But he could still admire a woman like her. On top of being intelligent, driven and unwilling to compromise her ethics, she was petite with long wavy hair that had him itching to run his hands through it. And those curves of hers were far more appealing than the starving skinny girls that were all the fashion in his usual social circles.

"Spyder, R8. Did you have more questions for me, about your case? It's been a long day. I'd like to go home."

Her knuckles whitened on the satchel. "Actually, I have some *answers* for you."

"Answers?"

She nodded. "I'm risking my job by doing this. But I figure you deserve it. And it gives me some juvenile satisfaction doing this behind Jeffries's back. I can let you look at what's in this satchel, but only as long as I'm with you. And you can never tell anyone about this or I'll be fired. I'm crossing a huge line by even sneaking this out. I have to be careful, make sure I bring it back exactly the way it was."

"What are you talking about?"

"Your meeting tonight, and other nights. At the police station. You said you go there several times a year. Jeffries explained it was so you could pump them for information on an old case." She unclipped the satchel and reached inside.

He stared at her, afraid to hope as she pulled out a thick three-ring binder.

"Like I said, my boss was a total jerk to you tonight. To me too, not that *that's* anything new. I figure he owes you a look at this." She turned it around and held it up.

The tab on the folder had one word: *Prescott.*

His gaze flew to hers, his throat so tight he could barely force out the words. "Is that what I think it is?"

"It's the official case file, the murder book, the one you've never been allowed to see. It contains the details about the investigation into the murder of your wife seven years ago, and the disappearance of your infant daughter."

Chapter Five

Willow stood at the floor-to-ceiling bank of windows in Grayson's home office, marveling at the maze of British-style gardens spreading out beneath extravagant landscape lighting. It was a bit formal for her tastes, but beautiful just the same.

The view through the windows on the other side of the office was equally stunning. A pool that seemed more like a natural pond curved around the side of the house. Lush green, perfectly trimmed grass gave way to blankets of blue-and-white flowers that flowed like water to the tree line.

It was too dark to see the mountains, but as high as they'd driven to get here, she could well imagine the entire Smoky Mountain chain spreading out around them. No doubt the view rivaled the three-hundred-and-sixty-degree views she'd witnessed on her hikes to Clingmans Dome in the Great Smoky Mountains National Park.

The home itself was massive. She couldn't begin to guess how many square feet were contained behind its honey-colored stone walls. Seeing it as he'd raced his black sports car up the last of the mountain road to park beneath the portico had taken her breath away. And yet, he'd jumped out of the car, leading her along without even seeming to notice the beauty all around him.

What must it be like to live in a place like this and not gasp in awe every time you came home? Then again, maybe he normally did. But tonight, he'd been consumed with the need to review the murder book. He'd been desperate to see the information that had been hidden from him all these years, hoping to glean new clues about the tragedy that had taken his family.

Even now, he sat behind his L-shaped mahogany desk in the middle of the room, poring over every page, every picture, greedily soaking in each detail. He'd been doing that for the past two hours, long enough for the staff in his house to quit knocking on the door, asking whether they needed anything. Long enough for them to head down the mountain to their own homes, leaving this one entombed in silence, broken only by the occasional turning of a page that Grayson was reading.

Willow glanced toward one of the doors in the front corner of the room. She knew it was a bathroom. She even knew where the kitchen was if she got hungry, thanks to Grayson's housekeeper. She doubted he even realized his staff had spoken to her and given her a limited tour of the downstairs.

At the time, she'd taken that tour to give him privacy, even though technically she shouldn't have left him alone with the case file. But now she really wanted to go home. It was close to three in the morning and she was having trouble keeping her eyes open.

Thankfully, she didn't have to work tomorrow—or technically today. It was Saturday and she wasn't on call. And even though she didn't have her Taurus with her, she could easily call a car service to come get her. But every time she considered making that call, she'd glance across the room at Grayson, and she knew she couldn't do that to him. He'd waited seven years for access to that file. She couldn't make him stop reading until he'd finished.

Realizing she'd already made her decision, she headed into the bathroom. Unsurprisingly, she found everything she needed. After taking a new toothbrush out of a package from one of the drawers, she brushed her teeth and took care of her other needs. She tidied up, then headed back into the office.

The garden windows beckoned to her, so she chose the seating area in front of them for a much-needed nap. She set her shoes aside, then laid down on a gorgeous tapestry couch that was as big as some beds she'd seen. She tucked a throw pillow under her head and grabbed a delicate embroidered blanket off the back of the couch. It seemed too pretty to actually use. But the air-conditioning was a little chilly and she chose comfort over guilt.

She glanced around one last time at the opulence surrounding her. It truly was beautiful, stunning. And this was only the office. Still, in the short time that she'd been here, she'd become certain of one thing. She wouldn't trade places with Grayson Prescott even if she could, not if it came with that raw pain twisting his face right now.

His eyes had taken on a haunted look moments after he'd sat down and began reading. Even now, there were times when he'd scan a report, or glimpse a photo, and his face would go pale beneath his tan. The agony in his expression was almost more than she could bear. What must it be like to be him? A husband and father, seeing those details? Reliving the horror his wife had suffered. Wondering every day what had happened to their baby girl. It was beyond her ability to comprehend.

She sent up a silent prayer of thanks that she was so blessed. Her tiny little apartment, her life of penny-pinching and being budget-conscious was fine by her.

Because what she had was far more valuable than all his wealth. She had a loving family—parents, sisters, brothers, countless cousins, nieces and nephews. Most of them lived one state over, near Lexington, Kentucky. She could only afford a red-eye every couple of months to visit them. But at least she *could* visit them. And she had the peace of knowing they were safe, happy and healthy.

It seemed that she'd only just closed her eyes when a bright light had her raising her arm to block it. Blinking, she realized that the bright light was the sun, its rays coming through the windows on the other side of the room. Good grief, she'd slept here all night. She pushed herself upright and glanced around. Wait, where was Grayson? He wasn't sitting at the desk anymore. And he wasn't reclining on one of the other couches either.

She jumped up and peered out a window with a view of the front portico. The driveway was empty. The Audi, gone.

Good grief, what had she done? She'd snuck the murder book out for an ongoing investigation and left it with the victims' husband and father. Then she'd fallen asleep. If Grayson went downtown to confront her boss, or the chief, about anything in the file, her career was over. She might even face prosecution for interfering with an investigation, or some other charge that Jeffries wanted to throw at her.

She whirled around and ran to the desk. Her satchel sat neatly on top. *Please be here, please be here*, she whispered over and over as she grabbed it. She flipped open the top, then started shaking. The satchel was empty.

The murder book was gone.

Chapter Six

Usually, when Grayson came here, he brought a bucket of cleaners, granite polish, wipes. And flowers, fresh-cut flowers. For Maura, he always brought the hybrid-peach roses she'd grafted herself in the greenhouse he'd had built for her and still maintained to this day. But his last visit had been only yesterday. So there was no need to clean, to polish the granite to a dull shine. And the roses in the vase attached to the square of granite on the wall were still fresh. Besides that, he'd taken a long drive first to clear his head before stopping here on the way back to the house. He didn't have any supplies with him, even if he'd needed them.

He didn't start with Maura's tomb. He always saved his visit with her for last. It was tradition. Instead, he walked down the rows of granite squares with bronze plaques that announced the names, birth dates and when each of the Prescotts had taken their last breath in this earthly realm. He ran his fingers across the raised letters and paid homage to each of his ancestors, including his parents. They'd died ten years ago, together, in a car crash. He sometimes missed his mother. He never missed his father.

Three years after his parents had passed, the world

as he knew it ended. Maura was gone, along with their baby girl, Katrina.

Sometimes he wondered if there was something wrong with him, because he *hadn't* died of a broken heart after his wife was killed. How was it possible for him to function without her and without their little girl? He must not have loved them enough. And yet, he couldn't imagine loving them more. They'd been everything to him, filling the holes in his heart that his strict, distant parents had never filled. And he was still trying to figure out how to pick up the pieces of his broken life.

What had kept him going all these years were two things.

One: The hope that his little girl had been kidnapped, that she was out there somewhere, alive. He hoped she'd been placed with a loving family, desperate to adopt a child. Good people who didn't realize she'd been stolen. They would cherish her and give her a wonderful life.

And two: That the police really were doing everything they could to solve Maura's death and Katrina's disappearance. He'd been assured so many times that they were following up on every lead, reinterviewing, always seeking new clues that they firmly believed would one day result in them solving the case.

But that was a lie.

Everything they'd told him was a lie.

He paused at the granite square without any flowers, the one with the name Katrina Prescott. And a birth date. The death date was blank, an unknown. But he now knew that was wrong. He flattened his palms against the cool stone and pressed his forehead against it, closing his eyes as he remembered one of the reports he'd read in the murder book, a report written by a forensics expert involved in the investigation.

The pool of blood beneath Maura Prescott is a mixture of her blood, and that of her daughter, Katrina. Given the volume contributed by the daughter, and her age of three months, it's this expert's opinion that the infant was likely killed and the body discarded elsewhere for an unknown reason.

Grayson tightened his hands into fists. His daughter was dead, had been all this time. The police had hidden that detail from him, given him false hope.

And he had no idea why.

He drew a ragged breath and kissed his daughter's name. "I'll get you some flowers, little one. I've left your vase empty all these years. But now that I know you're in heaven, in your mother's arms, I'll bring you fresh flowers too." He pressed his palm against the polished surface, then moved to the next square, the one with peach roses stuffed to overflowing in the bronze vase.

His fingers trembled as he brushed them across his wife's name, then the ridiculously short span of time between the two dates beneath her name. Underneath that was a picture behind glass, the one her father had taken on their wedding day. He smiled, as he always did, at the look of rebellion in her eyes. Her father hadn't recognized that look, or understood it. But Grayson had.

She'd hated that her parents were so traditional, that they wouldn't let her get a tattoo or dye her hair. She'd argued that everyone in her family had the same straight black hair and brown eyes. Grayson had loved her long black hair, the beautiful slant to those mischievous brown eyes. But he'd also understood her longing to express herself.

On their honeymoon in Greece, he'd taken her to a salon where she'd had her long dark hair bleached blond and chopped off at the shoulders. And she'd gotten a butterfly tattoo on her shoulder, saying it was symbolic of her metamorphosis.

But when she'd seen her parents again, months later, her acts of rebellion weren't nearly as sweet as she'd hoped. Her mother liked her hair. Her father hated the tattoo but said it was her choice, that she was a grown woman now, a wife.

A few months later, she'd dyed her hair black again. She kept the tattoo. Every now and then, she'd chop off her hair and dye it blond, as if to relive her youthful rebellion. He never knew what color or length it would be whenever he came home from a tour of duty. The picture of her on his desk was taken during one of her blond phases. She'd given him that rebellious look he loved so much, standing at the airport in a sexy red dress before he boarded his plane for another overseas assignment. A month later, he'd received the terrible news and had flown home to bury her.

His smile faded as he traced the death date above the picture. He knew she'd been shot, that she'd bled out in the foyer. But he'd never seen the coroner's report before. The police had told him the details had to be kept secret so they could use the information to corroborate the killer's confession once they caught him.

That had always rankled, knowing they knew more about his family, and what had happened to them, than he did. He'd felt it was his right to know. That it was his duty to understand what Maura had endured in her final moments. That he should take on that burden, share the moments of her death as they'd shared their lives. Now that he had, the wound deep inside his heart was fresh all over again. It was as if they'd both died only yesterday.

He splayed his hand across her picture. Tears he didn't

even know he was still capable of shedding spilled down his face.

"I didn't know," he whispered. "My God, I'm so sorry that you went through that. I should have been there, should have protected you better. I didn't know."

Great racking sobs shook him as he slid to the floor. "I'm so sorry," he whispered, his breaths ragged. "So sorry."

When his tears finally stopped, he raised his head and wiped his face. The grief he'd been living with for so long no longer churned inside him. It had transformed into a cold knot of fury against those who'd been lying to him, those who'd withheld the truth.

Those who'd said they were investigating when they weren't.

There was plenty of information in the murder book that first year after the attack. But the only entries in the six years since then were notes about his meetings with the investigators. Nothing else had been added. No new clues. No new interviews. Nothing was being done to find his wife's, *and his daughter's*, murderer.

Nothing.

He shoved to his feet and tugged his suit jacket into place. He knew what he had to do now, or at least where to start. No one was going to stand between him and the answers he needed, not this time. And he sure as hell wasn't waiting another seven years to get those answers.

Chapter Seven

Willow was a stress-cleaner. That's what her mom called it. If she was stressed, she cleaned. Right now, her little one-bedroom apartment was the cleanest it had ever been. After hiring a car service to pick her up at Grayson's estate and take her to her car this morning, her first stop had been at a store to grab fresh cleaning supplies. She'd been cleaning ever since.

Then she'd turned her attention to the second-floor landing outside both her front door and her neighbor's. Still desperate for something to occupy her mind, she'd turned to organizing her closets. But with only two in the whole place, one of them being a minuscule entryway closet, that hadn't kept her busy for long—especially when she tended to be organized anyway.

She headed into the main living area and checked the time on her phone. Three o'clock in the afternoon. Half her Saturday was gone and she still hadn't heard from Grayson, even though she'd left him a note with her phone number and address, asking him to return the murder book. She hadn't heard from her boss either, so maybe that was a sign that Grayson hadn't ratted her out and she still had a job.

Maybe.

Groaning in frustration, she plopped down on her

couch and stared at her phone. This was ridiculous. She was a detective. She should be able to figure out Grayson's phone number. Unfortunately, it was unlisted. And it wasn't like she was part of an ongoing investigation where she could justify a subpoena to get it from the phone company.

His number was written in the interview notes from the River Road Rapist case. She sorely regretted not having copied it down. But she hadn't had a reason to at the time. Heading to the office to look at the case file would only raise suspicions, especially since she was off work this weekend.

It was going to be hard enough Monday morning to sneak the Prescott family murder book into the archival room. Then again, that was only a concern if she actually *got* the book back from Grayson. And he hadn't done something crazy, like call Sergeant Jeffries.

She raked her hands through her long hair, shoving it back from her face. All her life she'd been a rule-follower, not a rule-breaker. Rules existed for a reason. And those who broke them could pay a heavy price. If she came out of this with her career intact, she'd never do something like this again, that was for sure.

A knock on her door made her jump in surprise. Great. Let the weekend-pizza-and-hot-wing deliveries begin. College-boy down the hall was certainly consistent. Unfortunately, the delivery guys were just as consistent in mixing up their addresses. Their apartment numbers were the same, but one was followed by the letter *A* and one by a *B*. Why was that such a difficult concept to grasp?

She flipped the deadbolt and yanked open the door. "Apartment B is around the—" She gasped in surprise. Grayson Prescott stood in the opening, holding the answer to her prayers—the three-ring binder she'd pilfered from work.

She snatched the binder and held it in an iron-tight grip against her chest, just in case he tried to take it back. "Do you realize how terrified I've been all day after waking to find you, and this, gone?"

He leaned against the door frame, looking like a gorgeous Greek God instead of the jerk who'd nearly gotten her fired. Or maybe he *had* and she just hadn't gotten the call yet.

"My apologies," he said, not sounding all that sorry. "I should have followed your example and left a note."

"You shouldn't have stolen the murder book in the first place."

He arched a brow. "Like you did?"

She tightened her arms around the binder. "I *borrowed* it. For you."

"And I appreciate it."

"You have a funny way of showing it. Did you call Jeffries? Or Chief Russo? Please tell me you haven't gone to the police station to talk to them about anything you read."

"Not yet. But I will, after I leave here. I'm going to— Oof!"

She grabbed his arm and yanked him inside, then slammed the door shut behind him.

He stared at her, wide-eyed. "What was that about?"

She slammed the binder on top of the coffee table and put her hands on her hips. "You're trying to get me fired."

"No. I'm trying to find out, once and for all, what happened to my family."

"If that means saying anything about what's in that book—" she jabbed a finger toward it "—then, yes, you *are* trying to get me fired. What part of *you can never tell anyone about this* did you not understand last night?"

His frown turned thunderous. "What did you think I'd do after I read it? Ignore everything I found out? They've been lying to me for years."

She stared at him in surprise. "What do you mean they've been lying to you?"

It was his turn to look surprised. "You didn't read it?"

"That's a joke, right? You read it and it took hours. I literally had it in my possession for a total of thirty minutes yesterday before handing it to you. I skimmed just enough to know what the crime was. Period. When would I have read the whole thing?"

He let out an exasperated breath. "I guess I assumed you knew about the investigation. You're a Gatlinburg detective, after all."

"*Pfft*. Tell that to the people I work with. I'm pretty sure they think I'm a gopher. I'm still in training and they haven't deemed me worthy of being assigned to a case. I'm not even sure they realize I'm supposed to be one of them, instead of a glorified assistant." She headed around the peninsula that separated the living area from the kitchen. "You want a bottled water? Cleaning makes me thirsty."

"I, um, sure." He glanced around. "This place is spotless. What do you need to clean?"

She handed him a water bottle and moved past him to plop on the couch. "I already finished the cleaning. That's why I'm thirsty." She twisted off the cap on her bottle. "Twice," she grumbled before taking a deep sip.

He gave her an odd look as if he doubted her sanity. Then he glanced around, clearly trying to figure out where to sit.

She patted the cushion beside her. "Unless you want

to sit on the floor, you're sitting on the couch. There's no room for another chair in this place."

"Where do you eat?"

She pointed to the rack of TV trays to the left of the front door.

"Oh." He gingerly sat as if he thought the couch would break if he weren't careful.

"Not exactly Prescott manor, is it?"

"It's…nice. Cozy. And really clean."

She rolled her eyes. "It's cheap. That was my primary requirement when I rented it." She set her bottle of water on the coffee table and turned on the cushion to face him. "Explain your earlier statement about the police lying to you."

He set his untouched bottle of water down and braced his palms on his knees. "For one thing, I've been told for years that the case is still active."

"It is. They haven't moved it to cold-case status."

"They might as well. The only work they ever do is put notes in the folder whenever I have a status meeting with them. In the meantime, they tell me they're always looking at it and trying to generate new leads."

"Okay, well, that doesn't sound very good."

"No. It doesn't."

"You said for *one* thing. Was there something else?"

His Adam's apple bobbed in his throat. "My baby girl, Katrina. They told me she was probably kidnapped. The first few months, I kept expecting ransom calls, but none ever came. After that, they said maybe she was put on the black market, sold." His throat worked again. "So I clung to the hope that someone had taken her in, a family desperate for a child, through an illegal adoption."

Willow's stomach dropped at the mention of the black market. She'd seen enough in her short career, and during her college courses, to know that was far more likely to lead to something awful instead of a loving adoption. But she wasn't going to say that to a grieving father.

"That could be good," she managed, careful to keep her tone neutral. "She could be really happy somewhere, with a wonderful family."

He shot her an angry look, but it didn't seem directed at her. It seemed more…inward.

"She wasn't adopted," he said. "There was a report in the file, talking about blood found at the scene. I'd always been told there was no blood in my daughter's room, that her room seemed untouched. The assumption was that my wife was holding her when she answered the door. But I was specifically told no blood was found that matched my daughter. That report says the opposite, that so much of her blood was in the foyer she couldn't have survived."

Willow grimaced. "I'm sorry. But, seriously, take that with a grain of salt. I've seen enough blood spatter reports to know that, sadly, the conclusions aren't always accurate. Just do a quick internet search on issues with blood spatter analysis, lack of standardization and error rates, and you'll see what I mean. It's becoming the newest forensics controversy, like when the FBI admitted bite mark analysis was junk science."

"Really? I always thought the blood-stuff was unimpeachable. Like DNA."

"Don't get me started on DNA. It's not the holy grail people think it is. Again, search the internet for tertiary DNA transfer. Better yet, look specifically for Lukis Anderson. The guy was almost convicted of murder because paramedics treated him, then went to a murder scene after that and transferred Anderson's DNA to the scene. DNA has just as many potential problems as other scientific tools, maybe more. Trust me. Nothing is unimpeachable."

She motioned toward the murder book. "Show me the report about the blood."

He gave her a curious look, then pulled the coffee table toward them and opened the binder. After flipping about halfway through, he pointed to the relevant passage.

Willow read the details, cringing inside again when she thought about *him* reading it. When she looked up, he was carefully watching her, as if waiting for her to tell him he'd read it wrong. *Hoping* he'd read it wrong.

She closed the binder and cleared her throat. "Okay, I agree it looks bad. And I'm really sorry about all this. I thought I was doing the right thing when I gave you this binder. Now I know why they didn't want you to see it. A father should never read details like that."

He squeezed his eyes shut a moment before leaning back against the couch. "Maybe not. But it's my right to know. And now that I do, I can work through it, accept it. One day. But what I won't accept is that someone killed them and is still out there, unpunished, and no one is doing anything about it. I want justice. And I want to know *why*."

The pain in his voice had her instinctively putting her hand on top of his.

He pulled back his hand, just far enough so that she wasn't touching him.

Her face heated with embarrassment. "Sorry. Just trying to give comfort. I can tell you're hurting."

"Nothing personal. I'm not used to being touched. It's just…it's been a long time."

She blinked. "A long time since…anyone…touched you? At all? Not even a hug?"

He crossed his arms. "My only living relative is an older sister in Arizona and her family, whom I see once a year at Christmas. And I don't exactly walk around hugging strangers." He shoved to his feet. "Look, I wanted to return the binder. I'm going to demand an audience with the police chief but I'll try to keep your name out of it."

She jumped to her feet and ran to the door, pressing her back against it. "You'll *try* to keep my name out of it?"

He stopped in front of her. "If you get fired, I'll pay you, compensation for your loss."

"Seriously? Look around you. I'm obviously not in this job hoping to strike it rich and go on a spending spree. If I thought money would make me happy, I'd go into the private sector and start my own investigation company like a million other average Joes. But becoming a Gatlinburg police detective is a true accomplishment. I've worked my butt off to *earn* this, worked for years to rise through the ranks. I'm not ready to throw it all away." She searched his gaze. "What is it, exactly, that you expect from the police chief anyway? An apology?"

He shoved his hands in his pants pockets. "I don't want empty apologies. I want results."

"You've seen the results they can give you. You think complaining one more time will change things?"

His eyes darkened. "I'll push harder this time, demand details on what they're actively doing. Get them to move forward on the case. I gave them the benefit of the doubt before. I won't do that again. I'll bug them every day until they pay attention." He motioned toward the door. "Now, if you don't mind—"

"Wait. Please. Let's talk this through. There has to be another way. What you want is to solve your wife's murder and your daughter's alleged murder. Right? That's your goal?"

"And bring the killer to justice."

"Okay, okay. Then let's sit down and figure out the

best way to do it. Getting me fired isn't the solution. And, honestly, if you stir the pot, push the same people who've been working the case all along, I don't see how that's going to get different results. Like I said, there has to be another way."

"Don't you think I know that? I've hired people, a lot of them over the years, private investigators. No one's ever gotten any traction. All I know to do now is start over, go back to the source, the police. I'm going to put pressure on the mayor—"

"How would you do that?" she asked, alarmed.

"Media. I'll talk to the press, go national."

She winced. "Yeah, that'll generate leads. Hundreds, maybe thousands."

"And that's a bad thing? It's more than we have now."

"It's a very bad thing. You can pressure the mayor, get reporters involved. But if the same people ultimately work the case, you'll just end up with months, maybe years, of them following these so-called leads your media war produces. And odds are those won't create any real progress on your case. It will just send everyone around in circles, chasing down tips that are worthless and a waste of time."

He rested a palm against the wall beside her, crowding her. "You have a better suggestion?"

Her first instinct was to shove him back and tell him to stop trying to intimidate her. But when she saw the lost look in his eyes, the pain and frustration, and realized there were dried tear tracks on his face, it nearly broke her heart. This strong, courageous warrior had given his all for his country, only to come home to an empty house and have to bury his wife. He deserved better. Unfortunately, she was at a loss as to how to help him. Her first attempt had done more harm than good, and now her career was in jeopardy.

"You've read everything in the binder," she said. "I haven't. Let me read it and see what we're up against. I'll give you a call in the morning. Then we can brainstorm where to go from here."

She moved out of the way so he could leave, fervently hoping she'd gotten through to him and that he wouldn't go to her boss.

He stepped onto the landing, then looked back at her. "You've got one hour." He pulled the door shut with a loud click.

Chapter Eight

"Well, of course, Jeffries is the lead detective on the Prescott case," Willow grumbled as she flipped another page in the binder. "Could I get any luckier?" She quickly scanned the information in front of her, then turned to the next report.

Her back ached from sitting on her couch, hunched over the coffee table. But she couldn't afford the time to stretch and walk around. Her hour would be up far too soon, and she still hadn't had an epiphany about how to move forward on this case.

"An hour, wow. Thank you so much, Mr. Generous. There are like four hundred pages in this thing and it's not exactly easy reading." She swore a few unflattering things about Grayson, then immediately felt guilty. He'd been patient for years with absolutely nothing to show for it. Could she really blame him for being fed up, for wanting to go with the nuclear option?

"But is it too much to ask that I not be in the drop zone when you release the bomb?" She *really* didn't want to lose her job. She sighed and turned the page.

From what she'd gleaned so far, the crime itself was pretty basic. Young wife and daughter at home alone while the husband was on one of his army ranger missions out of the country. The staff that maintained the household had left for the weekend, which seemed to be the norm for the Prescotts. Willow remembered Grayson's housekeeper apologizing to her last night because she was leaving. She'd been worried that Willow might need something if she was still there on Saturday, which was why she'd given her that brief tour of the kitchen and the downstairs.

That same housekeeper, Mrs. Scott, was listed in the file as the first of the staff to arrive on that fateful Monday morning seven years ago. She'd found the front door standing open and Mrs. Prescott lying in a pool of drying blood in the foyer, clearly dead. The housekeeper hadn't even gone inside. She'd been too scared. Instead, she'd called 911 and sat in her locked car until police arrived.

They'd cleared the house, making sure no intruders were hiding anywhere. And at the housekeeper's urging, they'd searched for the Prescotts' three-month old baby girl, unsuccessfully.

And that was it. No suspects were listed. No witnesses. Maura Prescott had been shot twice—once in the chest, once in the head—and left to die. Or at least that's what was in the initial press release saved in the binder.

The coroner's report told another story.

Delicate, petite Maura had been brutally beaten and slashed several times with a knife. Even her blond hair had been hacked, with chunks of it found all over the foyer. Only then had she been shot, almost mercifully at that point. Willow wondered whether Grayson had already known about her suffering, the awful things done to her. Or had he discovered it because she'd foolishly given him the murder book?

She shook her head, adding that to her growing list of things to feel guilty about. Stupid decision. Stupid. She should have known there'd be things in the folder the police would keep from the family. It was standard operating procedure. Families didn't understand that. But police often held back details about crimes, especially ones like this.

They had to.

False confessions, unfortunately, weren't that uncommon. If an unbalanced person with a criminal record confessed to Maura's murder, the easiest way to determine if the confession warranted further investigation was whether the person knew intimate details that hadn't been released to the public. And in this case, it seemed more kindness than meanness to not have told the husband that his wife had suffered far more than just being shot.

Still, giving Grayson false hope that his daughter was alive seemed particularly cruel. Then again, Willow understood the reasoning after reading the report. It was one forensic expert's opinion that the daughter was dead. But there was a contradicting report, later in the file, that was inconclusive on that subject. Personally, Willow was betting the little girl had been killed. She knew the forensic expert who'd come to that conclusion, and he was one of the best around. The other so-called expert wasn't even in the field anymore. He'd retired not long after that opinion was written. But there really was no way to be sure.

She picked up her phone from the coffee table and checked the time. Her stomach dropped. Grayson would be here any minute and she'd only made it halfway through the binder. Even as familiar with cop-speak as she was, and able to quickly scan various forms for the sections she knew would have the most important information, she still needed another hour, maybe two, to get through all of it.

So many pieces of paper. So few that were actually

useful. Most of them were interview summaries, with the details behind each interview maintained in separate binders since they couldn't possibly all fit in this one. Family, friends, staff, neighbors—if people who lived over a mile away on the other side of Prescott Mountain could really be counted as neighbors. All had been questioned, multiple times. Not one of them had anything bad to say about the Prescotts, especially Maura. The twenty-eight-year-old wife and mother was adored by everyone who knew her.

So what had actually happened? What did it all say when taken as a whole?

A beautiful young woman had been assaulted and murdered in her own home, her daughter allegedly killed—either on purpose or by accident. No known enemies. No signs of breaking and entering, which led police to believe she either knew her attacker or had opened the door because he didn't seem threatening.

So who was he? Who would a woman living in an isolated house with a baby girl to protect open her door to?

A cop. That was the very first thing to pop into Willow's head. The idea that she could know and work with someone capable of such a crime sent a chill down her spine. But that was one theory that Jeffries had meticulously worked on this case. Everyone in law enforcement, from Gatlinburg PD to the park rangers in the nearby Smoky Mountains National Park had been interviewed, and alibis checked. Even his nephew, Brian, who was still in the police academy at the time, had to provide an alibi, which was solid since he was with his uncle, Sergeant Jeffries during the attack. Willow would have been questioned too, if she'd been working for Gatlinburg PD back then. But that was her last year in college and she'd been living in Tallahassee attending Florida State University.

Jeffries's conclusion? It wasn't a cop.

Of course, it could have been someone posing as one. There was no way to rule it out.

What else? A delivery person? How many people would question opening their door to someone in a well-known type of delivery vehicle, as long as they were wearing a uniform? Uniforms were easy to come by, or to fake. And with online shopping so popular these days, having packages delivered to someone's home was commonplace.

Once again, she couldn't fault Jeffries on that angle. He'd performed due diligence to rule it in or out. He'd reviewed credit-card receipts to prove some orders had been made. But when he followed up, none of them had been delivered on the day of the murder. Of course, as with the cop-as-the-killer theory, it was difficult to prove a negative. Even though they couldn't prove a real delivery driver had come to the house, they couldn't prove someone posing as one hadn't been there.

The odd thing was that there was no robbery. As remote as the home was, someone could have loaded up a huge truck with valuables and taken hours to do so, and no one would have noticed. But the staff, and Grayson after he flew back home, verified that nothing was taken. No jewelry, no credit cards or cash from the victim's purse upstairs, no priceless works of art or knickknacks scattered throughout the home. So what did that leave as the perpetrator's goal?

Murder.

Then again, maybe not.

If the killer had gone there to rob the place, he might have thought no one was home. But when his quick knock on the door was actually answered, he panicked and killed the mother and the child she was holding. After the murder, he could have been too scared and shaken to go through with the original plan and ran away. Willow could see that happening, especially if the killer was young and didn't have a mile-long rap sheet behind him yet. Plausible. Possible. But basically irrelevant since it didn't help solve the case.

Chimes sounded on her phone. It was the alarm she'd set. Time was up.

She sighed and pocketed her phone. Might as well meet Grayson outside. It would give her a chance to walk around and work out the kinks in her shoulders and back.

Leaving the murder book where it was, she grabbed her keys and headed out the door.

It didn't surprise her that the second she reached the bottom step, he pulled up in that gorgeous Audi. She'd pegged him as a type-A personality, just like her. Being punctual was important to her and she generally admired the trait in others. But this one time, she would have preferred he be late, maybe a couple of hours late.

He cut the engine and got out, a living breathing poster for a Matrix movie in his black suit, crisp white shirt and dark shades. Or maybe the devastatingly handsome, much younger brother of Tommy Lee Jones in the *Men in Black* movies. Too bad he was emotionally unavailable and wanted to get her fired.

After rounding the car, he leaned back against the hood. He tugged his shades down just enough to peer at her over the top. "Since you don't look thrilled to see me, I'm guessing you weren't able to come up with a brilliant plan to light a fire under the investigation."

She cocked her head. "You're saying women are usually thrilled to see you?"

His mouth quirked. "Touché. How about it? Any ideas?"

She crossed her arms. “I need more time. Giving me only an hour isn’t fair.”

“Do you honestly think more time would make a difference?”

“It might.”

“I said *honestly.*”

She huffed. “Maybe not. I don’t know. But I’d kind of like to try before you destroy my livelihood just because I was foolish enough to want to help you in the first place.”

“Ouch.”

“If the Louis Vuitton fits.”

He sighed heavily, then checked his watch. She couldn’t remember the last time she’d seen someone even wear a watch, especially a fancy one that looked to have a compass and no telling what else. Maybe it went along with his millionaire, or billionaire, image. Or maybe he just preferred a quick glance at his wrist instead of having to dig a phone out of his pocket. She could see the merit in that. It didn’t mean she’d take to wearing one though.

“Are you hungry?” he asked. “I haven’t eaten all day and my stomach’s burning a hole through my back.”

She gave him a suspicious look. “Why do you ask?”

He looked at her over the top of his shades again. “I prefer to destroy careers on a full stomach.”

“Well, if you put it that way, it sounds so appealing.”

He laughed, then sobered, seemingly surprised—which had Willow feeling sad. Did he laugh so infrequently it shocked him?

“Let’s have dinner,” he said. “Somewhere private so we can talk. I don’t want to hurt you, Willow. But I’m not letting this drop. Let’s talk it through, see if we can come up with a compromise.”

“Compromise? That sounds good. I like compromise.”

He rounded to the passenger side of the car, opened the door and waited.

"My purse is in my apartment—"

"You don't need it. Dinner's on me."

"Well, okay." She hurried to the car, smiling up at him as she slid onto the cushy leather seat. "Make it somewhere expensive then. I love lobster."

"I know just the place."

Chapter Nine

"I absolutely can*not* go in there."

The panic in Willow's voice had Grayson glancing at her as he parked in front of the restaurant. "You wanted lobster. You can't get better lobster anywhere else in Gatlinburg."

Her eyes, which he'd only just realized were a sea green, went wide with panic as she surveyed the parking lot. "The cheapest car I see is a Hummer. They probably wouldn't even let me park my Taurus on the road out front. Good grief, look at that woman's jewelry. I need sunglasses to keep all those diamonds from blinding me." She vigorously shook her head. "No way. I can't go in there. I'm wearing jeans and a blouse. They'll think I'm the help and shoo me through the back door into the kitchen."

"No one will care. It's okay."

"You can't make me get out of this car."

"You sure about that?"

She gave him a droll look and pulled up the leg of her jeans to reveal an ankle holster. "Positive."

He rolled his eyes as she smoothed her pant leg back into place.

"Let's go somewhere else," she said.

"I thought you wanted expensive."

"I was totally teasing. Good grief, Nob Hill Seafood and Steaks? Even the name sounds pretentious. I've never even heard of this place and I've lived here for six years."

"You win. We'll go somewhere else. Anything particular in mind?"

She frowned and gave him the once-over.

He glanced down, wondering if he had a spot on his tie or something equally egregious. "What?"

"Do you even *own* a pair of jeans? Never mind. Just take us into town, somewhere full of tacky tourists. Someplace so loud no one can hear anything we talk about at our table."

"As the lady wishes."

Twenty minutes later, they were tucked into a back corner booth in a seafood place just off the main drag. As requested, it was hopping with tourists. Reruns of sports games played on TVs hanging from nearly every available spot on the ceiling that wasn't already covered by an animal head. With the clinking of dishes, loud conversations and laughter, and equally loud music pumping out of the speakers, he could understand why there was closed-captioning running along the bottom of each television. There was certainly no way anyone would be able to hear them.

After the waitress took their orders, Willow gave him the once-over again, frowning.

"What now?" he asked.

"Can you lose the jacket?"

"You're embarrassed that I'm *over*dressed?"

"Pretty much. Yeah."

Shaking his head in exasperation, he took off his jacket and set it on the bench beside him. "Do I meet your low standards now?"

"Not quite. Ditch the noose."

"Oh, for the love of..." He shook his head. "Fine. Whatever. I'll take off the tie." He loosened it and yanked it over his head and tossed it on top of his jacket. "Quit stalling. We need to discuss our options."

She sighed and crossed her forearms on top of the table. "I wish I knew some options, other than the one you seem so fond of."

He leaned back, resting one arm across the top of the booth. "How much of it did you get through?"

"The binder? Half, maybe a little more than that. Actually, I did quickly *scan* through the whole thing first, before reading in more detail. I got a good feel for what's been done and I have to say, they spent a lot of time on this case. The first year anyway. There don't seem to be any leads left to follow."

"That's not what I wanted to hear."

She shrugged. "It's true. And believe me, I hate to say it. Because I'm no fan of my boss and he's the lead detective on this. But he was wickedly detailed, and that binder is just the summary. There are other binders with even more details to back it up." She glanced at him, then held up her hands. "Uh-uh. Don't look at me like that. You're assuming the other ones will have some magic key to solving this. I'm telling you, they won't. Everything is cross-referenced in the murder book we have. If there's a thread to pull, we'd find the end of it in the murder book itself."

Her eyes widened and she looked around, as if just realizing she'd said murder book out loud.

"Don't worry. You could scream in here and no one would hear you," he told her.

She scooted over in the booth until their thighs were touching. "I'm not taking any chances. We'll be able to keep our voices lower if we're closer."

He was glad the waitress arrived with their order just then, because the warmth of Willow's soft thigh pressed against his had temporarily robbed him of the ability to speak. He kept his expression carefully blank while she chatted with the waitress and asked for extra napkins and butter.

When they were alone once again, he watched her happily breaking the shell to get at the meat and realized it truly didn't faze her that they were sitting so close, that he could feel her body heat warming his, that her elbow occasionally brushed his side. For his part, it was almost all he could think about.

Until he glanced down at the gold ring on his left hand.

He stared at it a long moment, then reached across the table for the salt and used the movement to subtly scoot over just enough so they were no longer touching. When he caught Willow's questioning glance, he realized maybe he hadn't been as subtle as he'd hoped.

"Uh, did you want some? For your baked potato?" He raised the saltshaker.

She slowly shook her head, before turning her attention to her meal.

He let out a slow breath, and silently reminded himself why he was here. This unexpected attraction to the pretty detective was unwelcome, to say the least. He'd vowed to find Maura's killer years ago, and that had to be his priority. Not some fling that would only distract him from what really mattered.

Her warm hand pressed against his forearm. He forced himself not to pull away this time and simply arched a brow in question.

"Is something wrong?" she asked. "I mean, other than the obvious?"

He blinked. "The obvious?"

She motioned with her hand in the air. "The case. Is something else bothering you? You got quiet after the food arrived."

"No, just thinking. You know, about our options, or lack of them." He dug into his lobster, hoping that focusing on his meal would re-center him. He wasn't normally this easily distracted. But from the moment they'd sat beside each other on her tiny couch he'd been off-kilter. There was something so…refreshing about her, so honest, so…fun that he'd stormed out of her apartment for self-preservation.

He'd assumed once he'd put some distance between them that things would get back to normal. But the second he'd returned, he knew he was in trouble. Somehow he had to stay focused.

On Maura.

And Katrina.

"Ready to talk?" she asked, leaning in close.

"Yes," he said, perhaps a little too enthusiastically, judging by her wide eyes. He cleared his throat. "Let's discuss your impression of the case file. Are there questions I can answer for you?"

She nodded, took a deep sip of her sweet tea, then turned in the booth to face him. "Those interviews, there were a dozen or so people questioned who worked for you at your estate. Does that sound right? I have no idea how many people it takes to run a place like that."

"Too many. But twelve-ish sounds in the ballpark. The grounds alone require half a dozen gardeners. The housekeeper has a staff of four or five. Then there's the cook, who complains I don't use his services as much as I should. I think he's about ready to quit on me."

"Is he the same cook who was working there back then?"

"They're all the same people who worked for me back

then. At least the house staff is. The cook, or *chef* as he prefers to be called, has been there the longest, over thirty years. Mr. Baines, the head gardener, has been there almost as long. But I think the young people he uses for the physical labor come and go. Mainly college-aged kids earning extra money between semesters or while on summer break."

He idly traced a bead of water running down the side of his glass. "I've thought about selling, many times. It's a lot to keep up for one person. I offered it to my sister and her husband, but they don't want the place. Ashley prefers the climate in Arizona, the beauty of the desert. And she says the house reminds her too much of our parents."

She shot him a questioning glance. "Is that a bad thing?"

He considered her question. "Good and bad, I suppose. Our parents were…complicated. Life at home could be… difficult. They were extremely strict, old-school, formal." The way she was looking at him, he didn't think his vague references fooled her one bit. But instead of pressing for more information, she surprised him by smiling and flicking the collar of his dress shirt.

"And you're not? Formal?"

He scoffed. "Compared to them, no. I guess it's all relative." He cocked his head, studying her. "You and Ashley would get along great. She's the exact opposite of me." He motioned toward the boisterous tourists surrounding them. "She'd absolutely love a place like this."

She leaned in close. "Then there's hope for you yet. Maybe we can work some of that starch out of your collar before this is over."

"This?"

She motioned with her hands again. "You know. The investigation."

"Ah. Right. Somehow we keep getting off track. You

were asking about the interviews. Is there anything else that struck you?"

"Not really. I mean, it's all typical Jeffries, of course."

"Typical? In what way."

"Well, kind of like you and your sister, I'm guessing. You seem to approach life in different ways. My boss and I approach cases in different ways. Or at least if he'd let me work a case the way I want to. I'd definitely do it differently than him."

"How so?"

"It's just, well, he likes to do things the tried-and-true way, kind of old-fashioned. Not that it's wrong or anything. He's into solid gumshoe work, pounding the pavement, knock-and-talks—"

"Knock-and-talks?"

"Cop-speak. It's when you canvass a neighborhood, go door-to-door. You know, knock on the door and talk to whoever's there."

"Knock-and-talk. Got it."

She wiped her mouth with her napkin and shoved her plate back. "He's thorough. He really is, as far as interviews and fingerprints, stuff like that. It's just, well, I understand we have a limited budget and all, but if it were up to me, we'd do a lot more testing on any physical evidence in each case. Heck, I'd have the forensic team collect a lot more evidence than they currently do. I'd involve TBI more—"

"TBI. Tennessee Bureau of Investigation?"

"Right. State police. They've got a terrific lab, great scientists working for them. And they're not sloppy or stupid about how they handle the testing or interpret the DNA or blood spatter data. But it's expensive, really expensive. And they get backed up for months on testing. Sometimes you can go to trial without ever having your evidence tested because the lab couldn't get to it. That leads to plea deals and negotiations because the evidence is too weak without those lab results. You bluff and threaten without anything to back it up. It can be really frustrating."

"This happens a lot?"

"Well, yes. Like I said, it's about resources and budgets. You do what you can do with what you have. It's not just us. It's all of law enforcement, all over the country. Heck, probably all over the world. You have to make decisions about what to test, what evidence to collect. The realities are that those decisions often come down to what you can afford to process. I can't tell you how many rape test kits sit in evidence rooms, untested, for decades sometimes, because no obvious suspects have come to light in the investigation and the case isn't high profile or whatever. There just isn't enough money to test them all. Sad, but painfully true."

He stared at her incredulously. "That's terrible."

"I know, right? The sad thing is bad guys get off all the time because there's not enough money to throw everything you can at a case, forensically at least. But unless you've got bottomless pockets, I don't see how it can ever improve."

"Is that what was done in my wife's case? Evidence wasn't tested that should have been?"

Her hand froze with her tea glass halfway to her mouth. She slowly set it down and cleared her throat. "We've gotten off track. That's not what I was specifically talking about."

"Really? So if this were your investigation to run, as you see fit, you wouldn't have performed additional testing?"

A light blush stained her cheeks. "It's not my investigation."

"But if it were?"

"Look, I'm still a newbie, okay? Six years on the force, but only two months as a detective. And I already told you, they haven't actually assigned me any of my own cases. I've done knock-and-talks and I type interview notes, things like that. But in the end, my opinion isn't worth much."

"It is to me. Don't you get it? Everyone else I've spoken to downtown is more concerned about placating me and getting me to leave, rather than share any meaningful information." On impulse, he took her hand in his. She jumped as if startled, but he didn't let go.

"What do you want from me?" Her voice was so low he struggled to make out the words.

"The truth, Willow. I've been living in limbo for years, living with lies. Please, tell me the truth."

Chapter Ten

The silence grew between Grayson and Willow as he held her hand like a lifeline. He felt as if he were on a precipice, ready to fall, and this smart, bold, amusingly sassy woman was the only one who could save him.

He leaned in closer. “Please, Willow. Help me.”

She let out a ragged breath as she tugged her hand free. “I don’t know if I can.”

He squeezed his fingers against his palm, surprised at the twinge of loss that had passed through him when she pulled away. “Try. That’s all I ask.”

She sat there a long time, uncharacteristically serious and quiet as she stared at the tabletop. Finally, she said, “I honestly don’t know if it will make a difference. I truly don’t. But the only potential way of generating more leads that I can think of is if you can get Chief Russo to send everything, every piece of physical evidence that was collected in your family’s murder, to a lab for testing.”

“I saw something about DNA testing in the binder. One of the reports said that the killer didn’t leave any DNA at the scene.”

“No DNA *that the police found*. That doesn’t mean there wasn’t any.” She held up her hands as if to keep him from interrupting. “In most cases, it doesn’t make sense to test everything. Like when you already have a suspect, other corroborating evidence. But in your case, with no leads and nothing to go on, throwing everything you have at it is the only option. I’d like to see more testing done just in case there’s that one item with DNA on it that could break the case wide open.”

“Wide open? Really?”

“Well, a crack is more realistic. Even if DNA gives you a suspect, you still have to build a case, find out if they had motive, opportunity. But it could at least give you a starting point.”

“Which is more than I have now.”

“Exactly.”

“What evidence should be tested that wasn’t already?” he asked.

“I remember reading that there were some bloody, smeared fingerprints on the inside of the front door that were deemed not useful, meaning not enough detail to upload to AFIS.”

“AFIS?”

“Automated Fingerprint Identification System. It’s a nationwide database courtesy of the FBI. If there were good prints, with enough identifiers to upload to AFIS, then anytime potentially matching prints are found, either now or in the future, an alert would be sent to Gatlinburg PD.”

“What’s that matter if the prints that were found aren’t good enough to upload?”

“It doesn’t. But if this were my case, I’d send the prints to the FBI to examine. They’re the true experts in that field. Maybe they’d be able to identify more unique areas of the prints—whorls, arches, ridges, in specific sequences—that might make an upload possible.”

"You don't sound very hopeful."

She shrugged. "It's admittedly a long shot. No guarantees."

"You must have brought it up for a reason. You were talking about DNA when you mentioned the fingerprints."

"Right. I was kind of thinking out loud. It would have been great if those prints could have been swabbed for DNA testing. But it dawned on me that wouldn't work. Swabbing for DNA destroys fingerprints. Dusting for fingerprints degrades DNA." She sighed. "I wish they'd chosen the DNA route in this instance. But since they didn't, at least taking the prints to the FBI for further analysis is one more thing to try. Of course, that's only if we had access to test the evidence, which we don't."

He leaned back against the booth. "Then it probably *is* hopeless."

"I didn't say that. But I don't want to give you false hope, like Jeffries gave you, thinking Katrina might still be alive." She blinked. "I'm so sorry. I shouldn't have said it that way. She could be alive. She really could be. I sincerely mean that. It's just, well, being honest here, the odds aren't good."

"Willow, have you found something or not?"

She grew quiet as if gathering her thoughts, or deciding whether or not to say anything else. When she finally looked up at him, she had a determined look on her face. "Here's what I'd do, if I could do what I wanted. I noticed on the evidence logs that your wife's clothes were saturated with blood. Knowing now that she was cut, not just shot, those clothes should be tested again, more extensively. They should take swabs from every part of them to look for the killer's DNA."

He slowly nodded, understanding the logic of what

she was saying. "If the knife didn't have a substantial enough guard to stop his hand from sliding down the blade, it's highly *likely* he would have cut himself. The knives I carry on missions always have a guard for that very reason. My personal knife does too. I'm surprised the police didn't think about that."

"Your personal knife? You carry one with you?"

"Always."

"You didn't have one when I arrested you."

"Only because I'd just been at the police station. I didn't want to set off the metal detectors when I went inside. Normally, I do carry a knife."

"Okay, well, back to the DNA. The shirt was swabbed. But not extensively. It's a judgment call, a resource issue."

He shook his head in disgust. "Lack of resources is a poor excuse for not solving crimes."

"Agreed. But when you only have so much money to go around, you have to make tough choices. Do additional testing on a crime that seems solvable, or spend all your money on one that doesn't."

"Every case should get the same attention," he argued.

She held up her hands. "Just playing devil's advocate. I see these dilemmas every day at work. It's not fair to paint the police as the bad guys when they're doing the best they can with what they have."

"Then they need more resources."

"Yes. They do."

"What if I offer to pay for the testing?"

She shook her head. "That would open them up to lawsuits. Families who can't afford to supplement the police budget to help with their loved ones' cases would be disadvantaged. No police chief is going to touch that."

He swore. "So there's nothing I can do."

"That's not what I'm saying. If we can somehow steer

Jeffries toward realizing a specific test might yield him a suspect, he might argue for the budget for it. Like touch DNA, for example."

He shook his head. "I feel like we're going in circles. What's touch DNA?"

"It just means a really small amount of DNA can now be detected where we couldn't before. Like when you touch a piece of clothing and the oils on your skin are left behind. Touch DNA technology on that spot of fabric might yield a profile good enough to put in CODIS—"

"You're losing me with all this terminology. What's CODIS? Another FBI database?"

"Combined DNA Index System, and yes it's maintained by the FBI. It pairs DNA profiles with information on known violent offenders. It's searchable, like AFIS. My point is that if the person isn't in CODIS, or local DNA databases that don't link up with CODIS—"

"Isn't all law enforcement hooked up to the FBI databases?"

"Not even close to all. Big cities, sure. But there are thousands of small-town sheriff's offices or police stations that have only a handful of employees and little crime. It doesn't make sense to go all high-tech in their situations. Which means you could have collected prints but not get a match in the major databases, even though that person's prints are on file at some rural sheriff's office two counties over. I've heard of cases solved by homicide cops sending their fingerprint cards to fifty or more other jurisdictions to have them manually checked against their own systems."

"I'm starting to wonder how any crimes are ever solved."

"It's not as easy as crime shows make it look, that's

for sure. It's a lot of long hard hours. And you can only do what you have the budget to do."

"It all comes down to money again."

"And know-how. I'm not even sure TBI has the right people in their labs who can use the latest, greatest forensic techniques that science has to offer. The equipment alone is horrendously expensive. And the people have to be trained how to use it. The only reason I know about a lot of this stuff is because I'm a forensics nerd. I've studied all kinds of ways to solve crimes using the latest innovations. But most agencies, including Gatlinburg PD, can't afford to take advantage of them." She held her hands out in a helpless gesture. "I'm sorry, Grayson. I think we've hit a dead end."

He sat back, thinking about everything she'd said while she absently tapped at the ice cubes floating in her tea. She looked as defeated as he felt. It was unbelievably frustrating to think there might be some technology available to point to a suspect in his wife's and daughter's murders, but he was powerless to do anything about it, even though he had more money than he could possibly spend in ten lifetimes.

Wishing he'd ordered something stronger than tea, he turned to pick up his glass when a red newsbreak banner running along the bottom of one of the TVs caught his attention. It was an update on the River Road Rapist case. There'd been another attack late Friday night while he and Willow were reviewing his wife's murder book.

He caught Willow's attention and motioned to the broadcast. "I thought the police had the rapist in custody."

Her face drained of color. "No, no, no. That can't be. The guy confessed."

"One of those false confessions you mentioned earlier, maybe?"

She shoved her glass back, her expression a mixture of grief and anger. "I hate that someone else was hurt. Jeffries sounded so certain he had the right guy. Last I heard, they were waiting for his DNA results as confirmation. Maybe if they'd been able to get the tests done more quickly, they would have realized the real rapist was still on the streets. And they might have been able to do more to keep the public safe."

They sat silently as the waitress cleared their table, promising to return soon with the check.

"Grayson?"

"Hmm?"

"You mentioned earlier that you'd hired private investigators before but they came up empty-handed. Who did you hire?"

He laughed harshly. "Who did I not hire? I used six different companies. That's one of the reasons your chief and your boss are so sick of me. Each time I hire someone new, they start at the station, grill your boss with questions."

"Did any of them come up with anything at all that was useful?"

"No. Nothing. Not a single suspect has ever been identified, or even suggested."

"Maybe you need to hire different investigators."

"I wouldn't know where to begin. My track record isn't exactly stellar in that area."

"What about the Justice Seekers? They're a private company operating out of Gatlinburg. I'm not all that familiar with them but I know they do some types of investigations. Jeffries mentioned you might know the owner."

"Mason Ford. I sold him a parcel of land on Prescott Mountain to build his new home. I did speak to him once about working my wife's case. But he prefers to keep his team focused on helping the living, people who are victims themselves and in immediate danger. He provides bodyguard services and tries to figure out permanent solutions so they no longer have to live in fear—like a woman on the run from an abusive ex—cases where the law can't be proactive until after the crime occurs."

"He wouldn't make an exception to help you?"

He shrugged. "He probably would if he thought he could do any good. He doesn't feel that anyone on his team has the expertise to work something that cold with so little evidence to go on."

"That's a good point. I hadn't thought about it that way. You need someone with a proven track record working on cold cases. And, of course, you need access to all the collected evidence."

"What if I sue Gatlinburg PD for access?"

"I can't imagine you'd win. The police have every right not to turn over evidence. Testing can consume it, destroy it. If the defense team can't repeat the same tests, using their own experts, they can argue for the test results to be thrown out."

"What does it matter if we never even *get* to trial?"

She held up her hands. "I'm on your side. The problem is that you're a civilian. And civilians can't be responsible for evidence in an open investigation, cold or not." She frowned, idly tapping the table. "Civilian." Her expression turned guarded, but thoughtful. "I have an idea. It's pretty out there. I'm not even sure it's feasible. And it would cost a boatload of money."

"I'm not sure how much a boatload is, but money won't be a problem. What's your idea?"

She held up her fingers and ticked them off one by one as she spoke. "To solve a cold case, you need investigators experienced with cold cases. To have access to police evidence, you need someone active in law enforcement as a liaison. To get the evidence properly tested, using the latest techniques and eliminating the long wait times, you need a lab at your disposal." She grabbed his arm, excitement sparkling in her eyes. "Address those three things—cold-case experience, law enforcement access to evidence, private lab—and you've got everything in place to work your wife's case."

He stared at her. "Are you saying I should create my own company to solve cold cases, and partner with someone in law enforcement?"

"That's exactly what I'm suggesting. There'd have to be a contract between the company and the police. But if it's a partnership, with some kind of active law enforcement liaison who maintains the chain of custody on the evidence, it might work. And don't forget the lab. You'd probably need to fund your own, a private lab."

"Has that ever been done before? Do you think the police would go for that?"

"There are a handful of private cold-case companies in the country. But as far as I know, none of them have partnered with police the way I'm talking, where you'd get access to test all of the evidence and use your own lab."

"Why would they agree to it? You already said I can't just throw money their way for preferential testing."

"You wouldn't be giving anyone preference over anyone else. You'd have to agree the company would work on cold cases, *plural*, not just yours. They'd all be given the same treatment. I'm thinking you can limit the geographical area to the Eastern Tennessee region. That's thirty-three counties, but most of them are small without significant population centers, so it wouldn't be nearly as overwhelming as it sounds. As I said, every case would get the same attention, the same access to testing. It's a way to solve the resource issues without opening the departments up to lawsuits. The police get a better case-clearance rate. You get the best of the best trying to solve your wife's murder. Win-win."

"Yeah, well. Even if they'd agree to something like that, I don't know the first thing about cold cases. We both know my lousy track record of hiring the wrong investigators. I'd have to hire a consultant to get this right, to make sure I set up the company, and the lab, in a way that the police will agree to do business with me. I wouldn't have a clue who to hire to help me do that."

"Too bad I'm not in the market for a job," she teased.

He stared at her, considering.

Her eyes widened. "Don't look at me like that. I wasn't angling for a job offer."

"Why not? I could double, triple your current salary."

She blinked. "You don't even know how much I make."

"I've seen your apartment. You don't make much."

"Ouch."

He smiled. "Doesn't matter. Name your price. Like you said, I'd have no clue how to get something like this off the ground without you. I mean, sure, I know how to establish a business, hire the right human resources people, accountants, that sort of thing. I've got a dozen companies in my portfolio right now. But setting up a cold-case unit? I'm at a loss. I need you, Willow. What will it take to get you to work for me?"

"Pay off my student loans for starters." She chuckled.

"Done."

Her smile faded. "I was joking."

"I wasn't. I'll pay off your loans, triple your salary, and throw in a six-figure signing bonus. With standard benefits, of course, including a 401(k)."

She stared at him, her mouth open.

"The sooner you say yes, the sooner we can start working on our plans."

She grabbed her drink, then frowned when she realized it was empty. She grabbed his, and gulped down the last of it.

He smiled. "You seem a bit overwhelmed."

She clutched the edge of the table for a moment, then turned in her seat to face him. "I am. It's an amazing offer, truly. Mind boggling, even. But the answer is no."

Surprised, he waited for more. When she didn't explain, he prodded, "Because why?"

"Because… I already told you. I'm not in this job for the money. I'm in it to help people."

"You can help people in the private sector just as much as in the public sector. What do you have against making money?"

"Nothing. I'd love to not have to worry about bills, to have an apartment I can turn around in without bumping into a wall. But I don't want to throw away what I've been working for my entire adult life. Do you have any idea how hard it was to make detective? The last time Gatlinburg PD hired a new detective was fifteen years ago. Making the team was my holy grail. But I'm not done yet. I still need to prove I can cut it with the big boys."

"You said yourself they're not letting you run with any cases. You're a detective in name only."

"Wow. Thanks for that."

"Sorry. I didn't mean you aren't qualified, or that you aren't trying. Obviously you've won me over talking about how you'd approach my wife's case. What I meant was that you're not being allowed the opportunity to help people and prove yourself the way you want to. I can help with that. I can give you free rein, to be what you want to be, no one standing in your way. And before you say no, again, think about this. You said you're a forensics nerd, that you've been wanting your department to pursue new technologies. From everything you've told me, that will likely never happen."

Her mouth tightened. "Probably not."

"But if you help me, if you're in charge of all the detectives—"

"In charge? You want me to be the boss over your investigators?"

"Of course. This cold-case company is your idea. Your baby. I'll run the business part of it, all the stuff necessary to establish a corporation and make sure we're in compliance with tax laws and regulations. You'll be in charge of hiring decisions, establishing the team, setting policy for how to approach each case, how to choose what cases to work, whatever makes sense for an investigative unit."

"What about the lab?"

He shrugged. "We'll figure it out together. I can build a brand new one—"

"That would take too long. It would be better if you can partner with an existing one. Maybe fund a new wing, new techs. Make an agreement that your cases take top priority but they can use the new wing to supplement other cases when it's not being used for our cases. I mean, your cases."

"*Our cases* sounds better. What do you say?"

She still seemed hesitant. "It sounds like a dream. If you're serious about paying off my student loans—"

"I am."

"And the six-figure signing bonus?"

"I'll wire the funds to your account as soon as you give me your banking information."

She swallowed, her hands fisting in her lap. "If I quit my job, I'm burning a bridge with Gatlinburg PD. I'll never get a chance to be a detective again, not for them. Once your wife's case is solved—"

"I love the sound of that," he said wistfully.

She smiled. "I'd like nothing more for you. But I have to look out for myself, as well. After her killer is brought to justice, you have no incentive to keep the cold-case business going. It'll be hugely expensive, a drain on you financially. You could shut it down and I'd be unemployed with no prospects. It's not like I could go to another police department and start out as a detective. That's not how law enforcement works. You have to go through their academy, walk a beat, pay your dues and hope you eventually—years down the road—pass their detective's exam. After that, you still have to wait for a spot on the team to open up. Even then, you may get passed over and the position goes to someone else."

"Is that what's holding you back? Fear for the future?"

"That's a good way of putting it, yes. It's hard to turn down everything you've offered, especially because I'd get to mold a detective unit, establish it as cutting-edge, use the best technology science can offer. I'd be able to help far more people than I ever could in my current job. But if it's a temporary position, I have to say no."

"I see your point. And it's a valid one. I can't swear that I'll want to keep this new company going indefinitely. And it's not likely I could sell it to someone else who would. Few people can afford a cost center that doesn't produce revenue. Although I'd argue we could create a revenue stream eventually, by offering our services to civilians to solve their cases. But, regardless, I can offer you assurances, in writing. I can provide you with a golden parachute."

"A golden parachute? Like what CEOs get?"

"Exactly like what CEOs get. It's a clause I'd put in

your contract that ensures if you were ever fired—which of course would never happen—or if I dissolve the company, you'd be compensated financially so you can land on your feet. I'd make sure you have a generous enough severance that you can start your own private investigation firm, if that's what you want to do." He smiled. "And we haven't even talked about the best part."

"The best part?"

"If you agree to work for me, you'll no longer be working for Jeffries."

Her lips parted in a delighted smile. "You're right. That *is* the best part." She laughed and threw her arms around him, hugging him tight.

He froze, shocked to feel her soft curves pressed against him.

As if sensing his hesitation, she pulled back, but only slightly, her gaze searching his. "It's just a hug, Grayson. Nothing to feel guilty about. It's okay to hug me back. We're just two friends, celebrating."

He stared down into her sparkling emerald eyes, surprised she could read him so easily, that she knew he felt guilty even thinking about holding her. And yet, that's exactly what he wanted to do. He needed, *craved* the feel of her in his arms. And until this moment, he'd never even realized it.

Her smile turned sad. She loosened her hold.

No. He wrapped his arms around her and hauled her against his chest. She made a happy sigh and snuggled against him, her arms tightening once again. He let out a shuddering breath and rested his cheek on the top of her head. For the briefest of moments, he pushed away the concerns and worries, his conscience telling him this was wrong. Because it didn't feel wrong. It felt…wonderful. He closed his eyes, reveling in her warmth, breathing in the clean scent of her hair. And he allowed himself the fantasy of believing that he mattered to someone again, if only as a friend.

She was the one to end the hug and scoot back in the booth. It stunned him how empty he felt after she let go. He had to clench his fists to keep from reaching for her.

What the hell was wrong with him?

She smiled. “See, that wasn’t so bad, was it?”

He cleared his throat, twice, until he could trust his voice again. “Was that a yes, then? You’ll take the job?”

She chuckled. “That was definitely a yes.”

“Great. I’ll have the contract ready in a couple of days.” He forced a smile, uncertain what to do next. He knew what he *wanted* to do, pull her against him and hold her again. And that absolutely terrified him.

He desperately looked around for the waitress, but didn’t see her. “She should have brought the check by now.”

“I can go ask the hostess to find her.”

“No need.” He pitched an obscene amount of cash on the table, desperate to escape, to put his world back on its axis. “Let’s go.”

Chapter Eleven

Willow watched through her apartment's kitchen window as the black Audi sped out of the parking lot. Poor Grayson. She'd shaken him badly with that hug. When she'd pulled back, the look in his deep blue eyes had nearly broken her heart. He'd seemed so…lost, confused.

The conflict warring inside him was all too apparent in those stormy eyes. He'd wanted her—maybe sexually, maybe not. She wasn't sure. But he'd desperately wanted that human connection of holding and being held. Too bad he was drowning in guilt and couldn't free himself to live in the moment, to be happy.

She shook her head in wonder. What kind of love that must be, to not be able to move on after so many years. And what wouldn't she give to be loved like that one day? Her parents were probably the only couple she'd ever met who even came close to that kind of relationship. It melted her heart every time she saw them share a secret look across a roomful of people as if no one else were there. It had always made her smile and long for what they had.

But now, after seeing Grayson, and how much he was suffering, she wasn't so sure. She wouldn't want to be that miserable if the love of her life passed on before her. And she wouldn't want him unhappy, longing for her. She decided then and there that if she ever was lucky enough to fall in love and marry her soul mate, she'd customize her wedding vows. She'd make her groom promise not to pine for her. She'd make him swear that he'd try to find love again and not allow himself to feel guilty over it. After all, love was a gift, the kind that only flourished when it was shared.

"There you go, Willow," she chided herself. "Waxing poetic when you have a million things to do."

Like craft her resignation letter to turn in on Monday.

But first, there was something else she had to do, follow up on a hunch. It had been bothering her since noticing a faded picture on a bulletin board flyer at the restaurant. But she wasn't sure why. Now, little alarm bells were going off in her head as the puzzle pieces started clicking together. But she had to be sure.

She hurried into her bedroom for her laptop, then set it on the coffee table. As the ancient computer took its time booting up, she drummed her fingers impatiently. She really needed a new one. This one was barely limping along.

Once the screen finally flickered to life, it took another agonizing five minutes of searches to find a news website that actually had a picture of the woman who'd been attacked Friday night.

She was in her late twenties and small in stature. Her hair was long, brown and hung in waves halfway down her back. She appeared to have a mixture of Caucasian and possibly Korean ancestry. In the picture, she was well-dressed, the quality of her clothes clearly better than average. And the gold earrings she wore didn't look cheap by any stretch.

Willow pulled the piece of paper out of her pocket that she'd taken from the restaurant and smoothed it out on the coffee table. It was old, faded and wrinkled, but the picture was still good enough to make out the woman's features.

This couldn't be a coincidence.

She grabbed her phone and punched the speed dial for her boss.

He answered on the first ring. "What do you want, Mc-Cray?" He'd obviously recognized her number. "We're kind of busy here. There was another attack last night and the whole River Road Rapist team is here trying to figure out what we missed. 'Cause the guy who confessed obviously ain't the perp."

"I saw a news report about it. You've seen her picture, right?"

"I'm working the case. What do you think?" His tone dripped with sarcasm.

"Sorry, right. Of course, you have. Will you please bring up her picture on your monitor?"

"McCray—"

"Please. It's important."

He sighed heavily, but she could hear him tapping his computer keyboard. "Okay. It's up. Now what?"

"Split your screen and pull up another picture beside it. It's from an old missing person's case, the one where the single mother went missing."

"Erin Speck? From two or three years ago?"

"Four, actually. And, yes. That's the one."

"That's a cold case. I don't have time for that right now."

"It'll only take a minute."

"Like I have a minute to spare." He mumbled something about rookies, but once again he tapped away at the keyboard. "What's got you thinking about that old case anyway?" He tapped a few more keys.

"I was in a restaurant tonight and noticed one of the

old Speck flyers when I was heading to the ladies room. I'd just seen a news report about the latest attack and—"

"Holy crap."

"You have it? Both pictures?"

"In living color. Holy. Crap."

She tightened her hands on her phone. "You see what I see, then? It's not my imagination, right?"

"No, McCray. It's not your imagination. Erin Speck and last night's rape victim could be twins."

"Erin was an only child, and she wasn't adopted. So they definitely aren't. I know Wagner had already theorized the rapist has a specific physical type he goes after—mid-twenties, pretty, nice clothes, nice jewelry. And they all have long dark hair. But we all thought the rapes started six months ago."

"I'm not a newbie, McCray. I can connect the dots. But I don't like where they're leading."

"I know, I know. We thought we had a serial rapist on our hands, who went too far with one victim and killed her. If Speck is dead, which seems likely, and her case is linked—"

"Then our serial rapist is also a serial murderer," he said. "And he's been operating in our area a lot longer than we realized. Dang it. We're already up to our elbows in this. Going back four years to work a cold case isn't going to make it any easier. We don't have the resources for that."

"I know. I'm sorry."

"Don't be. McCray, I know I'm hard on you, probably harder than I should have been. But this, this is good work. I'm glad you called and told me."

She blinked. "Um, thank you, sir. I appreciate that."

"Enjoy the rest of your weekend off. It may be the last one you have for a while. Come Monday morning, I'm putting you to work on this case along with the rest of us. The training wheels are coming off. We need you." *Click.*

Willow slowly lowered the phone. Training wheels? *We need you?*

Her hand shook as she shoved her hair back over her shoulders. Had she misjudged Jeffries this whole time? Had he been giving her gopher duties as part of her training, trying to ease her into becoming a full-fledged detective? All along, she'd thought he was being petty, punishing her because his boss had forced him to hire her when he'd wanted to hire his nephew instead. Could she have been wrong?

Monday morning, he planned to assign her to a case—*the* case—the most important one they had. She was finally about to become a detective in reality, not just name, something she'd despaired of ever doing while working for Jeffries.

And she'd just promised Grayson Prescott that she would work for him, and quit her job with Gatlinburg PD.

What had she done?

Chapter Twelve

Willow took a long look in the restroom mirror, trying to get excited about returning to the Gatlinburg PD conference room down the hall for the supposedly final round of negotiations. If everything went as planned, she and Grayson would leave today with all of the contracts signed. *Unfinished Business*—cop slang for a cold case, and the chosen name for Grayson's new company—would finally take off.

But even though Willow's fancy new business suit and hair styled into a single braid that fell halfway down her back made her look professional and polished, the butterflies in her stomach told the real story.

She was terrified.

Terrified that she wasn't good enough. That she'd given up her job three months ago for nothing. That she would let Grayson down, that a year from now, two years from now, he'd still be living in limbo with no one brought to justice for the murder of his family.

She braced her hands on the granite countertop. Three months. Had it really only been three months ago that she and Grayson had come up with this outlandish plan to start a cold-case company? After that night at the restaurant, she'd somewhat reluctantly resigned from her job as a detective, which Jeffries seemed to take as a personal affront, saying she was quitting at the worst possible time. But she couldn't turn her back on Grayson. Jeffries had a team to help him. Grayson had no one.

Looking back, it had been the right decision. The link between the River Road rapes and the Speck case, though seemingly strong, had yielded nothing new in their search for the rapist and killer. Gatlinburg PD was getting nowhere with their investigation. But in that same time, she and Grayson had made tremendous strides toward the start of something special that would help so many hurting families.

If they could just get the contracts signed.

The men and women here today were the proxies with the final say-so about making the partnership agreement for the entire East Tennessee region. But instead of signing the contracts in front of them, they'd spent the last hour listening to the lowest ranking person in the room—Sergeant Jeffries.

He really knew how to hold a grudge.

He obviously couldn't stand that the lowly detective he'd once berated was now rubbing elbows with millionaires, a governor—courtesy of an introduction by Mason Ford—and higher-ups in TBI who wouldn't even take Jeffries's calls. No doubt, part of that resentment was also because she'd earn more in a year working for Grayson than Jeffries would in a handful of years in the public sector. And as a result, as an invited guest of the Gatlinburg police chief, her former boss was doing everything he could to sabotage Grayson's chance at justice for his family.

The alarm went off on her watch, which she'd taken to wearing at Grayson's suggestion. She had to admit, it looked great with her suit. And it seemed more professional to subtly glance at her wrist instead of hauling out her phone when she wanted to check the time. Right now, the alarm was telling her the break was over. Everyone would be heading back to the conference room. Which meant she couldn't hide in here any longer.

She drew a deep steadying breath, then headed for the squad room to get to the conference room on the far side. But as soon as she stepped into the squad room, she stopped. The sight of Brian Nelson, the nephew of Sergeant Jeffries, sitting at the desk that used to be hers shouldn't have bothered her. After all, she'd known he was her logical replacement since he'd scored the second highest on the detective's exam—right below her. But knowing it, and seeing it, were two different things.

Brian said something to the detective at the next desk, then noticed her standing by the doorway. He smiled and waved as if they were old friends. She waved back, pretending—like him—that they didn't despise each other. They'd never been friends. Not even close.

There'd certainly been an attraction, on his part, several years ago. And he'd been relentless in his pursuit of her, asking her out so many times she'd lost count. But even though he checked off all the boxes on paper, in person there was something about him that made her stomach churn with dread. Admitting to him that she wasn't physically attracted to him had stopped the date requests. But it hadn't been a good strategy for forging a successful working relationship on the rare occasions that their paths actually crossed.

And when they'd both gone up for the detective slot, and she was the one hired, his resentment of her had only gotten worse. Now, seeing that he'd taken her old job, she couldn't help feeling bothered by it. And a little icky, knowing he was touching the chair, the desk, sticking his hands inside drawers that had once been hers. She shivered and rubbed her hands up and down her arms.

"Ready to get this done?" Grayson stepped beside her from the hallway. "I think just about everyone's back from break. Are you ready?"

"I think so. But I'm not looking forward to it. Things have gotten pretty intense in there."

"Negotiations often are. Don't worry. They'll cave soon and sign on the dotted line."

"I hope you're right."

"Trust me."

"I do." She squeezed his hand, something that would have made him pull away in panic weeks ago. But now he simply squeezed back. Baby steps. He was slowly rejoining the land of the living, smiling more, growing comfortable around her. She'd given him hope. And she prayed that hope wouldn't die today at the hands of Jeffries, or someone else in the meeting determined to end the promise of Unfinished Business before it even started.

Half an hour later, in response to yet more questions from Willow's nemesis—Sergeant Jeffries—Grayson was reviewing the proposal again for the twenty-odd people stuffed into the conference room.

He fanned out the files on all of the investigative professionals who'd tentatively agreed to sign on as part of their new company, assuming the cold-case unit became a reality. He tapped them one by one, discussing their merits, trying to get the meeting back on track.

"Ladies and gentlemen, you and your respective agencies have been consulted and kept up to date on everything Ms. McCray and I've been doing to create Unfinished Business. We've shared our preliminary plans for the headquarters facility that will be built on Prescott Mountain. We've received verbal agreements with all thirty-three counties in Eastern Tennessee to partner with the new company."

He raised another folder. "This is a contract with one of the best private labs in Tennessee. I'm funding the creation of a new wing of equipment and professionals to focus on testing for cases being worked by Unfinished Business. But I'm in no way taking away from their ability to help other agencies. Instead, I'm adding to their capabilities by allowing them to use that new wing to augment their other work when they aren't conducting tests for us. It's a win-win, for everyone. So why are we still debating this? What's the real issue here?"

Willow leaned back in her chair, watching all eyes turn toward Jeffries again. Sure enough, he crossed his arms over his chest and gave Grayson a doubtful look.

"All of us met earlier today without you, a pre-meeting," Jeffries announced. "We wanted to see where we stand on this endeavor, see if we're in agreement. We realized the majority of us have the same concern. Namely, the involvement of Ms. McCray."

Willow stiffened, shocked that he'd let his dislike of her jeopardize something this important, something that would help the people in his own county.

Grayson's jaw tightened, a subtle signal that he was angry. But he did his best to cover it. "What exactly is the concern about her?"

"We're not confident in her ability to oversee your team of detectives when she has all of two months of experience as a detective herself. We think this cold-case unit would be doomed to failure if it's led by her."

Willow squeezed her hands together under the table. Jeffries had just vocalized the same fears she'd had herself on many occasions. But she knew her limitations, and because of that had researched extensively to find the right people to hire—people with far more experience than her, people specifically skilled with cold cases and impressive solve rates. She'd purposely taken on more of an administrator role to compensate for her lack of experience as an investigator. But apparently that wasn't sufficient for her old boss.

While she remained silent and focused on keeping her composure, Grayson wasn't nearly as accommodating.

The chill in his blue eyes should have frozen Jeffries where he sat. "Ms. McCray has years of experience in law enforcement, not to mention a master's degree in criminology with a minor in psychology. Do you have a master's degree, Sergeant Jeffries?"

Jeffries's face flushed. "My qualifications aren't pertinent here."

"Aren't they? You hired her as a detective on your team and yet here you are, criticizing her. Are you saying you made a mistake, that your opinions are flawed, unreliable?"

"Now, look here, Prescott."

"No, Sergeant, you look here. I'm not about to let your petty jealousies over your former employee's success destroy our chance to help families in Eastern Tennessee obtain the justice and closure that has been denied them for years. Through no fault of the TBI or any of the agencies represented in this room, budget constraints and lack of resources have meant the cold-case load is growing, not shrinking. Unfinished Business is the solution, a way to clear those cases and get dangerous kidnappers and murderers off the streets."

Grayson tapped the folders again. "Which of these investigators do you take issue with? Which one of these hiring decisions that Ms. McCray made doesn't meet your high standards?"

When Jeffries didn't answer, Grayson gave him a look of contempt, then addressed the others in the room. "We're ready, right now, to move forward. Even without our headquarters built, we can work out of my home. I've got contractors there right now converting my library into the work area we'll need. The investigators will have the latest, most advanced computer equipment. The team is ready to be here within days of us signing these contracts and will start working cases shortly after that. All you have to do is sign on the dotted line. Or is there something else holding you back that we haven't discussed?"

Jacob Frost from the TBI cleared his throat, gaining everyone's attention. "Let's lower the temperature in here a few degrees, shall we?" He gave Grayson a respectful nod. "First, I'd like to express my condolences again on the great loss you've suffered. I can well imagine how your frustration with your family's case going unsolved so long has led you to come up with this cold-case company as a possible solution. And I think I speak for us all when I say we genuinely appreciate that you're willing to front the resources to help countless others in similar situations."

There was a round of head nods and murmured agreement from the men and women sitting at the table.

"I sense a *but* here," Grayson said dryly.

"You'd be correct," Frost continued. "Regardless of whatever resentments may exist between Jeffries and his former detective, I can assure you those resentments have had no impact on the issue regarding Ms. McCray's qualifications."

Frost nodded at Willow. "Ma'am, no disrespect intended. I think you've done an incredible job helping Mr. Prescott with this idea. But there's a gap that has to be addressed. He doesn't have either a law enforcement background or experience as an investigator. And even though your education and experience in law enforcement are a tremendous advantage, you *are* relatively inexperienced, especially with investigations. Cold cases are some of the most difficult to solve, even with the most experienced of detectives. And you're asking all of us here to believe that the two of you have the combined ability to hire the right team for this job. That's just not realistic. I don't think any of us feel comfortable with what's been presented."

Grayson shot Willow a questioning look. But all she could do was shrug. She didn't know what to say.

He speared Frost with his hard gaze. "Every investigator we propose to hire has years of experience, much of that specifically working cold cases. We plan to liaison with law enforcement via your chosen TBI representative who will be an integral part of the team," Grayson reminded him.

"Understood. And I appreciate that. But that TBI rep isn't an employee of your company, and he or she won't have the power to oversee how the investigative team is being run, or to countermand the decisions. His or her job will be to focus on the legalities of whichever cases you're actively working and to ensure chain of custody is maintained on evidence. Your lead investigator will coordinate which cases to focus on and assign priorities. That requires someone experienced enough to judge the merits of each cold case presented by the various counties and determine which ones are potentially solvable. The success or failure is directly tied to the lead's decisions."

He gave Willow an apologetic smile. "I'm sorry, Ms. McCray. But all of us, without exception, believe it's safer, less risky, to have someone far more experienced in law enforcement *and* investigations to act as that lead."

He looked at Grayson. "We'd like someone other than Ms. McCray to take on that role."

Grayson's jaw clenched. "Is that all or do you have more demands?"

"Not demands. Concerns and a few minor requests. The first is that before going public with this partnership and signing the final contracts, we'd like your team to solve some cold cases to prove that everything's in place that needs to be. We'd sign temporary contracts so you'll have access to the evidence in the chosen cases, of course. And then we'll make a decision about our continued partnership based on the success, or failure, of those investigations. That will be the true proof that the lead we're recommending, and the infrastructure you've put in place are compatible."

"The lead you're recommending?" Grayson gritted out.

Frost seemed unfazed by Grayson's less than receptive tone. "When we all discussed this earlier, the one name that kept coming up, the only one we could all agree on, was Ryland Beck."

Grayson frowned and glanced at Willow. "Who's Ryland Beck?"

Her face heated. "His name never came up during my search for investigators. I've never heard of him."

"Which goes toward your lack of experience, Ms. McCray." Frost smiled, as if trying to take the sting out of his words, before turning back to Grayson. "Beck is probably the best investigator we've ever had at the TBI. He began his career in Knoxville and eventually transferred to TBI where he worked exclusively on cold cases, for years. He quit because he was frustrated at the lack of resources to do his job, which makes me think he'd likely jump at the chance to work for your company, where resources won't be an issue. Another advantage is that since he's not active in law enforcement right now, you won't be poaching him from other agencies as you're doing with many of the investigators you plan on hiring." He chuckled, not seeming particularly upset over their so-called poaching.

"Getting Beck on board as your lead will go a long way toward making us comfortable with this planned partnership. Unfortunately, we really must insist that Ms. McCray no longer be in your employ, going forward, to ensure that she's not in a position to influence the investigative decisions."

Grayson stiffened. "Wait a minute, Frost—"

"This isn't up for argument," Frost insisted, his expression hardening. "Those are our terms. Obviously, it's your company. It's your choice to go along, or not, with our recommendations. But if you don't, then you'll proceed without the support of law enforcement."

Grayson's eyes flashed with anger. "You know damn well we can't be successful without access to case evidence, access we'll only get if you sign those contracts."

Frost pushed back his chair and stood. "Then I guess you have to weigh that with everything else. I look forward to hearing your decision."

Willow sat frozen as everyone filed out of the conference room, leaving her and Grayson alone. She remained in her chair six seats down from him, her face flaming with embarrassment over what had just transpired. He sat rigid in his chair, his hands fisted on top of the table, lost in thought as he stared at the far wall. Neither of them spoke. What was there to say?

Three months ago, Jeffries had told her to enjoy her weekend off, saying it would be her last for a while. His prediction had turned out to be right, though not in the way he'd expected. Instead of working on the serial killer/

rapist case, she'd been working with Grayson to make the cold-case company a reality.

They'd both toiled day and night, with her sometimes sleeping in a guest room at his mansion so they could get up early to work out some issue or brainstorm late into the night. She'd extensively researched investigators, searching for the cream of the crop, the best of the best. She'd interviewed dozens over the phone, then flew around the country with Grayson for the second and third rounds of interviews, whittling down their list.

Next, it was time to research labs. That part had been easier, since she and Grayson had agreed to narrow the scope to those within a three-hour drive of Gatlinburg. That would make it easy to transport evidence to and from the labs, considering their headquarters would be built here in Gatlinburg. But it had still taken weeks of phone calls, meetings and tours to narrow it down to two potential labs. The final decision had been difficult. But they felt good about their choice. Contracts had been signed, and the next step, the hardest one, lay before them.

Getting the TBI and thirty-three counties of law enforcement agencies to agree to their terms.

But they'd done it.

They'd met with the governor and dozens of other politicians to smooth the way and win their support. Then they'd conducted meetings with dozens of police chiefs, sheriffs and Jacob Frost—the all-important head of the TBI. It had culminated in today's final meeting with the leaders representing the agencies of Eastern Tennessee. Everything had finally come together. The pieces of the puzzle all fit. Except one.

Her.

She wasn't sure how long the two of them sat there

in silence. Thirty minutes? An hour? Longer? But when Grayson finally let out a deep sigh and turned in his chair to face her, she read his decision in his tortured gaze, the tension lines carved around his mouth.

"Say it," she whispered. "I need to hear you say it."

"Willow, you have to understand. I can't live like this anymore, always wondering, never having closure. You've worked so hard. I know that. And this is killing me. But we're so close. We may never get this chance again and—"

"Say it, Grayson."

He swallowed, hard, shaking his head with regret. "I'm sorry, Willow. You're fired."

Chapter Thirteen

Grayson had spent an exhausting two months setting up the new cold case company without Willow's help. Between welcoming each member of the team, helping them find housing and pushing the contractors to finish converting the library into a squad room, he'd had little time for anything else. But now, finally, he had time to focus on what was most important, Willow.

He pulled his Audi into the parking lot and cut the engine but didn't get out right away. Instead, he allowed himself the guilty pleasure of watching Willow through the windshield.

She was sitting at a picnic table perfectly positioned beneath an oak tree where the sun wouldn't glare on her computer screen. Judging by the dark marks scored in the grass, she'd dragged the picnic table to that spot. He couldn't help smiling as he pictured her huffing and puffing, struggling to move something that outweighed her twice over. But that's the kind of person she was: driven, focused, determined to never give up until she'd reached her goal.

Kind of like him.

Except that *unlike* him, she hadn't betrayed the trust of someone she cared about in order to get what she wanted.

He sighed heavily and put his shades on before getting out.

He knew the exact moment when she realized he was there. Her hands froze on the keyboard. Her mouth flattened in a hard straight line.

"Hello, Willow. It's been a while."

She slowly looked up. "Two months isn't nearly long enough."

"I've been to your apartment a dozen times during those two months, but you never answer the door."

"Maybe I haven't been home."

"Your car was parked out front."

"I was probably washing my hair."

He chuckled. "What about all the phone calls? You never answer. Not even my texts."

"Maybe you dialed the wrong number."

He gave her a grudging smile. "Maybe I did."

She crossed her arms. "How did you find me anyway?"

"I bribed your neighbor down the hall. He said he's seen you in this park before and suggested I give it a try."

"Next time I'm keeping the pizza when they knock on my door," she grumbled.

"What?"

"Never mind. Now that you've found me, what do you want?"

"To talk. You look great, by the way. But then you always did."

Her eyes widened. "What are you doing? Sucking up to me? Let me guess. There's a report you need or minutes to a meeting that you can't find. It's all in that massive library of yours. Do the work. Hunt it down. Don't expect me to dig through drawers and cabinets for you. Or are you afraid you'll get your Armani suit dirty?"

"You do realize I spent years in the army right? In fatigues and combat boots. Hunkered down in rain and mud and burning hot sand, dodging bullets and taking out bad guys. Not a Louis Vuitton or Armani suit to be had. I'm not the snob you seem to think I am."

She rolled her eyes and bent over her keyboard.

He stepped closer to see what was on the screen. "Erin Speck? You're working on her case? On your own?"

"Not that it's any of your business, but yes."

"Why?"

She gave him an exasperated look. "Because I'm a detective. That's what detectives do. They investigate. Except I'm working for myself these days. Thanks to you convincing me to give up the job I'd worked for all my life, then, oh, yeah, firing me."

"Ouch."

She snapped her laptop closed. "Don't you have a headquarters building to design? Or lab equipment orders to place? Oh, wait, it's almost lunchtime. Maybe you and your buddy Frost have reservations, lobster for two at Nob Hill." She made a shooing motion with her hands. "Don't let me stop you. I wouldn't want you to be late."

"The whole bullets-and-fatigues speech didn't make a dent, did it?"

"Nope."

He sighed heavily. "You're not going to make this easy on me, are you?"

"Make what easy? I didn't invite you here. I don't *want* you here."

"I'm sure you don't. Lucky for me, it's a public park." He settled onto the bench across from her.

Her eyes narrowed. "You like this picnic table so much, take it." She tapped her computer. "By the way, thanks for the new laptop. I bought it with my golden parachute." She grabbed her satchel and flipped it open.

As she was reaching for her computer to stuff it inside, he put a hand on hers to stop her. "Willow, wait. Please. We need to talk."

She shook off his hand. "The last time we talked, you said *trust me*. Then you fired me. I'm not interested in anything else you have to say. We have nothing to discuss."

"I want to hire you back."

She paused with her laptop half inside the satchel and slowly raised her gaze to his. "Excuse me?"

"Firing you was reactionary, stupid and wrong. I've regretted it ever since." He looked at her over the top of his shades. "I'm not good at groveling. What will it take to get you to come back?"

"Don't insult me by offering more money."

"I wouldn't dare."

She folded her arms on top of her satchel, pinning him with her stare. "Having been burned, I've no intention of ever putting my hopes and dreams in your tender care again."

He winced.

"But," she continued, "I have to point out that you have a lot to learn in the art of groveling. You haven't even said you're sorry."

"I am, you know, sorry. More sorry than you can imagine."

"*Pfft*. Right. Let me guess. Something went wrong and you think I'm the only one who can fix it?"

"Actually, no. Everything's going like clockwork. Ryland Beck agreed to lead the team. Half the investigators are at my house. They're working in the converted library with the IT guys, setting up our computer system for tracking cases. The rest will be here in another week. Rather than having to wait for the lab's new wing to be built, I rented another building down the street from the current lab. Equipment's being set up. Techs are being hired. The team has already started on some initial so-called *easy* cold cases that Beck chose, to prove to Frost that Unfinished Business is worth partnering with. Plus, they're working one that's a lot more difficult, the same one you're working on—the Speck disappearance. With the potential tie-in to the active River Road Rapist case, he feels it would be a huge boon to the company to solve it."

Her eyes widened. "Congratulations. You definitely don't need me. Jeffries was right." She shoved the computer in the satchel and zipped it closed.

"No. He wasn't. He was wrong, Willow. They all were—me included. I never should have given in to their demands. Without you, I'd still be floundering, with no direction, no hope. You're the reason Unfinished Business exists. And it's not right that you're not a part of it now. I'm sorry for what I did to you. I hope someday you'll be able to forgive me."

She stood and settled the satchel's strap across her shoulder and hip. "Your groveling's improving. You get points for that. Not that it makes a difference." She started to move past him.

He grasped her arm and waited until she looked up. "I don't want points, Willow. I want you."

Her eyes widened. "You...you what?"

He framed her face with his hands. "I didn't fight for you when I should have. But I came to my senses a few days later. I had a private meeting with Frost and convinced him to change the terms of our arrangement. As long as we have Ryland Beck on board, and we prove ourselves with the initial cold cases, he and the others will sign the formal contracts making things permanent. I want you back, Willow. Back at Unfinished Business."

She dropped her gaze to his chest and let out a shaky breath. "Wow. Okay. I'm confused." She pushed his hands down and stepped back. "About a lot of things," she mumbled.

"Like what?"

She opened her mouth to say something, then seemed to think better of it and cleared her throat.

"Willow? What questions do you have?"

"Um, mainly, how did you get Frost and the others to agree that you could hire me back? Assuming I'm even interested, which of course I'm not." She crossed her arms over her chest.

"I threatened him."

"You what?"

"I told him if he didn't back down from his stance about you, I'd go to the press and give them an exclusive on how a multi-million-dollar privately funded cold-case unit had been turned down by TBI, and that the escalating numbers of unsolved murders and missing persons cases in Eastern Tennessee would continue to rise out of control."

"You did *not*."

"I totally did. I even showed him a planned press release. He flipped immediately."

"Would you have done it, if he hadn't flipped? Would you have gone to the press?"

"In a second. Come back to work with me. You can be Beck's boss if you want, or choose another role. I don't care, as long as you're there. We'll be a better team with you on it. And if it takes groveling every day to make you happy and earn your forgiveness, that's what I'll do."

She raked a hand through her long dark hair, tossing it back over her shoulder. "You don't even need me."

"That's where you're wrong. Can Unfinished Business be a success without you? Maybe. Probably. But I know it can be better with you there, with your ideas, your creativity. And it's eating me alive that your creation is coming to life without you there to steer and guide it, and enjoy it."

She cocked her head, hands on her hips. "So, what you're saying is you want me to work for you so you don't feel guilty anymore. It's all about you."

He grinned. "That's one way to look at it, I suppose. What do you say? Will you do it?"

"Maybe. Let me sleep on it."

"I can live with *maybe*. Thanks, Willow. You won't regret it. Promise."

At her skeptical look, he winced again. "I know a promise from me doesn't hold a lot of water. But let me prove it to you. You really can count on me going forward. I won't let my desperation to solve my family's case influence how I treat people again. I've learned my lesson."

She blew out a long breath. "Okay, okay. I'll do it. But I get a ten percent raise."

"I thought more money would be an insult?"

"I changed my mind."

He laughed. "Deal."

He kept in step with her as she headed to her car.

"Speaking of your family's case..." She put her satchel in her back seat. "How is the investigation going?" She shut the back door and turned around, brows raised in question.

He focused on keeping his tone upbeat when he replied. "We aren't working on that case yet. Ryland was worried that it might not be solvable." He shrugged, trying not to let her see how crushed he'd been to hear the veteran investigator tell him that. "Since we need some quick solves under our belt to get the contracts signed, he chose cases he felt had a lot more promise. I can see his reasoning. We'll get to it, eventually. So, when will you be back at work? Can I look for you tomorrow morning?"

"Sounds good." She smiled. "And Grayson?"

"Hmm?"

"Thanks. The timing really sucked, but you finally stood up for me. I appreciate it."

Unable to resist the impulse, he leaned down and pressed a kiss against her cheek. "See you tomorrow."

WILLOW HELD HER smile until Grayson's Audi disappeared around a corner. Then she closed her eyes, holding on to her car door for support. Just seeing him again had sent her heart racing. She'd been ready to forgive and forget the second he'd stopped by the picnic table. Which, of course, only made her angry at herself, so she'd disguised her eagerness by forcing him to work for whatever it was he wanted.

And then he'd said he wanted *her.*

She'd been so stunned she couldn't put a coherent thought together. Thankfully, before she could throw herself in his arms, he'd clarified that he wanted her as his employee.

What was that for her now? Strike three? Four? Had she ever even been in the game?

She should have been immune to her ridiculous attraction to him that had morphed into a near-obsession during their three months of working together. Him firing her should have been the cure. Instead, she'd pined for him. She was living proof of that absence-and-the-heart-growing-fonder thing. While talking to him beside her car, she'd just managed to get her emotions under control when he'd decimated her again with one tiny soft kiss. On the cheek.

If he ever really kissed her, it would probably kill her.

Not that there was any chance of a real kiss. He was always a gentleman, refusing to give in to the desires and longing she'd seen in his gaze. There was no room in his heart for her, only for a ghost.

She wiped her eyes, dismayed to realize tears were spilling down her cheeks. Crying over a man had never been her thing. But this man, Grayson Prescott, was worth a few tears. Not because he could slay her with a smile or make her shake with desire after a stupid hug or a friendly peck on the cheek. He was so much more than that. Smart, strong, caring, able to admit when he'd made a mistake. Well, eventually anyway.

And he didn't deserve to suffer the way he had, the way he was still suffering. It was so unfair that just when he thought he was going to get the dream team working on his cold case, Ryland Beck had steered them toward something else. Once again, Grayson had to wait for justice for himself, for his loved ones. She kind of hated Ryland right now and she'd never even met him.

She started up her car, which took three tries. Maybe she should spend some of that golden-parachute money to replace her old Taurus instead of just her computer.

When she reached her apartment, she sat in her usual spot in front of the coffee table. Then she closed out of her investigation file labeled Erin Speck: Missing, Presumed Dead and opened the other file she'd been working on for the past two months—Maura and Katrina Prescott: Murder on Prescott Mountain.

Chapter Fourteen

Willow sat in the elevated glass-walled conference room in Grayson's converted library, looking from Grayson to Ryland as they filled her in on what she'd missed. Downstairs, a small team of investigators was working at their desks, a few of whom she'd interviewed months ago. Others, she'd never heard of until today.

"I don't understand. I thought we were going to have thirty-three investigators—one to work cold cases in each of the counties that we'll support."

Ryland shook his head. "That's too many. I know it seems counterintuitive, but less is more. With investigations, you need a manageable-sized team that can become close, a tight unit, complement each other's weaknesses and magnify each other's strengths."

He slid a folder across the table to her. "I know you introduced yourself to everyone in the squad room before coming up here, and seemed surprised that you hadn't met some of them during the interviews."

"Some of them? Try most of them."

He glanced uncertainly at Grayson before continuing. "Right. So the first page in that folder is a list of the final team members. All of their résumés are in the folder too."

She read through the list of names, then flipped the

page over to see the rest. The back was blank. "Ten investigators? That's it?"

"That's the core team, the permanent positions. That includes you, of course, but not Grayson since he isn't an investigator. I'm also counting our TBI liaison to help with investigations since the liaison workload will fluctuate, depending on the needs of each case."

"I don't… I'm… confused. It seems like everything that Grayson and I worked so hard to plan has been tossed or completely changed."

Grayson leaned across the table and gently squeezed her hand as if to reassure her. "The basic infrastructure you and I came up with is still there. Just smaller."

"Exactly," Ryland said. "You did a great job, honestly. And I would have picked most of the investigators you wanted to hire if I wanted a team that large."

"*Most* of them? Meaning you don't approve of some of my hiring decisions?"

"No, no. Any of the ones you picked would have been fine. I just preferred some others, investigators I'd met over the years and with whom I was familiar."

She held up the piece of paper he'd handed her. "Those *others* are over half this list."

Ryland gave Grayson a help-me look.

Willow held up her hands to stop whatever he was about to say. "Don't. I get it. You both did what you felt was best in the months when I was gone. I'm just struggling to absorb all of this. Ryland, can you explain what you meant about a core team of *permanent* positions? That implies there will be others who come and go?"

"Exactly. The team will grow or shrink as needed, outside the core group. With each case we work, we'll bring in temporary experts if or when we need them. Like, say, a car accident scene reconstructionist. Useful for some cases, but probably not for most of the ones we'll work."

She slowly nodded. "Okay. That makes sense." Kind of. She decided not to argue about it since she didn't want to seem completely negative on her first day back. She held up the list again. "I see the TBI liaison is Rowan Knight. I remember meeting him. He seems like a great fit."

"I agree," Ryland said. "Once a year, TBI will rotate that position with a new special agent, just as you proposed."

Yay for her. He'd kept *one* idea she'd had.

Grayson motioned to another folder on the table. "I've hired administrative staff as well, assistants, a human resources manager, that sort of thing. They all start next week and will work out of another part of my home until our headquarters is built. We wanted the computer system and construction work completed before they got here."

"Sounds like a great plan." Had she made a mistake coming back? Had her feelings for Grayson clouded her judgment? They didn't seem to need her and she wasn't sure how she was going to fit in. It was obvious Grayson and Ryland had thought of everything with their plan to grow and shrink the team based on workload. She eyed the list of team members again, and the roles each of them filled.

"Anything else I can explain?" Ryland asked.

She glanced up. "Actually, I wanted to ask you about the Erin Speck case. I did quite a bit of work on that on my own and Grayson asked me to share it with you. I gave a flash drive to Faith, um—"

"Lancaster." Ryland smiled encouragingly. "Don't worry. You'll learn everyone's names in no time at all."

"Lovely." She gritted her teeth. It was the closest to a smile that she could manage.

He cleared his throat, clearly uncomfortable.

Grayson chose that moment to grin, which had her wanting to kick him beneath the table. She knew she was being childish. But was it really too much to ask that this Ryland guy could have at least one major flaw?

"Regarding the Speck case," she said, trying hard to keep the little green monster at bay. It wasn't Ryland's fault that he was offered the job she'd wanted for herself. But that didn't mean she had to warm up to him right away. "Grayson told me you only just started working on it a few days ago. But I wonder whether you've thought about what kinds of forensic tests you plan to run on the evidence collected from her car? That was the last place anyone saw her so I feel it's important not to overlook even the smallest item."

"Couldn't agree more. The first thing I did in her case was check on her car. The police returned it to her parents after processing. But her father was so distraught he parked it in the garage and wouldn't allow anyone near it."

His eyes lit with excitement. "It's basically a four-year-old *pristine* potential crime scene. That never happens. One of the forensic techs we hired at the lab went over every inch of the car, inside and out, and gathered prints that were missed by Gatlinburg PD. They swabbed every surface for potential touch DNA testing. One small fiber on the back seat appears consistent with a fiber found on one of the River Road Rapist's victims, which of course strengthens your theory that the cases are connected."

"I'm so relieved," she said dryly.

He shot her an uncertain look, obviously not sure

whether she was being serious or sarcastic. At this point, she wasn't sure either.

"Right," he said. "Um, so we're also exploring a relatively new technology that might get some usable prints from the heavily patterned car seats. The computer software cancels out the repetitive sequence of the patterns to reveal latents. We're testing dirt and minerals from the tires and undercarriage to compare against soil-sample databases of the area. That might tell us where she'd driven the car most recently. If we can match that to any areas the rape victims traveled, it can help us expand our geographical profile as to where the perpetrator might live. Aside from that, of course, we're reinterviewing everyone who knew her, reconstructing the timeline of the weeks before she disappeared, looking at financial and cell-phone records, triangulating places to search based on last cell-phone tower pings. You know, all the standard stuff."

Her inner mean girl wanted so badly to criticize him for something. But he was doing everything she'd have done, and then some. "Sounds like you're on top of things, Ryland. I appreciate the update and am sure I'll have more questions later. But I need to talk to Grayson in private for a moment, if that's okay."

"Of course. I've got plenty to keep me busy. Let me know if you need anything."

If she smiled any harder, her face would probably break.

When the door closed and Ryland jogged down the stairs to the main floor, Grayson burst out laughing.

She crossed her arms. "I fail to see what's funny."

"*You*, sweet Willow. If looks could kill, Ryland would be a lump of burning coal right now."

His unexpected endearment had her belly fluttering.

But what he'd said about Ryland had her cringing with embarrassment. "Was I that obvious?"

"He couldn't get out of here fast enough."

She groaned. "Dang it. He'll hate me now."

"He'll love you. How could he not?" He winked. "What did you want to talk to me about? Or was that an excuse to save Ryland's life?"

She had to force herself to breathe after the how-could-he-not-love-her comment and the devastating wink. One day soon, she'd have to tell him to stop smiling so much and not to wink, hold her hand or—God forbid—hug her. Otherwise, her heart would never survive. Would he ever be able to let go of his past and see what was right in front of him? See *her*?

"Willow?"

"Sorry. Still trying to take everything in." She tapped the member list. "I noticed no one's taken the victim's advocate position. Seems like an essential role to me. I wouldn't want the family of a victim to hear that a cold-case company is working their case by hearing about it in a press conference."

He leaned back in his chair. "You're right. We haven't hired one yet. I didn't see the urgency since we're keeping the company a secret until the final contracts are signed. You disagree?"

"No. That makes sense. And I'm kind of glad you haven't filled the position yet. I'm having a hard time seeing how I'll fit into the team. Maybe the advocate slot would be good for me, and Ryland could hire another investigator to replace me in that role. I've got a minor in psychology. That should come in handy."

"I think you'd be a great victim's advocate. But I thought you wanted to be more hands-on with the detective work."

"I did. I do, eventually. But I'm also a realist. You've got some of the best investigators in the business on this team and I'm still a novice. I can contribute more in the advocate role than as an investigator. At least until I—"

Her phone chimed. "Sorry. I'm expecting an important text so I kept the sound on. Just a sec."

"No problem."

She checked the screen and her stomach dropped as if she'd just leaped off a cliff.

Grayson leaned forward, his brow furrowed with concern. "What is it? Did something bad happen?"

"That depends on your perspective."

"Business or personal?"

"Business."

"I'll get Ryland—"

"*No.*" She winced. "Sorry. That came out louder than I meant it to. It's just, I think you should hear this first. Without him."

"Okay. What's going on?"

She tapped the table, trying to figure out the easiest way to explain it. "Have you ever heard of the Golden State Killer?"

"I'd be living in a cave if I hadn't. He's been all over the news for the past few years. He raped and murdered people in California, in the '70s and '80s, I think."

"That's right. Then he disappeared off the radar. No one ever even had a suspect in the case and decades passed. Then a cold-case unit took a fresh look. They already had a DNA profile of the perpetrator from evidence collected at the scenes. But it never generated any hits in those FBI databases I told you about."

"But they caught him using DNA, didn't they?" he asked. "If I remember it right."

"They did."

"You're not suggesting he's the guy we're looking for are you? He's been in prison a while."

"No, I'm not. The only reason I brought him up is because of how he was caught. I think it could be the key to catching our guy too. It's called forensic genealogy. It's where you take a known DNA sample, like from a rape kit, and you upload the DNA profile to one of those popular ancestry family tree database websites."

"I've used those myself," he said. "Helping my niece trace our roots. She's convinced if we look hard enough, one day we'll find she's royalty."

She smiled. "How old is this little princess?"

"A very precocious six." He motioned for her to continue. "Didn't mean to sidetrack you."

"I just wanted to point out that if someone in the extended family of our serial rapist happened to have uploaded their DNA profile to one of these websites, and we upload the DNA profile of the rapist, we can get a familial match. We know these two people are related somehow, so to figure out who the rapist is, we work on the family tree of the known familial match to try to eventually trace to the suspect. That's how they caught the Golden State Killer."

She held her hands out to the sides. "I'm hugely oversimplifying the process. It takes a ton of work to build the tree and find those links between the two DNA samples. It's based on a combination of math, probabilities and genetics as well as old-fashioned detective work, interviewing people, performing surveillance to get more information on various family members. You build an online genetic profile and extrapolate from there. It's grueling work. If I tried it on my own, it would probably take me a year, if I'm lucky. And once you narrow it down you could potentially end up with a large number of people who could be your perpetrator. Then you weed them out by figuring out who lived where and when, who had opportunity, things like that. If you get a workable number of potential suspects, then you try to get their DNA samples to see if there's a match."

He nodded. "I remember they followed the Golden State guy until he spit on the sidewalk to get his sample."

"You're probably thinking about another case where they did that. But his was similar. They swabbed the door handle of his car while he was shopping in a Hobby Lobby. And later they tested a tissue from his trash, to confirm their findings. Both samples matched their rapist's DNA profile, so they were able to get a warrant to get an official DNA sample they could use in court. The rest, as they say, is history. He's never getting out of prison."

"I take it you want to try this family-tree stuff on the rapist case."

"I do. I know it's not technically a cold case, but since it appears that our cold case—the Erin Speck case—may have been done by the same guy, it makes sense to use the DNA profile from the rapist case and move forward to save time. And once Ryland gets test results from Speck's car, if he's able to get a DNA profile, that will hopefully match the one we already have. Solve one case and you solve both of them. And hopefully get the perpetrator to tell us what he did with Erin."

"Sounds like a solid approach to me. We'll need to hire one of those experts—"

"A forensic genealogist."

He nodded. "I can't imagine Ryland having an issue with that."

"Actually, he won't need to hire one. I already did. During the past few months when I was working the Speck case by myself, I used part of that ridiculously generous golden parachute money you gave me to hire the best person I could find."

"Why didn't you say that to start with?"

"I wanted you to understand the context before I explain this next part." She leaned toward him, her excitement warring with dread. "Grayson, that's what the text I just got was about, an update from the genealogist. A while back, she found a familial match on an ancestry site and she's been building the family tree ever since to come up with a pool of possible suspects. She just texted me that she's narrowed our potential DNA contributor to six males on the family tree."

His eyes widened in surprise. "You've got a list of suspects, and there are only six?"

She nodded.

"Good grief, Willow. That's fantastic. Why didn't you want to tell Ryland?"

"There's a...complication."

He waited.

"Keep in mind, with this ancestry thing, the genetics only get you so far. The bulk of the work after you get your starting and ending points is to build a family tree, which is based on siblings, marriages, births, all of that. The tree starts with science, but after that it becomes an exercise in drawing a map, essentially showing different branches of the tree that the genes would have gone down. Are you following?"

"I'm trying."

"Think of any typical family tree. It's like an umbrella. Your great-great grandfather and great-great grandmother are at the very top. But as you follow it down, you have to trace their siblings, then their children, and their children, all the way down each rib of the umbrella. You could end up with hundreds of people on that one little tree. All you know for sure is that each of those tips on the bottom has a very distant relationship to the great-greats at the top."

"Now I'm following. I think. You're saying this genetic expert knows our killer is one of those points at the very bottom, because they're related to someone who uploaded their DNA to this database at the very top of the tree."

"Pretty much. Our genealogist works through that math I was telling you about in order to eliminate some of the branches of the tree. And she can eliminate some others because of obvious things—like a certain branch ended with all females. Or another one ended when all of the males in that line died before the timeline for our crime."

"I'm with you," he said. "She figured out the suspect has to be at the end of a handful of specific branches, but she can't narrow it down any further. Our investigators will have to do that."

"Exactly. We have six people, all male, who fit an age range where they could be capable of committing these rapes and murders. Because of marriages all along the tree, they don't all share the same last name either. We're talking distant cousins who may not even know each other. Investigators need to look at each of the six to try to rule them in or out. Of course, getting a DNA sample from each one would be ideal so they can zero in on a specific suspect more quickly."

"All of this sounds like that magic clue we've wanted all along to make the pieces of the puzzle fall into place," he said. "So why do you seem so worried?"

"Not worried, exactly. More like...concerned...at how this is going to play out. It could actually hurt our company's reputation before we've even begun because they'll question the research."

"They?"

"You'll understand when you see this." She opened the text app on her phone. "Here's the suspect list we need to research." She slid the phone across the table.

He looked at the screen and swore.

"My thoughts exactly."

He shoved his chair back and stood. "We need to talk to Chief Russo. Right now. I'll call him on our way downtown so he can clear his calendar."

She hurried after him. "Should I grab Ryland, tell him to come with us?"

"No. Your instincts on this were spot on. The fewer people who know about it for now, the better. At least until Russo decides how he wants to proceed."

Chapter Fifteen

Police Chief Russo sat behind his desk, staring at the text on Willow's phone for a full minute as if the names would change if he looked at them long enough. Finally, he handed it back to her without saying anything.

Grayson glanced at Willow to judge her reaction. She flashed him a worried look, obviously unsure what to do next.

Grayson cleared his throat. "Chief Russo—"

Russo held up his hand to stop him. "Don't worry. I'm not going to shoot the messenger." He glanced at Willow. "Or in this case, messengers, plural. And you don't need to go into another drawn-out explanation about the science behind forensic genealogy. When that Golden State Killer case made the news, the first thing I did was study up on how they figured out who he was. Seemed like a clever way to catch someone. I just never thought it would be used to catch one of my own guys, or his *son*." He shook his head. "What a mess."

He stared down at his desk. "If one of my men *is* the perp, it's going to shake the foundation of trust between the police and this community. It could take years to rebuild." He swore. "I don't get it. It doesn't even make sense. If it's a cop—or even the cop's family—you'd think he'd know to be careful, not to leave behind trace evidence that could point back to him—especially DNA."

"These days," Willow said, "it's exceptionally difficult not to leave any trace evidence behind. The amount of DNA required to yield a viable profile is minuscule. A drop of sweat, a hair with the follicle attached, saliva. He *did* try to be careful. He used condoms, covered his features until he got his victims blindfolded so they couldn't identify him. But it's almost impossible to attack someone so violently, to lose control and get in a frenzy the way his victims have described, and not leave something of himself behind. His Achilles' heel, the thing that will bring him down, is that he thinks he's being careful and covering his tracks when he really isn't."

He shook his head in disgust. "This animal, regardless of who he is or who he works for, needs to be locked up before someone else is hurt or killed. Grayson, you said we can use your lab for the testing. And they can get the results back in hours instead of the days or weeks we're used to? Heck, months sometimes."

"Absolutely. Since we know three of the suspects are in Gatlinburg, I've already got a tech on the way here. Once the samples are collected, he'll head back to the lab. It's a couple of hours away, so the drive time will delay us. But we may still be able to get results on these first three by nightfall."

"And the other three? You don't have addresses for them?"

"Not yet. As soon as Willow gave me the list, we called you and headed here. I still need to brief my team about what's going on and get them working on locating the others."

"We can help with that."

"Thank you, sir."

"I don't like waiting, Grayson. We've got DNA collection kits here. One of our guys can collect the samples and an officer can hightail it down the highway, lights and sirens, to intercept your lab tech. Your guy can take custody of the samples and head back to his lab and start the testing. You okay with that?"

"Better than okay. Are you sure you can convince your men to provide a sample without a warrant?"

He made a derisive sound. "They don't have a choice if they want to keep their jobs. That's part of the agreement when they sign on here, that if they're ever a suspect in a crime they'll fully cooperate with the investigation and submit to any required tests. If they refuse, I can fire them immediately. And I don't even need a union rep to do it. The hard part will be the son, since he's not an employee here. But I don't see him wanting to jeopardize his father's job. He'll agree to provide the sample."

He punched a button on his desk phone. "Molly, have one of our crime scene guys come up here with two DNA swab kits. And tell Sergeant Mike Jeffries and his nephew, Detective Brian Nelson to come to my office, ASAP."

Twenty minutes later, a visibly shaken Sergeant Jeffries watched as the tech who'd swabbed his mouth for a DNA sample sealed it in the test kit and signed it.

"Where's your nephew?" Russo demanded. "He should have been here by now."

"He's not at his desk and didn't answer my text yet. Maybe he's interviewing a witness out in the field and has the sound off on his phone." Jeffries cast a worried glance at Willow and Grayson. "But you don't need to test him. Not if you're going by that ancestry tree thing Mr. Prescott talked about."

"Explain," Russo said, his tone brooking no disobedience.

"Brian's not my sister's biological child. He's adopted."

Russo sat back in surprise. "Well. That's something I didn't know. Mr. Prescott, I'm no expert but that does seem to rule him out. No blood link. No DNA link. No need to test. Do you agree?"

Grayson glanced at Willow. "Are you okay with that?"

"I can't think of a reason to argue otherwise. Looks like Brian is in the clear."

"Excellent," Russo said. "One name off your list." He gave Sergeant Jeffries a hard stare. "Your DNA should clear you from that list."

"Yes, sir. It will."

"It had damn well better. What about your son? Steve? How fast can you get him here for his test?"

Jeffries swallowed. "Should be here soon, sir. When I texted, he said he had to find his boss to let him know he was leaving. His job is ten minutes from here."

"When he arrives, send him downstairs to our techs. They'll swab him there. I want to know the second it's done so I can have a uniform drive both of your samples to Mr. Prescott's lab."

"Yes, sir." He headed to the door.

"Jeffries?" Russo called out, stopping him. "Kick your team into gear and catch this guy so I can get the mayor off my back, will you?"

Jeffries gave him a nervous smile, nodded at Grayson and Willow, then hurried out the door.

Russo tapped his desk. "Even though I don't like you finger pointing at anyone in the department, I must say, Grayson, I'm already impressed with your new company.

You figured out this rapist has been operating for years instead of months as we'd originally thought. And you've provided suspects when we had none. When we get this guy, we'll get some flak from the media for not getting him sooner, considering how quickly your company was able to solve this thing. But I don't even care. What matters is getting this monster off the streets. I look forward to seeing what you do next."

"Thank you, sir. The praise goes to Ms. McCray. Not only was the company her initial idea, she's the one who linked Erin Speck's disappearance and the River Road Rapist. And the forensic genealogy part was all her too."

Willow aimed a grateful smile at him.

Russo stood and leaned over his desk, holding his hand out to her. She looked surprised, but she got up and shook his hand.

"Thank you, *Detective*. I say that title out of respect, regardless of who you work for. You've earned it."

She blinked, her eyes suspiciously watery. "I really appreciate that, sir."

"No one here ever doubted you'd do great things. I know Mike—Jeffries—can be a pill to work for. But behind closed doors, he bragged on you all the time. It's our loss that you decided to go into the private sector. But we'll reap the benefits as you help solve our cold cases."

She glanced at Grayson again, clearly rattled.

Grayson shook Russo's hand. "As soon as the lab calls us with the DNA results, I'll have them call you too."

"See that you do."

In the car on the way back, Willow sat uncharacteristically silent, staring out at the rising little puffs of white mist that gave the Smoky Mountains their name.

"You're shocked that Sergeant Jeffries bragged on you to the chief, aren't you?" he asked.

"I don't think shocked quite covers it." She looked away from the window. "What surprises me even more is that Brian's not our guy. As soon as I saw his name on the suspect list, everything clicked. I was sure it was him. He always put off a strange vibe, gave me the creeps."

"You don't think it's Jeffries? Or his son?"

"No on Jeffries. He can be a jerk, but he's a cop to the core. As to his son, I didn't even know he had one until today. We didn't exactly sit and swap family stories when I worked for him."

He chuckled. "I imagine not. Jeffries doesn't strike me as the bad-guy type either. And I've never met Steve or Brian. But I trust your instincts. We'll keep Brian in mind for future cases."

She laughed. "Sounds like a good idea. Honestly, it's a really good thing that we have DNA so we can tell the good guys from the bad guys. We've become so civilized that we've lost the ability to rely on our instincts about people. We open our doors because someone's dressed nice or has a friendly smile, never suspecting the evil that can lurk just beneath the surface."

Grayson tightened his grip on the steering wheel.

Willow's hand was suddenly on his shoulder. "I'm so sorry. I swear I wasn't thinking about what happened to your wife and daughter when I said that."

"It's okay. And it's not like I haven't wondered about the same thing. I've never been able to make sense out of why she opened the door. She had to trust whoever was on the other side, especially since the blood evidence shows she must have been holding Katrina at the time. She had to know her killer. But I've spoken to everyone I can think of, let alone whoever the police spoke to. No one has ever come up as a suspect. It just doesn't make sense."

She settled back in her seat, turning to face him as much as her seat belt would allow. "Before we got the suspect list and went downtown, there was something I wanted to talk to you about. When we get to the house, after we brief Ryland on what happened, can you squeeze me in on your calendar for a private meeting?"

He steered around a curve in the mountain before glancing at her. "You sound worried. Is it about Unfinished Business? Your role on the team?"

"No, nothing like that. It's something I've been looking into for the past few months that—"

Her phone chimed. She silenced it without looking at the screen. "I've been working on another case and—" Her phone chimed again. She swore.

Grayson chuckled. "Maybe you'd better check it. Someone's determined to get in touch with you."

"Sorry. I'll make it fast."

Grayson maneuvered the Audi around another treacherous curve as Willow's fingers flew across her screen, texting back and forth with someone. He doubted it was about the case. They couldn't have DNA results back yet. As far as he knew, they were still waiting for Steve Jeffries to show up at the police station for the cheek swab.

Her warm fingers were suddenly branding him through his shirtsleeve. "Grayson?"

The despair in her tone had him glancing sharply her way. She'd gone pale, her green eyes luminous with unshed tears. "What is it, Willow? What's wrong?"

"We're too late."

"What do you mean? Who was on the phone?"

"Chief Russo." She drew a shuddering breath. "Another woman's been abducted. It looks like it's the River Road Rapist."

Chapter Sixteen

"The missing woman's name is Nicole Paletta," Grayson announced to the Unfinished Business team in the converted library of his home, after introducing Willow more formally than earlier, and explaining what had happened at the police station. Willow stood beside him on the steps to the conference room, so they could both see everyone as they briefed them.

"Paletta matches the same general description as the other victims of the River Road Rapist," he continued. "She's young, in her mid-twenties, well-dressed, upper middle-class and has long dark hair. She's single, no children, which is consistent with some of the previous victims, although some, like Erin Speck, did have children. What makes this particular victim so important is that we have a witness to her abduction, and we know it's one of five possible suspects."

He held up his hands to stop the flood of questions that he could sense was coming. "Willow can brief you on the pertinent details and answer questions. I just want to make clear, first, what our role will be in terms of helping bring Ms. Paletta home safely."

Willow gave him an encouraging nod as he continued.

"I know you all signed up to work cold cases. And you're doing a great job working to clear some so-called *easy* ones already. Plus, you've made great inroads on the Speck case. But we've all learned, thanks to Willow's observant eye, that our cold case—the Speck investigation—is related to the active case, the hunt for the serial rapist and murderer. I feel it's far more important to help the police find Ms. Paletta than to focus on our cold case. I hope you're all in agreement with that."

Ryland stood at his desk and looked around at the others before responding. "We're all ready and willing to do whatever you need us to do."

"Thank you. I appreciate it. The police are in charge of the search for Paletta. They'll coordinate with search-and-rescue teams, the TBI, and they'll have every law enforcement officer who's available out looking for her. They're the lead on the case, as they should be. Our role is different. We're going to use every resource at our disposal to suggest places for the police to search, based on our in-depth knowledge of each suspect."

"What in-depth knowledge?" Ryland leaned back against his desk, ankles crossed. "None of us have even been told about any suspects. Plus, if there's an eyewitness, can't they pinpoint which of these suspects you mentioned abducted the victim?"

"That question's my signal to let someone actually experienced in investigations and police procedures take it from here. Willow?"

He stepped back and leaned against the railing while she brought the team up to speed on the work she'd done with the genealogist. Her explanation was much shorter and to the point than when she'd explained it to him. Likely that was because everyone else in the room already knew about the science behind forensic genealogy.

"Regarding the witness," she said, "I think it's a waste of our time to pursue that angle. Maybe the police can get a better description or more details from her. But what I was told was far too generic to be helpful. Paletta was jogging down a street just off River Road when the witness saw someone yank her around the corner of a building. As is typical of this serial rapist and murderer, the man who accosted her was dressed all in black with his face covered. The witness didn't know whether the suspect forced her into a car or into one of the buildings. She just disappeared. That's it. The only reason we even know we have a victim, and know it this fast, is because the witness was her friend and saw the attack. They were jogging together, but the friend had fallen behind. She wasn't close enough to help but she immediately called 911."

Ryland motioned to let her know he had a question. "How can we be sure that the man who abducted Paletta is the serial rapist? If we make that assumption, and we're wrong, couldn't we be heading down the wrong path and wasting our time?"

Willow gave him a pained look. "Believe me, that's my worry too. One of the hallmarks of what we're doing here, working cold cases, is that we should have the luxury of taking the time we need to look under every rock, sift through all the evidence, explore every possible scenario. We don't have that luxury with the Paletta abduction. This man has killed before and could kill again. Time is not on our side. We have to make that uncomfortable best guess and do what we can to help. Grayson spoke to Chief Russo a few minutes ago on the phone. Russo specifically requested that we focus on the list of rapist suspects, so that's what we're going to do. Now, for that suspect list."

She held her phone out toward Ryland. He hurried forward and she pitched it to him.

"That text shows their names," she said. "Ryland, it's your team. How do you want to proceed?"

His fingers seemed to fly across her phone screen. Then he jogged up the steps and handed it to her before turning to face everyone else. "Guys and gals, I just texted that list to our message group. You should all have it on your phones now."

Willow chuckled. "Guess I need to get in on this message group for future reference."

He smiled. "Quick question. There are six names on the list, but you said there are only five suspects?"

"Brian Nelson can be eliminated. We found out he's adopted, so his DNA wouldn't be a match."

"Got it. Okay, this is what we're going to do, folks. We'll split into five teams with each team focused on one suspect. Use that fancy computer system Grayson bought for us that links up dozens of law-enforcement and private databases. Tap into social-media accounts, online newspapers, ancestry records on the public family-tree sites—all the usual places."

Willow touched his shoulder, interrupting him. "I can have the forensic genealogist send the team the tree information on these suspects. That should save some time in coming up with family members to contact."

"Thanks," Ryland said. "That'll definitely help. Nobody worry about making reports or presentations perfect or pretty. This isn't about documenting evidence for a prosecution. It's about saving a life. I don't care if your final research notes are chicken scratches on a napkin, as long as you can interpret them for the rest of us."

Ryland glanced at a large digital clock on the back wall. "It's a quarter till. Let's huddle up in exactly one hour and info-dump what we have. I want to know everywhere these guys have gone in the past month, from sunup to sundown and everything in between. Give me real-estate holdings, favorite fishing spots, where they each go on vacation. If they've got a lover on the side, I want to know where they go to fool around and all of the lovers' hidey-holes."

There was some good-natured snickering around the room.

Ryland grinned. "You know what I mean, ladies and gentlemen. Hiding places, love nests. That's the name of the game. We want a list of locations to give the police to search for Paletta, and we need it fast. Questions?"

Adam Trent, or Trent as he was known to everyone, stood to ask a question. "If we can narrow down the geography, that could cull the list of places to something more manageable for the police. We don't want to mention a cabin in Montana if the perpetrator wouldn't have the time or means to get there. Willow, can you tell us how soon after the abduction the police got moving on this? Did they lock down the highways, alert bus stations, airports?"

"Great question," she said. "Russo believes we caught a real break on this one. Within minutes of the abduction, highway patrol was stopping traffic and setting up checkpoints on all the roads in and out of Gatlinburg in a fifteen-mile radius around the city. They locked everything up tight and fast. He's confident our perpetrator is still in the area. Rangers in the Great Smoky Mountains National Park are patrolling campsites and hiking trails in case our guy tries to hoof it on foot. Police are going door-to-door downtown and in the foothills, checking every hotel room, business and doing their best to check private residences too. Any homeowner who isn't cooperative and won't allow a search is noted so police can keep a watchful eye for signs of our suspect in that location, or potentially return with a warrant if they have probable cause. The media has also been alerted, so that will put additional pressure on the bad guy to hunker down somewhere. Any other questions?" she asked.

Trent shook his head. "I'm anxious to dig in. I think we all are."

"You're speaking my language, Trent." Ryland threw a number out to each investigator, lightning fast, assigning them to five different teams. "Look at your suspect list. Team one takes the first suspect. Team two, the second and so on. Remember to ignore the Nelson fellow. Let's roll."

He hopped down the stairs and jogged to his desk. Soon the room was buzzing with conversations and the sound of tapping keyboards as each team huddled around a computer monitor.

Grayson shook his head in wonder as he stepped beside Willow again. "I wish the employees at my other companies were this enthusiastic about their work. No telling what we could accomplish."

She smiled, but it didn't quite reach her eyes. "Are you comfortable leaving them in Ryland's hands? I'd like to steal you for a bit."

"Investigating is growing on me, but it's not my wheelhouse. They're in good hands with Ryland." He arched a brow. "Is this about what you said in the car, before Russo's call? That you wanted to talk to me about something once we got to the house?"

She nodded. "Although wanting and needing are two entirely different things. Can we take this outside? Maybe scarf down one of your cook's amazing sandwiches by that English-garden maze while we talk? I always loved his creations when you and I were working here alone those first few months."

He gave her a sad smile. "I'm sorry about everything that happened."

"Don't be. We're past that now. I'm back, and I'm not going anywhere. To the garden then?"

His eyes took on a teasing light. "You always spent more time in that garden than I ever do. Maybe I should ask my head gardener if there's something going on between you two."

She rolled her eyes. "I'm not Mr. Baines's type. I don't have leaves or branches."

He chuckled. "I'll grab the brown bags and some bottled water and meet you out there."

Chapter Seventeen

Grayson strode toward where Willow and his head gardener were sitting at the opening to the main garden maze.

"Thanks so much, Mr. Baines." Willow leaned across the little table that separated their patio chairs and squeezed his hand. "But be warned. If your advice can get my mom's violets to actually bloom again, she'll probably hop on the next plane and whisk you back to Lexington to solve all her gardening problems."

He chuckled and slowly climbed to his feet, knees popping like Bubble Wrap. "Better get back to work. The boss can be a real tyrant." He ambled toward one of the paths in the maze.

Grayson stopped beside Willow's chair. "You know I heard that, right, Mr. Baines?"

The gardener's laughter floated back to them.

"He seems like a really nice guy," Willow said. "Did he teach you a lot when you were growing up here?"

He set the bagged lunches and water bottles on the table between them and took the seat that Baines had vacated. "He taught me plenty. With a willow switch on my backside."

Her eyes grew big and round. "He spanked his employer's child? With a switch?"

"More times than I can count. And I deserved every single swat. I was a terror, trampling his flower beds, nearly setting the woods on fire while lighting bonfires or trying to roast s'mores."

"Wow. Where were your parents?"

"Good question. I didn't see them a whole lot growing up. They traveled extensively, usually out of the country. And before you go feeling sorry for me, I had way more fun without them than I did when they were here. Baines was the perfect substitute father. He even built me an old fort way out in the woods, with real doors and windows. Pretty impressive. My mother would have been scandalized to know that I spent many a night there in a sleeping bag on the dirty floor with nothing to eat but the fish I caught in one of the ponds—courtesy of Baines and some of the other staff who taught me to fish and cook it too."

She blinked. "You can cook?"

He grinned. "I'm pretty good at it."

"But…you have a cook, a chef."

"Who worked for my parents even before I was born. If I have to pretend I can't feed myself so he feels useful, it's a small price to pay to salvage his pride. Besides, it wouldn't be fair to make him leave. This is his home." As she stared at him, his face grew warm. And it wasn't from the sun. "Stop looking at me like I'm being noble or something. Anyone would do the same. It's the right thing to do."

She suddenly stood and crossed to him. Before he knew it, his arms were full of soft, curvy Willow, pressed against his chest, hugging him. He couldn't have pushed her away even if he knew it would cost his entire fortune to keep holding her. He didn't *want* to push her away. As he held her tight, he could almost feel the wall around his heart cracking open.

What was she doing to him?

When she stepped back, she shook her head in wonder. "You're a really good man, Grayson Prescott. Far better than most people know."

He cleared his throat. "Maybe we should eat before the sandwiches grow cold. Or warm. Or whatever. Heck, I don't even know what he packed for us."

She laughed and they both devoured their food, which ended up being hot ham and cheese on rye with some kind of fancy French sauce that elevated it to cuisine.

When they finished, the easy conversation was over and her expression took on an all-business look as she grabbed a folder from under the table.

"Ready?" she asked, her hands on top of the folder.

"That sounds ominous."

"It's just… It's some research I wanted to discuss with you."

He shifted his chair to face the table better instead of the shrubbery maze. "You do know about my lack of investigative skills, right? Harvard business school grads aren't the best equipped to solve murder mysteries."

"Harvard? Wow. No wonder you're such a snob." She winked to let him know she was teasing. After flipping open the folder, she pulled out a stack of pictures.

"Those look familiar."

"They should. This first one is Erin Speck. These others are the known victims of the River Road Rapist, including the woman who was killed."

Dread settled in his gut. "Known victims? You're implying there are more?"

"I am." She lined up the five known ones in a single row, side by side.

"It's amazing how similar they all look," he said. "Definitely a victim preference there."

"Part of his MO, his modus operandi."

She formed another row beneath the first, all new pictures he'd never seen before. And yet, they seemed achingly familiar. Young, female, with long brown or black hair.

"All these women were raped?" The idea was appalling, horrifying. And when she nodded, the sandwich he'd eaten seemed to sour in his stomach. "Any killed?"

"One." She tapped the middle picture. "Peggy Lidow. This other one—" she pointed to the picture to the left of Peggy "—is Samantha Stuckey. She's officially a missing person. Disappeared two years ago near Knoxville. All of them were either abducted, raped or killed in neighboring counties. They never came up on Gatlinburg PD's radar, or ours, until I went on a hunt to see if there were more victims we didn't know about."

"Why did you do that? Try to find more?"

"The gap between Speck's disappearance and the recent rapes was too long. The time between the rapes has been escalating. He's devolving, becoming more and more unstable. It didn't make sense to me that he'd abduct one woman, go three and a half years without attacking any others, then escalate so much in the past six months."

"Okay," he said, considering. "Using my fledgling detective skills, which are based solely on what I've seen on television, I have to ask what proof you have that these are connected? With Speck, the physical similarity to another victim was so strong it was creepy. And I know some fibers later proved it's the same guy. But what about these? You said they're from other counties. Is there DNA or something like that to link them?"

"The DNA from the one who was killed was too degraded to yield a useful profile. Rape kits were collected from the other victims but never sent to a lab for testing."

He fisted a hand on the table. "Resource and budget constraints again."

"Even you can't afford to fund every police agency out there. Resources will always be a problem in law enforcement no matter what we try to do to help. But in these specific cases, the similarities of their attacks, the fact that each was blindfolded, how their attackers subdued them, it all seems the same to me."

"Are you asking me to sanction testing their DNA, as part of the cases we're already looking into?"

"I am."

"You had to know my answer would be an emphatic yes. I completely trust you to use the company's funds in any way that you see fit. So what's the real reason I'm here?"

She reached for the folder again. As she flipped through it, alarm bells started going off inside him. When she pulled out yet another picture, he eyed it warily as she slid it facedown beneath the second row she'd created.

"The Speck case isn't the only one I worked on during my...break. I'd read a coroner's report about another potential victim of our serial rapist and murderer. And even though everything about the victim fit with the case we're working, one thing didn't. Her hair. At the time of her death, it was short, and blond." She searched his gaze. "But that wasn't always the case. When I was in your office one day, months ago, I noticed a picture on your desk. It was a picture of Maura. Something about it bothered me but I wasn't sure what, until I was researching your family's case on my own and thought about that picture. I searched the internet and found a copy of that same picture. You must have shared it with a reporter, because it was in a story he did about your family."

She slowly turned the picture over.

He stared down at the picture of his wife, the one he saw every time he visited the mausoleum. The one her father had taken the day of their wedding. It shook him to his core as he scanned the two rows of victims above her. Every one of them could have been sisters.

And he'd never even considered a link, until now.

"She thought of herself as a rebel," he said, half smiling as he always did whenever she'd reminded him of that fact. "Her family emigrated here from Japan when she was a little girl. Like my parents, hers were strict, old-fashioned. They forbade her to dye or cut her hair. Or get a tattoo. So, of course, she did all of that. But out of respect for them, she'd waited until after we were married. Being rebellious at that point wasn't the big thrill she'd thought it would be. And she didn't like the work involved in constantly dying her roots. So for the most part, she kept her hair its natural color, black. And she'd grow it out. Until she got bored and cut it and bleached it blond again."

He forced himself to look up from her photo. "Mid-twenties, well-off, nice clothes, expensive jewelry. Long dark hair most of the time. But not when she was killed."

She gave him a sympathetic smile. "There's another difference too. Her hair, her blond hair, was violently hacked by the killer. There were tufts of it all over the foyer. It's one of the things that didn't fit, something that puzzled me. So I called a friend of mine, someone I met in my psychology classes. She's a consultant now, works with law enforcement. In her opinion, it's entirely possible that whoever killed your wife saw her first with long dark hair and fixated on her."

"Then what?" he asked. "He decided to kill her because she dyed her hair blond?"

"What's more likely is that he chose her as his next

victim, possibly even his first victim ever, when her hair was dark. He didn't know she'd dyed it. When he knocked on the door, he expected the woman he'd fantasized about. Instead, a woman with short blond hair answered. It incensed him, destroyed his fantasy. He went into a frenzy, chopping her hair. She's the only victim who was shot, but she was also stabbed, which is consistent with the other attacks. I could be wrong—"

"But you could be right."

"If I am, then we need to have her clothes tested, like we've wanted all along. We need to do everything possible to try to find some DNA the killer left behind. The good news is that if we can get the profile, and it matches the one from the River Road Rapist cases, we already know the killer's identity. Or, we will, once your lab tests the swabs and provides the profiles."

"The suspects from your list."

"Exactly."

He sat back and stretched his legs out in front of him. "I should be relieved that we might be close to solving her case. But I kind of want to break something right now. It's revolting and infuriating that my wife, and my little girl, could have been killed because some sick animal liked, or didn't like, her hair."

He pushed to his feet. "Thank you. This is incredible, everything you've found. But I have to say, I don't know how you do it, day in and day out, dealing with this ugliness. I saw horrible things in combat, awful things. But this, somehow this is worse. Maybe because it's women, and in one case, a child. I don't know. If I investigated this stuff all the time, I'd be a complete basket case. Hell, I *am* a complete basket case. I need a minute."

He didn't wait for her reply. He strode back to the house and didn't stop until he'd reached his office. He stared for a long time at the picture on his desk, the same one that Willow had shown him in the gardens. He feathered his hands over it, then grabbed a round crystal paperweight sitting beside it. He clenched his hand around it, over and over, as hard as he could, trying to calm the rage inside him.

Such a senseless, useless waste of life. Over *nothing.*

He crossed to stand a few feet from one of the floor-to-ceiling windows, trying hard to cage the beast that Willow's words had set free. It was a beast he was familiar with, the rage and cruelty he could unleash on an enemy on the battlefield and never blink an eye. It was the pent-up frustration and resentments from his childhood that hadn't been nearly as idyllic as he'd allowed Willow to believe.

He'd had a love-hate relationship with his parents, mostly hate where his father was concerned. And he'd dreaded every time they returned from one of their trips. When they left again, he'd hide away in his room until the bruises faded. Once they had, he'd try to forget he even had parents. He'd play in the woods, spend his nights in the fort, exchange ghost stories with the staff.

But the rage was always there.

It was why he'd joined the military, hoping he could channel that anger into something constructive. The medals gathering dust in some closet upstairs proved that he had. But now he wanted nothing more than to let go, to let it fly, to scream to the heavens about how unfair it was that all those people—especially Maura and Katrina—had suffered and died at the hands of a crazed killer, over something as random and petty as whether he liked, or didn't like, their hair.

A knock sounded and the door opened behind him.

"I'm so sorry to bother you," Willow called out. "But

I thought you'd want to know this right away. Some of the DNA test results are already back. Grayson, we've got a match."

He slowly turned to face her, his fingers tightening around the paperweight. "Is it Jeffries?"

She hesitated. "Yes."

He stared at her, the rage building. "Your old boss, a cop, raped and killed those women? Maybe even my wife? My child?"

"No, Grayson. He didn't. His *son* did."

He let out a guttural roar and hurled the paperweight through the window.

Chapter Eighteen

Willow sat beside Grayson in Chief Russo's office, waiting for him to arrive. She slid another sideways glance at Grayson before looking away.

He let out a deep sigh. "I'm not going to break another window."

"I didn't think that you were."

He speared her with his stormy blue gaze. "Are you afraid of me now?"

She stared at him, sensing the pain and worry beneath the thin veneer of civility he was struggling to maintain ever since she'd waved the red flag of his wife's murderer's name in front of him.

Desperate to break through the wall he'd erected around himself since learning about Jeffries's son, she did something she'd wanted to do since the first moment she'd realized he really was trying to save her in that back alley. She did something crazy, completely inappropriate given the current situation. And the only thing she could think of to try to reach the sweet, gentle man drowning beneath all that anger and pain.

She kissed him.

Really kissed him.

She leaned across the arms of their chairs and plastered her breasts against his chest. She poured all the love she'd been trying to deny into that kiss, letting him know without words that he *was* loved, that he mattered, that she trusted him. Completely. Unconditionally. No matter what.

And that he could trust himself.

He wasn't the animal he thought himself to be after losing control in his office. The self-loathing and shame that had crossed his face after he'd shattered the window had been quickly hidden behind a wall he'd thrown up between them ever since. She knew he was hurting, that he was embarrassed. And she wanted him to know he didn't need to feel guilty about anything.

He made a strangled sound deep in his throat, and then he was kissing her back. He was wild, almost savage in his response. But he didn't hurt her. Never that. His hands speared through her long hair, pulling her head back, giving him better access. Then he thrust his tongue inside, stroking her into a frenzy as his hands slid down, down, down.

She jerked against him, his expert touch setting off a fire inside her, sizzling across her nerve endings. Good grief, if they didn't stop she was going to tear off his clothes and straddle him right there in the police chief's office. With an unlocked door. And half the police force in the squad room just outside.

She broke the kiss, her chest heaving as she stared wide-eyed at him from six inches away, her hands clutching the arms of his chair to keep from falling. "Ho… ly…cow."

His lips curved in a slow sexy smile. "I'm guessing this means you're not afraid of me."

She snorted, then gasped in dismay at the ugly sound.

He grinned. "You're utterly adorable. If you were trying to distract me, mission accomplished." His smile faded as he gently smoothed her hair back. Then he cupped her face and kissed her again. A soft achingly sweet kiss that had her wanting to weep from the beauty of it.

When he pulled back, he ran his thumb across her lower lip in a caress that was almost as devastating as his wild kiss. She shivered in response, then lightly bit his thumb.

He drew a sharp breath, his body taut as a bow against her. "When this is over, we really, *really* need to talk."

"Or...something." She winked.

He laughed, then sobered at the sound of approaching footsteps.

She plopped down in her chair, hastily smoothing her shirt and hair. Grayson simply tugged his suit jacket and shoved a hand through his hair. Once. It fell expertly into place. No one would look at him and suspect he'd been practically devouring her thirty seconds ago. And here she was, still frantically finger-combing her hair.

When the door opened, she quickly dropped her hands. Russo marched in, followed by one of the court reporters Willow had met a few times before. Sergeant Jeffries slinked in behind them. He shut the door, no doubt not wanting his peers to hear the upcoming conversation. Not that they wouldn't find out eventually.

Grayson watched Jeffries's every move like a predator ready to attack. Willow placed her hand on his forearm, not caring one bit if Russo or her former boss noticed or what they thought of it. She wanted Grayson to know she was there for him, no matter what.

Russo plopped into his chair and ordered Jeffries to sit in a chair on the left side of the room, beside the court reporter who set up her steno machine on the edge of the desk.

Willow and Grayson were sitting on the right side. Luckily for Jeffries, it was out of slugging range. Because no matter what Jeffries planned on saying, neither she nor Grayson believed he couldn't have known about his son and what he was doing to those poor women.

Russo introduced everyone for the court reporter's benefit. After explaining that an official record was being made of the meeting, he motioned to Willow.

"Tell us what the lab told you. To save time, I already told our court reporter, on the record, about the whole genealogy thing you explained earlier today. You can add to that and then I'm going to fill in some blanks you don't even know about."

She glanced in confusion at Grayson, then turned to the chief. "I'll keep it as brief as I can. The genealogy work indicates that one of the six suspects we've come up with is the rapist and killer we're all looking for. This morning, DNA swabs were taken from two of those people—Sergeant Mike Jeffries and his son, Steve Jeffries. I received a call from the lab this afternoon stating the test results were back on those samples. Both were negative. They didn't match the killer's profile. However, Sergeant Jeffries's profile revealed a close familial link to the killer's profile, a father–son link. So the lab concluded there *is* a match, to Steve, pending a retest. His original sample must have been contaminated somehow and he'll need to provide a new sample. In the meantime, it would be prudent to arrest him now—if you haven't already—to ensure he doesn't go on the run."

Russo crossed his arms on top of his desk. "And I agreed with that suggestion when you explained that on the phone earlier. So I've got Steve downstairs on a twenty-four hour hold. But there's a problem. You see, while waiting for your lab to perform the testing earlier today, our guys did some digging on Mike and Steve, alibi checking, pending those DNA results. At the time of three of the attacks, Steve has a rock-solid alibi. He was out of the country for work."

Grayson straightened. "Then you need to check his alibi again. Something's not right."

"I agree with you. Something's definitely not right. So I had my guys recheck the alibi. There is no mistake. Mike's son, Steve, couldn't have raped or killed those women." He speared Sergeant Jeffries with a frosty look. "Which is why I sat down with Mike, here, and asked him to explain what the hell was going on. DNA doesn't lie. Turns out, Mike's a liar. Steve isn't his only biological son. His *other* son is Brian Nelson."

Grayson swore. "You son of a—"

"Couldn't agree more," Russo interrupted. "Brian is Mike's son by his mistress. He had his sister adopt him so they could keep him in the family, without breaking the news about the affair to Mike's wife, so she doesn't know he's a total slimeball. Did I get all that right? Sergeant?"

Jeffries had gone alarmingly pale. "Yes, sir."

Grayson swore. "You idiot. You flat-out told us that Brian was adopted, that we didn't need to test his DNA or look at him as a suspect. But you knew all along he was the killer. The rapist. Didn't you?"

Jeffries violently shook his head. "No, no, no. It's not like that. I swear. I never, in my worst nightmares, thought either of my boys capable of something so vile. I was sure they were both innocent. But I didn't want my wife finding out Brian's real connection to me because of some unnecessary DNA test. I couldn't risk the questions it would raise if the lab questioned why my DNA and Brian's came out looking like father–son instead of uncle–nephew. I figured once you tested the other guys on your list, one of them would match the killer's profile and there'd be no need to test Brian. I wasn't trying to protect a killer. I was trying to protect my wife. Brian knows I'm his dad. But my wife doesn't. I didn't want her hurt."

Grayson narrowed his eyes at him. "You weren't protecting your wife. You were protecting yourself. *You* didn't want to get hurt when your wife left you."

"Enough," Russo said. "We can throw around accusations and blame later. What matters right now is finding Brian Nelson and our missing woman, Nicole Paletta."

Willow's hand tightened on Grayson's arm. "What do you mean *find* Brian? You don't know where he is?"

Once again, Russo glared at Jeffries. "Want to answer that one?"

He twisted his hands together, looking miserable. "Mr. Prescott, the chief told me what you and Willow figured out. That the River Road Rapist may be the one who killed your wife and daughter. I'm so sorry—"

"I don't want to hear how sorry you are. In addition to the DNA lies, you provided an alibi for Brian during my wife's attack. Cut to the chase, Jeffries. Where's Brian?" Grayson bit out.

He swallowed. "I don't know. Truly, I don't. I told him to lay low until the DNA came back on the other suspects. I said I'd tell human resources that he's out sick. He's supposed to come back in a couple of days."

Grayson shook his head, rage warring with disbelief in his expression. "Nicole Paletta is out there somewhere, kidnapped by your son. If you hadn't warned him about the DNA testing, he could have been taken into custody at work today. Instead, thanks to your lies, he's probably doing unspeakable things to her before he kills her and drops off the radar to pop up somewhere else and start raping and killing all over again. How many more will be hurt or killed because you weren't man enough to own up to a stupid affair?"

Jeffries turned ashen. "I'm so sorry."

Russo rapped his knuckles on his desk to get their attention. "We've got a BOLO out on Brian Nelson. Everyone in law enforcement will be on the lookout for him. It's all hands on deck. We're turning over every rock we can to find this guy and rescue Ms. Paletta."

Grayson turned away from Jeffries, effectively dismissing him as beneath his contempt.

"Chief," Willow asked, "have you contacted the phone company, tried to track Brian's cell phone to locate him?"

"We're working with the phone company on that right now."

"I'll get our team to switch gears," Grayson said. "They've been researching five of the original suspects, everyone except Brian. We'll get them digging into his background to try to suggest places where he might hide."

"My team's doing the same. Let's keep each other posted on our progress. Jeffries and his sister will sit down with my detectives and tell us everything they know about Brian, as well. Isn't that right, Sergeant?"

"Yes, sir. Of course, sir. I'll go call her right now, tell her to come to the station." Jeffries rushed from the room.

Grayson and Willow exchanged an uneasy glance.

"Chief," Willow said. "Are you sure you can trust Jeffries not to take off? If he knows where Brian is, he could go warn him."

A slow smile spread across Russo's face, the first he'd had since he'd come into the room. "Like I said earlier today, Detective. You're an excellent investigator. I came to the same conclusion as soon as I spoke to Jeffries about this fiasco. Except I don't think he'd try to warn

Brian. He'll want to bring him in himself, to make sure he doesn't get cornered by some other cop and get shot."

"You're tailing your sergeant," Grayson said.

"I've got two of my best guys on it. And a GPS tracker on his car."

Chapter Nineteen

Grayson walked into the converted library the next morning with a tray bearing three coffee cups. "Wake up, sleepyheads."

Ryland didn't stir. He was snoring, facedown across a stack of papers on his desk. Grayson left a cup for him on the far corner, out of the danger zone for flailing arms so Ryland wouldn't knock it over when he woke up. He was betting the smell would wake him soon.

Willow wasn't in much better shape than Ryland. But at least she'd been smart enough to curl up on one of the couches by the front bank of windows instead of falling asleep in a chair.

She opened one bleary eye and held out her hand. "Coffee. Now."

He chuckled. "Sit up first. And maybe next time the whole team works until the wee hours of the morning, you'll take my advice and use one of the guest rooms."

She gulped down half the cup without coming up for air. Her eyes narrowed suspiciously as he stared at her. "What?"

"Your hair. It's, ah, interesting this morning."

"Medusa or windblown goddess?"

"I'll go with windblown goddess."

"Smart man." Her eyes widened. "I have to pee." She shoved the cup in his hand and took off for the bathroom.

Grayson was still chuckling when he heard Ryland yawning. He turned around, sipping from his own cup. "Morning."

"Morning." He yawned again. "Where is everyone?"

"It's Saturday, Ryland. I ordered everyone to head home at about 3:00 a.m. and not to come back for at least eight hours. Although, to be honest, I expect Trent will sneak back long before that. He gave me quite an argument about not wanting to stop working."

Ryland smiled. "Sounds like Trent."

"Hopefully he'll heed my advice anyway. The whole team's running on empty. You all need your rest. I would have made you and Willow go too but you were both already asleep."

Ryland scratched at the five o'clock shadow on his face. "Did they find Paletta? Brian Nelson?"

Grayson settled in a chair one desk over. "Not yet. The police and search teams are working in shifts, doing everything they can. Jeffries hasn't done anything suspicious yet. He brought his sister in to give a statement about Brian, then went home to wait and see if Brian calls him. He hasn't left his house."

Ryland pulled his keyboard toward him.

"It's okay to take a break like everyone else. Go upstairs. Crash on the first bed you find."

"I may in a bit. Just want to check one more thing. I figured Brian will hunker down someplace familiar. People tend to gravitate to places they know, especially in times of stress. With half the county searching for him, he has to be feeling stressed."

"Okay, and…?"

"Well, if I can get someone in the human resources

department at Gatlinburg PD to answer a phone on a Saturday, I'd like a copy of Brian's original job application from when he started there, six years ago. I'm hoping it will list the jobs he worked during summers or breaks from college, maybe even some he had in high school. If he worked in a warehouse, for example, maybe if that warehouse is closed down now, out of business, he might use it as a hideout. Or if there's some vacant land near a place he worked before, that could be a place to look too." He held his hands out. "Long shot, I know. But I can't think of much else left to try. And since the police still haven't found him, we might as well go for the long shots."

"Sounds reasonable to me." Willow strode into the room, her hair brushed and looking much closer to the windblown goddess he'd lied about earlier. "If HR doesn't answer the phone, you could call Chief Russo and ask him to rustle up someone to get what you need." She stopped by Ryland's desk. "I'm going to grab something to eat on the run and head outside for some fresh air to get my brain firing again. Anyone want to join me?"

"Maybe. After I make that phone call," Ryland said.

Grayson stood. "Hold on. Both of you. We all want to catch this guy. Me, as much or more than anyone."

Willow gave him a sympathetic look.

"But," he said, "we can't help if we can't function. Eating and sleeping aren't optional. They're a requirement. Even in Special Forces, we tried to make sure we got a full eight hours and a hot meal whenever possible. You work better that way."

"I'm waiting for the punch line somewhere," Willow said.

"The *point* is that you don't need to grab breakfast in a bag. The cook is off today, all the staff is off since it's a weekend. So now I get to cook. Omelets and fresh-baked homemade croissants anyone?"

He headed toward the door, grinning when he heard Willow and Ryland enthusiastically running to catch up.

"Nothing like sunshine and the smell of roses to clear the cobwebs in your brain." Willow eyed Grayson beside her as they strolled down one of the manicured paths by the gardens. "That amazing breakfast helped too. You know, if you ever get tired of being a gazillionaire businessman, you'd have a great future as a chef."

He chuckled. "I'll keep that in mind."

She pulled him to a stop in front of the last greenhouse, where the path ended and the woods began. "Things have gotten pretty crazy since I told you my theory about Maura maybe being the killer's first victim."

Tiny worry lines crinkled at the corners of his eyes. "They have. You've thought of something else, something that might help the police find Brian?"

"A thread to pull. It may or may not lead anywhere. The thing is, Brian would have still been in college when that happened. A senior, I'm guessing, so around twenty-one or two. If my psychologist friend is right and Brian fixated on Maura, fantasizing about her looks for a while before he got the nerve to approach her, he had to have seen her somewhere on a regular basis. But not so regular that he would have known she'd dyed her hair and cut it. He thought she still had long black hair. Can you think of any way to explain that? Would he have seen her in a grocery store maybe, but she only went there every few weeks and not the week after she changed her hair?"

He leaned back against the greenhouse. "Doubtful. Our cook was in charge of all the grocery shopping. He's picky about his fruits and vegetables. I suppose it's possible she might have gone shopping for clothes or accessories. But she wasn't a fan of the small boutiques we have around here. She liked to go on shopping trips, to Sevierville or Knoxville, places with much bigger stores, more variety."

"Did she go to the same stores all the time?"

"Honestly, I don't know. I can't imagine I'd have charge card receipts going back that far either. But now that I think about it, even if she did, she wouldn't have gone to any of them in the months before her death. The baby was only a few months old and neither of us wanted to expose her to crowds and the germs that come with them. She didn't even go to her salon that last time she had her hair bleached. They came here."

"They? More than one person? Like, maybe Brian worked in the salon? Wait, that wouldn't make sense. Then he'd know she'd changed her hair. My psychologist friend doesn't think he would have reacted the way he did, chopping at her hair, if he'd known ahead of time she'd changed it. Dang. I was hoping we were on to something."

"You might be," Ryland called out, jogging up to them. He was breathing a little heavily, trying to catch his breath. "The acoustics out here are almost as bad as when the wind snatches your voice at the beach and you can't hear people ten feet away. I was yelling, but neither of you heard me. Maybe it's the trees or the cladding on the greenhouses absorbing the sound."

"Did you find something?" Grayson asked, pointing to the paper in his hand.

"Right. Sorry. It may or may not help but it sure is interesting. This is the previous work experience portion of Brian's job application. He worked *here*."

"Here?" Willow and Grayson both said at the same time.

"Yep. The address he gave is your home address and he listed Mr. Baines as his boss."

"Baines," Grayson said. "The gardens. Brian must have been one of the college kids Mr. Baines hired as temp help. Maura was in these gardens all the time. She spent hours in the greenhouses, cultivating hybrid-roses. That must be where Brian saw her." He swore. "All this time, I thought I'd let her down by not having good enough security at the house, when it should have been the gardens—and the people working there—that I should have guarded her against."

Willow stepped closer to him. "The only way to have protected her from every possible evil person in this world was to lock her away and never let her outside. She'd have been a prisoner in her own home. That's not a life, Grayson. And her death is *not* your fault."

He gave her a crisp nod of thanks, but she wasn't sure he agreed with her.

"What else did you find out, Ryland?" she asked.

He shot Grayson a sympathetic look before continuing. "He listed Baines as a reference, not that anyone at the police station followed up on that. If they had, they might not have hired him."

"Why not?" Grayson asked.

"Because I called Baines and asked him about Brian." His face flushed a light red. "I, ah, hope you don't mind. I wanted to save some time, so I checked the files in your office, figuring you'd have the payroll information there for your household staff so I could get a current phone number for him."

"I'll have to get a lock for that drawer," he said dryly. "What did he tell you?"

"Brian Nelson worked here for three summers. But the last one was cut short, because Mr. Baines fired him. Get this. The main reason was because he was acting inappropriately with some of the female staff. They felt uncomfortable around him."

Willow rubbed her hands up and down her arms. "No surprise there. I felt uncomfortable around him too. There was always something odd about how he'd look at me."

Grayson frowned. "Did he ever hurt you?"

"No, no. I made it clear I wouldn't put up with his unwanted attentions early on."

The worry in his eyes faded and he addressed Ryland. "You said that was the main reason. There was another one?"

"This is the *really* interesting part. Apparently, Brian didn't have much of a work ethic. He goofed off a lot and would disappear for hours at a time. Baines said he'd often see him coming out of the woods after disappearing for a while. When asked, he said he was studying the plants, to help him become a better gardener. Baines said if that were the case, it didn't help. He was terrible."

Willow put her hand on Grayson's sleeve. "This could be it. Maybe Brian had some hideaway out there. And he's still using it even now."

Grayson's expression was less than enthusiastic. "Even if he did, we wouldn't know where to begin looking. These woods cover the back half of the mountain and meet up with the Smoky Mountains National Park on the other side. We're talking thousands of acres of uninhabited land, most of it nearly impossible to hike because the brush is so dense, with steep drop-offs."

"I don't think we have to worry about searching thousands of acres," she said. "Just the ones with something that might provide a good place to hide someone. Something that's close enough to the gardens for relatively easy access, but not so close that someone might accidentally stumble upon it. Some kind of structure, perhaps. Like a fort?"

His eyes widened.

"How far away is it?" she asked.

Ryland glanced back and forth between them. "It? What are we talking about?"

Grayson considered. "Far enough not to hear someone scream. Especially if the acoustics are like Ryland mentioned. He's probably right. I've never thought about that before."

"Uh, guys. Catch me up here?"

Willow hiked her pant leg up, revealing her ankle holster.

"No." Grayson grabbed her wrist as she pulled the gun out. "If anyone goes out there, it's the police."

"Grayson. I *am* the police. Which way to the fort?"

He swore viciously, not letting go of her wrist.

"He could be killing her right now," she argued. "Let me go. Trust me. I know what I'm doing."

"Ah, hell. Ryland, call Chief Russo and tell him there's a fort, an old building in the woods where I used to play as a kid. There's only one room, about twenty-by-twenty, two windows, two doors. It's a hundred yards in from where we're standing, due east through heavy brush. If I remember right, it's about fifty yards south of a creek. Brian Nelson may be using it to hold Paletta hostage, and no telling what else. He needs to get a team up here to thoroughly search the area, but make sure he knows we're out here. If we don't call you, or if we don't come back to this exact spot, in the next fifteen minutes, something's gone wrong. Have Russo send in a tactical team. Hell, send the whole freaking police department."

Ryland took out his cell phone and swiped through his contact list for Chief Russo.

Willow tugged her gun arm free and sprinted toward the woods.

Chapter Twenty

Grayson snatched the gun out of Willow's hand and spun her around, backing her up against a tree.

She stared at him in shock. "How did you do that? I didn't even know you were right behind me."

"Exactly. You didn't hear me, didn't know I was there. I could have snapped your neck and you'd be dead before you hit the ground."

Shock gave way to anger, her green eyes practically flashing sparks at him as she shoved at his chest.

He didn't budge.

"What is this?" she demanded. "Some male chauvinist way of putting me in my place? Telling me women shouldn't be cops or something? That we're the weaker sex?"

"You *are* the weaker sex. It's simple biology, not some chauvinistic insult. Pound for pound, men have more muscle mass. It's how we're built. It sucks, but there it is. Which means you have to be smarter, keep your wits about you and rely on your training. I'd rather have a smart well-trained woman with me on a battlefield any day of the week over some knucklehead brute who's like a bull in a China shop. But what you're doing right now isn't going to help Paletta. It's just going to get one or both of us hurt, or killed."

He handed her gun to her and stepped back, scanning the bushes and trees around them as he did. Lowering his voice, he said, "You don't know this terrain. Neither do I, not anymore. If Brian's using the fort as his base of operations, he's likely been doing it for years. He knows these woods inside and out. Does that police training of yours tell you it makes sense to run in blind in circumstances like this? Because that sure isn't what my army training tells me."

Her face went pale as his words sank in. She glanced around, scanning their surroundings as he'd done. "Okay, okay," she said, keeping her voice low too. "You're right. I shouldn't have taken off like that. But I'm not waiting around for Russo's guys to get here either. Brian could be hurting Paletta right now."

"Agreed. Waiting isn't an option. So we need to work as a team. If you'd waited back there instead of taking off, you'd have heard me tell you to silence your phone like I've done. No one wants to get killed because a text chimed on their phone at the worst possible moment."

She blinked. "Crap. I didn't even think of that." She quickly silenced her phone, then shoved it back in her pocket.

"We need to look out for each other," he said. "Watch each other's backs."

"How? You don't have a gun."

He held up his hands. "I have these. That's all I need."

Her eyes widened.

He checked the compass feature on his watch, then pointed. "Due east is that way. We use hand signals from here on out. Step softly and try to make as little noise as possible. I'll lead—"

"But—"

"*I'll lead.* Maybe it's that male chauvinist thing coming out in me. But I'm not about to let you lead this time. If the killer's out here, I'd rather be the one to run into him first."

Her eyes widened. "Then at least take my gun—"

"Hell, no. I'm not leaving you defenseless. Silence from here on out. All right?"

She cleared her throat. "Fine. Can we go now? *Sir?*"

He nodded, and waited until he'd turned around to smile.

WILLOW FOLLOWED GRAYSON, her embarrassment at going off half-cocked like a rookie overshadowed by her deepening respect for him. During the months they'd worked so hard together to make Unfinished Business a reality, he'd amazed her with his business acumen and ability to juggle that along with his daily conference calls and split-second decision-making for his other companies. But that all seemed inconsequential compared to watching his survival and reconnaissance skills here in the woods.

Even with all those impressive muscles, he could step like a deer, placing his feet in just the right spots to avoid snapping a twig or crunching a dry leaf. And he was constantly on the alert, like a jungle cat sniffing out danger. As an adversary, he'd be mind-numbingly terrifying. She was extremely grateful to have him as an ally. She just hoped she didn't let him down, like making too much noise as she followed behind him or not reacting quickly enough if it came to a gun battle.

She really wished they both had a gun.

He suddenly stopped and held up his hand, signaling her to stop too. She tried to keep her breaths even and quiet as she carefully scanned the nearby trees and bushes like he was doing. A full minute passed before he finally gave the signal that all was well, and they started forward again.

She was getting used to how he operated, so it didn't surprise her the next time he stopped and gave a signal for them to turn. They each rotated in complete circles, her with both hands wrapped around the butt of her gun, ready to fire if Brian suddenly came crashing out of the trees at them.

After what seemed like an eternity later, but was probably closer to five minutes, they stopped and crouched down in the tree line at the edge of a small clearing. She expected to see the fort he'd spoken about, but all she saw was a long mound of dirt about six feet away. Another one was spaced about ten feet from the first, off to the right. Were they burrows? For a raccoon or some other woodland creature? She leaned over, peering between some branches to see the rest of the clearing. This time, she didn't see a dirt mound. Instead, the ground had sunken in, but it was the same shape as the others.

She blinked, and glanced at the mounds again, then realized Grayson was watching her. The grim expression on his face confirmed what she'd just figured out. These weren't animal burrows.

They were graves.

Chapter Twenty-One

Grayson texted Ryland a picture of what he was sure would prove to be graves of some of Brian's victims. Ryland texted back that he would update Russo and that a tactical search team was already on the way, ETA twenty minutes.

Ryland also texted something else, some bad news. Sergeant Jeffries had slipped his tail. The officers assigned to watch him had been worried that they hadn't seen any sign of him for far too long. He hadn't walked past the windows in his house, even though his wife had, several times. So even though his car was still sitting in the driveway, they made the decision to blow their cover and knock on the door.

The panicked look on his wife's face had confirmed their fears even before she let them inside to perform a search. She quickly caved, admitting that Jeffries had snuck out the back of their house a few hours earlier. He'd climbed a neighbor's fence to get away without being seen. But she claimed he'd refused to tell her where he was going or what kind of trouble he was in.

He'd left his cell phone at home and they didn't know what kind of vehicle he might be driving. If he was going to wherever Brian was, to warn him—which everyone believed—they had no way of tracking him.

The police were going door-to-door, talking to his neighbors to see if anyone had loaned him their car. Hopefully, they'd find out what he was driving, soon, so they could put out a BOLO.

Grayson figured the best-case scenario was that Brian had left Paletta out here but that he wasn't around right now. Unless Brian had built some kind of shelter on his own, which Grayson doubted. Given his penchant for not wanting to work, the fort seemed the most likely place to stash Paletta. If they could find her and get her to safety before Brian returned, it would be far safer for everyone involved.

With Jeffries possibly in the mix though, that added a whole new level of risk. Would Jeffries fire at his former fellow officer, and Grayson, if it meant protecting his son? Or would he do the right thing and take him down? Grayson fervently hoped that Willow wouldn't get to find out.

He motioned her close and whispered the updates. The red spots on her cheeks told him she was furious with her former boss. She probably felt his betrayal even more acutely, since they'd worked so closely together.

Grayson squeezed her hand in solidarity. He understood all too well how critical it was to be able to trust and rely on your fellow soldiers, or in her case, her fellow officers. Even though, technically, she *wasn't* a cop anymore. Her heated declaration earlier about being the police meant she still thought of herself as one.

They circled the clearing, keeping to the cover of the trees. He consulted his compass a few times, making corrections to their course as needed. The ground cover and bushes out here had grown up considerably since he'd been a kid. Maybe because he hadn't been out here, regularly hacking them back with a machete so he could keep a path open to his so-called fort.

The going was slow and difficult, and he worried that no matter how quiet they were trying to be, if Brian was out here, he might already have heard them and was lying in wait.

Which made this little scouting expedition even more dangerous.

If it weren't for the possibility that a woman's life was in imminent danger, he'd pull Willow with him and get her back to safety. He didn't doubt her capabilities, now that she'd calmed down and was using her training. What he doubted was *his* ability to focus without letting his concern for the woman he'd grown to care about making him too cautious, which could be just as dangerous as being too bold and rushing in without assessing the situation.

She jogged to his side and motioned to the right. There, less than fifty feet away, was what they'd been looking for. The fort. It was in better condition than he'd expected after all these years. But then Mr. Baines didn't do anything halfway. He and his precocious employer's son had built it with attention to quality and making sure it would withstand the elements. The siding was gray and weathered, but aside from a few rotting boards near the eaves, it looked sound.

They crouched down, watching and waiting. With no sign of Brian, or Jeffries, they crept through the trees until they were parallel to a sidewall, just out of sight of the open window, should anyone look out. He turned to motion to her to wait here, just in time to see her running out of the trees a few yards down, not stopping until she reached the fort.

He really wanted to swear right now. But at least she

was being cautious, ducking down, gun out in front as she eased closer to the window opening. It had been left open, like the doors, probably to provide ventilation.

Since he was left as her wingman, he kept an eye out, scanning left and right, while she carefully eased up to peer through the opening. She ducked back down and nodded.

They'd found Paletta.

Unfortunately, Brian Nelson had found them.

He stepped out of the tree line on their left side, pointing his gun directly at Willow.

Grayson dove out of the trees, dropping and rolling on the ground, purposely drawing Brian's startled attention away from her.

Gunshots rang out as she laid down cover. Brian fired back, but his shots went wild as he sprinted into the woods.

Grayson jumped up and grabbed Willow, lifting her and running even as she continued shooting toward where Brian had disappeared. He skidded around the far corner of the building, out of Brian's sight line.

He set her down, and together they ran through the open doorway into the building. They had to act fast, get the victim out of the danger zone before Brian worked up his nerve to come after them.

The victim's eyes had grown big and round when they ran inside. Her mouth was gagged. Her hands were zip-tied together, as were her ankles. Several more zip ties had been used to connect the ones around her wrists to a metal hook bolted into the floor. She was naked, with dried blood on her breasts and thighs.

Willow swore a thorough list of obscenities about Brian.

Grayson couldn't agree more.

Willow positioned herself by the second door, the one facing the woods where Brian had gone. Grayson ran to the woman and dropped to his knees beside her as he pulled out his pocket knife. She made noises behind the gag, jerking back. Guilt flooded through him as he realized he'd just traumatized her even more. She was shaking and looked absolutely terrified.

"NICOLE PALETTA, RIGHT?" He kept his voice soothing and gentle, as if he had all the time in the world and everything was okay.

She didn't nod or shake her head in response. He wasn't even sure she could see beyond her terror and understand him, but he had to try.

"We're not going to hurt you. We're here to get you out of here. I'm Grayson Prescott. And that's my friend over there, Detective Willow McCray." He didn't figure the lie about Willow still being a cop mattered if it would help put the victim at ease.

Her wide-eyed gaze darted toward Willow, still standing by the doorway.

"I'm going to cut your restraints, okay? I promise I won't hurt you."

Hoping she understood, he quickly sliced through the zip ties, freeing her. She scrambled backward until her back pressed against the wall near the open window.

Grayson wished he had his hands around Brian's neck right now.

"Nicole, help is on the way. The police are sending a team up here to rescue you. But the thing is, we can't wait for them. Officer Willow is protecting us from the man who tied you up, the man who hurt you. But he's going to come back. And we need to get out of here before he does."

She shook her head, her hair flying around her face. He realized he hadn't taken off her gag. And she seemed too scared or confused to do it herself. "Is it okay if I take that off?" He pointed at her mouth.

She hesitated, then nodded.

Progress.

"Hurry," Willow called out. "I've seen movement out there. I think he's about ready to try something."

Grayson tore the gag off and she started coughing, trying to spit out another piece of cloth stuffed into her mouth. He pulled it out and threw it aside.

"Come on, Nicole. Let's go."

"No, no. You said he's outside." Her voice was raspy and raw, her words barely above a whisper. "Wait here for the police."

"If I thought they could get here in time, we would. The problem is there's no cover in here. Nothing to stop a bullet. Those walls are better than nothing, but not by much. The trees will offer much better protection. It's our best chance."

"He's on the move," Willow called out. The pop of her gun firing sounded, followed by answering gunfire from outside. Then *click, click, click.*

Grayson jerked around to see Willow running toward him.

"Bad news," she announced as she dropped to her knees beside them. She held up her gun. "I'm out of ammo."

Chapter Twenty-Two

Willow spoke soothingly to Nicole, who was clutching her hand so hard it ached. But Willow wasn't about to tell her that. The poor woman had obviously been through a horrible ordeal.

And it wasn't over yet.

Grayson jogged over to them from the doorway where Willow had been moments earlier. "I don't see him. I think the sneaky little coward may be circling through the woods to get to the other side of the building. We have to get out of here before he reaches it. Meaning right now."

He scooped Nicole up in his arms. She let out a little squeak of terror and started batting at him with her arms.

"Nicole, Nicole, stop," Willow told her. "He's trying to help you."

Grayson shifted her in his arms, ducking his head to the side to avoid a flying fist. "I'm sorry. But there's no time to make this easy on you." He tossed her over his shoulder and he and Willow took off for the same doorway they'd entered earlier.

Grayson swore savagely and they both skidded to a halt in the middle of the building.

Sergeant Jeffries stood in the doorway. And he was raising his gun. Very slowly, Grayson lowered Nicole to the floor, then shoved her behind his back.

"Sergeant, don't. Please," Willow called out, raising her arms as if that could stop a bullet.

But Jeffries didn't point his pistol at her, or Grayson and Nicole, who was timidly peeking around Grayson's side.

He pointed it toward the opposite doorway.

Willow slowly turned. Brian must have stepped inside while their backs were turned. His pistol was pointed at them, as if he'd been about to shoot. But then he slowly turned it toward his father.

"Here to join in on the fun, Dad?" Brian smirked.

Grayson softly nudged his shoe against Willow's, getting her attention. He motioned almost imperceptibly with one of his fingers, toward the back open window. It was plenty big enough for someone to jump through it.

She blinked once, to let him know she understood. Grayson slowly eased back, bumping into Nicole. But she'd been paying attention, and now seemed more than ready to go along with what he had planned, anything to get her to safety.

The three of them started slowly backing up, trying not to make any sudden or obvious movements that might turn either Brian's or his father's attention on them.

Jeffries's face twisted with pain. "Don't talk like that, son. This isn't you. You don't want to hurt anyone."

"I don't?" Brian motioned toward the woods behind him. "Tell that to all those special gals I've got out there feeding worms." He chuckled.

A keening moan whistled between Jeffries's teeth. He shook his head. "No. No. You're trying to shock me. You wouldn't do something like that. You're not the monster they're saying you are."

He smiled. "You don't think so? I'll bet if you ask Nikki, she might disagree with you." He nodded toward

Nicole, who was once again peeking around Grayson. Brian swung his pistol toward them. "Stop right there. Don't take another step."

They stopped. Willow tried to step in front of Grayson, hoping to shield him. He jerked her back, his glare letting her know in no uncertain terms that he wouldn't allow her to do that.

"Leave them alone," Jeffries ordered.

Brian slowly turned his gun back toward his father. "Or what? You're going to shoot your own son?"

"You know I don't want to do that. I want to protect you. I'm here to bring you in. You can't outrun this forever. You need to give up before some gun-happy SWAT guy shoots you."

Brian made a show of looking around. "I don't see any SWAT guys pointing a gun at me. Only you."

"Brian—"

"Shut up. Don't pretend you care about me. I'm your dirty little secret, the one you're too ashamed of to tell your wife about."

"I'm so sorry—"

"Enough. How did you even find me? And why did you bring them with you?"

Jeffries's eyes widened. "I didn't bring them. I went searching for you. When I couldn't find you, I thought maybe you'd head here, to hide out by our favorite fishing hole."

"*Our* favorite fishing hole? The creek out back? The one I brought you to a handful of times in college? It hardly qualifies as *our* favorite spot since you haven't taken me fishing in years."

Jeffries's face reddened and he started blubbering through another apology.

Grayson tugged on Willow's shirt, pulling her with

him and Nicole toward the window again. When they reached it, he mouthed one word. "Go."

She glanced at the opening, then back at him, before shaking her head. "Not without you," she mouthed silently.

Nicole tugged on Willow's arm, her eyes pleading with hers.

"I should have paid more attention to you, son," Jeffries continued talking to Brian. "I should have done more things with you. Work's just always so busy and—"

Willow tuned him out. Grayson had just mouthed something else. *Trust me.* The situation was impossible. She was terrified that if she and Nicole jumped through the window opening, they'd be leaving Grayson to die in a hail of gunfire. She instinctively knew he wouldn't dive through with them. He'd want to stay and buy them some time.

He'd asked her to trust him, and she did. He'd been in Special Forces, had fought the enemy overseas and had come back safe and unharmed. She also knew that if he didn't have her and Nicole to worry about, he'd be free to do whatever he was planning, to somehow bring an end to this horrible situation. Although what exactly he planned was beyond her. Trust him. She had to trust him.

She nodded, letting him know she was ready even though the idea of leaving him there was killing her.

Nicole glanced back and forth between them and nodded, letting them know she was ready too.

"Just how did you expect this to end, Dad?" Brian asked, their conversation continuing.

Grayson silently counted down. Three. Two. One. Go.

Willow dove out the window. Grayson shoved Nicole through the opening after her, then disappeared back into the building.

Shouts sounded from inside, followed by a guttural yell. A single gunshot echoed. Willow bit her lip, desperately wanting to know what had just happened, and desperately wanting to help. But she had to do what Grayson wanted her to do. She had to get Nicole to safety.

She grabbed Nicole's arm and yanked her to standing. Nicole wobbled, the adrenaline that had given her strength moments ago seeming to fail her now. Willow grabbed her waist and pulled her arm around her shoulders. Together, they hobbled as fast as they could toward the cover of the trees.

Chapter Twenty-Three

Grayson slowly raised his hands as he stared down the barrel of Brian's gun. He counted himself lucky that Brian was such a lousy shot. But as red as Brian's face was, it was only a matter of time before he pulled the trigger again.

"Don't," Jeffries pleaded. "Please, Brian. Don't shoot. Put your gun down."

"Don't shoot? Are you kidding me, old man? He helped them escape! And he threw a frickin' knife at me!" His knuckles whitened on the grip of the gun. "The only reason I haven't shot again, yet, is because I want to know how he figured out I was here." He motioned with the gun at Grayson. "Does anyone else know?"

"Just Willow and me. We were talking about my childhood and I wanted to show her the fort."

"Fort? What fort?"

"This building. I called it a fort when I was a kid."

Brian rolled his eyes and said something about crazy rich people. He'd bought Grayson's lie about no one else knowing they were here. That would buy some time for Russo's guys to reach this place before Brian bailed. But it didn't do anything to buy Grayson time.

He glanced at Jeffries, who was still pointing his pistol at his son. *Pull the damn trigger.*

Brian snickered. "I heard you were supposed to be some badass Special Forces guy. What happened? You were sick the day they taught knife-throwing class?"

Keep talking, kid. It gives Russo's team more time.

He shrugged. "Maybe I did." He'd have buried that knife in Brian's throat if he hadn't been both trying to shove the victim out the window to safety and whirling around to avoid being shot while pulling his knife out of his pocket. Too bad he didn't have a second knife with him. At least if Brian killed him now, Willow and Paletta were out of the line of fire, hopefully halfway to the safety of his house.

He'd rather give them enough time to make it all the way, to be certain they were out of danger. Keeping Brian talking could buy them that time. And he knew just what to talk about, something that had been eating him alive for over seven years.

"Why did you kill my wife? What did you do with my daughter?"

Brian's face reddened. "I don't want to talk about that."

Grayson clenched his fists in frustration. "At least tell me what you did with my little girl. Is she here? Buried in the ground like the women you murdered?"

Jeffries made a strangled sound in his throat, his face flushed with shame. Was it because he felt terrible about what Brian had done to Maura, to Katrina, to the others? Or because he felt guilty for doing nothing? Even now, all he had to do was pull the trigger to end this. But he still refused to do the right thing.

Grayson shook his head in disgust. The only hope of getting out of this alive was if he took Brian out himself.

The one thing on his side right now was that Brian had moved closer to Grayson after that first shot went wild. He probably didn't want to risk missing his target again.

Which meant he was almost close enough for Grayson to jump him. Almost. Grayson needed to edge just a little closer to make sure he could reach him. But he needed to turn Brian's attention elsewhere first. He needed him to focus on Jeffries.

"Sergeant," Grayson said. "Why are you here? The real reason? Are you stalling, trying to get Brian to hang around until backup arrives?"

Brian's gaze darted toward his father. "Did you call the cops?"

Jeffries shook his head, his eyes widening. "No. No, Brian. I wouldn't do that. I told you, I'm here to bring you in myself. I want to protect you so you don't get hurt."

Brian scoffed. "Where was all this tender care when I was growing up? You left me with your stupid sister. Screw it. If the cops are coming, I'm out of here. Just two loose ends to wrap up first." He swung the pistol toward his father.

Grayson darted forward, then lunged.

Bam!

Bam! Bam!

His arms met empty air as he fell to the floor. He rolled and jumped to his feet. Then slowly straightened.

Brian was gone. He must have run out the back doorway, because Ryland stood in the other doorway, pointing a gun where Brian had been moments earlier.

And behind him, in a spreading pool of blood, lay Sergeant Jeffries.

WILLOW SPRINTED THROUGH the back doorway, both hands wrapped around the thick length of wood she'd found, holding it like a baseball bat. She skidded to a stop, shocked and confused at what she saw. Grayson and Ryland were crouched over Jeffries's body, feeling for a pulse, even though it was obvious he couldn't possibly be alive with a wound like that. She looked around, but didn't see anyone else. Had Brian escaped?

Grayson slowly rose to his feet, his gaze riveted on her makeshift weapon. "Willow?" His voice held an odd huskiness to it that was a bit…disconcerting.

"Um, yes, Grayson?"

"What exactly did you plan on doing with that stick?"

She straightened and pitched the wood aside. "Tree branch actually. I was going to hit Brian. Where is he?"

He gave her an incredulous look. "You ran in here, hoping to fight a gunman? With a tree branch?"

Her face heated. "I was trying to save your life."

He swore.

Ryland cleared his throat. "I was just telling Grayson that Trent arrived at the house as I was grabbing my gun from my desk. We ran up here to help and found you struggling to half-carry Paletta through the woods. Trent carried her back to the house while I continued on to the building." He gave her a wounded look. "You promised me you'd follow Trent to the house."

Her face heated even more. "Yes, well, I planned to. But first, I figured I might be able to help even the odds."

"With a tree branch," Grayson gritted out.

She crossed her arms. "You really seem fixated on that. What happened here after I left?"

He turned away, dismissing her. He took the gun from Ryland and shoved it in his pocket. "Did you bring extra magazines?"

"Never thought I'd need extra ammo at your estate. I conceal carry and keep the gun, and the one magazine, locked in my desk while I'm working."

"I'll manage. Did you see which way he went?"

"Guys? What happened?" Willow stopped beside

them. She glanced at Jeffries and winced. “Brian shot his own father?”

Ryland nodded. “I was a second too late. Didn’t have a clear shot anyway without hitting Grayson. I fired far right to make Brian dive for cover. He ran out the door instead.”

“And he’s escaping while we’re talking,” Grayson said. “Which way?”

“North, toward that creek you mentioned.”

“All right. Here’s what we’ll do. When Russo’s guys get here—”

“*Grayson.*” Willow put her hands on her hips. “You are not going after Brian. Wait for Russo. Let him handle it.”

The skin along his jaw turned white, as if he was clenching his teeth. Without looking at her, he crossed the building and retrieved a knife from the floor. After folding it and putting it in his pocket, he strode back to Willow, finally giving her his full attention, which had her wincing and wishing maybe she’d kept her mouth shut. His expression was hard, like granite, his eyes so dark they were almost black.

“Willow, you could have been killed.” His voice was clipped, vibrating with anger. “You shouldn’t even be here.” He leaned down until his stormy eyes were inches from hers. “*Get off my mountain.*”

She drew back in shock.

He turned his back to her again. “Ryland, get her out of here. Don’t let her out of the house until Russo arrives. Have a couple of his guys take her back to her apartment. She doesn’t leave until I get there. Understood?”

“Understood. Come on, Willow. Let him do what he needs to do.” He grabbed her arm.

“No, stop it.” She tried to evade his hold, but Ryland was determined and a whole lot stronger. He half dragged, half carried her out of the building, with Grayson stopping just outside to examine some footprints in the dirt.

"Grayson, don't do it," she called out. "You can't go after him alone." She looked over her shoulder, as Ryland pulled her toward the woods. "You're a businessman, for crying out loud. Leave this to the police."

He stiffened and slowly turned. "Did you forget the Special Forces part of that equation, Willow? I'm not caught unprepared in an alley this time. I know who I'm after and what they're capable of." He motioned to Ryland. "Go."

Ryland tugged her into the trees.

"Grayson, wait!" She pushed at Ryland and whirled around. "Grayson!"

He'd already disappeared.

Chapter Twenty-Four

"My gun's right there, on my coffee table," Willow argued, aggravated with the two Gatlinburg PD officers currently taking up precious space in her tiny apartment. "Seriously, this is ridiculous. You've checked my minuscule hallway, bathroom, even under my bed. And you searched my closets—*both* of them. Brian Nelson isn't here. He's up on Prescott Mountain with Grayson and half the police force searching for him."

"Kitchen," one of them told the other. "Did you check *all* the cabinets? He's not a huge guy. Pantry. Maybe he's hunkered down, hiding behind some boxes or something." They drew their guns and rounded the peninsula into her kitchen.

"Oh, for Pete's sake," she told them. "A mouse couldn't hide in that so-called pantry. I can barely fit food in there, let alone a person. And you already checked the cabinets."

They searched again, the whole apartment, which took all of twenty seconds. When they came back into the main room, they re-holstered their weapons.

She faced them with hands on hips. "See? There's no place to hide. I don't even have a balcony and there's no way Brian could crawl up the siding to try to climb through a window. I'm telling you, your boss is being paranoid, sending you here to guard me."

The younger one shook his head. "Russo's not the paranoid one. It's *your* boss, Prescott. Ryland told the chief if something happened to you, Prescott would make his life a living hell."

She threw her hands up. "Come on. Even if Brian could miraculously evade a massive search party and escape, he doesn't have any reason to come after me."

The older officer crossed his arms. "Revenge. From what I hear, you're the one who figured out that Brian's the killer. Maybe he's come to realize that."

The younger one nodded his agreement. "And you're just his type. Long dark hair."

"Okay, that's it. Out. You can guard me from the landing outside my door, or better yet, your car in the parking lot. I've got enough to worry about—namely whether Grayson is safe—without having to deal with tripping over you in my tiny living room. Go."

She shooed them out the door.

"Lock it," one of their muffled voices called through the door.

She rolled her eyes and flipped the deadbolt. Finally, with her audience gone, she could quit trying to appear unaffected and brave. Her shoulders slumped. She plopped onto the couch and clutched a pillow to her chest.

Raw fear, unlike any she'd ever known, coursed through her, making her shake so hard the couch was vibrating. She drew deep breaths, struggling to keep it together. But it was no use. She was a mess, because Grayson was up there on the mountain with a murderer.

She didn't care that he was former Special Forces. That was years ago. And even though he obviously took care of himself, with an amazing body to prove it, that wasn't the same as running dangerous missions every day. The most dangerous thing he faced at the office was a paper cut. How dare he scare her like this and go off hunting a serial killer, with no backup. A sob escaped her and she buried her face in the pillow.

Please be okay, Grayson. Please be okay. You have to come back to me. Please.

She didn't know how long she lay there, but when she finally let go of the pillow, she wasn't shaking anymore. The fear was still there, but she'd managed to get it under control. She let out a long slow breath, then stepped toward the kitchen to get a bottle of water.

"Hello, Willow. *Nice hair.*"

She whirled around. Impossibly, Brian stood in the hallway, his lips curved in a feral grin that had her blood congealing in her veins.

She dove for her gun.

Chapter Twenty-Five

Grayson pulled his Audi into a visitor parking space two buildings down from Willow's apartment, because a police cruiser had taken her usual spot in front of her building. No doubt it was the officers he'd asked Russo to send over to guard her.

He couldn't help smiling as he cut the engine, picturing the feisty argument they'd no doubt have about him ordering her to get off his mountain. She was probably fuming about having the police at her apartment too. It would seem insulting to her to have two police officers guarding her when she was a cop herself, or had been. But just knowing that someone else was there to help keep her safe had given Grayson the peace of mind to focus on the hunt for the killer.

His smile faded. Unfortunately, that killer was still on the run. Grayson had finally had to admit that Brian gave him the slip, no doubt because he knew the woods up there far better than Grayson. He'd been using that fort as his headquarters for years, and the land surrounding Grayson's home as his killing field.

Before Grayson had left, cadaver dogs had already alerted on the three areas he and Willow had believed to be graves, plus two more. He could only assume that Erin Speck was buried in one of them. No telling how many more they would find. And although it hurt his heart to think about it, one of them very likely could be his daughter's grave. Hopefully, once they captured Brian, he'd finally tell the truth, the whole truth, about that awful day and what exactly had happened to Grayson's family.

He fisted his hands as he got out of the car and started toward Willow's building. Even knowing she was protected, he wouldn't be able to relax until he saw her for himself. He couldn't shake the fear that had taken hold of him when he'd thought of all the times that she'd walked the gardens by his house. Brian could have been out there at the same time, watching her from the woods. Thank God he'd never gone after her. Which was surprising, considering Willow's physical attributes were like a laundry list of features that appealed to an animal like Brian.

He nodded a greeting at one of the yard guys working outside the building he was passing, automatically scanning the man's features to make sure he wasn't Brian in disguise. Willow would probably call him paranoid when he told her about that later. But he was nothing if not cautious. Being in combat did that to a man, had him bracing for danger everywhere he went. So did caring deeply about someone, the way he was only now beginning to realize he cared about Willow.

Russo had Prescott Mountain locked down tight. No one should be able to get in or out without going through a checkpoint. Even Grayson's car had been searched before he'd been allowed to leave. And the mountain was crawling with tactical teams trained for that kind of terrain. On paper, Brian wasn't getting off the mountain unless he was handcuffed or in a body bag.

But Brian was a cop.

He knew what to expect in a situation like this, the standard operating procedures the police would follow.

Grayson couldn't help wondering if he'd had a plan B all along, an escape route in case anyone ever discovered him up there. And what worried Grayson the most was that, if Brian was angry enough, he might decide to seek revenge against anyone he felt was responsible for him becoming a hunted man.

Like Willow.

He jogged up the stairs toward the landing outside her apartment. Whether she liked it or not, when he left today, he was taking her with him. To the airport. They were going to hole up somewhere secluded and safe until Brian Nelson was no longer a threat.

When he reached the top of the stairs, he slowed, every muscle in his body going on high alert. There weren't any policemen outside Willow's door and their car parked out front was empty. He couldn't imagine her letting them wait inside. She'd be too keyed up, too annoyed to allow them to hover over her.

He was about to try her door, when he looked down. Two bright red drops of blood stained the wood on the landing. Another drop dotted the wood a little farther away, leading toward her neighbor's apartment.

Chapter Twenty-Six

Willow desperately tried to scream, but the cloth Brian had stuffed in her mouth was held in place by another cloth tied behind her head. All that came out was a muffled sound. She had to let her eyes do the talking, pouring all her hatred and loathing into her glare. Brian chuckled as he checked the zip ties fastening her arms and legs to her bed frame.

"Uh-oh," he said. "This one's a little loose. Wouldn't want you slipping your arm out and punching me right in the middle of our fun." He winked, making bile rise in her throat.

He yanked the zip tie. It bit into her skin, cutting into her. She cursed viciously against the gag.

"Go ahead," he crooned. "I like my girls to fight."

As long as they're tied down and can't fight back.

She wanted so badly to scream and curse at him, to tell him he was nothing more than a coward. She wanted to tell him that he could hurt her, and no doubt kill her, but he'd never conquer her spirit. As long as there was breath in her lungs, blood in her veins, she'd fight with every ounce of strength she had.

How had he managed to escape from Prescott Mountain? From Grayson and the police? There must have been another way out of the woods, a road no one knew about. A way to slip past anyone if they ever found his sick little hideout. She just prayed that he hadn't hurt anyone else during his escape.

Especially Grayson.

He climbed on top of the bed, straddling her. She bucked, hard, trying to throw him off. He retaliated by sitting on her stomach, pinning her in place. His weight squeezed her diaphragm, pressing against lungs already starved for oxygen with the gag blocking most of her airway. She sank back against the bed, conserving precious energy, letting her arms and legs go limp. Drawing in precious air, struggling to draw a breath past the gag with his weight constricting her lungs, suddenly became her only focus.

"There you go. Works every time." He held up a jagged knife, turning it so the metal winked in the light shining down from above her bed. Then, as if he couldn't resist the temptation, he leaned down, down, down, burying his face in her hair. "You smell so good," he whispered against her ear.

She shivered in revulsion.

He laughed and pulled back, once again pressing against her diaphragm.

"In, out. In, out. In, out," he mocked. "Makes you appreciate life, doesn't it? The struggle to breathe?"

Tears ran down her cheeks, and she hated him for it.

He captured one of them on his finger, staring at it as if fascinated. "It's such a shame that I don't have my playhouse anymore." He rolled his fingers where the tear had been, back and forth, back and forth. "I take all the special ones there, the ones worthy of more than a quick screw in an alley. I keep them for a long, long time. So we can…enjoy each other. Over and over again." He leaned down again, his breath hot against her neck, like a rabid dog. "You're one of the special ones, sweet Willow. I had great plans for you. It's a pity we have to speed this up, that I can't keep you, treasure you the way I'd like to."

Nausea roiled inside her. She turned her head to the side, worried she'd throw up and choke on her own vomit.

"I can't stay long. Too many people after me. Thanks to you and your stupid lover." He yanked her hair, making her arch up to relieve the awful pressure. "What should we do in the little time that we have?" he asked as casually as someone asking what she wanted to watch on TV.

Breathe. Breathe. Don't throw up. Breathe.

"Oh, I know. How about I show you what happened to Russo's little foot soldiers? Stupid beat cops who thought they could outsmart me. They were so busy watching the stairs they didn't think to check the other apartment behind them." He arched his brows. "What? You didn't think of that either?" He held up his phone, then started tapping through some menus on the screen. "I must say, your next door neighbor is a real slob. Well, he was a real slob." He turned the phone around, holding the gruesome bloody picture in front of her face.

She screamed against the gag, bucking and jerking, not even caring anymore if it meant wasting precious air. Her lungs seized in her chest. Her eyes widened. She desperately fought for air. Spots swam in her vision, everything going dark.

"Now, now. Can't have you dying on me just yet. We have a lot more to do before that happens." He raised himself up on his knees, still straddling her, but no longer pressing on her belly or chest.

Air rushed in, her lungs finally filling. She nearly wept with relief as she greedily sucked in air through her nose and around the gag.

When her vision cleared, she realized he was stroking her hair, his fingers like claws as he combed them through the long strands, then lifted her hair to his mouth and sucked.

She closed her eyes, determined not to watch whatever else this sick man wanted to do. She was so tired of fighting. She just wanted to let go.

No, what she wanted was Grayson. She wanted to see him one last time, to make sure he could go on without her, that he'd find someone to love. She couldn't bear the thought of him going back to the way he'd been, so closed-off, starved for something as simple as a hug.

"Shall I tell you what I did to your lover?"

Her eyes flew open. *No! Grayson had to be okay. No, please. No.*

Brian rested the flat of the blade on her breast, the cold steel leaving a trail of goose bumps across her skin. He turned the blade, the jagged edge cutting into her skin like fire.

She cried out against the gag.

His eyes danced with laughter as he drew the blade down. Hot liquid trickled down her ribs and sides. "This is the same blade I used on him. I carved Grayson up into little pieces. Starting with his skin. Did you hear that, Willow? I skinned him alive."

"*Liar.*"

They both jerked their heads toward the doorway. Grayson swooped down on Brian like an avenging angel, very much alive. He grabbed the wrist holding the knife and jerked it up and back. The knife fell to the mattress. Brian screamed with outrage as Grayson lifted him off her and slammed him to the floor.

Willow bucked and strained against the zip ties, desperately trying to see what was happening on the floor beside the bed. Arms and legs flailed as the sound of fists slamming into flesh filled the room. A solid thunk was followed by another of Brian's screams, this one so pitiful and raw with pain it almost made Willow feel sorry for him. Almost.

A thump sounded. Grayson swore and Brian was suddenly on his feet, cartwheeling around the corner into the little hallway. Grayson was a blur as he jumped up and sprinted after him.

A bloodcurdling scream filled the apartment, followed by a boom and a crashing noise.

"Police, don't move!"

More crashing and thuds echoed from the other room. Willow curled her fingers against the sheets, her body heated with embarrassment at the idea of anyone seeing her there, naked, vulnerable. But more than that, she was terrified that they hadn't gotten there in time. Where was Grayson? Was he okay? She watched the doorway, cold fear making sweat break out all over her body.

Footsteps sounded in the hallway. The familiar figure that suddenly appeared had tears of relief flooding down her cheeks. He was alive. Brian hadn't killed him. Grayson was alive.

"It's okay, sweetheart." His voice was infinitely gentle and soothing. "Everything's okay." He bent over the footrail, slicing through the zip ties on one of her ankles.

She sobbed against the gag.

His tortured gaze shot to hers as he freed her other leg. "It's okay, Willow. It's okay. He can't hurt you now." He quickly freed her from the rest of her restraints, then pulled the cloth from around her head.

She spit out the gag, her chest heaving as she drew her first deep breath in…forever.

"I've got you," he whispered, as he wrapped a blanket around her. Then he scooped her up and carried her out of the bedroom.

Her face heated again when she realized the SWAT team and dozens of her former Gatlinburg PD colleagues were squeezed into her apartment, many of them staring at her as they passed, no doubt wondering what awful things she'd endured.

"Look away, damn it. Give her some privacy." Grayson flipped the edge of the blanket over her head, but not before she saw what was left of Brian Nelson on the floor.

Grayson was right earlier today when he'd told her the only weapon he needed was his hands.

She buried her face against the side of his neck as he carried her outside.

Chapter Twenty-Seven

Willow glanced up from her desk as the library door opened. Ryland and the team began filing in, which meant the celebratory press conference announcing the partnership between law enforcement and Unfinished Business had finally wrapped up.

It had been a month since Brian's rampage of violence had ended on the floor of her apartment. And it had taken every bit of that month for Gatlinburg PD to tie up the loose ends in the investigation. Which had basically put all of the plans for Unfinished Business on hold. But now the company was officially, and publicly, moving forward, finally getting its day in the sun.

Ryland had pressured her to be with them at the press conference. But Grayson had come to her rescue, telling Ryland to respect her decision. Grayson understood, even if the others didn't. Although she was thrilled for all of them, she couldn't stomach the part of the press conference where Chief Russo was going to tell the press the final conclusions of the investigation, including that Sergeant Jeffries had died with honor, in the line of duty.

Russo had done it, partly, to protect the sergeant's family from the vitriol the public would send their way if they knew the truth. But mainly he'd wanted to ensure that Jeffries's widow received survivor's benefits. Noble reasons, sure. But it still rankled for him to be praised like a hero.

Willow supposed there was some validity to Russo's claim that Sergeant Jeffries had died in the line of duty. He'd acted like a cop, confronting the bad guy and trying to save others. And he'd tragically lost his life in the process. But, all told in the final count, after the police dug up half the mountain, fourteen women had lost their lives. And they still didn't know, might never know, what had happened to little Katrina. Her body wasn't found with the others.

One good thing was that fourteen families now had closure, of some type. At least they could bury the bodies of their loved ones, visit a grave someday. Grayson didn't even have that comfort for his little girl.

Nicole Paletta had been rescued, which was another good thing to be grateful about. And there was no denying it was partly due to Jeffries showing up, confronting Brian, distracting him while Grayson helped her escape. But Willow didn't give her former boss much credit for that. He didn't purposely try to distract Brian. His interference, trying to *save* Brian, almost got Grayson killed.

If Jeffries hadn't lied all those years ago, providing Brian with a false alibi during Maura's murder, so many lives would have been saved. And all those women he'd brutally attacked since then wouldn't have had their lives forever changed, or ended, in such a horrible way. Willow's young neighbor would still be alive too, and the police officers assigned to guard her. The damage her former boss's lies had done could never be undone.

But Willow was making an effort to undo the damage, at least in her own life. Although Grayson had encouraged her to stay at his mansion, she'd been determined to go home, to try to get back to her normal routine and banish the images of Brian from her apartment. She didn't want to give him any more control over her life. She didn't want him to win. But too many sleepless nights, jumping at shadows, afraid to even close her eyes, had made her realize that staying in the apartment wasn't the way to win. Living, enjoying life again, was how she would defeat the evil that was Brian.

A few days ago, she'd signed papers to turn in her apartment at the end of the month. And she'd scheduled a moving company to pack everything up and store it, at least until she figured out her next steps. The first step would be packing a bag, today, and heading to a hotel. Then, after that, who knew? Maybe she'd see if that offer of moving in with Grayson was still open.

One of the investigators, Trent, stopped beside her desk, grinning. "Is it true? Did Grayson really tell you, *Get off my mountain*?"

"Grow up." She shoved him, but smiled to let him know she was teasing as he chuckled and retreated to his side of the room.

Grayson had never once brought up that order he'd given her back at the fort. And she had no intention of bringing it up either. He'd done what he felt he needed to do to keep her safe. And she certainly didn't expect an apology for that. Looking back, it was kind of endearing, although she certainly hadn't thought so at the time.

Once the investigators had all returned, she realized that Grayson wasn't with them. She caught Ryland's attention and waved him over.

He perched on the edge of her desk with a friendly smile, as always. Which, of course, made her feel guilty when she thought of all the horrible things she'd said to him as he was dragging her off the mountain. It would be a while before she atoned enough for that and felt comfortable around him again.

"What's up, Willow?" he asked. "You need something?"

"Grayson didn't come back with you from the press conference?"

"He stayed behind to sign the contracts."

"Oh, right. I forgot about that."

"He'll be here soon. He said it wouldn't take more than a few minutes." He stood to return to his desk but she motioned for him to wait.

She scooped the papers she'd been reviewing into a folder. "I have a favor to ask you. And it's a big one."

He glanced at the folder, curiosity lighting his eyes. "You have a new case you want me to work?"

"More like a pet project. It's really important. But it's…sensitive. I'd rather that Grayson doesn't know about it."

His expression hardened, and his usual smile was nowhere to be seen. "He's my boss. I respect him far too much to hide something from him."

"Believe me. No one holds him in higher esteem than me. I'm not saying I'll never tell him about this…project. Just that we can't tell him right now."

"Willow, I don't—"

"Just hear me out. Let me explain. Then you can decide for yourself whether you agree with my reasoning, and whether you'll help me."

"Fair enough. What have you got?"

She pushed back her chair and stood. "Let's discuss it in the conference room."

Ten minutes later, Ryland was typing furiously at his computer, busily and eagerly working on her *pet project*. Willow smiled her thanks again, but he didn't seem to notice. A true investigator, he was already trying to figure things out and make the puzzle pieces fit.

Willow was grateful that Grayson hadn't come home while she and Ryland were still in the conference room. That would have led to some awkward questions. But as she passed one of the front windows, she saw his Audi parked under the portico. There was no sign of Grayson though. Had he come inside without her realizing it?

She was about to go on the hunt for him when a flash of movement on the far side of the driveway caught her attention. It was Grayson, heading into the woods, disappearing into the tree line.

This wasn't the first time she'd seen him do that. She figured he wanted to stretch his legs, take a stroll in the shade, which was the best place to be if one was outside, as the weather became increasingly warmer. And it didn't surprise her that he was wearing a suit for his walk. She'd still never seen him in a pair of jeans. She smiled. Maybe she could iron out some of the starch in him and teach him to relax someday. If she was lucky enough to have someday with him.

Maybe this was a good time to talk about the future. Her heart swelled with hope as she hurried outside and jogged to catch up. She was ready to take the plunge, to bare her soul, to finally tell him how she felt and pray that he felt the same way.

He'd been achingly patient with her since… Brian. She wasn't ready to talk about what had happened, aside from what she'd had to tell Chief Russo for his investigation. And she hadn't been ready to talk about her and Grayson. She'd felt too fragile, too confused.

But she was stronger now. Not healed, exactly. Maybe she never would be. Trying to sleep through the night without reaching for her gun in a cold sweat was still a problem. But the good memories were coming back, slowly pushing out the bad ones. The memories of Grayson, how gentle and sweet he'd been. How passionately they'd kissed in Russo's office when she was trying to bring him back from his own nightmares of the past.

He'd told her, after that life-altering kiss, that they needed to talk when this was all over. Well, it was over, or as much as it ever would be. And she was ready for that talk.

She sure hoped he was too.

There he was, just up ahead. A little too far for her to call out and be sure he'd hear her. But not so far that she couldn't quickly catch up. He went behind a thick stand of oak trees, spurring her to jog again so she wouldn't lose him.

When she rounded that same group of trees, she stopped so fast she had to grab a sapling to keep from falling down. About ten yards ahead, an elaborate black wrought-iron fence surrounded a small rectangular building. Gorgeous stained-glass windows were set between Greek-style columns. Well-maintained ivy climbed the walls, lending a regal, old-world elegance to the structure. But that didn't hide what it was.

A mausoleum.

And Grayson had just stepped inside.

It must be the Prescott family mausoleum, no doubt housing ancestors of old. And, of course, his wife, Maura. This was a private moment. She shouldn't intrude. But if he turned around and he stepped out in time to see her disappearing into the woods, it would seem like she'd been spying on him. Rather than risk a misunderstanding, she straightened her shoulders and stepped through the open gate.

At the entrance to the building, she saw him standing

inside, facing one of the engraved marble squares with his back to her. There were fresh flowers in the vase, those peach greenhouse-raised roses the head gardener had said that Maura was fond of. Although Willow couldn't read the name beside the vase, she knew it had to be his wife's.

She was just about to step inside when Grayson bowed his head and pressed his palm against the tomb. And that's when she heard him. He spoke Maura's name. He told her that he loved her, that he would always love her, that she would be forever in his heart.

Willow covered her mouth to hold back the sob that wanted to escape. She was such a fool. A stupid fool who'd fallen in love with a man with room in his heart for only one woman—his dead wife.

She quietly backed away, then took off running.

Chapter Twenty-Eight

Willow stuffed another shirt into her travel bag. It had been far too long since she'd hopped on a flight to Kentucky to see her family. And she could really use their love and support right now, more than ever before. Unfortunately, she doubted her mom's famous homemade chicken noodle soup could fix her broken heart. But that didn't mean she wouldn't give it a try.

Her family didn't know what had happened to her here. Russo had promised to do everything he could to keep her name out of the news. And so far, he'd been successful. She didn't want to have her family worry after the fact. She was okay. Or she would be, one day.

Heading into the main room, she took a final glance around to make sure she hadn't forgotten anything that she might need. She was relieved that she'd already arranged for the movers to pack her apartment before getting her heart broken today. It made taking off on an impromptu visit back home much easier. She could really use easy right now.

The only change she'd had to make was a call to the apartment manager a few minutes ago, arranging for him to let the movers in and lock up after they were gone.

She took one last slow walk through her little apartment. She'd been happy here once, with hopes and dreams for her future. It was bittersweet and ironic that this phase of her life was ending, and that those hopes and dreams had completely changed, then died. She was starting over, again, and had no idea what she was going to do next.

Maybe this place could still be a good home for someone else, though, as it once had for her. Anyone looking around wouldn't have a clue about the violence that had happened here. Repairs had been made. A solid wall had been built in the attic by the apartment management, making sure no one could ever cross from one apartment to another as Brian had done. The manager had assured her they were reviewing all of the apartments in the complex to make the same alterations, to keep everyone safe.

Grayson, of course, was the one who'd saved her, twice—at the fort and then here. When he'd arrived at her apartment building that fateful day and saw some blood drops on the landing, he'd known that Brian must already be there. He'd followed the trail to her neighbor's and discovered the bodies of the two officers who'd done nothing but try to protect her. And he'd found her neighbor, right alongside them. She hadn't even known his name and felt guilty now for being so aggravated about all those pizza deliveries.

She squeezed her hands together. Grayson had snapped a picture of the bodies and texted it to Russo, knowing that would bring help faster than even a call to 911. Then he'd gone on the hunt for Brian.

He was a hero. He'd saved her, then held her hand in the emergency room as the doctor treated the cuts on her wrists and ankles, and the path of the knife where it had cut into her chest.

A hot tear slid down her cheek, startling her out of her walk down a scary yet somehow sweet version of memory lane. Grayson had been her hero and she'd always love him for that, even though he couldn't love her back.

For someone who wasn't normally a crier, she'd sure gone through a ridiculous amount of tissues lately. She wiped at her eyes before strapping the travel bag across her shoulder and hip and hurrying to the front door.

She yanked it open, then froze.

A devastatingly handsome man in a charcoal gray suit stood in the opening, his hand raised to knock.

She swore.

Grayson peered at her over the top of his shades as he lowered his hand. "Not what I was going for, but it's a start." He pocketed his shades and motioned toward her bag. "Going somewhere?"

"I'm going to see my family, actually. In Kentucky. A visit is long overdue."

Instead of moving back, he lounged against the door frame, one arm braced on the opposite side, making it impossible for her to escape.

"The sticky note you left on my desk was a bit cryptic," he said. "I was hoping you could explain it to me."

She blew out an exasperated breath and pulled her bag off and let it drop to the floor. "I don't see how I could have made it any more clear."

"*I quit. Goodbye.* That's all I get? No reason?"

"I didn't know a reason was required."

"Why are you crying?"

She wiped her cheeks, swearing again. "There was a sad movie on TV. It's one of my vices. I cry over the stupidest things."

He arched a brow. "Am I one of those stupid things?"

Her chin wobbled. She crossed her arms, deciding to ignore the tears dripping off her cheeks. "Will you please leave? I have a plane to catch."

"Willow?"

"What?"

He stepped inside and shut the door behind him. "Why did you quit?"

She threw up her hands in frustration. "Maybe I need a change of scenery, okay? Ryland's running everything fine on his own and—"

"I meant why did you quit *us*?" He took a step toward her. "I'd say that maybe I misread you, that my rusty instincts in the relationship department are even rustier than I'd realized. But that kiss we shared before everything went to hell was like a flashing neon sign. I'm pretty sure even I couldn't misread that."

He cocked his head, studying her. "I wanted to give you time to heal, time to come to terms with everything that happened. Did I wait too long? Tell me I'm wrong to think that you want me, that you care about me. Tell me I'm wrong and I'll walk right out that door and never bother you again."

"You're wrong."

He blinked. "Okay. Well. I guess I lied about walking out the door. Because I'm not ready to give up on you, to give up on us."

"There is no us, Grayson." She wiped at her eyes. "There's only you and Maura. That's all there will ever be." She fisted her hands. "I saw you. Earlier today."

He frowned in confusion. "You saw me? Where? Doing what?"

"In the woods. I was looking for you and glanced out the window. You were stepping between some trees just past the driveway. I thought you were going on a walk, stretching your legs. So I decided to join you."

Understanding dawned in his eyes. "You saw me go into the mausoleum."

"I not only saw you, I followed you. I was about to step inside, let you know I was there. But then you started talking…to her. Telling her how much you loved her, crying." She stepped close, until she was almost touching him.

"This probably sounds crazy. But I love you, Grayson. I have for a long time. I'm so totally in love with you that I can hardly breathe sometimes."

His eyes widened.

She lightly pressed her hand against his chest. "I've been hooked on you since that first hug in that obnoxiously loud restaurant downtown. But it doesn't matter." She tapped the spot, just over his heart. "Because there's no room in here for me. There's only room for a ghost. And I can't compete with that."

She started to drop her hand, but he covered it with his, keeping it pressed against his chest.

"To say there's no room in here for you means you didn't stick around to hear everything I said to Maura."

She looked down at the floor. "I heard enough."

"What you probably heard was me telling my wife I loved her, which I do, and always will. I make no apologies for that. If you'd stuck around, you'd have also heard me update her about Brian Nelson, tell her that we'd finally caught the man who'd hurt her, who took our baby girl from us." His throat worked before he continued. "I told her he was evil enough and mean enough to take the knowledge of what happened to Katrina to his grave, that I may never know the truth. But I've made my peace with it, as much as possible anyway."

He drew a deep breath before continuing. "I told her that justice had been served. She could rest in peace and move on." He gently tilted her chin up until she met his gaze. "Then I told her about *you*, Willow."

She stared at him, stunned. "I don't… You told her… about me? Wh-what did you say?"

"I explained that something extraordinary had happened. That I'd closed my heart long ago. But then I met a smart, feisty, beautiful woman who showed me I still had the capacity to love and be loved. This woman gradually worked her way into my heart, my mind, my very soul. She showed me it was okay to take a chance again, that even though there are no guarantees, and there will always be the risk of being hurt, love is worth that risk. This incredible woman showed me how to laugh again, to find joy in the little things. She taught me to *live*."

He cupped her face in his hands, his stormy blue gaze searching hers. "And then I told her the most important part of all. That I'd learned it's possible to find your soul mate twice, because that's what happened to me. I told her goodbye, Willow."

He pressed a whisper-soft kiss against her forehead. "Maura is my past. You're my future, if you'll have me. I love you, and it took almost losing you to figure that out." He smiled. "Timing has never been my superpower." He squeezed her hand on his chest. "This is yours, Willow. It beats for you. I love you with *all* of my heart. Please, please tell me I haven't waited too long to realize that, to see what was right in front of me? Tell me I haven't lost you."

She tugged her hand free and threw her arms around his neck. "You're so much better than chicken noodle soup."

"I don't… Chicken noodle soup?"

"I'm saying your timing is perfect. You're exactly what I need, who I need, right when I needed you the most. Kiss me, Grayson. Kiss me and make these tears go away."

A smile grew like sunshine across his face as he lowered his mouth to hers.

Epilogue

Willow sat on the edge of the bed in their honeymoon suite, watching Grayson with hungry eyes as he toweled off in the bathroom doorway. Never in her deepest fantasies had she ever *really* believed she could call someone like him *hers*. Sexy as hell? Absolutely. A sensual, teasing smile that could make her toes curl with wanting him? The goose bumps on her arms answered that question.

But he was so much more than that.

He was a man who loved deeply, generously and who'd found room in his heart for both of the women in his life—past and present. His love for Maura was a part of him, and always would be. But it didn't diminish his love for Willow. It formed a solid foundation for their love to grow and flourish. And she couldn't wait to see what would happen next as they started a new life together.

Still, as she clutched her phone in her hands, she couldn't settle the butterflies in her stomach. What she was about to tell him was going to change…everything.

His towel hung low on his hips as he padded barefoot into the bedroom. He was heading toward the closet when he stopped in surprise, then veered toward the bed instead.

Leaning over her, he pressed a hungry kiss against her lips, making her sigh as he pulled back. His blatantly male grin told her he'd heard that sigh and knew exactly how smitten she was with him.

"Hey, beautiful. What are you still doing in your nightgown? I thought you wanted to head into town for dinner. Or was there something else you wanted?" He waggled his brows, making her laugh.

"I'm still hungry, for you and for food."

"Well, I can fix one of those problems right now." He winked and reached for his towel.

"Grayson, wait. We need to talk first."

The concern that suddenly filled his eyes had her heart breaking, just a little. He loved her so much and was fiercely protective. Given his past, the terrible losses he'd suffered and what they'd both gone through together, she understood his obsession with keeping her safe. He was still healing, learning to be carefree and not worry all the time. And she was about to throw a curve in front of him, one that was wonderful and bittersweet and frustrating all at the same time.

The mattress sagged as he sat beside her, gently feathering her hair back from her face. "What is it? Do you feel okay?"

She pressed a hand to his chest and leaned into his warmth, selfishly delaying her announcement for a few more precious seconds of just the two of them.

"Willow, sweetheart, you're shaking. What's wrong?" He got down on his knees in front of the bed and started to take her hands in his. He frowned when he realized she was clutching her phone. "Did someone call with bad news? Is your family okay? What is it? Tell me."

To her dismay, tears started flowing down her face.

His eyes widened. "Willow?"

She set the phone aside, and threaded their fingers

together. "While you were getting your shower, Ryland called."

He frowned. "Ryland? You're working on our honeymoon?"

"Yes and no. A month ago, when you signed the contracts for Unfinished Business, I asked Ryland for a favor. I wanted him to try to track someone down by working with that forensic genealogist I used on the last case. It was a long shot. I didn't expect anything to come of it, but I had to try. I knew the odds were a million to one that there was even anything to find, but he uploaded the DNA profile from an old case file and got a hit."

He gently rubbed his thumbs across her palms as he listened to her, the worry still there in his wrinkled brow, the crease lines around his eyes. "He got a hit? On what?"

"It's a…missing-persons case. Someone who was missing, presumed dead. For years." She tugged her hands free and cupped his face. "Grayson, it's Katrina. Your daughter. She's *alive*."

He froze, his eyes turning a stormy blue as he stared at her in disbelief.

"It's true," she told him. "She's alive. And she's beautiful and healthy and happy and is growing up in a loving family and—"

"She's alive?" he rasped, barely able to speak.

"She is. We'll never be able to get Brian's side of the story, of course, but from what Ryland was able to piece together, along with what the genealogist found on the ancestry site, we think that Brian may have hurt Katrina by accident and felt guilty about it. None of his other victims were children. But, of course, he wouldn't have wanted to call 911 to get help for her, fearing the police would catch him. So instead, he took Katrina somewhere else."

"What did he do to her?"

The fear in his voice nearly broke her.

"It's a complicated story, but he patched her up as best he could until he got her to a doctor in Missouri. He wouldn't have wanted to take her to anyone in Tennessee who might have heard about Maura and connected the dots. The doctor he took her to worked at a free clinic in an underserved community, the kind of clinic where no one asks for your ID or delves into your past. As the doctor was working to save Katrina, Brian snuck out and left her."

Grayson squeezed his eyes shut, his expression mirroring his pain at hearing his daughter had been hurt, kidnapped, then abandoned.

She took his hands in hers and waited until he looked at her again. "He seems like a kind man, with a successful practice. He and his wife had been trying for a baby for years and had given up. They'd despaired of ever having a child. Then Katrina was left in his care and it must have seemed like the answer to their prayers. He took her in and they raised her as their own. From everything that Ryland's been able to find out, she's had a good life, Grayson. And she's so beautiful. She has Maura's dark hair and your deep blue eyes."

He stared at her in shock. "You've seen her?"

"A picture. Ryland took it this morning, outside, across the street from their home. He just sent it to me with an update on the investigation. It's a little blurry since he was zooming in but—"

"Show me."

She grabbed her phone and brought up the text that Ryland had sent just a few moments ago, then turned it around.

Tears filled Grayson's eyes as he took the phone and

held it close, his greedy gaze drinking in every detail. "My little girl. My little girl." He traced the outline of her face, shaking his head in awe.

"Grayson? I know this is a shock. I hope you don't hate me for interfering and—"

"Hate you?" His expression turned incredulous. "I could never hate you, Willow. For any reason."

"Okay, maybe *hate* is the wrong word. It's just, I know this isn't going to be simple. She's over seven years old. She's with the only family she's ever known, or that she remembers. It's going to be complicated and messy and stressful and—"

He pressed a gentle kiss against her lips and set the phone aside. Then he speared his hands through her hair, his eyes filled with love. And joy.

"Dear sweet Willow. You've given me the best gift a father could ever receive. The knowledge that his child is safe and healthy, and happy. I can do complicated and messy. And don't worry about Katrina. I'm not going to selfishly traumatize her by ripping her from the arms of the only family she's ever known. It wouldn't be fair to her, or the people who've taken care of her all these years. We'll take it a step at a time. Figure it out. Together." He kissed her again, then pulled back, with so much love in his eyes, it stole her breath. "You took a broken man and made him whole. I love you, Willow. I love you so much."

"I love you too. But there's another problem we have to deal with."

His smile dimmed. "What is it?"

"I'm still hungry."

He laughed and squeezed her hands. "Well, we can't have that. I'll hurry and get dressed and—"

"That's not the kind of hunger I was talking about."

She tried to waggle her eyebrows, but judging by his laughter, she failed miserably.

That's when he pounced.

They both fell back on the bed, laughing.

* * * * *

CONSPIRACY IN THE ROCKIES

CINDI MYERS

To Winston and Lucy.

Chapter One

The man lay facedown in the ditch, green water flowing over and around him, his gray hair flowing out from his head like a mantle of weeds. His hat, a tan felt Stetson, was caught in a raspberry bush just out of the water, the ripe fruit staining the brim like fresh blood.

"I wanted to pull him out, but I could see he wasn't breathing, and I figured I'd better call you." Perry Webber, the ditch rider for this part of Rayford County, wiped at his hatchet of a nose with a yellow bandanna. "It was a shock, seeing Sam Russell there like that. I've known him over fifteen years. One of the really good guys, solid as a fence post."

Deputy Chris Delray only half listened to Perry's rambling. He studied the body in the ditch and the trampled grass mingled with mud around it. "What time did you find him?" he asked.

Perry pulled out his phone. "It was maybe twenty or twenty-five minutes before I called you, so about ten after seven? I had to run all the way back to my truck, then drive to where I could get a phone signal."

Chris looked around at the cattle pens and crude sheds constructed of rough cedar logs, the wood weathered silver by years in the dry air. A hot breeze sent a dust devil dancing across the empty corrals and bent the tall grass alongside the irrigation ditch. "What brought you out here?" he asked.

"I had to open the number seven gate so Russell could irrigate his south hayfield," Perry said. "Sam called me last night to tell me he wanted to irrigate first thing this morning."

Chris looked down the deep, narrow irrigation ditch that ran parallel to the gravel track where he and Perry had parked. "Where is gate number seven?"

"It's down that way, about a quarter mile." Perry pointed downstream. "I opened it a little after six fifteen, but the water wasn't moving like it should. That usually means a blockage, so I got out my shovel and started walking upstream, looking for whatever was impeding the flow." He stared glumly at the body. "I guess I found it. You reckon his heart gave out or something and he fell in?"

"We'll have to wait for the coroner to find that out," Chris said. He took Perry's arm and steered him away from the ditch and the body. "Did you see anyone else on your way to this spot, or since you arrived here? Any other vehicles pass on the road?"

Perry shook his head. "No." He looked around them. "I don't see Sam's pickup, either, and we're a ways from the house. How did he get here?"

No sign of a horse or a four-wheeler, either. Chris had never known a rancher to walk when he could ride. He wasn't sure how Sam Russell had died, but he needed to secure the scene to save any evidence that would help them figure that out. "Can you drive until you get a good phone signal and call the sheriff's department?" he asked. "Tell them what happened. I'll stay here with Mr. Russell."

"All right." Perry stuffed the bandanna in his pocket. "But who's going to tell Willow?"

"Who is Willow?" Chris asked.

"She's Sam's daughter. She moved back home a few weeks ago, from somewhere out East, I think."

"Someone from our office will contact her. Don't worry about that now. Just call the sheriff for me."

Perry nodded and headed for the battered red truck parked on the road, Rayford Irrigation District stenciled in fading white letters on the door.

When Perry was gone, Chris took some photos with his phone, placing his steps carefully, alert for any evidence. In the few criminal law classes he'd taken in law school, as well as in the state's law enforcement academy, it had been drilled into him that any unattended death had to be treated as a crime scene until ruled otherwise. Though he had ended up specializing in water law, that information had stuck with him.

The law itself interested him, but after a year spent stuck behind a desk researching every arcane aspect of Colorado's complicated water law for more senior attorneys, he had had enough. He met a sheriff's deputy in eastern Colorado whose job involved enforcing that law and decided that was the job for him. So he'd quit the legal firm, enrolled in the law enforcement academy and here he was, Rayford County's newest deputy and a fully qualified water cop. In four months on the job, he'd gotten to know the officers of the irrigation district and the farmers and ranchers who were the primary members of the district, as well as the five ditch riders who were responsible for managing the water, releasing it for members as they needed it and were entitled to use it. Chris's job was to mediate disputes between members and issue citations to unauthorized users. So far, he'd broken up one fistfight and been shouted at by one angry man, but he never thought he'd have to deal with a dead body.

Just over an hour later, a plume of dust foretold the arrival of another vehicle on the scene. Chris walked out to meet what he hoped was a fellow deputy. But the vehicle that emerged from the dust wasn't a sheriff's department SUV, but a brown late-model F-250, a top-of-the-line King Ranch edition. The vehicle skidded to a stop behind his SUV. The driver's door opened and a woman slid out. She had a braid of black hair that hung past the center of her back and the kind of figure Chris guessed was what people meant by "hourglass"—full breasts and hips and a small waist. He knew he was staring, but had a hard time pulling his gaze away.

"What's going on here?" she called, then started toward him. "Is there some kind of trouble?"

Chris stepped out to intercept her. The last thing he wanted was for her to see the body in the ditch. "I'm Deputy Chris Delray," he said. "Who are you?"

"I'm Willow Russell. My father owns this ranch. Have you seen him?" She pushed her sunglasses up on her head and fixed him with a direct gaze. She had green eyes and olive skin, and lacy dark lashes—a beautiful woman, and a very worried one, from the look of things.

"Why don't we sit over here and talk?" He put a hand on her arm, intending to lead her toward his SUV.

She wrenched out of his grasp. "I'm not going anywhere until you tell me what's going on," she said.

He wasn't going to get away with stalling or lying to her, and he was ashamed of himself for even thinking it. She deserved the truth, even if it was unpleasant. "The ditch rider found your father earlier this morning," he said. "I'm sorry to have to tell you, he's dead."

Her eyes widened and she gasped, then put a hand to her mouth, as if to cover the sound. He hovered, ready to steady her if she looked faint, but she stood firm. She swallowed, then lowered her hand. "What happened?" she asked.

"We don't know yet. I'm waiting for more deputies and the coroner to arrive."

"I want to see him," she said. "Where is he?" She looked around, trying to see past him.

"I don't think you want to do that," he said.

Again that direct gaze. "If it was your father, would you believe he was dead if you didn't see it for yourself? And who better to identify the body than me?" She must have read the hesitation on his face, and pressed her point. "I won't scream or faint," she said. "I'm not that kind of woman."

He nodded. "All right. But you can't touch anything. You can't touch him."

She followed him to the canal and stood beside him, her shoulder almost touching his, staring down at the man in the ditch. Already the body had taken on the stiff appearance of a mannequin. Something not quite human. Her breath hitched, and she put her hand to her mouth again. "That's him," she said, the words muffled.

He gently turned her away. "Let's wait over here for the others to arrive," he said.

He led her back to the trucks, retrieved a bottle of water from the cooler in his back seat and handed it to her. She didn't open it, just held it, looking back toward the ditch, though they could no longer see the body from here. "What do you think happened?" she asked. "Did he have a heart attack or a stroke? He's never sick, but I guess at his age, you never know."

"I don't know," he said. "I'm waiting for help from the sheriff's department. It's better not to touch anything until they get here. Do you know what your father was doing out here this morning?"

She shook her head. "No. He was gone when I got up." A ghost of a smile flickered on her lips, then vanished. "He can't sleep past six and is usually up by five," she said. "But he's always back for breakfast by eight. When he didn't come in, I went out looking for him. He tells me I worry too much, but this time..." She pressed her lips together and looked away, but not before he saw the sheen of tears in her eyes.

The sound of tires on gravel made them both look down the road. Two sheriff's department SUVs parked across from Chris and Willow. A black 4Runner pulled in behind them. The sheriff emerged from the lead SUV. Deputy Jamie Douglas and Deputy Wes Landry got out of the second one. A portly man with a black doctor's bag followed from the 4Runner.

"This is Willow Russell," Chris said. "She's identified the man in the ditch as her father, Samuel Russell."

"I'm very sorry for your loss, Ms. Russell." Sheriff Travis Walker had a solemn maturity that made him seem older than twenty-nine. And he had a reputation as a smart, thorough lawman. "It would be best if you return home to wait while we process the scene. I can send Deputy Douglas with you."

"I'll wait here," Willow said. "I won't get in your way, but I won't leave, either."

Travis paused, then nodded. "All right."

He waited until she had climbed back into the driver's seat of the Ford, then returned to Chris. "What have we got?"

"The ditch rider, Perry Webber, called me at about seven thirty to tell me he'd found rancher Sam Russell's body in the ditch near his loading corrals."

The portly man with the doctor's bag joined them. "Butch Collins," he said to Chris. "County coroner."

Chris nodded. "Deputy Chris Delray."

"Any relation to Ted Delray?" Collins asked.

"My father." Most people in the county knew his dad, one of only a handful of attorneys in the area.

"Wes, you and Jamie wait here," Travis said. "Keep an eye on Ms. Russell." He and Collins followed Chris to the ditch, all of them careful to stand back from the body.

"How long has he been there?" Collins asked. "Anyone know?"

"His daughter says he is usually up between five and six and he wasn't in the house when she came down from her room at seven," Chris said. "Perry found him about ten after seven."

Butch nodded and looked around. "I need a board or something across that ditch so I can examine him before you pull him out."

Travis pried a loose section of fencing from one of the corrals and carried it over to form a bridge over the ditch. The coroner crouched awkwardly over it and began examining the body. Chris looked away, back toward the Ford. Sun glinted off the windshield, making it impossible to see Willow's face, though Jamie stood next to the open driver's-side window, talking.

"Help me turn him over," Butch said. "Easy now."

Chris and Travis knelt in the mud of the ditch bank and eased the dead man on to his back. Chris winced at the gaping wound in Russell's chest, and quickly looked away, his gaze falling on the shotgun beneath the body. "Suicide?" Travis asked.

"I'd say the shotgun blast killed him," Butch said. "Though whether it was self-inflicted or not, I won't know until I get him to the hospital, where I can take a better look." He stood. "Get all the photos and whatever else you need. While you're doing that, I'll call the ambulance to transport him."

"Estimate on the time of death?" Travis asked.

Butch made a face. "You know that as well as I do. He's been there two or three hours, which matches with what the daughter told us."

He walked away. Travis signaled for Wes and Jamie to join them, and they set about photographing and measuring the scene, and combing the surrounding area for evidence. Travis pulled Chris aside. "Let's talk to the daughter," he said.

Chris suspected Willow was watching them as they crossed to the truck. When they stopped beside her, she leveled her same direct gaze. "Well?" she asked.

"What was your father's mood this morning when he left the house?" Travis asked.

"I already told your deputy here that I wasn't awake when Dad left, but I imagine his mood was good," she said. "It usually was."

"Nothing worrying him lately? No concerns about money or his health?"

"No. Why are you asking?"

"Does your father own a shotgun?"

"Yes."

"Do you know where that gun is now?"

"No. Why are you asking this?" Not waiting for the answer, she shoved open the truck door and got out to stand in front of them. "How did my father die?" she asked.

"He was shot in the chest with a shotgun," Travis said.

There was no way to cushion a blow like that. Chris saw the impact of it in the shrinking of her shoulders, and the slight hunching as if she'd taken a hard punch. But she quickly straightened, and inhaled a deep, though shaky breath. "Who shot him?" she asked.

"Do you know someone who would have wanted to do so?" Travis asked. "Did your father have any enemies?"

"Dad has lived in Rayford County for almost seventy years," she said. "There may be people here who don't love him, but I never heard of anyone who hated him."

"Can you think of any reason your father would have taken his own life?" Travis asked.

Another blow, this one blanching the color from her face, but she lifted her chin and held the sheriff's gaze. "No," she said. "My father wouldn't have killed himself. Someone else killed him and you'd better find out who that person is."

Chapter Two

Willow refused the sheriff's offer to have Deputy Douglas drive her back to the ranch, and had declined his suggestion that he call someone to stay with her. "I'd rather be alone right now," she said. "I have a lot of things to think about."

"We may have more questions for you after we get the doctor's report," the sheriff said. She remembered Travis Walker from high school—a tall, good-looking athlete, whom all the girls had crushes on. His reticence made him that much more desirable in their teenage minds. She wasn't as easily impressed these days—looks weren't everything, and she had had her fill of men who wouldn't talk.

"I want to know what the coroner has to say," she said. No tiptoeing around reality with that softer word, *doctor*. "Though my father did not kill himself." She climbed back into the truck and turned the key in the ignition. They stepped back, and let her pass.

She was still replaying the morning's events in her mind a few minutes later when she steered the truck through the gates leading to the ranch house. Before she had even parked, movement by the machine shed across from the house caught her eye. Ranch hand Von King emerged from the shed, a shovel in one hand, a five-gallon bucket in the other. He looked over as she slid out of the truck, and she felt the impact of that gaze.

She didn't like Von—not the hungry way he looked at her when her father wasn't around, or his sullen answers to her attempts to make conversation. She had shared her opinion with her father who, as usual, dismissed her concerns. *Von's all right*, he'd said. *He's a good worker.* That was the highest praise a man like her father could give.

Her impulse was to go inside and avoid Von, but her father's death—his murder, she was sure—didn't give her that luxury. She couldn't be sure Sheriff Walker and his deputies would go out of their way to find out what had happened to her dad, so she would have to do so.

Von looked up at her approach, his eyes hooded, his expression unreadable. Then, when she was almost to him, he grinned. The grin caught her off guard, so different from his usual surly glare. "Willow," he said. No greeting attached, just her name, almost drawled off his tongue, as if he was tasting each letter.

"Have you seen my dad this morning?" she asked.

"Nope."

"He's not in the house and I can't find him anywhere."

"He's probably out on one of the four-wheelers, checking fence or something." He set down the bucket, which she saw now contained a mixture of oil and sand. He plunged the shovel into it, working it up and down. "He likes to do that."

"He's always back by eight for breakfast," she said.

"Before you came home, he'd sometimes stay out all day. Maybe he decided to do that today. I imagine he'll come home when he's ready."

"I'm worried something may have happened to him."

"He's been looking after himself for years."

"Well, I think you should look for him." That would get him out of her sight for a while.

"Can't." He lifted the shovel from the sand and inspected the blade, clean now, with an oily sheen. "Your dad wanted me to clean and sharpen all the hand tools today and he's the boss." *Not you* hung in the air between them, unspoken.

She turned and headed for the house, aware of his gaze burning into her all the way across the yard.

Inside, she switched on the coffeepot to reheat and looked around at the cluttered kitchen, their uneaten breakfast on the table, dirty dishes in the sink. A pair of her father's muddy rubber boots stood by the back door, and a stack of mail was piled on one end of the kitchen counter.

The phone rang and she jumped. The old-fashioned wall-mount phone had a loud bell and a long cord that, when she was a teenager, had allowed her to carry the handset down the hall and lock herself in the bathroom, where she could talk privately, until her father decided she had talked too long. Then he would simply unplug the phone, silencing her conversation. If she objected, he'd say, *Next time, maybe you won't talk so long.* But next time invariably brought the same scene.

She shook herself out of her paralysis and rushed the pick up the handset. "Hello?"

"Willow, let me speak to Sam." Darla Russell—the former Mrs. Samuel Russell, who had stepped in after Willow's mother died—didn't waste time with friendly greetings.

"Dad's not here right now," Willow hedged. Let the sheriff or one of his men give her stepmother the news that her ex-husband was dead. Willow had made a policy to say as little as possible to Darla and she saw no reason to deviate now.

"Well, where is he?" Darla demanded.

"I don't know." That much was the truth, at least.

"When you see him, tell him to call me. Right away."

"Okay."

"Don't forget, okay? This is important."

"Sure. Goodbye." Willow hung up the phone and stared at the white plastic handset, amber around the edges with age. She could call people her father knew and try to find out what he might have been up to. She should call a friend and ask for help.

But she had no friends in Eagle Mountain anymore. She knew most of the neighbors, of course. She had grown up with them and with their sons and daughters, a few of whom had even stayed in the area. But she had not spoken to any of them in years and felt no connection.

When she did run into one of them in town, they were polite, even friendly, but she could feel all the questions behind the greetings—*What brought you home after so long? What happened to you in that eastern city?* A few of them were more direct.

We sure were surprised to hear you were back in town, Shayla Wayne had said at the grocery store last week. *I was sure once you left you'd never come back.*

Willow had believed that, too. There was nothing for her here in Eagle Mountain. She had only returned because she had no place left to go.

WILLOW RUSSELL'S FACE stayed with Chris as he left the Russell's Double R ranch and headed back toward town—a beautiful face full of pride and grief. Pain showed clearly in her eyes, but she fought against it, determined to stand strong.

After the ambulance had arrived and collected Sam Russell's body, the sheriff dismissed Chris. "You have things to do," he said. "Don't let me keep you from them."

Chris wanted to point out that, while his primary duties were related to the water district, he was still a fully certified deputy, able to do the law enforcement work of any other deputy. Travis must have read the sentiment on his face. "Depending on what Butch finds, I may need you on this investigation," he said. "Meanwhile, keep your ears open among the other ranchers you call on. Could be one of them knows something about this."

Right now, however, Chris wasn't on his way to a ranch, but to a new housing development in the shadow of Dakota Ridge. A rancher in the area had reported decreased water flows and the ditch rider had noted the same. After checking for leaks or blockages and finding none, the ditch rider had contacted Chris. "I think we probably have a homeowner in one of those new houses out there who needs a little education on Colorado water laws," the rider, Shirley Jacobson, had said. "It sounds better coming from you than from me."

Chris had been down this road before. Colorado water law was convoluted and complex. The rules regarding who had rights to water in the state dated back to the Gold Rush and seldom made sense to anyone who hadn't spent years studying the subject.

He followed the river for several miles, then turned in at a large granite sign proclaiming Welcome to Idlewilde Estates. He drove slowly past large lots with stucco or log homes set back from the road in groves of cottonwood or aspen trees that thrived along the banks of the Daimler Ditch. The ditch was one of a network of irrigation canals, some of them a hundred years old, that crisscrossed the county, carrying water from the Ute River and Centennial and Skyrocket creeks to area farmers and ranchers and a few residential water systems.

He spotted what he was looking for at the sixth house along the canal—a row of sunflowers along a back fence, fronted by a jungle of colorful blooms. He parked in the driveway of the house and walked around the side to get a better look. Drip irrigation hoses threaded through the plants and he could hear the chug of a pump.

A small white dog woke from a nap beneath a swing and began barking furiously. An attractive older woman, long gray curls pulled back from her face, emerged from the house and stared at him. "Who are you?" she demanded, fear tingeing the words.

"Deputy Chris Delray, Rayford County Sheriff's Department." He held out his identification. "I need to ask you a few questions, Miss…?"

"Howell. Melissa Howell." She walked out to the edge of the porch to meet him.

"I was noticing this irrigation setup you have," he said.

"Yes. What about it?"

"I'd like to take a closer look at it," he said, already moving toward the sound of the pump.

She followed him, the dog at her side. "Is there something wrong, Deputy?" she asked.

He walked to the edge of the ditch, and the hose leading from a submersible pump in the water. He reached down and hit the off switch, silencing the pump.

"Why did you do that?" she asked.

"You're not allowed to take any water from this

ditch, ma'am," Chris said. "The water rights belong to a rancher downstream from here."

"But the ditch is on my property," she said. "And there's plenty of water in there. It doesn't hurt anyone if I use a little."

To her, it was perfectly logical. But logic didn't always dictate Colorado water law. "The ditch belongs to the irrigation district," he said. "They have an easement through your property. You're not allowed to use the water and if you continue to do so, you could be fined up to seven hundred and fifty dollars a day, and you could even face time in jail."

She stared at him, mouth agape in disbelief.

"Do you understand, ma'am?" Chris asked. "You can't use this water. For anything."

"But if I don't water my flowers, they'll die," she said.

"I'm very sorry about that, ma'am. I can give you the name of a bulk water supplier. You can install a water tank and he'll deliver water to fill it. You can water your flowers from that tank." He took a business card from his wallet and handed it to her.

She frowned. "That sounds expensive."

"It's not too bad," he said. He looked down at the pump. "You need to disconnect all of this right away. I'll be checking back, and if I find this hooked up, I'll have to issue a citation."

"This is ridiculous," she said, anger replacing shock. "I never heard of such a thing."

"Where are you from?" he asked.

"Florida."

He nodded. "I understand in Florida they have more water than they know what to do with, but it's a different situation here, and the laws are different."

"I'm going to contact my lawyer about this," she said.

"Please do." Chris took out his ticket book and began writing. "Maybe he can help you understand the situation."

"What are you doing?" she asked.

"I'm issuing you a warning. It states you need to cease taking water from this ditch immediately or you'll be fined." He tore off the ticket and pressed it into her hand.

"I'll have to wait until my husband gets home to unhook everything," she said. "There's no way I can lift that heavy pump."

"I'll get it for you." That wasn't in his job description, but he doubted the woman's husband was much younger than her, and it was a heavy pump to haul uphill. He inched his way down to the edge of the ditch and crouched, prepared to heave the pump out, when a flash of something caught his eye. Gold metal, glittering bright in the clear water.

Ignoring the pump for the time being, he knelt beside the ditch and plunged his arm into the surprisingly cold water. The water reached past his elbow, soaking the short sleeve of his uniform shirt as his fingers closed around the item. He brought it up and dropped it on the bank beside him.

The little watch, bright gold and as big around as a plum, was worn smooth across the cover, the etched design so faded Chris couldn't tell what it was supposed to be. With the knuckle of one finger, he nudged it over, and stared at the initials embossed on the back side. *SRR* in elaborate script. Samuel Russell?

He did a quick calculation. This section of the ditch was maybe two miles from the place where Russell had been found. How had it not been caught in a gate between there and here? He pulled out his cell phone. The signal here was strong, and he dialed the sheriff's direct number.

"What you got, Chris?" Travis answered.

"I'm on a call in Idlewilde Estates." He gave the address. "I found something in the Daimler Ditch that runs in back of the property that you probably need to see."

He ended the call, and stared at the watch, gleaming in the sun. *How did you get all the way out here?* he wondered.

Chapter Three

Willow stared at the gold watch, shining in Deputy Delray's palm like a big gold button. "Yes, that's my father's watch." She looked up, into his serious brown eyes. "Where did you find it?"

He laid the watch, in a clear plastic evidence bag, on the kitchen counter between them. "First, where were you this morning between 5:00 a.m. and 7:30 a.m.?"

"I was here—asleep, most of that time."

"Is there anyone who can verify that?"

"What are you saying? Do you think *I* killed my father?" Tears stung her eyes, as much from anger as sorrow.

"Is there anyone who can confirm that you were home during that time?" he asked again.

"I sleep alone, Deputy," she snapped.

Something flickered behind those serious eyes—embarrassment? Amusement? She didn't care. "Where did you find that watch?" she asked again.

"The watch was found behind a house in Idlewilde Estates. In the irrigation canal."

She had a vague idea of the location of the fancy new housing development on what had once been farmland. "How did it get there?" she asked.

"Did your father have the watch with him when he left the house this morning?" Delray asked.

"If he was awake and dressed, he had that watch." She looked away, fighting emotion again. "My mother gave it to him." Her father's first wife, the woman he had really loved, and would still be married to if she had lived. That was the story Willow always told herself, the only one she would believe.

"Can you think of any reason your father would have been near Idlewilde Estates this morning?" the deputy asked.

"No." She studied him, trying to decide if it would be worth trying to make him understand. He was watching her, too, as if waiting for her to say more. Fine. She'd give him a chance. "My father worked his whole life on this ranch," she said. "This *was* his life. And it's a lot of work, running a place like this. He had a routine. He got up early, had a cup of coffee, then went out to work. He would check on the cattle, or ride fence, or see to the irrigation ditches, or supervise a work crew—whatever needed doing. He would come back to the house about eight, eat breakfast, and go out to work some more. Some days he worked until dark. Other days, when it wasn't so busy, he would come in during the hottest part of the day and rest. Sometimes he went into town to run errands, but that was in the afternoon, after the work on the ranch was done. He didn't have a reason to go anywhere else that early in the day. And I can't imagine he'd ever have a reason to go over to that development. Whose house was the watch found behind?"

"Melissa and Doug Howell. Did your father know them?"

"I don't think so. I never heard him mention them."

He looked away from her, at the living room that

looked nothing like it had when she was a girl. Darla had redecorated after she moved in, and though she and Sam had divorced three years before, he hadn't bothered to replace anything. So the white leather sofas, plush red chairs and chrome-and-glass tables remained, amid piles of ranch catalogs, bits of old harness and the globe Willow had given her dad for Father's Day. "Did your father leave a note when he left this morning?" the deputy asked.

"No. He didn't feel the need to tell me where he was going or what he was doing." She had asked him to keep her informed, but he had scoffed at the idea, so she had let it drop.

The deputy's gaze met hers once more, softer this time. "Have you looked on his desk or in his bedroom for a note?"

His meaning hit her like a punch, and she took a step back. "Do you mean a suicide note?"

He nodded. "You should probably look. Or I can do it, if you'd rather."

"How long have you lived in Rayford County?" she asked him. She couldn't recall seeing him around when she lived here before, and she thought she would remember. Chris Delray was a good-looking man, clean-cut and fit, with a bit more polish than the boys she had grown up with. The kind of man women noticed.

"A couple of months," he said.

"Then you don't know my father. You don't know the kind of man he is—was." She swallowed. "He wouldn't take his own life. And he had no reason to. It doesn't make sense."

"So no financial problems? No health problems?"

"None. The ranch was doing well. And I nagged him into getting his first physical in five years recently and afterward he bragged about how the doctor said he was in better shape than men twenty years younger. He never took any medication stronger than an aspirin."

"What about relationship problems?" He looked around the room again. "You mentioned your mother. Is she no longer in the picture?"

"My mother died when I was thirteen. My dad remarried after I left for college, but they were only together six years. Since then he hasn't dated anyone that I'm aware of."

"Do you know of anyone who would want to kill him?"

"No!" She clenched her hands in frustration. "I'm not saying he was a saint, or that everyone loved him, but why would someone want to murder him?"

"Who inherits the ranch?" he asked.

"I assume I do. I'll have to speak to his lawyer." The idea exhausted her. What did she want with the place, especially without her dad here?

"You don't know for sure?"

"Why should I? Do you know the terms of your parents' wills?"

He looked uncomfortable. "No."

"I'm his only child, and I never heard him talk about leaving the place to anyone else, but he was free to make his own decisions."

"What kind of work do you do?" he asked.

The shift in topic caught her off guard. Her cheeks grew hot. "I'm unemployed at the moment."

"What did your father think about you coming back here to live?" Delray asked.

"He was happy to have me here." Which was partly true. Dad didn't like her tendency to fuss over him.

If you're going to stay here, you need to find some-

thing to focus on besides me, he had said only the night before.

"I haven't moved back permanently," she said. "I'm only using this as a base while I look for a new job."

"What kind of work did you do?"

"I taught cultural anthropology at Hemphill University, in Connecticut." Her father, though proud of her education, had also believed she had chosen a particularly useless career. He would have preferred she study business, or veterinary medicine—something that would have been useful to him on the ranch.

"What will you do now that your father is gone?" the deputy asked. "Will you continue to operate the ranch?"

"I don't know. I haven't had time to think about that." The ranch was her father's most prized possession, not hers—but it was also a big part of her life. Her heritage. She couldn't imagine simply letting it slip away.

"It's a big place," he said. "I imagine you'll need help."

"My father has employees. They do most of the heavy lifting, though Dad would have hated to admit that."

Deputy Delray took out his phone. "What are their names? I may want to speak with them."

"Von King is the only full-time hand right now. There are a few other men who work during haying, or when it's time to move cattle, but they aren't employed right now."

"What does Von King do?"

"Whatever needs doing. He was cleaning and sharpening tools at the machine shed earlier."

Delray tucked his phone away. "Maybe I'll stop and talk with him on my way out."

"I haven't told him yet that Dad is…is dead." Saying the word was harder than she had expected.

"Why not?" Delray asked.

"I was upset and I didn't want to talk about it." She didn't want to talk about it now, with him, but she had no choice.

"I can tell him, if that would be easier for you."

The kindness in his voice caught her off guard. Up until now, he had seemed so businesslike, even accusatory. "I should do it," she said.

"You don't have to."

"I'll go with you and tell him, then you can talk to him." Having him there, adding authority to her words, might help. She feared that knowing her father was gone, Von would see her as vulnerable. She wasn't, but she didn't want the hassle of making that clear to him, not with everything else she had to deal with now.

They walked together to the machine shed. She was very aware of him beside her, the way he shortened his stride to match her own, the solid bulk of him casting a shadow over her, his calmness.

Von was sharpening the point of a pickax on a grinder and didn't notice when they first entered the shed. Delray stepped to one side, casting a shadow across the workbench, and Von looked up and took them in. He returned to his work and a full minute passed before he shut off the grinder and turned to them. "What is it?" he asked.

"This is Deputy Delray," Willow said. "I'm afraid my father…" What? Had an accident? Was killed? She tried to force the words past the knot in her throat and couldn't.

"Samuel Russell died earlier this morning," Deputy

Delray said. "His body was found in one of the irrigation ditches."

Von's face registered no emotion. "That's too bad," he said.

"Did you see Mr. Russell this morning?" Delray asked.

Von shook his head. "Nope. The only person I saw was her." He pointed the pickax at Willow. "Leaving early in Sam's truck."

She froze. Was Von accusing her of something? She couldn't look at the deputy, afraid of what she might see in his expression.

"When was the last time you saw Mr. Russell?" Delray asked.

"Yesterday, before supper," Von said. "He told me he wanted all the hand tools cleaned and sharpened today." He studied the point of the pickax.

"What was his mood?" Delray asked.

Von shrugged. "He seemed normal to me."

"He wasn't upset about anything?"

"He was a pretty grumpy old coot most of the time, anyway," Von said. His gaze flickered to her and she wondered if he had intended to hurt her with the criticism of her father.

"Where were you between five and seven thirty this morning?" Delray asked.

"I got up at six, had breakfast and came here to work," Von said.

"Where do you live?"

Von turned to Willow. "She can tell you that."

She wanted to refuse to take part in whatever game Von was playing, but the deputy was looking at her, expectant. "He lives in a cabin a couple of miles from here," she said. "You passed the entrance on the way in."

"Is there anyone who can verify your alibi?" Delray asked.

Von snorted. "Am I being accused of some crime?"

"Is there anyone who will confirm your whereabouts this morning?" Delray asked again.

"No."

Delray turned to leave and Willow hurried after him. They had only taken a few steps when Von called after them. "How did he die?"

"We're still waiting on the coroner's ruling," Delray said.

Von grunted. Before they were out the door, Willow heard the grinder start up again.

"What's his story?" Delray asked. "How long has he worked here?"

"He's been here about nine months, I think," she said. "The man who worked for Dad before moved back to New Mexico to work on his family's ranch. I'm not sure how Dad found Von."

"What's his background? Do you know?"

"Dad told me he'd been in prison."

Delray's gaze sharpened. "Your dad didn't have a problem with that?"

"He said everybody deserved a second chance. And he said Von is a good worker."

"Are you comfortable, having him around?"

Again, his kindness touched a soft place inside her she didn't want to reveal. "I'll be all right. I know how to take care of myself."

He took a business card from his shirt pocket and passed it to her. "If there's any trouble, call me," he said.

She nodded, and then stood on the front steps and watched while he got into his SUV and left. She didn't know what to make of the deputy, who had all but accused her of having a good reason to want her father dead one minute, and had handled the exchange with Von with sensitivity. He'd said to call him if she had trouble, but she could have told him she had had nothing but trouble over the past few months. She had hoped coming home would give her space to regroup and refocus, to get her life back on the right track. That wasn't happening. Without her father here, she was more lost than ever.

"HE WAS SHOT with his own gun, at close range." Dr. Butch Collins indicated the wound on Samuel Russell's body with the tip of a felt-tip pen. The sheriff had invited Chris to accompany him to the medical examiner's office in the basement of the hospital the next morning. It was Wednesday, and Chris was trying to focus on the injury as separate from the man whose daughter he had spoken to only hours before. He'd seen death before, but never this naked and clinical. It wasn't a usual part of his job.

"How do you know it was his gun?" Chris asked.

"His name's engraved on it," Butch said. "And I've been pheasant hunting with Sam Russell. I know that weapon."

"So, is it suicide?" Chris asked.

Butch looked to the sheriff, who stood across from Chris and the doctor, on the other side of the body. "What do you think, Travis?"

"I'm waiting for you to tell me," Sheriff Travis Walker said.

"Then take a look at this." Butch walked to the top of the exam table, and tilted Russell's head to one side. "You see that bruising?" he asked. "There, under the hair."

Chris forced himself to look, at the pattern of darkened flesh beneath Russell's thick white hair. "What's that from?" he asked.

"Somebody hit him with something heavy and flat—a board, a big flat rock—not sure."

"Hard enough to knock him down?" Travis asked.

"Hard enough to knock him out," Butch said. "The bruising isn't just external. There's a cerebral hemorrhage under there."

"Could it have happened after he was shot?" Chris asked. "He fell back and hit his head on a rock or something?"

Butch shook his head. "He was found facedown in that ditch, right? And I checked the scene and didn't see any rocks that could have done this damage. One more thing." He moved to Russell's hands. At the scene, the techs had slipped a plastic bag over each hand to preserve any evidence. The hands were bare now. "No residue on his hands from firing a weapon recently," Butch said. "But dirt and scratches, the kind I'd expect if he fell back and tried to catch himself, maybe thrashed around a little before he lost consciousness."

"So—somebody hit him over the head, then while he was out, took his gun and shot him?" Chris asked.

"Then arranged his body in the ditch with the gun beneath him to make it look like suicide," Butch said.

"Anything else you can tell us?" Travis asked.

"Whoever shot Sam Russell was standing very close," Butch said. "If he didn't get blood on him at the time of the shooting, it would have been hard to avoid it when he—or she—moved the body and arranged it in the ditch."

"I guess his daughter was right when she insisted her father wouldn't kill himself," Chris said.

"A lot of people say that," the sheriff said. "Most of the time it isn't true." He looked at Russell's body. "Maybe this time it is."

"Sam Russell didn't take his own life," Butch said. "You two have a murder on your hands."

Those words still rang in Chris's ears as he walked out of the hospital with Travis. "Do you want to be part of this investigation?" the sheriff asked when they reached the parking lot. "Technically, you were hired to primarily deal with water issues, and back up other cases. But your experience dealing with local ranchers could be helpful."

"I can handle my water work and this investigation, too," Chris said. His job kept him busy, but it wasn't overly demanding. "I feel like I'm already in hip-deep, anyway."

The sheriff nodded. "You talked to Willow Russell more than any of us. What's your feel for her? Does she have a motive to kill her father?"

"She's unemployed, recently moved back home. She says she doesn't know the terms of her father's will, but she's his only child, so it stands to reason she would inherit at least part of the ranch. She says she was home alone this morning, but no one can verify that." He rubbed the back of his neck. "On the other hand, she insisted her father's death wasn't suicide, and urged us to find his murderer."

"He turned his back on whoever hit him, so he probably knew and trusted them, or at least didn't suspect any ill will," Travis said. "But she's not a big woman, and it takes some force to knock a man out. Sam was older, but I wouldn't call him frail."

"She wouldn't be my primary suspect," Chris said.

"Who would that be?"

"He's got a hired hand, an ex-con named Von King. Struck me as a generally unpleasant fellow. He doesn't have anyone to vouch for his alibi, either. I'm not sure what he would stand to gain from killing his boss, however. He did say Russell was a 'grumpy old coot.'"

"Check into him. You should also question Trey Allerton. He's leasing a section of the Russell ranch and living in a trailer on the property with a woman named Courtney Baker and her little girl."

"I remember," Chris said. "He was linked to Talia Larrivee's murderer somehow, right?" Chris hadn't been actively involved in that investigation the month previous, but he had heard plenty of talk.

"Talia's killer, Tom Chico, and Allerton were business partners in the lease with Russell, and supposedly Allerton plans to build a summer camp– type ranch for disadvantaged youth," Travis said. "But I haven't seen much sign of progress."

"Why would he want to kill Russell?" Chris asked.

"That's what I want you to find out," Travis said. "Take Shane with you. He worked the Larrivee murder and knows Allerton and can fill you in."

Chris rode with Travis back to the sheriff's department, making a mental list of everything he needed to do. He planned to start with pulling Von King's criminal record, but before he could make it to his desk, office manager Adelaide Kinkaid waylaid him and the sheriff. "There's someone here to see you, Sheriff." Adelaide, a white-haired dynamo who wore outlandish earrings and bright colors, kept the office running smoothly. She knew everyone and everything in town and as the widow of a police officer, had a firm grasp on the way law enforcement was supposed to work.

Chris turned away, but Adelaide reached out and

snagged him. "She wants to talk to you, too. About Sam Russell."

Chris followed Travis toward the front lobby of the building. A well-preserved older woman with a cap of black hair and deep lines on either side of her mouth stood at their approach. "I'm Darla Russell," she said. "And I want to know what happened to my husband."

Chapter Four

"I don't think much of local law enforcement. They wouldn't tell me anything about Sam's death, despite the fact that I'm his widow." Darla Russell made this announcement approximately two minutes after dropping her suitcases in the middle of the ranch house living room Wednesday afternoon. She and her adult son, Emmet, had arrived less than a day after guilt had induced Willow to call and inform her former stepmother of Sam's passing.

"But you're his ex-wife, not his widow," Willow said. She still stood by the door, wishing she had never opened it to these two.

Darla drew herself up to her full five foot nine, the teased bouffant of her ink-black hair adding a couple of inches. "Neither Sam nor I ever remarried," she said. "I think that entitles me to call myself his widow."

This wasn't worth arguing over. "What are you two doing here?" Willow asked. She glanced at Emmet, who had already settled on the sofa, his long legs stretched out in front of him. Twenty-nine years old, pale and sullen, what hair he had left in a bad comb-over, Emmet was perpetually "between jobs" and lived with his mother in Albuquerque.

"Someone has to get to the bottom of this," Darla

said. "The police never tell the family anything in cases like this unless someone holds their feet to the fire. Besides, Sam would have wanted me here with you."

"Thank you, but I'm fine on my own."

"Don't be ridiculous." Darla sat in the recliner—Sam's chair. Willow wanted to tell her to move, but didn't have the energy for the argument that was sure to ensue. "The first thing you need to do is contact that pretty-boy sheriff and tell him he has your permission to share details of the case with me. They have you listed as Sam's next of kin."

Because I am his next of kin, she thought, but didn't waste her breath pointing this out. "I really don't think you need to bother with all this," she said instead. "You should go home and I promise to let you know if anything happens that affects you."

"You don't think Sam's death affects me?" Her voice rose and inwardly, Willow cringed. "Sam was the love of my life and I will mourn him forever. I don't know how you can be so cold. I did my best to be a good mother to you and this is how you repay me." She dug a tissue from her purse and pressed it to her eyes.

Willow had been twenty and away at college when Sam married Darla. She hadn't needed a mother and had only interacted with Darla and her son on holidays and brief visits home. What she had seen then hadn't impressed her, though she had told herself that if this woman made her father happy, it was none of Willow's concern. When Sam and Darla had divorced, Willow had been relieved, if a little sad for her father. She didn't need, or want, Darla and Emmet here now. "It was very kind of you to travel all this way to help me," Willow said. "But there really isn't anything you can do. Until the sheriff's department has finished their investigation, we can't even plan a funeral service."

"We were already in the area," Darla said. "When I called yesterday morning, it was to tell Sam we were coming for a visit." She narrowed her eyes. "Did you know then that Sam was dead? And you didn't tell me?"

"I had just found out," Willow said. "I was still in shock."

Darla seemed to consider this, then patted the sofa cushion beside her. "Sit down and tell me what happened."

Reluctantly, Willow sat on the end of the sofa. "I told you on the phone last night that the ditch rider found Dad in the irrigation ditch near the loading chute and cattle pens," she said.

"You said he'd been shot. But who shot him?"

"I don't know." Willow shook her head. "That's what the sheriff is trying to find out."

"And how long is that going to take?" Darla asked.

"I don't know," Willow said again. "I can't think of anyone who would want to kill Dad." She didn't mention suicide. No matter what Deputy Delray said, she couldn't believe her father would take his own life.

"Can they issue a death certificate without knowing who killed him?" Darla asked.

Willow frowned. "I have no idea. Why do you ask?"

"You have to have a death certificate in order for the will to go to probate," Emmet said. Willow stared at him. He shrugged. "I'm just saying."

"Have you looked at the will yet?" Darla asked.

"No. Dad has only been gone a day."

"There's nothing to be gained in putting it off," Darla said. "And I suppose you've already looked for any cash he kept around." She turned her head to survey the living room.

"What cash?" Willow asked.

Darla fixed her gaze on Willow once more. "Sam always kept cash on hand. In case of emergency."

"I'm sure he had some money in his wallet," Willow said. "But I guess the sheriff still has that." She'd have to ask next time she spoke to someone from the sheriff's office.

"I'm not talking about a few bills in his wallet," Darla said. "I'm talking hundreds, probably thousands of dollars Sam kept here."

"Do you mean in the safe?" Willow didn't remember her father keeping cash in there, but maybe he had started to do so. She hadn't thought to look.

"Not in the safe," Darla said. "He kept the money hidden."

"Where did he hide it?" Willow said. "This is the first I've heard of it."

"You didn't know?" Darla widened her eyes. "I thought everyone knew. Sam had quite the reputation as a bit of a miser."

This was the first Willow had heard of this. Yes, Sam was frugal, but she had never thought of him as stingy. "So you saw him hide money?" she asked.

Darla pressed her lips together, the lines on either side of her mouth deepening. "Well, no, I didn't actually see him. But other people told me about it."

"What other people?" Willow couldn't believe this.

"Oh, just people." Darla waved her hand. "My hairdresser mentioned it, and one of the ranch hands said something about it. I asked Sam about it, but of course he denied it. But he would, wouldn't he? I mean, the whole point of hiding the money was to keep other people from finding it."

"I don't think Dad hid money around here," Willow said. "I've never found any of it. Besides, what difference does it make to you?" She was weary of making nice to this annoying woman.

"Don't get ugly with me," Darla said. "For your information, Sam promised Emmet a share of this ranch when Sam passed on. And I think that includes any cash you find."

The idea was so outrageous Willow couldn't breathe for a few seconds. "Why would my father leave part of the ranch to Emmet?" she asked.

"We negotiated it as part of the divorce," Darla said. "I wouldn't ask for spousal support if he agreed to leave half of the Double R to Emmet."

She couldn't believe her father would do such a thing, but then, she still couldn't understand what Sam had seen in Darla in the first place. "Why would Emmet even want half the ranch?" she asked.

"All this real estate must be worth a lot of money," Emmet said. "I figure I could sell it."

She swallowed down a wave of nausea. Her father would be horrified at the idea. "I'll have to speak to Dad's lawyer," Willow said.

"I can call him." Darla pulled out her phone. "What's his name and number?"

Willow was about to refuse when her own phone buzzed. She slid it from her pocket and didn't recognize the local number. "Hello?" She stood and walked out of the room, the phone pressed tightly to her ear.

"Hello, Willow? It's Chris Delray."

She entered the kitchen and shut the door behind her. "Deputy Delray. What can I do for you?"

"The coroner has made his report and I wanted you to know before we release anything to the press."

Fear climbed her throat. "What did he say?"

"I'm sorry to tell you that your father was murdered."

Hearing the word out loud, instead of only in her head, shocked her more than she would have thought possible. She groped for a kitchen chair and sank into it, and clamped one hand over her mouth, trying to hold back a sob. "I'm sorry," Delray continued. "Losing a loved one is hard enough. Losing them to murder is that much worse. We'll be doing everything we can to find his killer. I'll probably have more questions for you soon."

"Thank you," she managed to choke out the words.

"Are you going to be all right? Is there anyone I can call to come be with you?"

"I'm okay." She struggled to pull herself together. "Dad's ex-wife is here. She and her son just showed up a few minutes ago."

"They stopped by the sheriff's office," he said. "She wasn't too happy when the sheriff told her he couldn't release any information to her."

"So she said."

"Well, it's good that you're not alone right now."

"I'd rather be alone. I think she only came here because she has a crazy idea that my dad left half the ranch to her son."

"I'm sorry you're having to deal with that on top of grieving for your father and answering all our questions," he said. "If you like, I could come over and question her and her son. I could annoy them into leaving."

She almost smiled at the image of him doing just that. "Thanks, but I can deal with them. It's a good distraction."

"I'll be in touch," he said. "Call me if you need anything."

It was something people said to the bereaved, but she thought Deputy Delray might mean it.

She tucked her phone back in her pocket and went to the sink and filled a glass with water. While she drank it, she watched out the window as Darla, trailed by Emmet, crossed the yard toward Von King, who had just emerged from the equipment shed. Willow couldn't hear the conversation, but body language told the story. Darla gestured with both arms held wide. Von scowled and shook his head. Darla, hands on hips, unleashed another torrent of words. Von waved his arms and stormed off.

A few minutes later Darla, minus Emmet, burst into the kitchen. "You need to fire that insolent hired hand. He called me a very ugly word just now."

"What did you say to upset him?" Willow asked.

"I told him I wanted him to give us a tour of the property, and he refused."

"He has work to do," Willow said. "He's not a tour guide."

"He doesn't have to be rude," Darla said.

"I guess Dad didn't hire him for his personality."

Darla folded her arms over her chest. "Then you can show us around the ranch. I want to see what Sam did with the place since I lived here."

Willow set the empty water glass in the sink and turned to face Darla. "I have other things I need to do now," she said. She needed to call her father's lawyer, and she needed to take something for the headache hammering in her skull. She moved past Darla, toward the door.

"I don't understand why you have to be so unfriendly," Darla said. "I blame your father for not remarrying sooner after your mother died. A woman would have taught you that charm is the most powerful weapon a woman can have. It's no wonder you've failed to attract a man."

"I guess lack of charm explains why Emmet is still single, too," Willow said. She left before Darla could fire back a retort. She shouldn't let the woman get to her this way. She had a fight on her hands to keep the ranch and to help find out who had murdered her father. She couldn't let a couple of unpleasant not-quite-relatives distract her.

DEPUTY SHANE ELLIS was a former major-league pitcher who had been sidelined by a career-ending injury, returned to his hometown of Eagle Mountain and signed on with the sheriff's department. That was all Chris knew about his fellow officer, except that Shane had been involved in the hunt for Talia Larrivee's killer the month before, while Chris had been primarily focused on working with local ranches during the busy summer irrigation season.

"How much did the sheriff tell you about Trey Allerton?" Shane asked as he rode with Chris toward the Russell ranch Wednesday afternoon.

"He said Allerton was leasing part of the ranch from Russell, and that he planned to build some kind of summer camp for kids?"

"I learned more about him when my fiancée, Lauren, asked me to help her find her former sister-in-law, Courtney Baker, and Courtney's daughter, Ashlyn. Supposedly Allerton and Courtney want to build a camp where kids who've experienced some kind of trauma can come and have a break," Shane said. "Horseback riding, hiking, counselors, that kind of thing. Sam Russell agreed to lease them part of the north section of the Double R."

"Did Allerton and Sam have a disagreement over the lease or something?" Chris asked.

"Not that I know of," Shane said. "But we'll want to ask about that."

"What's Allerton's connection to Talia's murder?" Chris asked. He should have paid more attention to that case, but it wasn't his, so he hadn't memorized the details.

"Allerton was supposedly business partners with Tom Chico, the man who admitted to killing Talia," Shane said. "Chico and Talia hung out with Allerton and Courtney for a couple of weeks before Talia disappeared. Tom Chico is a suspect in the murder of another young woman in Colorado Springs at the same time Allerton was stationed there. We think the two men might have met up when they were both in Colorado Springs, but we haven't found any real proof of that."

"So Allerton may or may not have a questionable past," Chris said.

"Right. He doesn't have a criminal record that we're aware of, but he comes across as a schemer. He has big plans for this ranch, but so far he's mainly talking other people into giving him money."

"Some people call that good business," Chris said.

"Yeah, they do. And Sam seemed okay with Allerton, as long as he was paid what he was owed, which he was. But he's worth questioning, if only because he and Courtney live closest to Russell's ranch house."

They passed the entrance to the Russell ranch. Chris couldn't see much from the road—the ranch house itself was much farther up the drive. He wondered how Willow was faring with her stepmother, who had come across in the sheriff's department as loud and demanding—the opposite of Willow.

But soft-spoken wasn't the same as weak. So far, Willow had radiated strength and determination. In a war of wills, Chris would bet on Sam's daughter as the winner.

A few miles farther on, Shane turned the cruiser into a second drive, this one pocked with deep ruts. He stopped the cruiser in front of an old mobile home with turquoise siding, a small wooden landing and steps sitting crookedly in front of the door. "It doesn't look as if they've done anything in the three weeks since I was up here," Shane said. He and Chris got out and made their way to the door.

The door rattled in its frame when Shane knocked, and a few moments later, heavy footsteps inside moved toward them. The door opened and a tall, broad-shouldered man with sandy brown hair looked out at them. "Hello," he said, his voice without inflection.

"Hello, Trey," Shane said. "This is Deputy Delray. We wanted to ask you and Courtney a few questions."

"Courtney isn't here," he said. "What is this about?"

"Can we come in?" Shane asked. "This won't take long."

Allerton hesitated, then held the door open wider. "Sure."

The interior of the trailer was clean, but worn. The sofa sagged and the only other seating was a single folding chair. Allerton picked up a blanket from the floor in front of the sofa. "I was taking a nap," he said, and sank onto the sofa.

Shane perched on the other end of the sofa and Chris took the folding chair. "Did you know Sam Russell died yesterday morning?" Shane asked.

"Von King was by here late yesterday and he told us." Allerton sat forward, clasped hands on one knee. "He said the old guy killed himself."

"He didn't kill himself," Chris said. "He was murdered."

Allerton sat up straighter. "Really? Who did it?"

"We're trying to find out," Chris said. "Have you heard of any disagreements between Sam Russell and anyone else?"

Allerton shook his head. "I didn't know him all that well."

"But you're leasing this land from him," Chris said.

"Yeah, but that's just business. It's not like we were friends or anything."

"Are you friends with Von King?" Shane asked.

"He's done some work for us around the place, that's all."

"How do you know Von?" Chris asked.

"I told Mr. Russell I was looking for someone to help with some cleanup and stuff around here and he told me I could hire Von, so I did."

"Where were you between five and seven thirty yesterday morning?" Chris asked.

Allerton didn't appear surprised or upset by the question. "I was here. In bed."

"Is there anyone who can verify that?" Chris asked.

"Courtney will. She was with me."

"Where is Courtney?" Shane asked.

"She and her little girl took some laundry to town, and planned to buy some groceries."

"Lauren would like to see her and Ashlyn," Shane said.

"That's up to Courtney," Allerton said. He stood. "Sorry I can't help you with the whole Russell mystery. I'm too busy here to pay attention to what's going on with other people."

Chris and Shane stood also, and followed Allerton to the door. "How is the youth ranch coming?" Shane asked. "Have you started building yet?"

"It's a slow process," Allerton said. "But I'm courting an investor and that should give us the money we need soon. It's going to be great."

Neither officer said anything until they were back on the road. "Courtney was married to Lauren's brother, Mike," Shane said. "He was killed in Afghanistan and the two women were close until Courtney took up with Allerton and she and her daughter, Ashlyn, moved here. Allerton says he was Lauren's brother's best friend, but Lauren never heard him mention Trey."

"I'll ask Sam's daughter what she knows about her father's relationship with Allerton," Chris said. Trey Allerton hadn't impressed him as the kind of person who could pull off a big project like his proposed youth ranch, but that didn't make him a murderer.

"I think it's suspicious that Allerton is pals with Tom Chico, a murderer who has a pretty long rap sheet," Shane said. "And now he's pals with Von King, another ex-con."

"Sam Russell told Willow that Von had been in prison," Chris said. "But when I tried to find information about him, I drew a blank."

"It's not the sort of thing a person lies about to impress a potential employer," Shane said.

"Maybe King heard Sam had a soft spot for ex-cons," Chris said. "He had supposedly hired them before."

"Or maybe Von King isn't his real name," Shane said.

"Sounds like we need to talk to him again," Chris said. "I want to interview the ex-wife and her son, too. Willow said they showed up today asking about the will. They said Sam promised to leave half the ranch to the son."

"People have killed for less," Shane said. "Let's stop by the ranch now and see what they have to say."

Chapter Five

"I was very sorry to hear of your father's death. Sam was a great man, and he will be missed by many in this community." Ted Delray, Attorney at Law, sounded suitably grave when he took Willow's call Wednesday afternoon.

She had been prepared to break the news to Ted herself, but apparently the community grapevine had already gotten the word out. "How did you find out about it?" she asked.

"It's on the newspaper's website," Ted said. "Murder is big news in a county this small. And even more shocking following the murder of that young woman last month. And your father was so well-known and well respected."

"Yes, it is shocking," she said.

"Does the sheriff have any idea who did it?" She heard the eagerness behind the question, and realized this was the first of many such inquiries from the people she knew. Murder held a fascination, and carried with it a desire to be a little closer to the mystery. Or maybe Ted had another reason for asking.

"Are you related to Chris Delray?" she asked. "He's a sheriff's deputy."

"Chris is my son," Ted said. "Is he involved in the murder investigation?"

"Yes." She wondered why Ted didn't know that. Then again, maybe Chris didn't talk about his work with his father.

"Was Chris able to tell you anything about who might have killed your father?" Ted asked.

"No one seems to know anything," she said. "I can't think of anyone who would want to harm Dad, much less kill him. Can you?"

"I can't. But a man doesn't get to be almost seventy without making a few enemies."

"Who were Dad's enemies?"

"Maybe *enemy* is too strong a word. But you know your father wasn't happy when the Carstairses sold the family ranch to that developer who built Idlewilde Estates. He and Bud Carstairs were good friends for years, but they never spoke to each other again after that."

"I heard Bud sold the place to pay for Mary Ann's care in that special Alzheimer's facility in Junction," Willow said.

"He did. But your father took a hard line about things like that."

"Bud Carstairs didn't murder my father." She pictured the neighboring rancher as he was the last time she had seen him—an almost elfin figure with a cap of white hair and a warm grin. When she was little, he would slip her sticks of the cinnamon chewing gum he carried with him since he'd given up tobacco years before.

"I'm sure he didn't," Ted said. "I'm just offering that as one example of how Sam had had disagreements with people that left hard feelings. Maybe there's something like that we don't know about."

"Maybe." Willow knew her father wasn't a saint, but had he really done something that made someone so angry that person decided to kill him? "That's not really why I called," she said. "I need to know about Dad's will."

"Of course. Well, I'll need a copy of the death certificate, and we'll go before a judge and ask her to issue letters testamentary, declaring you the executrix, which will give you authority to act on behalf of the estate. The will has to go through probate, but I can handle all of that for you."

It sounded overwhelming, but people dealt with this sort of thing every day, so she would, too. "Can you tell me the terms of the will?" she asked.

Ted paused, so long she wondered if they had lost the connection. "You don't know?" he finally asked.

"No." Her stomach roiled. This didn't sound good.

"I did advise Sam to discuss this with you, but as we've already talked about, he had very strong feelings about how things should be done, and no one could persuade him differently."

"What provisions did he make?" she asked, steeling herself for the worst.

"Several years ago—about the time they broke ground for Idlewilde—your father placed the entire ranch in a conservation easement."

"What does that mean?"

"It means you are free to live on the ranch, to continue to operate it and derive income from it, but it cannot be divided or sold for any other purpose but ranching."

"Does any part of the ranch go to Emmet Caspar?"

"Who is Emmet Caspar?"

"Darla Caspar Russell's son from her first marriage," Willow said. "Darla was Dad's second wife."

"I know who Darla is," Ted said. "And she and her son aren't mentioned in the will. There is a small bequest to the county ranching museum and that's it. Everything else goes to you."

Willow sagged in her chair, weak with relief. "Darla is here now," she said. "She told me my father promised to leave half of the ranch to Emmet if she didn't ask for spousal support."

"I handled the divorce for your father and there was no such agreement. He did pay a generous settlement to her at the time of the divorce, as outlined in their prenup."

"Dad and Darla had a prenup?" She didn't know why the idea surprised her so much, except that her father—who had never owned a computer, or even a smartphone—had seemed so firmly fixed in the past, where things like prenuptial agreements didn't exist.

"Your father was a shrewd businessman," Ted said.

"I'm relieved to hear it," she said. "And I'm pleased about the conservation easement."

"Not everyone is," Ted said. "I've dealt with heirs who are absolutely furious they won't be able to make their fortunes by selling the family estate. So do you intend to stay and continue to operate the ranch yourself?"

"I don't know about that," she said.

"If you decide the day-to-day operation of the place isn't for you, I can put you in touch with some people who can help you find a manager," Ted said. "Or you can sell the property to someone who will continue to operate it as a ranch. They would still be bound by the terms of the conservation easement, but there are people who look for that kind of thing."

"I'll have to think about it awhile." She had never been that interested in ranching, but could she really sell off her father's legacy, even to another rancher?

"No rush. In fact, I would advise you not to make any hasty decisions. In the meantime, let me know when you have the official death certificate and I'll start the proceedings for probate."

"Thank you, Ted." She hung up the phone, feeling much less burdened. And she couldn't wait to find Darla and give her the good news.

CHRIS AND SHANE located Von King at the corrals and loading chute near where Sam's body had been found. Crime scene tape still fluttered from stakes around the irrigation ditch. Shane parked the sheriff's department SUV on the side of the road, behind Von's truck, and they ducked under the barbed wire fencing to reach the ranch hand. "When I was driving by last night, I saw someone had cut this fence wire," Von said as they neared. He hammered a staple into a wooden fence post. "One of your crime scene people, I expect."

"Was the wire cut yesterday?" Shane asked Chris.

Chris shook his head. "I think Von's right, and the crime scene team cut it to get their equipment in. You can file a claim to get the sheriff's department to reimburse the ranch for the damage," he told Von.

"It's just wire and a few staples." Von tugged at the strand of wire, shiny against the rusted strands on either side of it. "What do you two want?"

"We've been talking to Trey Allerton," Shane said. "He told us you've been doing some work for him."

"I have." Von straightened and faced them. "What of it?"

"What kind of work?" Chris asked.

"Grunt work. Moving rocks and dirt, propping up broken-down fences."

"Did you know Tom Chico?" Shane asked.

"Never met him."

"He and Allerton were business partners," Shane said.

"Trey is the only one I dealt with. Don't know about the other guy." He moved along the fence, tugging at the wire at each post. Most people found being questioned by two uniformed officers unsettling, but not Von, maybe because he'd been questioned before.

"We know your real name isn't Von King," Chris said.

Von fixed him with a hard gaze. "My name is Von King. I can show you my driver's license if you like."

"There's no law against changing your name," Shane said. "We're just curious what you went by before."

"My name is Von King," he said again, and moved to the next section of fencing.

Chris and Shane exchanged a look, silently acknowledging this line of questioning was going nowhere. "How are things at the ranch house today?" Chris asked.

"The ex-wife and her boy showed up, circling like vultures."

"Did you know them when she was married to Sam before?" Shane asked.

"Wasn't around then. But she made a point of telling me they'd been married."

"When did she arrive at the ranch?" Shane asked.

"Around noon. The two of them moved in, suitcases and all, and she started giving orders."

"Had she visited the ranch before this?" Chris asked. "I mean, since you've worked for Sam?"

"Nope." He moved down the fence line and they followed.

"Did Sam ever mention anyone he had a disagreement with?" Chris asked. "Anyone he was angry at or worried about?"

"He wasn't my best friend, he was my boss," Von said. "We talked about the work he wanted me to do and when he wanted me to do it. We didn't stand around baring our souls."

"So you don't know anyone he argued with?" Chris pushed.

Von stopped, one hand on top of a fence post, and faced him. "He and Willow argued plenty," he said.

"What about?" Chris asked.

"I don't know. But I could hear the raised voices from the house. They were both yelling."

"When was this?" Shane asked.

"Night before last," Von said. "Right at dark. I went to put away the tools I'd been using, replacing some broken fence posts on the south pasture, and I heard them going at it."

"Did that alarm you?" Chris asked. "Hearing them fighting?"

"It wasn't the first time. And it wasn't any of my business, either." He turned away. "I've got work to do and I think you do, too." He didn't wait for an answer, simply walked away, long strides over the sagebrush-dotted ground until he reached his truck and climbed in.

"We'd better talk to Willow and find out what this argument was about," Shane said, leading the way to the cruiser.

"If Von was even telling the truth," Chris said.

"We have to check it out," Shane said. "If the two of them were arguing and the next morning Sam was killed, we can't ignore it."

"Of course not." So far, this was the first they had heard about Sam Russell arguing with anyone. It didn't mean Willow had murdered her father, but it did indicate she hadn't been entirely truthful with them, and that troubled him even more than doubts about her guilt or innocence.

WHEN WILLOW EMERGED from her bedroom after her telephone conversation with Ted Delray, she found Darla and Emmet in the living room, preparing to leave. "We're going into town to eat, since you haven't offered us anything," Darla said.

"Suit yourself."

"You don't have to be so rude!" Darla huffed.

The little patience Willow had left deserted her. "You're the one who's rude—showing up here uninvited," she said.

"We have every right to be here," Darla said.

"I don't think you do," Willow said. "I just got off the phone with Dad's lawyer."

"Oh?" Darla crossed her arms over her chest and looked at Willow expectantly. "What did he have to say?"

"We discussed the terms of Dad's will."

"And? Don't be coy, Willow. You're too old for it to be cute."

"Everything comes to me, and it's in a conservation easement so it can't be sold for development or divided."

She had expected Darla to be upset, maybe even to fly into a rage. Instead, she uncrossed her arms and smiled. "There's another will," she said.

"There isn't," Willow said.

"There is." Emmet, who had been lurking behind his mother until this point, finally spoke. "Mom has a copy."

"I can show it to you, if you like," Darla said. "After we've returned from dinner."

"After you return from dinner, you can pack your bags and leave," Willow said. "My lawyer will be contacting you."

"You can't throw us out." Darla's veneer of calm cracked.

"I can and I am," Willow said. "This is my home, not yours."

"Your father would be appalled to know you were treating us this way," Darla said.

"Your ex-husband would never have let you in the door in the first place," Willow said.

"I can't believe this." Darla stood and faced Willow, who became very aware that this woman was six inches taller and probably fifty pounds heavier than her. "I came here to help you!" Darla's voice rose. "And this is how you repay me!"

Emmet stood, too. "You're upsetting Mother," he said.

Willow glared at the two of them. She wanted to tell them exactly what she thought of them, but that would only anger them more and escalate the situation. Instead, she took a deep breath and took out her phone. "There's a motel in Eagle Mountain," she said. "You can stay there, or you can go back to Albuquerque. But you have to leave. And if you don't, I'll call the sheriff."

She expected Darla to object again. "We'll talk in the morning," she said, and headed out of the room. "Emmet, come," she barked as she passed her son.

Willow stared at the closed door and listened to Darla's car starting up outside. She was probably stuck with those two for tonight, but in the morning she would make them leave, if she had to contact the sheriff's department for help. What would they think of this new family drama? she wondered.

She went into the kitchen and put water on to boil for tea. She should probably eat something, but she couldn't imagine what. She felt hollow inside, as if the loss of her father had left a vacancy she feared might never be filled. All she really wanted was to crawl into bed, pull the covers over her head and wake up tomorrow to find this was all a horrible nightmare.

She was staring into the refrigerator, seeing nothing, when she was startled by a knock on the back door.

"We saw you through the window, so I came around here," Deputy Delray said after she opened the door. Another officer stood at his shoulder, a good-looking man with blue eyes.

"Come in." She held the door open wider. "You may be just in time to help me."

The two moved past her, filling the small kitchen with their bulk. "This is Deputy Ellis," Deputy Delray said.

The other officer nodded. "What do you need our help with?" Deputy Delray asked.

"I've just told my dad's ex-wife and her son that they need to leave," she said. "They said we'd talk more after they returned from eating in Eagle Mountain, which I suspect means I'm stuck with them one more night, but I'm going to try again in the morning. Can I call the sheriff's office if they give me trouble? I mean, if I don't want them here, they're trespassing, right?"

"What have they been doing that has you so upset?" Deputy Delray asked.

"I don't want them here. Isn't that enough?"

He nodded, those warm brown eyes studying her. She felt that gaze, as if he was trying to see past the surface to what lay beneath. "Have they done something in particular to upset you?" he asked after a moment.

"I talked to Dad's attorney, Ted Delray. I believe you know him?"

A flush spread across the deputy's cheeks. "He's my father."

"He's handled all of Dad's legal affairs for years," she said. "I asked him about Dad's will and he said several years ago, Dad placed the ranch in a conservation easement. Do you know what that is?"

"Yes. It's a way to keep properties from being subdivided and sold off."

"Right. Dad left everything to me, except for a small cash gift to the history museum, and I'm free to continue to operate the ranch, to hire someone to manage it for me or to sell it to someone who will keep it as a working ranch. There's nothing at all in the will about Darla or her son, Emmet. I told Darla that and she says there's another will—one that does give Emmet half the property."

"Did she show you this will?" Deputy Ellis asked.

"No. And I don't want to see it. I don't believe it exists. I told her to take it up with Ted."

"Is it possible she's right—is there another will?" Deputy Delray asked.

"Why would Dad make another will that Ted doesn't know about?" she asked. "Dad used him for everything. He even handled Dad's divorce from Darla." She shook her head. "She has to be bluffing."

"We can't help you with legal advice," Deputy Delray said. "But we're here if your unwanted visitors give you any trouble about leaving. Though we'd like to question them before you kick them out."

"Of course. Is that why you're here?" She put aside her agitation about the will to focus on him. "Or have you learned something new?"

He shook his head. "Nothing new. And we wanted to talk to you again, too." He moved to the kitchen table and pulled out a chair. "Why don't we sit and talk for a few minutes?"

She sat and they took the two chairs across from her. "How are you doing?" Deputy Delray asked, real concern in his expression.

"I'm still in shock," she said. "So much has happened so quickly. Right now I'm just powering through, and not quite believing Dad is gone."

"You don't have to do everything by yourself," he said. "Ask your friends for help."

She pressed her lips together, fighting for control. "I don't have many friends here," she said. "I've been away a long time."

"How long have you been back living on the ranch?" Deputy Ellis asked.

"Four weeks."

"How was that going—you and your father living together after you had both lived on your own so long?" Deputy Delray asked. "Or did you live on your own?"

"Dad and I got along well. For years after my mother died it was just the two of us, so we've always been close."

"So you didn't argue?" Deputy Ellis asked.

She shifted, then told herself not to squirm like a guilty child. "We were making it work," she said.

"We have a witness who says he heard you and your father arguing," Deputy Delray said. "The night before your father was killed."

A chill settled in the pit of her stomach. "We weren't fighting," she said. "Not really."

"The witness says the two of you were shouting," Deputy Ellis said.

She looked away, blinking back tears. "Dad and I both have tempers. But it was nothing, really."

"What was the argument about?" Deputy Delray asked.

"Dad thought I was wasting my life looking after him. He accused me of hiding here." Her father's words had stung, maybe because they were at least partly true.

"What were you hiding from?" Deputy Delray asked.

"I was fired from my teaching job at Hemphill University. At first, I thought I would stay here with Dad a couple of weeks, but that turned into a month."

"I'm sure being fired was painful," Deputy Delray said. He sounded more sympathetic than accusatory. Was he playing "good cop" or did he really care?

"Dad yelling at me about it was his way of getting me moving forward with my life again."

"But the two of you argued about it," Deputy Ellis persisted.

She nodded. "We argued. But it wasn't real anger. It was the kind of disagreement that two people who love each other have—they're not on the same page, but each of them is coming from a place of caring. I thought Dad needed me here and he believed I was wasting my talents hiding away here." She forced herself to meet his gaze. "I loved my father. I can't even imagine anything he could have done or said that would have made me angry enough to hurt him. I just..." She shook her head. "It wouldn't happen. He was my father. The only parent I'd had for years and years." She began to sob, unable to hold back the tears any longer.

"What time did you leave the house yesterday morning?" Ellis asked after a moment.

She sniffed and tried to focus on answering him. "About eight forty-five," she said. "Dad is usually in for breakfast by eight, so when he hadn't come in forty-five minutes later, I was worried. I tried calling his cell phone, but didn't get an answer." She frowned. "That isn't so unusual, since there are a lot of places around here where the signal isn't very good. But I was so worried I decided to go out and look for him. When I saw he hadn't taken his truck, I was even more concerned."

"Why was that?" Delray asked.

"If he was riding a horse or on a four-wheeler, he might have been thrown and hurt. Dad liked to think he was bulletproof, but he was almost seventy and he's not as strong as he used to be. I thought if I moved back here I could make sure he ate better and got his rest and didn't overdo it—but it was hard." She almost smiled. "Dad could be very stubborn, but so could I. It's why we sometimes clashed."

"Where did you go looking for him?" Delray asked.

"I walked over to the horse barns first. The mare he usually rides was in her stall, so I thought that meant Dad was out on one of the four-wheelers. I knew he wouldn't strike out on foot."

Neither of them argued with that assumption. They had probably spent enough time around local ranchers and cowboys to know that was true.

"Where did you look for your father next?" Ellis asked.

"I drove over to Von King's cabin, to ask if he had

seen Dad. But he wasn't there, so I figured maybe he and Dad had gone somewhere in Von's truck. That made me feel a little better, so I started back for the ranch house. But then I saw all the law enforcement vehicles over by the corrals and drove over to find out what was going on."

"What did you think when you saw the vehicles?" Ellis asked.

"I thought Dad had been in an accident," she said. "I was scared."

"You mentioned your father's temper," Delray said. "Do you know of anyone else he argued with recently?"

"No. I asked Ted that also and all he said was that a person didn't live to almost seventy without making enemies. I don't know if I agree with that, but someone disliked my father enough to kill him, didn't they?"

Deputy Delray looked at Deputy Ellis. "Do you have any more questions for Ms. Russell?"

"No." Deputy Ellis slid back his chair. "I've got a couple of calls I need to make, so I'll meet you outside in a bit."

He left the room and silence wrapped itself around Willow and the deputy. "We're not purposely being hard on you," Delray said after a long moment. "We have to gather as much information as possible, in order to find out who killed your father."

"I know." She gripped the edge of the table. "It's just hard, having strangers judge every part of your life. I'm not proud that my dad and I argued, but I'm not ashamed, either. He and I were a lot alike, and that meant we clashed. It didn't mean we didn't love each other." She shifted toward him. "I wish you could have known him, Deputy Delray. He could be stubborn and set in his ways, but he was also the first to help someone in need. Just like Von King—I wouldn't have hired him, but my dad wanted to give him a second chance. And if there was any kind of fundraiser in town for someone in need, everyone knew my dad was good for a generous donation."

"Could you call me Chris?" he asked. "It's what almost everyone else in the county calls me. I found out pretty quickly that most people don't stand on formality here."

"All right, Chris." Calling him by his last name always made her think of his father, anyway. "And you can call me Willow."

He nodded, a hint of a smile at the corners of his mouth and glinting in his eyes. "I met your father a couple of times, in my duties enforcing water laws," he said. "But he never broke those laws, so we only talked in passing. He welcomed me to the job when I first started, and he wished me luck. I never heard any of his neighbors say a bad word about him."

She nodded. "Which makes it even harder to understand who would have shot him. I don't even understand how someone could have gotten his gun away from him and used it to kill him. Not without a real struggle."

"The coroner says someone hit Sam in the back of the head and probably knocked him out."

"So they snuck up on him."

"Or he trusted the person enough to turn his back."

"That makes me feel even worse." She looked up at the ceiling, willing the tears not to fall. Her eyes and head ached from crying. "Though why it's easier for me to think he was killed by someone he hated than someone he liked—I mean, he's still gone, either way."

"I'm sorry," Chris said.

"That helps a little," she said. "Knowing other people hate that this happened and that some of them will miss him, too."

Chris stood. "I'd better go. But just remember—you and I are on the same side. We both want to find out the truth about what happened to your father."

She nodded. "Finding out who did this won't bring Dad back, but not knowing just adds to the loss. Does that make sense?"

"It makes a lot of sense." He rested his hand on her shoulder. The touch was brief, but reassuring. She still felt its warmth long after he had left her alone in the kitchen.

Chapter Six

Every encounter with Willow Russell unsettled Chris. He was confident he knew how to perform his job well, but that confidence faltered when it came to dealing with her. He told himself it was essential to put aside emotion and personal feelings to focus on facts in order to bring justice to Sam Russell's killer. That meant considering everyone who had come in contact with the man as a possible suspect. Willow Russell was probably closer to her father than anyone, she had no alibi for the time of his murder, she had admitted that she and her father had clashed, and as her father's only heir, she would inherit a lot of money and land worth even more. He had to look at her very closely and keep digging, yet when he was with her, he had a tough time believing she had hit her father over the head, then shot him at close range with a shotgun.

Maybe that just proved Chris didn't have what it took to be a criminal investigator. He knew as much as anyone in the state about water law, and never hesitated to enforce that law, even in the face of opposition from angry ranchers or irate homeowners. But murder was a very different story, with so much more at stake, both for the victim and the accused.

Willow had caught him off guard mentioning his

father, and her connection to him. Of course, Ted Delray had lived and practiced law in this county a long time before Chris took the job with the sheriff's department. Chris had thought his moving closer to his parents would be a good thing, but he wasn't so sure. His father and he seldom saw eye to eye when it came to plans for Chris's future. Ted Delray had made it clear he thought his son was wasting his time in law enforcement.

Not unlike Willow's clashes with her father over her own plans for the future, he mused. Chris and his dad had certainly had their share of loud arguments on the subject—but that didn't mean they didn't love each other. If anything, that love made the disagreements all the more acute. He believed Willow when she said she could never be angry enough with her father to harm him.

But someone had been angry with Sam Russell, and Chris wanted to do his part to find that person. Because it was his job and he wanted to prove he had what it took to do the job. And maybe, he could admit, if only to himself, because he would like to be the one to bring a small measure of comfort to Willow Russell.

WHEN CHRIS AND Shane returned to the Russell ranch early Thursday morning, they found Willow waiting in the living room with Darla Russell and Emmet Caspar. "This is Deputy Delray and Deputy Ellis," Willow introduced them. "Darla and Emmet agreed to wait here until you had a chance to talk with them, then they're leaving."

"We're moving to a bed-and-breakfast in town," Darla said. "Much nicer and more conveniently located than here."

Willow nodded to the officers and left the room.

Chris focused on Darla and her son. They stood close together, Darla's arms hugged tightly across her chest, fine lines fanning out from her heavily lipsticked mouth. She frowned at them.

"We appreciate you waiting to speak with us," Chris said, hoping to put her at ease.

"Do you have information about poor Sam?" she asked. "When will you release his body, so we can have a proper funeral? Do you know when they'll issue the death certificate? Have you found the person who did this?" She fired off the questions one after another, as if afraid she might lose her ability to speak at any moment.

"Sit down, Mrs. Russell." Shane gestured toward the sofa. "We'll do our best to answer your questions, and you can give us some more information about Mr. Russell."

The combination of Shane's leading-man good looks and charming warmth melted away much of Darla Russell's agitation. "Thank you, Deputy," she said. "It's nice to have someone acknowledge how much this has distressed me." She directed a sour look toward Chris. "Even though Sam and I were no longer married, we were still close. I want to help in any way I can."

Shane moved a chair from the dining table and set it up close to her. Chris sat in an armchair a little farther away, content to observe and let Shane take the lead.

"Let's start with getting some basic facts out of the way," Shane said. "Where were you between 5:00 and 7:30 a.m. Tuesday?"

"Oh, my." She put a hand to one cheek. "I'm sure I was asleep. I do require my beauty sleep, you know." She didn't exactly flutter her eyelashes, but somehow the gesture was implied.

"And where were you sleeping?" Shane asked.

She laughed. "Where do you think, Deputy? I was at home in my own bed."

"And where is home?" Shane asked.

"Albuquerque." She rattled off the address.

Shane looked to Emmet. "And what about you? Where were you Tuesday morning?"

"I was home." Emmet looked at his mother, as if for confirmation.

"Emmet lives with me," Darla said. "He's a great help to me."

"What kind of work do you do, Mr. Caspar?" Shane asked.

"Well, I—"

"Emmet is between jobs right now," Darla said. "It's something he and Willow have in common."

"When was the last time you spoke to Sam, Mrs. Russell?" Shane asked.

"You can call me Darla."

"When was the last time you spoke to Sam?"

She looked thoughtful. "I can't be absolutely positive, but I think it was about a week ago." She nodded. "Yes. We talked about Emmet and me coming to visit."

"Was that something you had done before?" Shane asked.

"Oh, yes. Sam and I were still good friends, and I still think of him as a father to Emmet."

Emmet's pained expression hinted that he didn't share this feeling, Chris thought.

"When you last spoke to Sam, was he upset or worried about anything?" Shane asked.

"He was worried about Willow," Darla said. "She moved home and didn't give any indication that she ever intended to leave. As if she expected Sam to support her for the rest of her life."

Chris shifted in his seat. He was tempted to point out that she appeared to be supporting her son, but Shane, probably wisely, didn't bring this up.

"Was anything else bothering him?" Shane asked. "Did he have any enemies you were aware of?"

"No. Sam was a wonderful man. He was generous and hardworking. Everyone thought very highly of him. We couldn't go anywhere around here where people didn't come over to talk to us or offer to buy us a drink." She laughed again, a high-pitched titter so out of keeping with her otherwise severe demeanor, it startled Chris. "It was like being married to a celebrity."

In his brief tenure on the job, Chris had heard many ranchers complain about their neighbors. So-and-so was greedy and Mr. Such-and-such was cheap. Mr. X cut corners and Mrs. Y thought she was better than everyone else. But he had never heard anything but admiration for Sam, who most often was described as hardworking, fair and honest.

"Chris, do you have any questions for Mrs. Russell and her son?" Shane asked.

"When did you learn of Sam's death?" Chris asked.

"Willow called me Tuesday night," she said. "I was upset that she waited so long. Poor Sam had been gone all day and I didn't know." She looked away, blinking rapidly.

"And what time did you arrive in Eagle Mountain yesterday?" Chris asked.

"I came straight to the sheriff's office," she said. "So—just before lunch?"

"You drove from Albuquerque?" Shane asked.

"That's right. I couldn't sleep, so we left very early."

"Why did you decide to come here?" Chris asked.

"I couldn't leave Willow to deal with this all by herself," she said. "Not that she's been appreciative of my efforts. In fact, she asked us to leave."

"Why did she do that?" Shane asked.

"I think she wants to hide the truth from me," Darla said.

"Why?" Shane asked. "What truth do you believe she's hiding?"

"The truth about what really happened to Sam. I believe she knows more than she's telling."

"Why would she want to hide that from you?" Chris asked.

"She was always jealous of me, Deputy. She couldn't accept that her father could love another woman. I blame her for destroying our marriage. Her jealousy and resentment put Sam in a terrible position."

"I thought Willow was already living on her own, out of state, when you and Sam married," Chris said.

"She called her father regularly and said terrible things about me," Darla said. "And when she visited she was very rude to me. After a while, it was too much for Sam. But I know he still loved me."

"Why do you believe Willow knows things about her father's death that she isn't telling anyone?" Shane asked.

"She was the only one here the morning he died, wasn't she?" Darla said. "She's in such a hurry to get us out of the house she must be hiding something. And she's already been on the phone to talk to Sam's lawyer about the will, as if she can't wait to get her hands on this place. I think that's suspicious, don't you?"

"How do you know she's talked to the lawyer?" Shane asked.

"She told me!" Darla drew herself up to her full height. "If I were you, I'd take a much closer look at her."

"Anything else?" Shane looked at Chris, who shook his head. He didn't have anything more to say to this woman.

Darla stood and Emmet followed. "We'll be staying in Eagle Mountain if you need to talk to us again," she said. "*Someone* has to keep an eye on Willow."

They left the room. "I get the feeling there's no love lost between Willow Russell and her stepmother," Shane said. "After I left you two alone yesterday, did Willow say anything more about why she asked Darla and Emmet to leave?"

"I think it comes down to she doesn't like them and she doesn't want to share her home with them."

Shane nodded. "Mrs. Russell seems to think Willow had reason to murder her father," he said.

"If not always getting along with your parents is reason enough for murder, then it's a wonder so many parents live to an old age," Chris said.

Shane quirked one eyebrow, but didn't comment on this. "We should try to verify if Darla and Emmet were really in Albuquerque when they said they were," he said. "If they believe Emmet is due to inherit half the ranch, that could be a motive for murder. Especially if they're having financial troubles. She said Emmet is unemployed."

Chris nodded. "We'll do that."

"Speaking of unemployed, what kind of work did Willow do?" Shane asked.

"She was a professor of cultural anthropology."

"Hmmm. Probably not a lot of call for that in Eagle Mountain. So she might be hurting for money, too."

"She never mentioned Sam being stingy about giving

her money if she needed it," Chris said. "And it doesn't seem the kind of thing to murder someone over."

"I think we might be surprised at how little it takes to push someone over the edge, but we need to see who else had a motive. Did Willow have any ideas?"

"No," Chris said. "We don't have much to go on so far."

He and Shane were walking out to the sheriff's department SUV when Chris's phone buzzed. The call was from the sheriff. "Where are you now?" Travis asked without preamble.

"We're just leaving the Russell ranch."

"Get over to Carstairs Park ASAP."

"Yes, sir," Chris said. "Where is Carstairs Park?"

"It's what they named that patch of greenspace at the far north end of Idlewilde Estates," Travis said. "There's a park there with some trails and a little pond. A fisherman spotted something in the water this morning. It's a side-by-side utility vehicle. I'm thinking it might belong to Sam Russell. You and Shane head over there and I'll meet you as soon as I can get away from this town council meeting."

"Yes, sir." Chris ended the call and looked at Shane, who was waiting by the SUV. "We need to head over to Idlewilde Estates," Chris said. "Carstairs Park."

"What's up?" Shane pulled open the passenger's door of the SUV.

"Somebody found a side-by-side in the pond." Chris took out his keys. "Travis thinks it might be Sam Russell's."

"Why does he think that?" Shane asked.

"He didn't say." Chris slid into the driver's seat and

fastened the safety belt. "But if it is Sam's, how did it end up in Carstairs Park?"

"Maybe the same way his watch ended up less than a mile from there in that ditch," Shane said. "Maybe his killer put it there."

WILLOW WATCHED FROM the living room window as Darla and Emmet drove away. She had expected to feel great relief at their leaving, but the tension within her remained tightly coiled. She didn't have to look far for the reason: Chris's questions from the day before still disturbed her. Did he really believe she had killed her father? And if he and the other sheriff's deputies believed that, would they stop looking for the real killer?

Chris had asked if her father had any enemies. She couldn't think of anyone, but she hadn't lived at home in a long time before she moved back only a month ago. Maybe there was someone she didn't know about.

She moved from the living room to the spare bedroom her father had turned into an office. As she opened the door she had to stand for a moment, overcome by a wave of sadness. This room, more than any in the house, was Dad's domain. The scent of his aftershave lingered in every corner, mingled with the smoke from the cigars he thought she didn't know about. An empty coffee mug sat on the corner of his desk, a scene from a Frederic Remington painting printed on the white china. She had given him that mug for his birthday one year. The fact that he had been drinking out of it not long before he died almost undid her.

She pushed back the grief and focused on the task at hand. Why hadn't Chris asked to see this place, to learn more about her father as a way of learning more about his killer? It would be up to her to search these things for some clue as to who had hated her father enough to kill him. But where to start?

Darla's comments about Sam's supposed penchant for hiding money came back to her, so she moved to the room's closet, at the back of which sat a small fireproof safe. She found the combination where she remembered it—written on a piece of paper taped to the underside of the desk—and spun the safe's dial.

Inside the safe she found titles for her father's truck and several other ranch vehicles, bills of sale for livestock, paperwork for the ranch itself and envelopes of other papers she would go through later. A handgun that looked antique inside a wooden box, a velvet bag half-full of silver dimes. No cash.

She closed the door to the safe and sat back on her heels. Had Darla been right that Sam had hidden cash in other places around the ranch? But where? And more to the point—why? While her father had always been careful with money, he had never been a miser. And why would he want to hide his funds, instead of investing them or keeping them safe in the bank?

Still puzzling over this, she sat at the desk, the worn leather chair creaking in protest. The top of the desk was almost obscured with stockmen's magazines, auction flyers, old issues of the local paper, and the numerous receipts and bills that were part of a thriving cattle ranch. Despite the attempts of herself and others to persuade him to use a computer for his ranching business, Sam still kept everything on paper.

She opened the top drawer to her right, and was confronted with a jumble of cow-calf notebooks—little notebooks designed to fit in a shirt pocket, in which a cowboy could note which cow had calved and a brief description of the offspring—a simple way to keep track of the stock during one of the busiest times of the year. The books dated back ten years at least, the numbers—and sometimes names, too—of a generation of cows and calves that had borne the Double R brand.

The next drawer contained files—branding and vaccination records, ledgers recording ear tag numbers, veterinary bills and breeding records.

The top drawer on the left side of the desk yielded a heavy green ledger. She cleared a space in the desktop clutter and heaved the ledger onto it. The pages were inscribed in her father's neat hand. He had penmanship worthy of a draftsman. When she had commented on it once, he said it came from having a mother who was a schoolteacher. *Mother said a neat hand was a sign of a gentleman*, he had said. *She made me practice every afternoon before she'd let me out of the house to ride my horse. The only way I could get what I wanted was to get good enough for her to decide I didn't need to practice anymore. I guess it stuck with me.*

She scanned the columns of numbers and the careful notations—twenty-eight dollars paid for salt blocks, eight hundred received for a load of hay, twenty-four hundred paid for a trailer, eight thousand for a cutting horse, one thousand for a saddle. Her father had made note in these pages of every dime spent or received. She couldn't calculate how much money had passed through the ranch over the years, but she had long known her father was a wealthy man, though he valued the land and the livestock on it more than money in the bank or fancy possessions.

Finally, in the bottom left-hand drawer, she found the spiral-bound black datebook, identical to the ones her father had used for decades. He purchased a new one toward the end of each year at the local office supply.

No fancy planners for him—a simple week-by-week calendar was enough.

She flipped through the weeks prior, where Sam had made careful note of appointments for haircuts, meetings of the local Cattleman's Association and lunch dates with friends. She reached this week. There was no notation for Tuesday, the day he had died. In fact, the only appointment recorded for the whole week was for today—a four-o'clock "Meeting with A."

Who was A?

She closed the calendar and contemplated the disarray around her. Dad's whole life was in these records, if someone took the time to study them.

She turned her attention to the piles of papers in a shoebox on one corner of the desk. This must be Dad's version of an inbox—things that needed to be replied to or filed away. There were a couple of bills she probably needed to pay, an issue of a magazine he must have intended to read and some correspondence—a request for a reference from a cowboy who had once worked for him, a request for a donation for a local political campaign and a thank-you from a 4-H student whose cow her father had purchased at auction.

At the bottom of the box was a brown envelope. It contained a collection of letters—from formal, typewritten missives to notes scrawled in slanted, hurried script. Willow's stomach sank as she read through the letters. All of them were between her father and Adam Treadwell. She didn't know Treadwell, but in his letters he was identified as president of the Idlewilde Estates Homeowners' Association. Sam had written a series of increasingly agitated letters that accused the residents of Idlewilde of polluting the irrigation ditch that ran behind the development with runoff from their lawns and gardens. At first, Sam merely pointed this out and asked that people be educated about the ditch system and their need to refrain from using chemical fertilizers and poisons that could pollute the water—some of which could kill the hay or other crops, or sicken the livestock that made use of the water. Treadwell at first denied the problem, then claimed he had no authority to do anything about it, then threatened to take legal action if Sam didn't stop harassing him.

The last letter in the pile was handwritten, the letters large and slanted, embossed into the paper by the force of the writer's hand. It was unsigned, and without an envelope, but the message was clear enough. "Mind your own business or you'll be sorry."

Chapter Seven

Chris, Shane and Travis watched as a wrecker winched the side-by-side all-terrain vehicle out of the pond at Carstairs Park. Water ran in sheets from the dark green paint and sluiced over the vinyl seats. Mud slicked the tread of the tires and left a trail as the wrecker pulled the vehicle over a grassy berm and onto the gravel of the parking area.

"I don't see how it could have gotten over that berm unless someone deliberately ran it up there," Shane said as the ATV came to rest in front of them.

"We'll canvas the neighborhood," Travis said. "Maybe we'll find an early-morning jogger or dog walker who saw something."

"This is five miles by road from the place where Russell's body was found," Shane said.

"It's only about three miles if you follow the ditches," Chris said. "There's room alongside them for an ATV. That's what the ditch riders use to keep an eye on things." He gestured to the pond. "This is actually a wasteway from the ditch system, where they drain excess water."

"How far is this from the place where you found Sam's watch?" Travis asked.

"Less than a mile," Chris said.

A blue Toyota pickup pulled into the lot and parked on the other side of Travis's SUV. A man with dark hair just turning silver at the temples and the body of a football player going soft got out of the vehicle and hurried toward them. "What's going on here?" he demanded.

"Who are you?" Travis asked.

"Adam Treadwell. Idlewilde Estates Homeowners' Association president." He looked around, like a kid trying to take in everything at once. "What's happened?"

"What do you know about this ATV?" Travis nodded toward the dripping vehicle. "We just pulled it out of the pond here."

Treadwell stared at the ATV. "Did some kids run it in there or something?"

"Did you know Sam Russell?" Travis asked.

Treadwell frowned. "I knew him. I heard he died. Is it true somebody shot him?"

"Have you seen Sam around here recently?" Travis asked.

The lines on Treadwell's fleshy face deepened. "Sam was around here a lot lately."

"Oh?" Travis waited while the one word hung in the air.

Treadwell rubbed the back of his neck. "Not to speak ill of the dead, but that old man was a pain in my rear."

"In what way?" Travis asked.

"He didn't like the fact that we—this neighborhood—even existed. I guess he thought it should have all stayed hayfields or pasture or whatever. Anyway, he got it into his head that the people who lived here were poisoning the irrigation ditch with chemicals from their lawns and gardens. He kept writing letters, threatening to sue if we didn't stop. I tried to tell him I didn't have the authority to tell people what they could and couldn't do in their own yards, but he wouldn't believe me."

"You don't have covenants and things like that?" Chris asked. "Regulations on what size houses there can be and what color they are?"

Treadwell turned to him. "Of course. But there's nothing in there about lawn chemicals. And you can't just add regulations willy-nilly. It's a long process. I tried to tell Sam that, but he wouldn't listen. I mean, it's difficult enough to get people to understand why they can't water their lawns and gardens with the water running right by their property."

"Water law doesn't always make sense to people who are unfamiliar with it," Chris said. "If you like, I could come to a homeowners' meeting sometime and talk about the subject." He handed Treadwell a card. A big part of his job was educating people, and this seemed like a good opportunity.

"Thanks." Treadwell tucked the card in the pocket of his polo shirt. "Anyway, the last time I saw Sam was last week. He was in the park here, taking a water sample from this pond. I saw him and drove over to talk, but he wasn't having any of it."

"Where do you live, Mr. Treadwell?" Travis asked.

"Just there, across from the park." He pointed to a house across the road.

"Did you notice anyone in the park Tuesday morning, early?" Travis asked.

He shook his head. "I had to go to Junction early, so I was gone most of the day. I stopped in Eagle Mountain for dinner and someone told me about Sam." He rubbed the back of his neck again. "I mean, I didn't like the old guy, but I'm sorry he's dead." He turned and looked at the ATV. "Do you think this was Sam's?"

"We don't know yet," Travis said. "We're going to be canvassing the neighborhood, asking people if they saw anything suspicious," Travis said.

"Is that really necessary?" Treadwell asked. "I'm sure you won't learn anything useful and people here really value their privacy."

"It's necessary," Travis said.

Treadwell shrugged. "It probably was old man Russell. It would be just like him to dump the thing in our pond. He was that ornery. I mean, once he had made up his mind about something, there was no changing it. Do you have any idea who killed him?"

"We're still investigating," Travis said.

"Can you let me know what you find out about this?" Treadwell gestured toward the pond and the ATV.

"We'll be in touch," Travis said.

The sheriff turned away and Shane and Chris followed. Chris's phone had vibrated while they were talking, so before getting in his vehicle, he fished it out and checked his messages.

"This is Willow Russell. I've been looking through my father's papers. I've found something. I don't know if it means anything, but I think you should see it."

"That was Willow Russell," Chris told the sheriff. "She says she found something in her father's papers she thinks we should see."

"What did she find?" Shane asked.

"She didn't say."

"Stop by and see what it is." Travis checked his watch. "Shane, you can ride back to the office with me. We'll all meet at four to look at what we've got so far on this case."

"Yes, sir." Chris turned toward his cruiser.

"Chris?" Travis called after him.

"Yes, sir?"

"Ask Willow if one of their ATVs is missing."

"Yes, sir." Maybe this would be his chance to show Willow that the two of them could work together to find justice for her father. Chris didn't want to be her enemy, though when it came to Willow, maybe it was better right now if he didn't think too much about what he did want. A certain beautiful brunette might figure too prominently in his answer.

WILLOW'S BREATH CAME a little easier when she saw that Chris had come by himself. He was easier for her to talk to than the sheriff or the other deputies. Maybe he believed she was capable of murder, but at least he seemed to listen to her answers to the tough questions he asked.

She met him at the front door and ushered him into the living room. "Let's go into Dad's office," she said, and led the way.

He stopped in the doorway to take in the room. She tried to see it through his eyes—the battered wooden desk covered with papers and books, tall shelves crammed with more books, the steer skull on the wall, one of her father's old hats hanging from one horn. It was a worn, serviceable room, a good reflection of the man who had worked here. "We should have looked at this sooner," he said.

"I thought if Dad really did have an enemy, I might find out more here," she said. She sat in the desk chair. "Dad kept almost everything having to do with the ranch in this room, and the ranch was such a huge part of his life."

Chris came to stand across the desk from her. "What did you want to show me?" he asked.

"These." She handed him the stack of papers she'd placed in the center of the blotter. "That's a collection of correspondence between my father and a man named Adam Treadwell."

"The president of Idlewilde Estates Homeowners' Association," Chris said.

"Oh. Do you already know about this?" Maybe she hadn't given him enough credit for his investigative skills.

"We spoke to Mr. Treadwell this afternoon," he said. "He told us your father had complained to him about Idlewilde homeowners polluting the irrigation canal."

"Dad apparently kept copies of all his correspondence with Mr. Treadwell." She stood and moved around the desk and looked over his shoulder as he flipped through the papers. "Treadwell's responses are in there. You'll see Dad wasn't the only one with a temper."

Chris stopped and read the last note out loud. "'Mind your own business or you'll be sorry.'" He flipped the paper over to check the back, which was blank. "Did Treadwell write this, or your father?"

"I don't think that's Dad's handwriting," she said. She touched the edge of the paper. "This sounds like a threat to me."

"Treadwell could have been threatening a lawsuit," Chris said.

"Maybe. But don't you think it's worth looking into?"

"Yes." He tucked the papers back into the envelope. "I'll need to take these to the station, but I'll give you a receipt. We'll probably want to take a look at all of this, but is there anything else right now that struck you as odd or significant?"

"Dad had a note on his calendar for today—'Meeting with A.' But I don't know who A is. Could it be Adam Treadwell?"

"What about Tuesday? Any meetings scheduled then, especially first thing in the morning?"

"There's nothing recorded for that day." She handed him the calendar. "You can see for yourself."

"Did your father keep an inventory of property?" he asked. "We're trying to determine if one of the ranch ATVs is missing. I think that's most likely how Sam got to those corrals when he left here Tuesday morning."

"Yes." She moved back around the desk and opened the file drawer. She found the file labeled Vehicles and handed it to him. "All the registration papers and tax receipts for every vehicle on the ranch, including the ATVs, should be in there," she said. "And the titles to all the vehicles are in the safe, though I haven't looked through them all."

"Thanks. This should be helpful." He set both folders on the corner of the desk and took out a receipt book. "Is there anything else?"

"Just one thing," she said. "Maybe it's nothing, but then again…"

"Even something that seems small could be important," he said.

"Darla said my dad had a reputation for hiding money around the ranch. She said thousands of dollars. She said it was common knowledge—her hairdresser mentioned it to her. I looked in the safe and the desk for money and didn't find any. And I'd never heard anything like that before. But maybe Darla wasn't the only person who heard that rumor. Maybe someone else did and killed Dad for that money."

"It's something to consider," he said. "We'll see about getting someone out here to go through your father's papers."

She held out her hands to indicate the office. "I know this looks like a mess, but Dad kept very good records, and they go back decades." She looked down at the open file drawer. "Somewhere in here there's probably a record of the car he bought me for my eighteenth birthday."

"Lucky you," he said. "I got a pen set and a new pair of jeans for my eighteenth birthday."

"This was an orange Vibe with primer on one fender. Not the cool ride of my dreams."

"Did you complain?"

She laughed. "I wouldn't have dared. I drove that car until I entered graduate school."

He laughed, too. Their eyes met, and she felt a zing of attraction that had her heart speeding up. She told herself to look away, but couldn't do it. The smile faded from his eyes, but he kept his gaze locked to hers. "How are you doing, really?" he asked.

"It's hard," she said. "But I'm stronger than I look. I'll get through this."

"I want to help," he said. "I know it's…awkward, sometimes. But don't let the fact that I wear a badge throw you. This job is all about helping, even if it doesn't seem that way."

She was finally able to look away. "Thank you," she said.

He put a hand on her shoulder, a brief, reassuring squeeze. "We're going to get to the bottom of this," he said. "We're going to find justice for your father, and for you."

She knew not every case was solved, and not every criminal was punished. But she wanted to believe Chris. Knowing he was working on her father's behalf made this horrible situation a tiny bit easier to bear.

"LET'S START WITH the timeline," Travis said, once the meeting of all available sheriff's department personnel convened Thursday afternoon. With a force as small as

Rayford County's, there was no homicide division or even a team of detectives to handle a murder investigation. Every officer worked to solve the crime, with assistance as needed from the Colorado Bureau of Investigation.

Sergeant Gage Walker, the sheriff's brother, stood at the whiteboard at the front of the conference room and ran through the timeline he had filled in earlier. "The medical examiner ruled that Sam Russell died between five and seven thirty on Tuesday morning," Gage said. "Willow Russell and Von King both say Sam left his house between six and six thirty most mornings."

Gage indicated the next point on the timeline. "Willow Russell, Sam's daughter, states she came downstairs at seven thirty. Her father wasn't there, but that wasn't unusual. Sam usually came back to the house for breakfast about eight. When he hadn't returned by eight forty-five, and Willow was unable to reach him on his phone, she set out to look for him.

"Meanwhile, ditch rider Perry Webber finds Sam's body in the irrigation ditch by the shipping corrals at approximately 7:10 a.m.," Gage continued. "He drives to where he has a phone signal and contacts Chris." Gage pointed to Chris. "Over to you."

Chris consulted his notes, though the facts of that morning were etched in his memory. "I met up with Perry at the corrals at seven forty-five," he said. "I sent Perry to contact the sheriff. At nine fifteen, Willow Russell arrived and explained she had been searching for her father. She identified his body and returned to the ranch. Later that morning I got a call about a water violation in Idlewilde Estates and drove over to talk to the homeowner. I found a gold pocket watch in the ditch that Willow identified as her father's."

"This afternoon, we received a report of an ATV in the pond at Carstairs Park in Idlewilde Estates." The sheriff continued the narrative. "We've since identified this, using records provided by Willow Russell, as belonging to her father."

"So what do we think happened?" Gage asked. "How did Sam's watch and his ATV end up so far from his body?"

Chris had spent a lot of time pondering those questions. "Sam met up with his killer at the corral," he said. "When Sam's back was turned, the killer hit Sam in the back of the head with a rock or a shovel or some other heavy, flat object, then shot Sam with his own gun—which Willow and Von both agreed he usually carried with him on the ATV. The killer then took Sam's watch and drove the ATV along the trail that runs alongside the Daimler Ditch. He lost the watch behind the Howell property in Idlewilde Estates. Maybe he hit a bump, or maybe he threw the watch away on purpose."

"Maybe he realized taking something from a man you killed wasn't very smart," Deputy Dwight Prentice said.

"Maybe," Chris said. "In any case, the killer took the ATV and ran it into the pond at Carstairs Park."

"Then what?" Deputy Landry asked. "How does the killer get home? And what about the vehicle he used to get to the corrals? That's not an easy walk from anywhere."

"Maybe he—or she—had help," Deputy Jamie Douglas said. "Someone gave the killer a lift from Carstairs Park back to the corrals, or they drove the killer's vehicle away from the corrals and met up with him at the park."

"The neighbors who live near the park didn't report seeing anyone on an ATV in the area Tuesday morning," Travis said. "There are a couple of people we haven't made contact with yet, so we'll need to follow up with them."

"I took a call out at Idlewilde Estates about a Peeping Tom Tuesday morning," Jamie said.

"What time was that?" Travis asked.

"Right after I came on duty," she said. "So, about seven thirty."

"It could have been whoever dumped the ATV," Chris said.

Jamie consulted her notes. "The woman—Julie Breck, on Ash Drive—didn't mention an ATV. She said her peeper was a man dressed in dark clothes, on foot. He stood outside her bedroom window for several minutes watching her, then left. She was home alone and by the time she pulled on clothes and called us, he had been gone several minutes. I talked to her neighbors, but no one else saw anything. And definitely no ATV."

"Talk to them again," Travis said. "Someone may have seen something and not connected it."

"We should also ask about hitchhikers on County Road 361 that morning," Jamie said. "Someone might have given the killer a ride back to his car. He might have stashed it somewhere between the park and the ranch and walked to his meeting with Sam earlier that morning. We don't know if it was a planned meeting. Maybe the killer knew Sam would be at the corrals and ambushed him there."

"We'll put out a public appeal," Travis said. "What else?"

"Why get rid of the ATV at all?" Dwight asked.

No one had an answer for that. "Let's talk about motive," Gage said. "Who gained from Sam's death?"

"Willow Russell inherits the ranch," Shane said. "It's worth a lot of money and she's currently unemployed."

Shane was stating facts, but Chris had to clench his jaw to keep from blurting out a defense of Willow. Instead, he said, "Sam's ex-wife, Darla Russell, claims her son, Emmet Caspar, inherits half the estate. Though that may not be true. I'm waiting for Sam's attorney to return my call about the will."

"Von King and Darla Russell both said Willow Russell had recently argued with her father," Shane said. "Maybe one of those arguments turned violent."

"Why at the corrals, so early in the morning?" Jamie asked. "If they had a domestic disagreement, it seems like it would have happened at the ranch house."

"The ME said Sam died where his body was found," Travis said. "But Willow could have followed her father to the corrals that morning."

"So could have Von King," Chris said. "Or Darla or Emmet. None of them have a solid alibi for that morning."

"Anybody else have a motive to kill Sam?" Gage asked.

"Sam had feuded with a former neighbor, Bud Carstairs, who sold the property that became Idlewilde Estates," Shane said. "They were friends and haven't spoken in three years, as far as anyone I talked to knows."

"More recently, Sam argued with Adam Treadwell, the president of Idlewilde Estates Homeowners' Association," Chris said. "Judging from the correspondence Sam had saved, the exchange got pretty heated."

"Sam was upset because he believed Idlewilde Estates homeowners were polluting the irrigation ditch," Travis said. "Maybe dumping the ATV in the pond at the park—which is a wasteway for the irrigation system—was related to that."

"Any fingerprints or other evidence on the ATV?" Jamie asked.

"Sam's prints are all over it, but that's no surprise," Travis said. "Nothing else. The killer probably wore gloves."

"Darla Russell said there was a rumor in town that Sam had hidden a lot of cash around the ranch," Chris said. "Someone who heard that rumor might have killed Sam in an attempt to get that money."

"I'd heard that rumor," Travis said. "Not recently, but years ago, when I was in high school even. I'm surprised it's still circulating, but we'll add it to the list of possible motives." He glanced down at his notes. "The ditch rider didn't see anyone else out that morning, did he?"

"No," Chris said. "And we should go through Sam's records at the ranch. From what Willow showed me, he documented every dime he spent and every appointment he had. We might find something there."

"I've asked CBI for help with this," Travis said. "But the state is in the middle of a hiring freeze and they're shorthanded. It could be a few weeks before they can spare an investigator. I'd like to solve this before then."

"Someone saw something," Gage said. "There are too many people out and about that time of morning."

"Then let's hope we can find that person." Travis directed his gaze to each deputy in turn. "This murder has cast a shadow over the town," he said. "We need to find the killer and get rid of that shadow."

Chris thought of Willow, and the shadow grief had cast over her life. He couldn't remove that shadow, but he would do what he could to lighten it.

WILLOW DIDN'T RECOGNIZE the man who visited the ranch Friday morning. When she answered his knock on the front door, his expression was one of deep concern. "Willow, I am so, so sorry for your loss," he said. "I've been in shock ever since I heard."

He reached out, as if to take her hand, but she stepped back. "Have we met?" she asked. He was a good-looking man—tall and broad-shouldered with thick brown hair, close to her own age.

"I'm Trey Allerton," he said. "I'm leasing the sixty acres at the north end of this ranch. We met once when I stopped by to speak to your father."

Embarrassed that she had forgotten all about Trey Allerton, and annoyed that he took for granted that she would remember him from a single encounter that had lasted less than a minute, she flushed. "What can I do for you, Mr. Allerton?"

"Please, call me Trey." He flashed a smile that she felt to her core. It was a smile meant to dazzle, and it was effective. "May I come in?" he asked.

"Of course." She stepped aside to let him in.

He stood a fraction too close to her, and studied her intently. "Sam was such a great man," he said. "Losing him is a tragedy for everyone who knew him. My life won't be the same without him in it."

The familiar way he spoke about her father grated. Trey Allerton had leased that section of property less than two months ago, and her father hadn't mentioned him since. How could this man pretend they were close?

"Thank you for your condolences," she said. "Is there something else you needed to talk with me about?" Maybe there was a problem on the land he was leasing. She would need to handle those kinds of things in the future, or hire someone to take care of them for her.

"We need to discuss the terms of my lease," he said. "Not to intrude on your grief, but now that Sam is gone, the terms have changed."

"What do you mean, the terms have changed?"

"Let's sit down and I'll explain." He gestured toward the sofa. She wanted to resist, to announce she would remain standing. But she recognized the irrational pettiness of this, so mutely followed him and sat on the sofa.

He settled next to her—not touching, but too close for her comfort. "You may remember that I'm leasing that section of the ranch as the site for a youth camp I'm developing," Allerton said. "A place where disadvantaged young people can come to relax and rejuvenate in the great outdoors."

She nodded, not bothering to mention that her father had dismissed the idea as a pipe dream.

"Your father was one of my biggest supporters," Allerton continued. "His encouragement and enthusiasm for the project meant so much to me."

"My dad wasn't the enthusiastic type." She looked him in the eye and dared him to contradict her. Sam Russell came from a family that believed outsized displays of any emotion were undignified and unnecessary.

"Well, he wasn't demonstrative, but he was definitely supportive," Allerton said. "He believed in our mission of helping young people and pledged to do all he could to help."

Light began to dawn. Allerton must be talking about money. Now that Sam was gone, he was hoping for a "donation" from Sam's estate. "You said the terms of your lease have changed now that my father is…gone," she said.

"Yes." He looked her up and down. "You take after your father, don't you? Direct and to the point."

"And your point is?"

The easy charm vanished, replaced by something harder. "Under the terms of the lease agreement I had with your father, in the event of his death it converted from a five-year lease to a forty-year contract at a cost to me of one dollar a year."

She couldn't hold back a gasp. "A dollar a year? My father was a better businessman than that."

"I'm sure Sam was a good businessman, but this was his way of showing support for what I intend to do with the land. And of course, he never expected to die so soon."

She stared at him, dumbfounded. "I'll need to speak to Dad's attorney about this." Why hadn't Ted mentioned this when they spoke Wednesday?

"Of course." Allerton stood. "I just wanted to give you a heads-up in case you were anticipating the next lease payment."

He said a few more things about how wonderful and generous Sam had been as she walked him to the door, but she scarcely registered them. Her mind whirled as she tried to unite the version of her father Trey portrayed with the shrewd, stern, sometimes fractious man who had raised her.

As Allerton's truck was pulling away from the ranch house, she was already punching in Ted Delray's number. "This is Willow Russell," she told the woman who answered the phone. "I need to speak with Mr. Delray. Now."

Ted didn't keep her waiting. "Willow? Is something wrong?"

Everything, she thought. "I've just spoken to Trey Allerton," she said. "He claims his lease agreement with my father converted to a forty-year contract for one dollar a year when Dad died."

Silence on the other end of the line.

"Ted?"

He sighed. "I told Sam it was the dumbest thing he'd ever done, but you know how he was—when he made up his mind about something, he did it, no matter what anyone else thought."

"So you're saying it's true?"

"Yes," Ted said. "In Sam's defense, I think he did it as a kind of joke—a way of teasing Allerton. Sam never expected to die. He used to brag about how his father lived to be ninety-eight. And you know as well as I do that he was as healthy as someone twenty years younger."

"Yes, he was." And Sam would never have seen himself as a potential murder victim. But then again, who did? Ted's explanation made sense. Her father had seen through Trey Allerton's smooth charm and decided to bait him a little. He would give Allerton a sweet deal that made no sense from a business perspective, believing the youth ranch would fail long before Sam was gone from this world. "Did you tell the police about this?" she asked.

"No. Why should I?"

"Ted! Someone killed Dad. Maybe Allerton did it because he didn't want to make any more lease payments."

"I'll tell them," Ted said. "I'm supposed to call Chris today, anyway."

She wondered what Chris would make of Trey Allerton. They were both good-looking men, close in age, yet Chris had none of Allerton's smooth charm and salesman's persuasiveness.

She much preferred the deputy's competent calm. "Let me know what Deputy Delray says."

"There's actually something else you need to know," Ted said.

The reluctance dragging at every word made her stomach sink. "What is it?" she asked.

"Darla Russell and her son came to see me. They had just left when you called."

"And?"

"And she brought a copy of a will that leaves half the estate to her son and the other half to you."

"Is it a legitimate will?"

"That's what we need to ascertain. It's dated after the last will I drafted for Sam, but I need to do more digging."

The thought that she might end up sharing the Double R with Emmet *and* Trey Allerton sent a shudder through her. "What was Dad thinking?" she asked out loud.

"I don't think he was, Willow," Ted said.

He hadn't been thinking of her. The idea hurt—and it angered her, too. If Dad was here right now, they'd have a shouting match that would make their previous disagreements seem like ordinary conversation.

Chapter Eight

Adelaide Kinkaid, office manager, chief authority on community gossip and general mother hen of the Rayford County Sheriff's Department, had decided to take Chris under her wing. "I know you have a fancy law degree and you went through the academy—top honors, I hear—but that doesn't mean you know everything you need to know about policing in a small town," she told him when he reported for work Friday morning.

"Did someone complain about me?" He searched his memory. Had Mrs. Howell protested his cutting off the water to her garden? He definitely had the law on his side in that case.

"No one has complained," Adelaide said. "I just want you to have all the tools you need to succeed."

"Such as?" Was she going to tell him he needed to join the Elks Club or go to the high school football games?

"Wipe that smirk off your face, Deputy. I may look like an old lady to you, but I was married to a police detective for forty years. I know a thing or two about solving crimes, even if I don't do it myself."

Chris assumed a serious expression. "Yes, ma'am. What do you think I need to know?"

"First of all, this job requires a lot of hours, and even

when you're not on the job, you carry the job around with you. Do you understand?"

"I think so," he said. "When people see me, they see the sheriff's deputy first."

"Exactly. Which can make it hard to have a personal life. The personal and professional bleed together." She waved her hand. "Don't stress about it."

"Don't?" Not that he had been.

"For instance, you might meet someone you're attracted to in the course of an investigation," she said.

"When I'm on the job, I need to put the job first," he said. "I need to remain professional."

"Well, of course," she said. "I'm taking for granted that you have enough smarts and class not to hit on a witness or a crime victim. I'm just saying it's okay to be human and have feelings. Things can work out."

"Is that how you met your husband?" he asked. "Were you a crime victim? Or maybe a suspect?"

She grinned. "I'll never tell. But yes, we met on an investigation. It happens all the time. In fact, I think every officer here met his or her significant other while conducting an investigation. It's almost like there's something in the water here."

"How is this going to help me be a better small-town cop?" he asked.

"It's going to help you remember that everything and everyone around here is related in some way—and that includes you. You can try to remain aloof and distant, but it won't work. People have to trust you, and that means getting in there and being one of them."

He nodded. "Okay. But I don't think I'm being aloof and distant."

"I didn't say you were. Just don't think you have to be."

"Adelaide, what prompted this sudden concern?" he asked.

She pressed her lips together in a thin line. He kept silent, waiting. She folded her arms over her chest and frowned at him. "I know you're trained to look at the evidence and put together a logical story, which is all very well and good. But you need to look at the people involved in a case, as well."

He nodded. "Is there a particular person you think I need to take a closer look at?"

"Willow Russell."

This wasn't what he had expected. "What about Willow?" he asked.

"If you get to know her, you'll learn she's a very smart woman. She was valedictorian of her class here and went to college on a full scholarship. Some people around here fault her for going off and leaving Sam to run the ranch alone, but she would have been wasted on that ranch. Sam probably wouldn't have taken her help with anything, anyway."

He nodded. "Yes, I think Willow is very smart."

"So, she's far too sharp to kill someone by bashing him in the head and shooting him with a shotgun." Adelaide shuddered. "Her own father? If she had wanted the old man dead, she would have slipped poison into his food or arranged an accident around the ranch. I'll tell you something—the kind of violence that was done to Sam was over-the-top and heavy-handed. Clumsy, even. You need to look for someone with those characteristics. Get to know the people involved in this case and take that into consideration, along with the facts."

"That's good advice," Chris said. "I'll certainly keep it in mind."

She nodded and left him alone again. He booted up

his computer and tried to focus on a report he was writing for the water board, but Adelaide's words kept replaying in his head. Her assessment of Willow—that she was smart, and that she wouldn't be the type to bash her father in the head, then shoot him in the chest—matched his own conclusions, but having his feelings confirmed flooded him with relief. He had worried that his definite attraction to Willow might have made him blind to something in her that pointed to her guilt.

She still had to remain on the list of suspects—she had gained the most financially from Sam's death, and she didn't have an alibi for the morning he died. But he would take Adelaide's advice and look for someone with a propensity toward, and perhaps even a history of, violence, as well as a reason to want Sam dead.

"Deputy?"

Adelaide was back in his doorway. Had she thought of some other pearl of wisdom she needed to share? "Yes?"

"There's a woman here to see you. Actually, she wanted to see Shane, but he isn't in, and everyone else is busy, so you're it."

"What does she want?" he asked.

"She says she wants to talk. And she's very pretty, so consider yourself lucky." She winked, then turned and left before he could say anything else.

The woman Adelaide escorted to his desk was indeed pretty—a platinum blonde with blue eyes and a shapely figure. But the woman's lovely face was troubled. "I wanted to speak to Deputy Ellis," she said, and looked around the room, and the other two empty desks.

Chris stood. "He's not in now. I'm Deputy Chris Delray. Can I help you with something, miss?"

"I'm Courtney Baker." She perched on the edge of

the chair in front of his desk, knees together, a worn leather shoulder bag balanced on her thighs.

"Is something troubling you, Ms. Baker?" he asked. "Is there something I can help with?"

"It's not me, really, it's my, uh, the man I live with. Trey Allerton. I think someone is trying to kill him."

This alarming statement both refreshed Chris's memory as to where he had heard her name before, and made him look over her shoulder toward the hallway. "Where is Mr. Allerton now?" he asked.

"He had a business meeting. He doesn't know I'm here. He keeps saying what's happened isn't really serious, but I don't think that's true."

Chris pulled a notepad toward him and picked up a pen. "Tell me what happened."

She took a deep breath, composing herself. "Yesterday morning, as Trey was leaving the trailer where we live, someone fired a couple of shots at him. I was standing on the front steps and the bullets whizzed right by Trey's head. I screamed and Trey dove to the ground. He shouted for me to go inside, so I did. A few minutes later, Trey came in and said everything was all right. I told him he needed to contact the sheriff, but he said it was just some stray bullets from a hunter and we would be foolish to make a big deal out of it."

Chris made notes on the pad. "And you live at the trailer on the Russell ranch, with Mr. Allerton?" he asked.

"Yes. We're staying in a mobile home, temporarily, until we can begin construction on the youth camp we're developing."

"When was this shooting, exactly?" he asked.

"Yesterday morning, about nine thirty."

"Could it have been stray shots from somewhere nearby?" he asked.

She shook her head. "That's never happened before, and I haven't heard any shots since. I think whoever was shooting was aiming for Trey. It was terrifying." She leaned forward, one hand on the desk. "I have a little girl—she's only three. She's with her aunt right now, but I'm afraid to let her play outside. What if the shooter comes back?"

"Could you tell where the shots were fired from?"

She shook her head.

"I can come out there and look around, but I doubt I'll find anything," he said.

"You probably won't. I looked after Trey had left, and he said he looked before he left, and neither of us saw anything. I was willing to accept that maybe it was an accident, and then this morning, something else happened."

"What was that?"

"Trey went out to his truck to go to work and when he opened the door, there was a snake curled up on the front seat. A big rattlesnake. He killed it with a big wrench, then threw it on the ground. I heard him yelling and came out."

"Maybe the snake crawled in through an open window?" Chris suggested.

She shook her head. "The windows were up. Someone put that snake in there. Trey thought so, too, though he lied and said what you did—that the snake crawled in there. Maybe he didn't want to frighten me, but I *am* frightened."

"Do you have any idea who would want to harm Mr. Allerton?" Chris asked.

"I don't know. And Trey says he doesn't know, either."

"I can talk to him, if you think that would help," Chris said.

"No. I just wanted you to know. In case something else happened." She stood. "Don't tell Trey I was here. It would only upset him."

"I'll keep your report on file," Chris said. "Let me know if anything else happens, or if Mr. Allerton changes his mind about wanting to talk to us."

She nodded, but didn't move. "Is there something else?" he asked.

"I heard about Mr. Russell," she said. "I didn't know him well, but the few times I met him, he was very nice. I can't imagine who would have wanted to hurt him." Her eyes met his, wide and full of fear. "You don't think these threats against Trey could be the same person, do you?"

"Do you think the same person who killed Sam Russell is threatening Mr. Allerton?" Chris asked.

"I don't know." She hugged her purse to her chest. "It just seems so strange, that Mr. Russell was killed and then, two days later, someone tries to kill Trey. We live on the same ranch. It seems like the two things could be connected."

"We'll definitely look into that," Chris said. She was right—the timing and the location of the incidents did seem too much for coincidence.

"Thank you," she said.

She left, and passed the sheriff on his way into the office. "What did Courtney Baker want?" Travis asked.

"She reported that someone shot at Trey Allerton yesterday morning, and today there was a rattlesnake on the front seat of his truck."

"Hmmph."

"She doesn't know who or why, but she wondered

if the incidents were related to Sam's death—maybe Sam's killer is going after Trey now."

"Someone who didn't like Sam leasing that section of the ranch to Allerton?" Travis asked.

"I haven't heard anyone complain about it," Chris said.

"What does Willow say about it?"

"She hasn't said anything."

"Maybe you should ask her."

"I will. But you said you knew Willow in school. Did she strike you as the type to go around taking pot shots at people or handling rattlesnakes?"

"Nope. But ask her, anyway. Maybe she knows someone else who isn't happy about the lease."

"I will." And he'd warn her to be careful. If the murderer had decided to target other people near the ranch, how long before he turned his attention to Sam's daughter?

WILLOW HAD STOPPED answering the house phone the day after her father died, weary of fielding condolence calls that inevitably morphed into attempts by curious friends and neighbors to glean more information about the horrible events. She still checked her mobile phone's screen when it rang, hoping to hear from Ted Delray. When she recognized Chris Delray's number on the screen, she debated letting the call go to voice mail. But she knew she needed to tell him about Trey Allerton's visit. And maybe the handsome deputy would have some good news for her for a change.

"Hello, Deputy," she answered.

"Hello, Willow." His low voice, with a hint of a drawl, sent warmth curling through her. "How are you?"

How many times had she answered that question in

the past few days? And had she really been honest with anyone? "This is all very hard," she said. "But I'm trying to keep it together."

"It's a lot for one person," he said. "Is there anything I can do to help?"

"Find whoever killed my father."

"I'm working on it. Can I stop by later this afternoon?"

She wished he was asking because he wanted to see her, but she knew better. "More questions?" she asked.

"I know it's tiresome, but you were closer to your father than anyone else. You know more about him and his activities."

"I don't mind the questions if they can really help."

"Could I come by about five thirty?"

"I'll be here." She ended the call and sat on the sofa, noticing the dust on the furniture and the clutter of old newspapers and magazines on the coffee table. She should probably clean, but she couldn't find the energy. She had tried, unsuccessfully, to talk her father into hiring someone to take care of the household for him, but he had argued that he didn't mind the clutter. *Besides, now that you're back home, you can do it*, he had said, which had led to another argument—one she had eventually lost. While he might have been able to live with the dirt, she couldn't. It wasn't the cleaning itself she minded so much, it was being forced into the role of unpaid household help.

She sighed and moved into the dining room, where she had set up her laptop. She logged on and checked on the half dozen applications she had made to various liberal arts colleges and universities around the country. Most of them hadn't bothered to reply, but her email did contain one response. She knew it was a rejection before she even opened it. If someone wanted to interview you for a job, they called first.

The rejection was from Mount Prince University. Her friend Cecilia had recommended her for the job, and she had had high hopes. She forwarded the rejection to Cecilia with a sad face emoji, then went to straighten the living room.

She was upstairs changing clothes when her phone rang. Cecilia's voice carried the soft accents of her Mexican birthplace, and a sharper accent of outrage. "I told them you were the best person for the job—that they would be so lucky to have you on staff," she said. "But someone heard about what happened at Hemphill and they got cold feet. I told the department head to his face that not hiring you because of that made it look as if they had something to hide. He had the nerve to tell me I didn't understand what it felt like to be a target."

"It's okay, Cece," Willow said. "It's not your fault. I really appreciate you putting in a good word for me."

"Someone will hire you. You're such a good teacher, they'd be crazy not to."

"Except I had the audacity to sue my former employer for sexual harassment. And lost."

"You didn't lose," Cece protested. "Rich Abrams resigned and the university paid you damages."

"Rich Abrams is still professor emeritus, still giving guest lectures, and my position was eliminated. They said it was part of restructuring, but we all know it was done to get rid of me." She took a deep breath, pushing back the bitterness.

"It isn't fair," Cece said. "I keep hoping you'll find a better position—one where you'll get the respect you deserve."

"I'm wondering if that's even possible."

"You can't give up."

"Sorry. I guess I'm all out of optimism right now."

"You've had a terrible time of it, I know," Cece said. "How's it going? You must have a lot to deal with at the ranch, settling your father's affairs and everything."

"I feel stuck until the sheriff's department finds whoever killed him, or wraps up their investigation. We can't even plan the funeral. And some stuff has come up with his will that is muddying the waters." She didn't feel like going into the details right now.

"Oh, honey, that is terrible!" Cece shifted to a teasing tone. "I don't suppose there's some big, handsome cowboy there at the ranch who can take your mind off your troubles?"

The image of Chris filled her mind. He wasn't exactly a cowboy, but he wore a Stetson and carried a gun, and had shoulders broad enough to bear any burden. "The only cowboy on the ranch right now is a forty-something ex-con with questionable hygiene," she said.

Cece laughed, as Willow had known she would. "Then I guess you're going to have to get out more." She sobered. "But seriously, I am so sorry about your dad. If there's anything I can do to help, even if it's just lend an ear when you need to vent, you call me. Anytime. And I'll keep my ear out for word of any job openings."

"Thanks. I appreciate it."

She ended the call and turned to finish applying her makeup when the doorbell rang. She glanced at the bedside clock—four thirty. Had she heard Chris wrong? Or maybe he'd gotten away early.

Chapter Nine

It wasn't Chris at the door, but Von King. He didn't bother with a greeting. "What are you going to do about the south hayfield?" he asked.

Willow stared at him blankly.

"It's overdue to be cut," he said.

"Then cut it."

"I don't cut hay. You need to get someone in to do it."

His belligerent tone grated, but she bit back an angry retort. "Who does Dad use?" she asked.

"That's up to you to find out."

"And I'm asking you."

He didn't answer, merely looked away, his jaw set. She wanted to tell him to leave—her doorstep, and the ranch. But then she'd be stuck with no one to feed the horses and look after the fences—two things she was pretty sure he was keeping up with, because she'd seen him doing both chores only yesterday. She took a deep breath and reminded herself that a little ego stroking could go a long way. "Now that Dad is gone, I'm going to be relying on you for help," she said. "You're obviously more knowledgeable about the ranch than I am. Of course, I'll pay you for the extra time and effort."

"Yeah, whatever. Just get someone in to take care of that hay before it's ruined." Not waiting for an answer he turned away, muttering under his breath. She thought she heard something about him having to do everything himself.

She shut the door and locked it. Though Von had never threatened her, he made her uneasy, and he knew she was here by herself. Better to be safe. She went into her father's office and sat behind the desk. In her fog of grief, she had forgotten that the ranch didn't stop for anything. There were still animals to take care of and hay and water to manage. Time for a crash course in ranch management.

An hour later, she was still engrossed in her father's records when the doorbell sounded again. This time her caller was Chris. She let him in, then headed back to the office. "I'm working back here," she said. "Von King reminded me this afternoon that there are a lot of things that have to be done to keep the ranch running smoothly, so I'm trying to get on top of all of that. I'm so grateful Dad kept such good records."

"That's helpful," Chris said, following her into the office.

"He did everything on a schedule," she said. "And he wrote it all down. Thanks to him I was able to get a haying crew in day after tomorrow, and I know it's time to call the farrier to see to the horses."

"It sounds like you're doing a great job," he said.

"I'm doing the job." She sank into the chair. "I don't know how great it is." But the necessity of getting to work had shaken her out of her funk. It felt good to accomplish something.

"Do you think you'll stay here?" Chris asked.

"And run the ranch?" She shook her head. "I think the best thing would be to find someone else to run it for me—someone with experience. Or I could lease this property to another rancher."

"The way your father leased part of the property to Trey Allerton?"

"I'm talking about a real rancher, not a big talker who, as far as I can tell, hasn't done anything." She rubbed the tight place at the bridge of her nose. "Mr. Allerton came to see me this morning."

"What did he want?"

"Sit down. You might as well be comfortable."

"Long story?" He sat.

"Just complicated. The short version is that the contract Allerton talked my father into signing had a clause that changed the agreement if my father died while it was active. Now the lease is for forty years at only one dollar a year."

Chris looked as dumbfounded as she had been. "That's an unusual arrangement," he said.

"I confirmed it with Dad's attorney. He thinks Dad meant it as a tease, since the original agreement was for only five years and he didn't expect to die anytime soon. Allerton says Dad did it because he really believed in the project."

"But you don't believe that."

She guessed she wasn't hard to read. "Dad was sure Allerton's ranch would never host a single kid," she said. "He even put a clause in the contract that said any improvements Allerton made would become Dad's property when the agreement ended."

"So Allerton came here this morning to remind you of this change in the lease agreement?" he asked.

"Yes." She looked him in the eye. "Do you think Allerton could have killed Dad? So he wouldn't have to make any more lease payments?"

"I'll certainly look into it." He shifted, the chair creaking. "I actually stopped by to ask you about Allerton, or rather, about that lease. Was anyone upset about that agreement? Someone who wanted that land for themselves, or who had other objections?"

She shook her head. "Dad never mentioned anything like that."

"What did you think of the arrangement?" he asked.

She shrugged. "I left the ranch to Dad. If he wanted to lease out part of it, I didn't care. Knowing Dad, I would have said he saw it as an opportunity to make money on land he wasn't utilizing for anything else. Though it doesn't sound as if the agreement was entirely to his advantage. Why are you asking?"

"Trey Allerton's girlfriend says someone has threatened Allerton twice in the past few days. She wondered if it was related to your father's death."

"Do you think it is?" she asked.

"It seems a big coincidence—your father is murdered, then two days later someone fires shots at a man who is leasing part of the ranch. I'm looking for a connection." He leaned toward her, his expression grave. "You haven't been threatened in any way, have you?"

She caught her breath. "No! Why? Do you think I'm in danger?"

"No, no. Just—promise you'll be careful."

She sat back and told herself to keep calm. "I'll be fine."

"Have you found anything else interesting in your Dad's papers?" he asked.

"Do you mean anything that might point to his killer?" She shook her head. "I'm afraid not. Just notes about when to move the cows and calves to new pasture, when to sell the steers, which auction house to take them to and what trucking company to use to ship them." She sighed. "He and I never talked much about the ranch. I wasn't interested in taking it over, so I never asked, and he had done things on his own for so many years, he wasn't going to ask me for help. But now, it's as if he's looking over my shoulder, telling me everything I need to know." Her voice broke on the last words.

"It's nice to think he's still looking out for you," Chris said. He stood. "I'd better be going."

"Are you headed back to the sheriff's department?"

"No, I'm off duty now."

Suddenly, she was anxious not to be alone with her grief. "Would you like to stay for dinner?" Heat suffused her face as soon as she made the offer. Would he misinterpret her invitation? Was he going to tell her she was out of line—that he had a wife or girlfriend waiting for him?

"That would be great." He smiled. "It gets old, eating alone all the time."

She returned the smile and stood. "Let's go into the kitchen and see what we can find."

"It doesn't have to be fancy," he said. "I'm good with a sandwich, or eggs."

"One thing about living on a ranch," she said. "We always have beef." She opened the freezer and started sorting through the packages wrapped in white paper. "We've got T-bone, rib eye, porterhouse…"

He laughed. "Any of those would be good."

She pulled out two rib eyes and thrust them into his hands. "You're in charge of the grill, which is right out there." She pointed toward the back deck. "Though you'll need to thaw those first."

He hefted a steak in each hand. "I think I can handle it."

While he thawed the steaks under running water, she made a salad and sliced and pan-fried potatoes. He seasoned the thawed steaks with whatever he found in the cabinets, and by the time she had everything on the table, he was taking the meat from the grill. A few minutes later, dinner was ready.

"This looks and smells amazing," he said, as he took a seat across from her at the kitchen table. She'd opted for this cozier setting over the dark and formal dining room.

"What would you have eaten if you'd gone home?" she asked.

He cut into the steak. "My specialties are fried egg sandwiches, canned chili or frozen burritos. And there's always takeout."

"Your poor arteries."

"Don't tell me you eat like this every night." He popped a bite of steak into his mouth.

She laughed. "I eat a lot of salad, grilled chicken and canned soup."

"Then I'm glad I gave you an excuse to take out these steaks."

"Oh, I've eaten plenty of steak since I moved back home," she said. "As far as Dad was concerned, it wasn't dinner if it didn't include beef."

"I guess you had to make a lot of adjustments like that, moving back home after living on your own."

"Oh, yes," she said. "It wasn't anything I ever thought I'd do."

"Why did you do it?"

Was he asking as a cop, or as a man she was having dinner with? She decided she wanted to answer him, either way. "I wanted to get as far away from Connecticut and my old job as possible. Eagle Mountain fit the bill."

"What happened?" He sipped iced tea, watching her, then added, "You don't have to tell me if you don't want to."

So he was the man sharing dinner, she thought. "I sued my department head for sexual harassment." The words came easily after so many months, though at the time she made her accusations she had struggled to detail all that had happened.

"That took guts," he said.

His assessment pleased her. "People who haven't been in that situation are sometimes quick to judge," she said. "But there are so many emotions surrounding harassment, or any time you're a victim, I guess. The first time the professor grabbed me in his office, I was in shock. I told myself I must have misread the situation. That sort of thing didn't happen to me. The next time, he threatened me. He told me no one would believe me and my career would be ruined if I tried to report him. I felt powerless. It took me a long time to get angry. Looking back, that still surprises me." She took a sip of water.

"What happened when you did complain?" he asked.

"The university had no choice but to listen. I made my accusations very public, and I'd kept a log of dates and times and situations. I refused to back down." She'd felt triumphant then, no longer powerless. But the mood hadn't lasted. "I ended up settling out of court and then the university eliminated my position. They said it was due to declining enrollment in the anthropology program, but I was the only person let go."

"What happened to the professor?"

"He agreed to retire, but did so with honors." She didn't try to keep the bitterness from her voice. "He kept his title and his pension and everyone pretended nothing had happened, even though I'm sure I wasn't the first woman he harassed. I was just the first who objected publicly. I ended up being labeled a troublemaker."

Chris had laid down his knife and fork and stopped eating. "That's infuriating."

"It was," she said. "It is. But it made me tired of fighting, too. I love my job. I enjoy teaching. But I don't like the politics involved. And it didn't stop when I left Hemphill. I'm having a hard time finding a new position. Academia is a small, insular world, and most people know what happened. I'm still viewed by too many of them as a troublemaker who cut short the career of one of the most eminent scholars in anthropology today."

"I'm sorry," he said.

"Thank you." She cut off another bite of steak. "I thought being in a completely different environment would help me sort things out, so I came home."

"Did your father know what happened?" he asked.

She shook her head and finished chewing. "I was afraid if I told him, he would either be so enraged on my behalf that he'd call up the retired professor and threaten him, or he'd tell me it must have been my fault."

"He wouldn't have," Chris said.

"Dad had very old-fashioned views of women," she said. "Anyway, I only told him my position was cut and I needed to stay here until I found a new job."

"He was probably happy to have you home," Chris said.

"He was. But he worried about me. I guess he sensed something was wrong, even if he didn't know what it was." She shook her head. "Now I wonder if I was so wrapped up in my own problems that I missed something wrong in his life—some clue that something, or someone, wasn't right."

"It's possible your father had no idea anyone was out to get him," Chris said. "We haven't found anything so far that points to him having a specific enemy. Not of the intensity you think would lead to murder."

She studied him across the table. He had rolled up the sleeves of his khaki uniform shirt and unclipped the radio from his shoulder. A breeze had ruffled his hair and a hint of five-o'clock shadow darkened his jaw. He looked relaxed and perfectly at home in her kitchen—and incredibly sexy, too.

She shifted, unsettled by her attraction to him. She scarcely knew him, after all. And she wondered if he still thought of her as a suspect in her father's murder. She wasn't going to ask. She was tired of talking about it. "How did you end up as a sheriff's deputy in Eagle Mountain?" she asked instead.

"I got a law degree, then discovered I hated almost everything about being a lawyer," he said.

"That's an expensive revelation."

"It's more common than you might think. Anyway, my area of expertise was Colorado water law. I read a newspaper profile of a water cop in another county and thought it sounded like something I would enjoy and would be good at. I did a little more investigating, went through the state's law enforcement academy, then started applying to various jurisdictions."

"Did you take the job here because your parents are here?"

A pained look she well recognized crossed his face. "It's great being closer to my parents, but…"

"But it's hard to have them close enough to scrutinize your every move," she finished. "Believe me, I understand."

"They moved here after I graduated college, so I never lived here," he said. "But I'd visited and I knew it was a great place. It was too good an opportunity to pass up, even though I might have preferred to start out in the job a little farther removed from them."

"What is your job, exactly?" she asked.

"Water law in Colorado—who has rights to use the water that flows on the surface or is stored underground—is complicated. Just because you've got a stream or an irrigation ditch flowing through your property doesn't mean you're entitled to use that water. My job is to educate people about the law, and enforce it when necessary. I make sure the people who have a right to the water—who have paid for that right in many cases—get the water they need to grow crops or water livestock or whatever."

"But now you're investigating a murder."

He nodded. "Your father was found in a local irrigation ditch. I was the first law enforcement officer on the scene. And I'm a fully trained deputy, so while water law is my specialty, it's not the only thing I do. And it's not as if I'm investigating this case by myself. In a department as small as ours, everyone works a case like this. And we have help from the Colorado Bureau of Investigation. Don't think we're not taking this seriously and putting every resource into it."

"I don't think that." Their eyes met and she felt such a pull she could imagine leaning toward him, though she remained very still.

He was the first to turn his attention back to his steak. They were silent for the rest of the meal, though tension hummed between them. Surely, he was aware of it, too.

After they finished eating, he insisted on helping with the dishes. They stood side by side in the cramped space between the sink and the dishwasher, him passing her the scraped plates to load in the machine. She caught the scent of him, warm and masculine, beneath the lemony aroma of the dish soap, and was aware of the hard muscle of his arm as he brushed against her.

"Thanks for inviting me tonight," he said when the last dish was loaded and she was drying her hands on a kitchen towel. "This was really nice."

"It was." She turned toward him and their gazes met and held. This time, she did lean toward him. Would one kiss hurt anything? she wondered.

Before she could find out, a reflection in the window opposite startled her. "What's that?" she asked.

He turned to see what she was talking about, then swore under his breath. "What is it?" she asked again.

He had already turned, and was moving toward the door. "Call 911," he said. "I think it's a fire. A big one."

Chapter Ten

Chris felt the heat of the fire while they were still some distance away. Flames engulfed the wooden posts on either side of the entrance to the Russell ranch, bright orange against the dusky sky. Sparks had ignited a pinion tree near the entrance and the fire was quickly reducing the tree to a skeleton. He looked around for a hose. By the time the fire department got here from town, the flames would have spread across the land—and the wind was blowing toward the house.

"We need to get some water on this," he called to Willow, who was hurrying up the drive after him.

"This way!" She turned and ran, back down the drive and across to the equipment shed. He caught up with her in time to help her push back the big doors at the front of the shed. "We keep an ATV with a water tank and a battery-operated pump for putting out small brush fires," she said. She flicked on the overhead light and started toward the back corner of the shed. "There are some shovels on the wall over there, and a pile of feed sacks we can wet down and use to beat out sparks," she called over her shoulder.

He went to pull down the shovels and gathered up an armload of the sacks. Willow met him again at the open doors. "The ATV is gone," she said. She shook her head. "I'm going to run back to the house and see if I can call Von at his cabin."

Chris scanned the shed. A tractor shared space with a cultivator and other implements, including a wheelbarrow and a cement mixer. But no ATV. While Willow returned to the house, Chris ran with shovels and feed sacks toward the fire and began attacking any sparks that leaped from the main blaze.

Soon Willow was back at his side. "Von isn't answering the phone at his cabin," she said. "Help me fill some buckets and we'll haul water over here in the truck."

He helped her gather up half a dozen five-gallon buckets and started to fill them from the water hose, but she called after him, "We don't have time for that. Get the water from the horse trough."

A pair of horses ambled over to observe as he and Willow plunged buckets into the trough to fill them with water. Willow struggled to carry a full bucket to the truck while Chris followed with two. When they had all six buckets loaded, Willow jumped into the driver's seat and shifted the truck into gear.

Though less than ten minutes had passed, the fire had spread, consuming most of the entry posts and the archway over it. Willow soaked the feed sacks in water and began beating at embers on the edge of the fire, while Chris soaked the bigger flames with water from the buckets. Then he grabbed a shovel and began scooping up dirt and throwing it on other areas of the fire. The two of them worked furiously, not speaking, for the next thirty minutes. Once the wood of the entryway was consumed and they had extinguished the trees on either side of the drive, the fire died down. They beat out or smothered the last of the smoldering embers, then stood, catching their breaths and surveying the blackened area on either side of the drive.

"Someone did that deliberately," Willow said. "I could smell the diesel when we first got close."

"I smelled it, too." Chris pulled out his phone. "I'm going to call this in to the sheriff's dispatcher."

"It won't do any good," she said. "Whoever did it is long gone, and we don't have any neighbors to see. You and I were closest, and we didn't notice anything."

"I'm going to call this in," he said again. "Then I'll take some pictures and look around."

"Okay." She looked up at what remained of the ranch entrance. "My father had that put up when I was a little girl," she said. "A man had a business in town for a while that did sandblasted wooden signs and Dad commissioned that from him."

She sounded so calm, but he thought about how all of this must make her feel—she had come home because it was a place that was safe and familiar, and everything was unraveling around her. "Will you be okay while I go in and make the call?" he asked.

"I'll be fine." She didn't look at him, simply remained standing there, looking at the damage.

Inside, he called dispatch to report the vandalism. He was on his way to the front door when the house phone rang again. He answered and Travis said, "I heard the call from dispatch. What's going on?"

"Someone—no idea who—set fire to the wooden archway at the entrance to the Russell ranch," he said. "I helped Willow put out the fire. It was definitely deliberate—we could smell the diesel."

"Has she had any threats from anyone?" Travis asked.

"She says no."

"Could be kids out for trouble, or it could be something worse. I think I'll come out and take a look."

Chris joined Willow just as the first of two fire trucks arrived. The assistant fire chief, a fit sixty-something with short-cropped gray hair, walked toward them, studying the blackened area around the gate as he moved. "What happened?" he asked.

"Someone set fire to the entrance gate," she said. "We could smell the diesel."

"We spotted the flames about seven o'clock," Chris said. "I don't think it had been burning long when we got here."

The chief nodded. "We'll mop up, make sure all the sparks are out and collect any evidence of arson." He glanced at Chris, taking in the uniform. "Are you with the sheriff's department?"

"Deputy Chris Delray." Chris shook the chief's hand. "I called in a report of vandalism."

"Tom Reynolds. I'll let you know what we find." Reynolds returned to his crew.

The firemen were at work when a battered green pickup swung into the drive. Von King pulled alongside them and lowered the driver's-side window. "What happened here?" he asked.

"Where were you?" Willow asked. "Why didn't you answer my call?"

"Wasn't home." He looked past her, at the blackened remains of the entrance arch. "I told Sam he ought to replace that with iron, but he stuck with the wood. Iron wouldn't have burned like that."

"Where were you?" Chris asked.

"Out." Von's gaze met his, defiant and letting Chris know he wasn't going to get any more of an answer.

"Have you seen anyone hanging around lately who shouldn't be here?" Chris asked.

"Nope," Von said.

"Did you pass anyone on the way in here?"

"Nope."

"Where is the ATV with the water and firefighting equipment?" Willow asked.

"It's in the shed, where it always is," Von said.

"No, it isn't."

Von finally looked at her again. "Are you sure?"

"Yes, I'm sure."

His gaze slid away again. "Then I don't know what to tell you."

Willow turned to Chris. "Did you call the sheriff's office?"

"Yes. They're sending someone."

"I'll be going," Von said. Not waiting for a reply, he rolled up the window and backed up the truck.

"Do you know of an experienced cowboy looking for work?" Willow asked as they watched Von drive away.

"No. But I'll keep my ears open."

"Do. Because I don't know how much longer I can stand having him around. So far he's been the very definition of unhelpful."

"I spoke to the sheriff," Chris said. "He's coming out to look at things."

"There's nothing for him to see," she said. "There's nothing for anyone to see. I think this is someone's idea of a bad joke—maybe kids trying to make trouble somewhere remote where they know they're unlikely to get caught."

"Maybe. But we don't see much of that kind of thing around here."

"There's always a first." She looked down at her

blackened hands. "I'm going inside to clean up," she said. "Do you mind?"

"Go ahead. I'll wait for the sheriff."

While he waited, he prowled the area around the entrance and along the road several hundred yards in either direction, but he found nothing suspicious. He returned to the equipment shed and found ruts where he thought the firefighting ATV might have been parked, but no sign of what might have become of the machine. He washed his hands at a spigot beside the barn, and refilled the horse trough while the horses looked on.

Travis arrived in his sheriff's department SUV, his brother Gage in the passenger seat. Gage looked to where the entrance arch had been and whistled. "I remember when Sam had that made twenty-five years ago or so. It was a big, thick piece of oak. Not the kind of thing to burn that easily."

"I think someone soaked the base of the posts with diesel, then lit them," Chris said. "The first was really hot and going good by the time we got out here."

"You're lucky it didn't spread," Travis said. "We've had some wind."

Tom Reynolds joined them. "Evening, Sheriff, Gage," he said. He turned to Chris. "You're right—this was deliberately set. We've got an investigator in Junction we use for suspected arson and I could have him come out and do a more thorough inspection, but his services aren't cheap, and since the fire didn't spread…"

"I don't think an arson investigation is going to turn up much more than we'll find on our own," Travis said. "Thanks, Tom."

"We've done our best to make sure the fire won't reignite, but you should be alert for any hot spots that might flare up," Tom said. He looked at the sky. "It's supposed to be a calm night, so I don't anticipate you'll have any trouble."

They said goodbye and the fire crew departed. When they were gone, Travis turned to Chris. "What do you think?"

Chris rubbed the back of his neck. "I don't know. It could just be kids, out to make trouble. But Willow said her dad kept an ATV outfitted to fight fires, and it's missing from the equipment shed. We ended up hauling buckets of water and beating out sparks with shovels."

"Did whoever set the fire steal the ATV?" Gage asked.

"Willow and I were in the kitchen, at the back of the house," Chris said. "I think we would have heard anyone in the equipment shed, especially if they started the ATV, or hauled it out on a trailer."

"So maybe they took it some other time," Gage said. "Or maybe there's no connection between the missing ATV and this fire."

"Maybe Sam sold the ATV and didn't tell Willow," Chris said.

"If Sam sold it, he'd have had another, better one in place first," Travis said. "He wasn't one to leave things to chance."

They walked the same path Chris had taken earlier, around the gate and along the roadside in either direction, scanning the ground for a tire print or cigarette butt or cap from a diesel can, anything that might be tied to their arsonist. But they found nothing but scorched earth and weeds.

"Was there anyone else on the ranch when this happened?" Travis asked when they were back in the drive, standing beneath where the archway had once been.

"Von King lives in a cabin not far from the corrals," Chris said. "When Willow called him, he didn't answer. He drove up after the fire was out and asked what happened. When he found out you were on your way, he left."

"I've been doing some digging," Gage said. "Von King is really Leroy Paige, from Oklahoma. He has a record for armed robbery, car theft and a few other minor crimes. But he's kept his nose clean since he got out of prison last year, as far as we know."

"Can't see why he'd do something like this," Travis said. "This is petty."

"Do you think it was meant as a threat?" Chris asked. "To frighten Willow?"

"Is she frightened?" Travis asked.

"She's hard to read," Chris admitted. Willow had seemed more annoyed than worried, but she struck him as someone who kept her emotions under wraps.

"Someone killed Sam on the ranch," Travis said. "Courtney Baker says someone's been threatening Trey Allerton, who lives on another part of the ranch. And now this."

"Maybe the target isn't any one person, but the ranch," Gage said. "Maybe someone is trying to run off everyone here."

"But why?" Chris asked. "The ranch isn't for sale, so it's not as if the people here are standing in the way of anyone or anything. The whole place is in a conservation easement, so it's not as if running off the owners would result in it going on the market."

"Maybe whoever is doing this doesn't know that," Travis said.

"Who would gain if Willow and Allerton left the place?" Gage asked.

"Darla Russell's son, Emmet Caspar, has a will that

leaves him half the place," Chris said. "Maybe he thinks if he can scare off Willow, he can get her half at a bargain price."

"Let's take a harder look at the two of them," Travis said.

Willow emerged from the house. She had changed from jeans and a blouse into a cotton dress with a long skirt and ruffled sleeves. She'd braided her hair and it hung over one shoulder. When she came to stand by Chris, he smelled the floral fragrance of her soap. "Did you find anything?" she asked, addressing her question to no one in particular.

"Nothing significant," Travis said. "Have you seen anyone around here lately who shouldn't have been here? Anyone who didn't belong?"

"I haven't seen anyone but a few neighbors who came to offer their condolences," she said. "And most of them I've known all my life. They wouldn't have any reason to do something like this."

"Where are your stepmother and her son right now?" Gage asked.

"I don't really know. They said something about staying in town, or they might have gone back to Albuquerque. Why? Do you think they would do this?"

"I'd feel better if I knew where they were," Chris said.

She shook her head. "This is stupid enough for Emmet to have come up with it," Willow said. "My dad used to talk about how dumb and lazy he was. Which is why I can't wrap my head around Dad leaving even part of the ranch to him."

"Do you think the will Darla gave your lawyer is a fake?" Chris asked.

"I think it has to be," she said. "Though proving so may be tough."

Travis and Gage took pictures and measurements, then left. Chris lingered. "I'm worried about you, here by yourself," he told Willow.

"I'll be fine," she said. She motioned toward the burned area. "This is just stupid. I can't even take it seriously as a threat."

"Still, after what happened to your father… I'm not trying to frighten you, but you should be careful."

"I promise, I'll be careful. And I'll call you if anything else happens."

"Call me," he said. "Call 911, too."

"I will." She put her hand on his arm. "Don't worry about me. I'm used to standing up to people who threaten me—I don't run."

He knew Willow didn't lack courage. But standing up to her department head had cost her her job—what if standing up to her current foe cost her her life?

Chapter Eleven

After a restless night, Willow woke determined to focus on the work that needed to be done. She started by walking up the drive to the burned area and assessing the damage. The acrid odor of burned wood lingered in the area, and ashes crunched underfoot. When Von swung his truck into the drive, she flagged him down. "I need you to clean this up this morning," she said. "The charred fence posts need to be replaced, and cut down the burned trees on either side of the drive."

She halfway expected him to argue with her, but he remained mute, so she charged ahead. "The farrier is coming at one o'clock to see to the horses, and the haying crew starts tomorrow." If she had expected him to be impressed, he didn't show it.

She returned to the house and spent the rest of the morning going through her dad's calendar, making note of upcoming tasks she would need to see to. She wondered if one of the neighboring ranchers would be willing to help her evaluate the stock and decide which should be sold and which kept. She'd have to think about that. After her father died, several neighbors had extended offers of help, but how serious had they been about that?

She was finishing up lunch when she heard the

crunch of tires on gravel. Expecting the farrier, she glanced out the window, only to see a familiar white sedan. The car stopped and Darla and Emmet climbed out.

Willow charged outside to meet them. "What are you doing here?" she asked.

"We talked to the lawyer and showed him the will," Darla said. "Half the ranch is going to be Emmet's, so we're moving back in."

"You can't make us leave," Emmet said, and heaved a large suitcase out of the trunk of the car.

Willow returned to the house, anger choking her. She punched in Chris's number. "Willow," he answered. "How are you doing?"

"Darla and Emmet just showed up," she said. "They're moving back in. Darla says since the ranch is going to be half Emmet's, I can't make them leave. That can't be right, can it?"

"My specialty is water law, not estate law," he said. "You should probably call my dad."

"I'm asking you," she said. She was annoyed with Ted for concealing so much from her already.

"If the will hasn't been probated, you could cite them for trespassing, I'd think," he said. "Though it might make things more difficult later, if the will does turn out to be legitimate."

"I can't stand them," she said. "Maybe you should come out here and question them about the fire last night."

"I'll do that," he said. "I have some things to take care of here first. Will you be all right until I can get there?"

"I'll be fine," she said. She already felt foolish, calling him so impulsively. "It's not as if those two are going to hurt me or anything."

"I promise I'll be there as soon as I can."

She returned to her father's office and tried to ignore the sounds of Darla and Emmet going in and out of the house. But she couldn't ignore it when Darla knocked on the office door and called, "Willow! There's a very good-looking man here to see you."

Her heart leaped. Chris must have gotten away from the office much sooner than he had thought. She smoothed her hair and hurried out to greet him.

Only to be met by a smiling Trey Allerton. "Willow!" He greeted her like an old friend, and pulled her close in a crushing hug.

She pushed him away and stepped back. "What do you need, Mr. Allerton?" she asked.

"Trey was just telling me that he's building a ranch for young people just down the road from here." Darla hovered at Trey's elbow, giving him her biggest smile. "That's so admirable."

"It's the least I can do," he said. "There's so much need in the world." He turned back to Willow. "And right now, I need to borrow a tractor. Just for a few hours."

"No, I can't lend you a tractor," she said.

"But why not?" Darla asked. "You don't even know why he needs it."

It didn't matter why he needed it, she didn't want to lend him anything. He smiled at Darla, who flushed pink and all but simpered. "Someone dumped a wrecked ATV and it's blocked my driveway," he said. "I need to pull it out of the way."

"Pull it out of the way with your truck," Willow said. "I can lend you some chain, if you need me to."

"A tractor would be easier," he said.

"Where did the ATV come from?" she asked. "Who dumped it there?"

"I don't know," he said.

"When did this happen?" she asked.

"Sometime last night. It was there when we woke up this morning. I had to take down part of the fence to get out of the driveway, then drive through the ditch."

"What kind of ATV?" she asked, a growing feeling of dread overtaking her.

"A big one. With a water tank or something like that on the back."

"Did you report this to the sheriff?" she asked.

"I didn't see any need to do that."

"I think that might be one of the ranch's ATVs," she said. "It's missing from the equipment shed."

"Huh," Trey said. "About the tractor…"

"I'm not lending it to you," she said.

"Of course you can borrow the tractor," Darla said. She turned to Willow. "Half of that tractor belongs to Emmet and I know he won't mind if Trey borrows it for a little while."

"Until my father's will is probated, as executor of the estate, I have final say in what happens here," she said. She wasn't entirely sure that was true, but it sounded good, and it wasn't as if Darla had a legal degree.

Darla made a face and started to argue, but Trey cut her off. "Where's Von? Can I at least ask him to come and help me?"

"He's supposed to be cleaning up around the entrance," she said. "Didn't you see him when you drove in?"

"No," Trey said. "I did notice the archway is gone. What happened?"

"Yes, what happened?" Darla said. "Don't tell me you're making changes to the ranch already. That can't be legal, executor or not."

"Someone set fire to the archway last night," Willow said. "Do either of you know anything about that?"

Trey shook his head. "I'll go see if I can find Von."

"I need to talk to you about where we'll be staying," Darla said. "I want to change to a better room."

"Which room?" Willow asked.

"The master bedroom isn't being used, and after all, it used to be mine."

"You're not moving into Dad's room," Willow said.

"I don't see why not. I—"

As far as Willow was concerned, this wasn't open for discussion. She shook her head and walked past them, toward the door.

"Where are you going?" Darla called after her.

"Away," she said. She had had enough of all of them. She had to get out of here before she said or did something she would regret.

"What if something comes up?" Darla called after her.

"Deal with it," Willow said.

CHRIS WAS SURPRISED to see Willow striding down the sidewalk toward him when he stepped out of the Cake Walk Café after a late lunch. Despite her diminutive stature, she made a striking picture, with her long braid of dark hair over one shoulder and her curvy figure. He hurried to meet her. "I was just headed out to the ranch," he said.

"You don't need to rush," she said. "Darla has dug in her heels and I don't think she intends to go anywhere anytime soon. And where she goes, Emmet follows."

He fell into step beside her as she continued down the sidewalk. "What brings you to town?" he asked.

"I came to buy new locks for the door of my dad's office and my bedroom door," she said. "I don't trust Darla or Emmet not to snoop in there the minute my back is turned. She's probably in there right now."

"I can ask her to leave," he said. "Tell her you have the option of pressing charges."

"No, don't do that," she said. She glanced at him. "I've decided I'm better off keeping them both where I can know what they're up to. You know the old saying—keep your friends close, and your enemies closer."

He would have laughed, but she looked too distressed for mirth. "Did something in particular happen this morning that has you so upset?" he asked.

"Everything," she said. "In addition to Darla and Emmet moving back in, Von has disappeared. When he showed up for work this morning, I asked him to clean up after the fire, to replace the burned fence posts and cut down the trees, and he left without doing anything or saying anything. And then Trey Allerton came by wanting to borrow a tractor. When I wouldn't lend him one, he asked if he could have Von help him for a while." She stopped and faced Chris. "Trey says someone dumped a wrecked ATV in his driveway last night, blocking in his truck. He had to take down the fence and drive through the ditch to get out. He said it was a big ATV with a water tank on the back."

"Like your missing ATV," Chris said.

"Yes. I'm betting it's the ranch's, and whoever set the fire put it down there. But I don't know why. It doesn't even feel like a threat, just annoying." She started walking again. "Anyway, I'm headed to the newspaper office to run an ad for someone to help me on the ranch.

Then I'm going to fire Von. My dad may have liked him for some unknown reason, but I never want to see him again."

"Fair enough," he said. "Why don't I go with you, and I'll follow you back to the ranch."

"Okay." She took a deep breath and she visibly relaxed her shoulders. "What have you been doing this morning?"

"It was ridiculous, really," he said. "I had to separate two ranchers who were having a fistfight over whose turn it was to draw down from an irrigation ditch that divides their property."

"I guess people get very passionate about things like that," she said.

"There's a fine line between passion and rage sometimes," he said. "Most of the time just talking to the people resolves things, but sometimes I have to get out the handcuffs."

"I don't think you'll have to go that far with Darla and Emmet, but who knows," she said. "I've given up trying to figure people out."

"Did you take a look at the ATV at Trey's place to see if it was yours?" he asked.

She shook her head. "I didn't have the heart. But we can drive down there when you're done questioning Darla. It didn't sound to me as if it was going anywhere anytime soon."

They entered the newspaper office and the woman at the desk gave Willow an ad form to fill out. Willow completed the form, paid for the ad, and she and Chris left again. "I need to stop by the office and get my cruiser," Chris said. "Then I'll drive you to your car."

But when they entered the office, Adelaide greeted

him. "I've been looking for you," she said. "Both of you, actually."

"What's up?" Chris asked.

"You need to get back out to the ranch," Adelaide said. "Darla Russell just called. She was hysterical, but she said something about a fight."

Chapter Twelve

Chris pulled his cruiser in behind another sheriff's department SUV in front of the ranch house. Willow drove past him to park in front of the garage. As they all exited their vehicles, Darla Russell ran toward them. "They're in the machine shed," she said. "You have to stop them before they kill each other."

Chris, along with Gage and Deputy Dwight Prentice, headed toward the machine shed. Willow stayed back with Darla, the two in earnest conversation. Emmet met the deputies at the door of the shed. "What's going on?" Gage asked.

"It's just a fight," he said. "Mom didn't really need to call you."

Chris and Dwight moved past him, to the rear stall where Trey Allerton and Von King were flailing at each other. Von had Trey in a headlock and was repeatedly punching the side of his head, but as the two deputies reached the combatants, Trey broke the hold and landed a solid blow to Von's stomach that doubled the older man over.

"Break it up, you two!" Dwight wrapped his arms around Trey and held him firm, while Chris dragged Von to the opposite corner.

"What was all that about?" Chris asked.

Von straightened and wiped the back of his hand across his nose, then pulled out a bandanna and began dabbing at his bleeding lip. "When I do a job for a man, I expect to be paid," he said.

"You'll get your money when you finish the job," Trey shouted. Dwight had released his hold on the man and he stood leaning against the wall.

"Who threw the first punch?" Gage asked.

"He did!" Trey and Von spoke at once, each pointing to the other.

Willow and Darla joined them. "I heard shouting and Emmet and I came out here and those two were trying to kill each other," Darla said.

"If I wanted him dead, he wouldn't be standing there," Von said.

"We're not done yet," Trey said.

"Both of you shut up," Gage said. "And stay away from each other or I'll haul you both in for assault."

The two men looked sullen, but said nothing else.

"Go home and cool off," Gage said. "Both of you."

Von was the first to leave. He sent a last malevolent look to Trey, then headed out of the shed. As he passed Willow, she called to him, "Von, wait!"

He stopped and looked at her, his expression sullen.

"You need to get your things and leave," she said.

"What?"

"You're fired," she said.

He drew himself up to his full height. "You can't fire me."

"I can and I am. Get your things and go. If you leave an address, I'll mail your final check in a couple of days."

"This place will fall apart without me," he said.

"I doubt that."

"You'll be sorry," he said.

Chris moved up behind Von. "If you cause any trouble for Ms. Russell, I'll arrest you," he said. "If you bother her in any way, you'll be in jail. Is that clear?"

Von grunted and moved on.

"I'll make sure he leaves without making trouble." Gage joined Chris and Willow.

"Aren't you going to arrest them?" Darla asked.

"Neither of them wants to press charges," Gage said. "Neither of them is badly injured and I don't see any property damage. Whatever the fight was about, let's hope they've got it out of their system." He turned to Willow. "Do you have any idea what the fight was about?"

She shook her head. "I know that Trey sometimes hires Von to work around his place. Maybe it's something to do with that."

Gage turned to Chris. "You make sure Trey goes to his place and stays there."

"Yes, sir," Chris said.

Gage and Dwight went after Von and Chris moved closer to Willow. "Will you be all right?" he asked. "Can you handle things here until you can hire someone?"

"I will." She turned to Darla and Emmet. "You two are going to have to pitch in to look after the livestock and keep the ranch going," she said.

Darla looked startled. "We don't know anything about ranching."

"Then you're going to learn. As long as you two are staying here, you might as well earn your keep." She turned and strode back toward the house, her long braid of hair swinging behind her. Chris grinned. Some people might have crumpled under the strain of all Willow had been through, but the adversity only seemed to make her stronger.

Trey Allerton limped past Chris. “Are you okay?” Chris asked.

Trey put a hand to his side. “My ribs are a little bruised, I think, but I’ll be okay. I figure Von is hurting at least as bad.”

“I’m going to follow you back to your trailer,” Chris said.

Trey didn’t even try to object. Chris waited while he climbed into his truck and started the engine, then got into his cruiser and followed him on the short drive to the trailer.

The first thing he saw as he approached the mobile home was the busted ATV and trailer with a water tank straddled across the drive, and a section of fence lying in the ditch. Trey drove past the driveway, then through the ditch into the bare dirt area in front of the trailer.

Chris parked on the road and walked over to the ATV. “Willow Russell is missing an ATV and trailer like this,” he said.

“Then she’s welcome to come get it,” Trey said. “It’s in my way.”

“How did it end up here?” Chris asked.

“Someone dumped it here.”

“Any idea who?”

Trey shoved his hands into the front pockets of his jeans. “I have ideas, but no proof.”

“Tell me and we’ll see about getting proof.”

Trey waved his hand toward the ATV. “Just get it out of here. That’s all I care about.”

“Do you think Von did this?” He would have had access to the ATV in the machine shed.

"I don't care if he did or if he didn't." Trey looked sullen, all of his easy charm vanished.

"Tell me what you and Von were fighting about," Chris said.

"I hired him to do a job for me, but he only did half of it. I told him I wouldn't pay him until he finished the work and he pitched a fit."

"What was the job?"

Trey looked around them. "Just some work around here. You can see this place needs a lot of work." He pointed behind the trailer. "All of that needs to be cleared, so we can build cabins and a lodge for the campers. We need new fencing and a front gate, some corrals and stables—all kinds of stuff."

As far as Chris could determine, no one had made a start on any of these projects. "It sounds to me like you need a whole crew of people to do all that."

"I do. But that takes money. I spend my days talking to people, persuading them to invest in the project. I'm make progress, even if you don't see it yet."

"Do you think Von King is the person who shot at you?"

"How did you know about that?"

"We had a report."

Trey scowled. "I told Courtney not to involve you people."

"Do you think Von fired those shots?" Chris asked.

"It was just hunters."

"And the snake?"

Trey looked at Chris, his expression bland. "What snake?"

"Your girlfriend told us someone put a snake in your truck."

"I don't know what you're talking about."

Chris looked toward the trailer. "Should I go inside and ask her?"

"She's not there."

"Where is she?"

Trey shrugged. "Visiting her sister? Shopping? I don't know."

"I understand Sam Russell's death put you in a better financial position," Chris said.

"You mean no more quarterly lease payments, I guess," Trey said. "That will be more money we can put to use to benefit the kids. I was touched Sam would do such a thing."

"You knew that provision was in your lease agreement," Chris said. "It didn't come as a surprise."

"No. I was still sorry Sam was killed."

"You don't know anything about his murder, do you?"

Another direct, cold look. "I didn't kill Sam Russell," he said. "But I hope you find who did. And I need to go inside and clean up now. I have a meeting this afternoon."

Chris looked back at the ATV. "I'll need to go in and use your phone to call this in." He had no cell service here.

"I don't have one," Trey said. "When I want to talk to someone, I do it in person."

"That's not very convenient," Chris said.

"It has its benefits. And its drawbacks. If I'd called Von instead of going over to the ranch to speak to him, maybe our tempers wouldn't have got the better of us."

"There was a fire at the ranch last night," Chris said. "Someone torched the entrance gate. Do you know anything about that?"

Trey shook his head. "I was here last night. With

Courtney and her daughter." He touched the split at the corner of his eye. "Something funny you might want to know about, though."

"What's that?" Chris asked.

"When I went into the machine shed, looking for Von, he wasn't there. But Darla's boy, Emmet, was."

"What was he doing?"

"He was half in a big bin they use to store chains and rope and stuff. When I asked him if he'd seen Von, he came out of there so fast, he hit his head. When I asked him what he was looking for, he turned all red and swore at me. Tough talk for a weakling like him. Then Von came in and told him to get lost. I guess he ran to Mama, because by the time Von and I took the first swings, she ran out there and started screaming at us."

"What do you think he was looking for?" Chris asked.

"I have no idea, but maybe you ought to ask him."

"I will."

Trey went into the house and Chris turned back to the ATV. He'd check the VIN with the list Willow had given him, but he was sure the vehicle belonged to the Russell ranch. When he got back to town, he'd see about getting someone up here to haul it in. Maybe they'd get some evidence off it, though he didn't hold out much hope.

He walked back to his cruiser, but stopped at the entrance to look back toward the trailer. The curtains twitched at the far window, and for a fraction of a second, someone looked out at him. Trey had claimed his girlfriend, Courtney Baker, wasn't home, but Chris could have sworn he had just seen her. But the window was empty again, the curtain still. Had Trey deliberately lied to him, or simply been mistaken? Maybe

Chris would ask Shane Ellis if his fiancée, Courtney's sister-in-law, had seen Courtney lately.

In the meantime, work was piling up on his desk, and he didn't feel any closer to finding Sam's murderer or helping Willow Russell.

WILLOW LED DARLA and Emmet to the horse barn and showed them how to feed and water the animals. "When you're done with that, you'll need to clean the stalls," she said.

"What are you going to do?" Emmet asked.

"I'm going to place an order for feed, then I'm going to pay bills."

"I could do that," Darla said. "Pay the bills, I mean. I'm good with paperwork."

Willow had no intention of letting Darla rummage through the ranch finances. Even if Emmet eventually ended up owning half the ranch, the financial details of her father's estate were none of Darla's business. "I'll handle the bills," she said. "If you want to do something else to help, you can clean up around the entrance. Von was supposed to rake up the coals and cut the dead trees, but he didn't do it."

"I'm not some ranch hand you can order around," Darla said.

"My father had a saying," Willow said. "You probably heard it when the two of you were married. He said, 'If you don't work, you don't eat.' Until I find someone to take Von's place, all three of us have to work to keep things going. If you can't agree to that, you can leave." She looked Darla in the eye, determined to stare her down.

"Come on, Mom." Emmet picked up a feed bucket. "We can do this."

Willow left them and returned to the house. She'd have to check their work later, to make sure the horses were properly cared for. Meanwhile, she kept her fingers crossed someone would respond to her advertisement for help.

She decided to take care of the bills before she left the house, partly to keep tabs on Darla and Emmet, and partly in case she needed to stop by the bank while she was in town and transfer funds between accounts.

She sat behind the desk, the worn leather chair embracing her, the leather-and-aftershave scent of her father faint in the air, as if his ghost lingered in this place where he had spent so much of his life. She pulled the ledger from the drawer and flipped through it. The pages were labeled for various spending categories—feed, veterinary care, supplies, repairs and so on. The last section was headed "Labor," with line after line indicating wages paid to various ranch workers, including Von King.

She studied the entries more closely. It appeared her father had paid Von a set amount per week, and withheld taxes, so that the check was the same amount each week. She simply had to prorate the amount for the partial week Von had worked.

She took out the checkbook for the ranch account, and flipped the ledger to a new page to record the payment, but stopped when she saw a note in her father's neat handwriting at the top of the page. The note was dated for the Saturday before her father's death on Tuesday, "Terminated," and below that, an entry for a payment, with the notation "Final Paycheck."

Chapter Thirteen

Monday morning found Chris poring over a spreadsheet recording water draws on the local irrigation district. The district manager sent him the reports each week and Chris always read them, looking for anything unusual that might indicate theft or misuse. But he never found anything, and reading the reports reminded him a little too much of his old law firm days.

Besides, he was too distracted lately by thoughts of Willow Russell. More than once over Sunday, his day off, he had started to call and check on her, but he didn't want to come across as pushy. She had promised to let him know if she needed his help, and while he knew she didn't especially like Darla and Emmet, their alibis for the time of Sam Russell's death had checked out, and he didn't think they would do more than annoy Willow. And their presence at the ranch might keep the real killer from trying to get close to her right now.

"Hey, Chris, do you have a minute?"

He pushed his laptop to one side and looked up at Deputy Jamie Douglas. "Sure. What can I do for you?"

She pulled up a chair and sat. "This morning I finished up questioning the neighbors who live near Carstairs Park," she said. "Only one of them had anything interesting to say."

"Did they see someone near the park the morning Sam Russell was killed?" Chris asked.

"He said he saw Adam Treadwell. He was sure it was Treadwell, because they sometimes play golf in the same foursome. But he was surprised to see him out so early."

"What time was this?"

"Seven thirty. Mr. Geary—Mick Geary—had knee replacement surgery scheduled for that morning and he was getting ready to leave for the hospital."

"What was Treadwell doing?"

"Mr. Geary said he was running, like he was running from something. He wasn't dressed for jogging, and he wasn't on the bike path. He was cutting across the grass from the pond, running hard. Geary wondered what was up, but he had to leave to get to the hospital and what with his surgery and all, he forgot about the incident until I questioned him."

"Did you ask Treadwell about it?" Chris asked.

"I stopped by his house but his wife said he wasn't at home. I asked her to have him call me, but so far he hasn't."

"Great." She stood as Shane walked past.

"Hey, Shane." Chris flagged him down.

Shane stopped beside Chris's desk. "What's up?"

"Has Lauren talked to Courtney lately?" Chris asked. "In the last day or two?"

"I don't know," Shane said. "Why?"

"Could you ask her?"

Shane pulled out his phone and typed out a text. "What's going on?" he asked Chris after he had sent the text.

"It may be nothing," Chris said. "But when I was out at their trailer Saturday, Allerton told me I couldn't talk to Courtney because she wasn't there. But as I was leaving, I could have sworn I saw her looking out the window at me."

"Was her car there?" Shane asked. "A white Toyota 4Runner."

"I didn't see it, but it could have been parked around back. Maybe Allerton didn't know she'd returned home."

Shane's phone buzzed and he answered it. "Hey… No, nothing's wrong. Just following up on Allerton's movements." He listened for a moment. "Okay. No big deal. Thanks."

He ended the call and looked at Chris and Jamie. "Lauren said it's been a few days since she's seen Courtney. Lauren has been busy at the clinic where she works. Why did you want to talk to Courtney?"

"I asked Allerton if Von King might have been the one to fire those shots at him," Chris said. "Allerton insisted the shots were from hunters and he said Courtney shouldn't have said anything to us. Then I asked about the snake someone put in his truck and he acted as if he had no idea what I was talking about. I wanted to get Courtney's side of the story, and that's when he told me she wasn't there."

"Trey Allerton always struck me as shifty," Jamie said. "Though his biggest mistake so far seems to be associating with questionable characters—first Tom Chico, and now Von King."

"Courtney seems happy with him," Shane said. "And it takes all kinds."

"He strikes me as someone who's full of a lot of talk and little action," Chris said. "He talks about how much work needs to be done on his so-called 'ranch,' but I never see him doing anything."

"I think Trey thinks of himself as the idea man," Shane said. "While other people do the heavy lifting. We think he's gotten a lot of money from Courtney, but we can't see that he's spent much on that ranch." He slid his phone back into his pocket. "Lauren and I will stop by soon to check on Courtney."

"See what you can find out about the feud between Allerton and Von." Chris stood. "Maybe Courtney knows something Allerton hasn't told us."

"I will," Shane said. "Where are you off to?"

"I'm going to track down Adam Treadwell. I want to find out what he was doing in Carstairs Park Tuesday morning—and why he neglected to tell us he was there."

CHRIS TRACKED DOWN Adam Treadwell at the driving range on Idlewilde Estates's golf course. Treadwell looked up at Chris's approach. "Hello, Deputy." Treadwell smiled, a toothy grin that showed no hint of unease. "Did you find out who dumped that ATV in our pond?"

Chris refrained from pointing out that the pond actually belonged to the irrigation district. "Not yet," he said. "But I did want to ask you some more questions about that morning."

"Sure." He straightened and slotted his driver into his golf bag. "Why don't we sit over here in the shade?" He led the way to a picnic table beneath a wooden shelter. He slid onto the bench and Chris settled opposite him.

"Tell me again where you were Tuesday morning," Chris said.

"I was at home."

"Alone?"

"Yes. My wife was in Denver, visiting a friend.

Why?" Treadwell laughed. "You don't think I dumped that ATV in the pond, do you?"

"We have a positive ID from a credible witness who saw you in the park Tuesday morning, around seven thirty," Chris said.

Treadwell's face paled beneath his tan, though his smile remained rigid. "Who told you that?"

"Our witness was positive about the identification. Why don't you tell me what you were doing in the park then."

Treadwell looked away, fingers drumming the picnic table. Then he relaxed. "I remember now. My wife has been after me to get more exercise, so I made a point of getting up early that morning and going for a walk. Unfortunately, the habit didn't stick." He shook his head. "I guess I got my days mixed up when you asked about it earlier."

"Did you see anyone else while you were out?" Chris asked.

"I sure didn't." Another grin. "Though I guess someone saw me."

"Our witness says you were running."

Treadwell's laugh sounded forced. "Right. At one point I thought maybe I should try jogging. I didn't get very far." He looked out over the driving range. "I guess golf is more my kind of exercise."

"The witness said you looked like you were fleeing—running away from something."

All pretense of an easy manner vanished. "Are you accusing me of something? It's not against the law to be in the park at seven thirty in the morning."

"You and Sam Russell exchanged some pretty harsh words during your argument about the homeowners' pollution of the irrigation ditch," Chris said.

"Alleged pollution," Treadwell said. "The water was never tested."

"Still, you both lost your tempers."

"We did." Treadwell bowed his head, silent for a long moment. Chris watched him, waiting. When Treadwell looked up again, his gaze was unflinching. "Look, I didn't like Sam," he said. "I thought he was one of those old-timers who is determined to oppose anything new. We were never going to see eye to eye about the water issue. But I didn't kill him. I wouldn't. I'm not a violent person."

Chris thought anyone might be pushed to violence, but Adam Treadwell had no criminal record of any kind. The man had never even had a traffic ticket. And the timing of the sighting troubled Chris. If Sam was killed at the earliest edge of the medical examiner's estimated time of death, a man racing the ATV alongside the Daimler Ditch might have made it to the park by seven thirty, but it would be pushing it. He stood. "We're still checking the ATV for prints and other evidence," he said. "I'll be in touch if we find anything."

Treadwell nodded. He looked relieved at this news. "I hope you find whoever did it," he said. "I never liked Sam, but I wouldn't wish murder on anyone."

WILLOW NEVER MADE it back to town that weekend. Shortly after her discovery that her father had fired Von King, the farrier arrived and she had to accompany him as he cared for the feet and teeth of all the horses. The next day, haying began. It was Monday afternoon before she could get away, and instead of going to Eagle Mountain, she set out for the cabin where Von King had lived on the ranch.

She drove her father's truck. Her own compact car

practically rattled her teeth loose on the rough gravel roads that cut through the ranch. Besides, she liked driving the big, powerful vehicle. She liked sitting up high above the road, and taking in the view through the broad expanse of windshield. Here, as in her father's office, his scent lingered—saddle soap and Old Spice and the cigars her mother had long ago forbidden him to smoke in the house.

Von, like a series of farmhands before him, had lived in a log cabin built in the early 1900s in a grove of cottonwoods by the side of the Daimler Ditch. The building was a squat rectangle, maybe thirty-two feet by sixteen feet, a series of three square rooms with a tiny bathroom cobbled onto the far end sometime in the 1950s. A small stable out back had room for a horse or two, though just as often these days one of the ranch ATVs parked in the stall. A personal horse wasn't an expense every hand could afford. When they needed to ride, they borrowed a mount from the ranch string.

Willow parked in the gravel in the shade of one of the leafy cottonwoods and studied the house. It looked empty. Certainly there was no sign of Von's truck around, and Willow had not seen or heard from him all weekend. She opened the door of the truck and slid out. Though she had driven past this place hundreds of times over the years, she had never been inside. She had never had a reason to come here. The men who worked for her father were usually solitary, older than her, without wives she might have befriended or children she could have played with. Some of the hands had been friendly to her, but most had ignored her.

Von had not ignored her. He seemed to have taken a dislike to her the moment she moved back to the ranch. She had thought it was because she was a woman, but she wondered now if he had another reason. Had he seen her as intruding on or influencing his relationship with her father? Hers were another pair of eyes to watch him and maybe see when he was up to no good.

She squared her shoulders and walked up onto the porch. The door was unlocked and she eased it open. She didn't know what she had expected to find, but the disorder inside was worse than she had feared. It took a moment for her to register that the jumble of items in the room wasn't the result of slovenly habits, but deliberate destruction. She picked her way through broken chairs, smashed dishes and scattered trash. Von must have thrown a regular temper tantrum. She took out her phone and snapped a few photos, then moved to the next room, determined to complete the inspection.

This was the bedroom, with an unmade bed and a dresser with every drawer pulled out onto the floor. She opened the closet and studied the jumble of items there—a boot with a broken heel, its mate lying on its side at the back of the closet. A power drill. A dented thermos. With a start, she realized these things had belonged to her father. She had given him the boots several Christmases ago, and when she turned over the thermos, her father's initials were engraved on the side.

She straightened, still staring at the sad collection. Had her father given Von these things? She shook her head. Her father wasn't one to pass along hand-me-downs.

Had Von stolen the items? That seemed a more likely explanation, and it could have been the reason Sam had fired Von.

But why had Von decided to keep working after her father died? With his perpetual scowl, it wasn't as if he ever appeared to enjoy the work.

But maybe jobs were hard to find for ex-cons and Von had wanted desperately to hang on to this one.

Desperately enough to kill?

Chapter Fourteen

Monday afternoon, Chris returned to the Russell ranch. He knocked on the door of the ranch house, but no one answered. He walked to the edge of the porch and surveyed the yard. There was no sign of movement anywhere. He walked over to the machine shed, which was empty.

When he started toward his cruiser again, he thought he heard music. He followed the sound to the horse barn, where he found Emmet cleaning a stall. The younger man wore cargo shorts, a T-shirt with a cartoon of an alien, and tennis shoes, unlikely attire for a ranch hand.

Emmet stopped his work and leaned on the shovel. "Need something, Deputy?"

"I'm looking for Willow."

"She drove off a little while ago."

"Where's your mother?" Chris asked.

"I don't know. I don't think she's speaking to me right now, which is fine by me."

"Why isn't she speaking to you?"

"I told her I wanted to go back to Albuquerque. But she's determined to stay, so I guess I'm stuck."

"I heard you could inherit half the ranch," Chris said. "Did you know about that before Sam died?"

"I didn't know anything about it until Mom told me while we were driving here, after the old man died."

"Were you surprised?"

"Well, yeah. I mean, I always knew Sam had pots of money, but he didn't like to part with it. He didn't even trust banks, just kept his loot hidden around the ranch."

Chris recalled that Darla had mentioned something like this to Willow. "Do you mean Sam kept a lot of money in his safe?" he asked.

"I heard he stashed it different places. He had so much money he probably didn't even keep track." Emmet shrugged. "Not that I've seen any of it."

"Is that what you were doing in the machine shed the other day?" Chris asked. "Were you looking for hidden cash?"

Emmet flushed. "Maybe. There's no law against looking, is there? And half of it's mine now, anyway."

"Did you see the will?" Chris asked.

"No. All that legal mumbo jumbo wouldn't mean anything to me, anyway."

"Why would Sam leave the money to you?"

"Mom says I'm the son Sam always wanted and never had, but really, I think she talked him into it. It's not like he ever liked me or anything. Or maybe he was upset with Willow and did it to get back at her."

This struck Chris as odd. "Why would he be upset with Willow?" he asked.

Emmet scratched the back of his head. "Well, you know she can be pretty smart-mouthed for a woman. If she doesn't like something, she's not shy about telling you to your face."

"And Sam didn't like that?"

"What man would? I like a woman who's a little easier to get along with. Willow is pretty enough, but when she opens her mouth to lecture you about something, it kind of spoils the effect."

The words grated, but Chris reined in his temper. He had never wanted a woman who wouldn't say what she really thought or felt. Why was that kind of honesty viewed as a negative trait by men like Emmet?

"Are you done asking questions?" Emmet straightened and gripped the shovel again. "Because I've got work to do. Willow will pitch a fit if I don't have this done by the time she gets back. Not that I'm afraid of her or anything. It's just easier to pick up the shovel than to listen to her harp at me."

Chris left him to the work. He was climbing into the cruiser when he spotted a vehicle headed toward him. He recognized the ranch truck, with Willow at the wheel. "I'm glad you're here," she said when he walked out to meet her, and for a moment his heart lifted at the words. Then he realized from her solemn expression that her words had nothing to do with personal pleasure at seeing him.

"What's up?" he asked.

"I found something else you need to see."

She led the way inside and headed for Sam's office, Chris at her heels. They both drew up short when the door opened and Darla emerged. The older woman gasped and put a hand to her chest. "My goodness! You startled me," she said.

"What were you doing in Dad's office?" Willow asked.

"I was looking for a stamp."

"That area is private. You need to stay out of it." Willow took a step forward and Darla scuttled past, but she stopped a few feet away and drew herself up to her full height.

"I'll go anywhere I like in this house," she declared.

Willow glared at her, then moved into the office. Chris followed and shut the door behind them. "I thought you bought a lock for this door," he said.

"I did. I just haven't gotten around to installing it. But I'll make it a priority now." She studied the desk, which was strewn with ledgers and papers. "I'm sure she was snooping around in here, but I left everything in such a mess I can't tell." She moved behind the desk, opened the bottom drawer and took out a ledger. "This is one of the things I wanted to show you." She opened the ledger, flipped through a few pages, then passed it to him. "Read this."

He studied the ledger entries, which appeared to be a payroll record for Von King. "Check the next page," Willow said.

He turned the page and blinked at the bold writing: "Terminated," followed by "Final Paycheck." "He fired Von."

"That's dated the Saturday before Dad was killed," Willow said.

"You didn't know about this?" Chris asked.

She shook her head. "Dad never said anything. I don't like Von, so I avoided him, and he has days off. I didn't think anything about not seeing him around that Monday. But he was working in the machine shed Tuesday morning, as if nothing had happened."

"Is it possible he had patched things up with your dad? Talked his way back into a job?"

"If he had, Dad would have made a note of it, I'm sure." She took out her phone. "There's something else. This morning, I drove out to the cabin where Von lived." She passed over the phone and Chris looked at the photos of broken furniture and general disarray.

"He trashed the place," Chris said.

"Check the last photo."

He scrolled to the image of a pair of boots, a drill and a thermos. "Those are all things that belonged to my dad," Willow said. "They were all stashed in Von's bedroom closet, like a pile of treasures assembled by a pack rat."

"Maybe Sam gave them to Von."

"I don't think so," she said. "I think Von stole them. He probably took other things, too. I believe that's why Dad fired him. Maybe Dad threatened to turn him over to the sheriff. If he had a prior conviction, wouldn't that make things worse for him?"

He nodded. "Do you know where Von is now?" he asked.

She shook her head and rubbed her hands up and down her folded arms. "But the sooner you find out, the better I'll feel." Her eyes met his. "If he killed my dad for firing him, what will he try to do to me, now that I've done the same?"

CHRIS HADN'T LIKED leaving Willow at the ranch. But she had assured him she would be careful, and she would call 911 right away if she spotted Von King. And she had pointed out that even though Darla and Emmet weren't her favorite people, their presence on the ranch with her offered some protection.

At the sheriff's department, Chris headed straight for Travis's office. "I think we should pick up Von King and bring him in for questioning," he told the sheriff. "Willow found evidence that her father fired Von the Saturday before Sam was killed. Apparently, Von had been stealing from the ranch and Sam found out about it. After Sam died, Von pretended he still had a job and didn't say anything to anyone."

Travis nodded. "All right. Pick him up and bring him in."

"We have to find him first." Chris raked a hand through his hair. "Willow fired him Saturday, before she found out her father had already done so. King cleared out, but not before he trashed the cabin where he'd been living. He didn't leave a way for her to get in touch. Now she's worried that if Von killed her father, he might go after her next."

"Is she alone at the ranch?" Travis asked.

"She has her former stepmother and the stepmother's son there with her, and she intends to hire a new ranch hand to replace Von." He hesitated. "And I intend to spend as much of my off-duty hours there as she'll let me." He hadn't really discussed this with Willow, but he'd made up his mind on the drive back to town that he needed to stick closer to her.

Travis nodded. "We'll put out an APB for Von. We can arrest him on theft charges and hold him on that while we question him."

Some of the tension eased from Chris's shoulders. "Thanks."

"We've got the ATV and trailer from the Russell ranch in our impound lot," Travis said. "Do you think Von was behind that also?"

"I think so. I think leaving it in Trey Allerton's way is part of his feud with Allerton—but we don't have any proof."

"It's one more thing to question him about. What's on your schedule for this afternoon?"

"Perry Webber left me a voice mail a little while ago.

He wants me to check out what looks like an illegal diversion ditch in Idlewilde Estates."

Travis nodded. "How did it go with Adam Treadwell earlier?" he asked. "Jamie said you went to question him about his activities Tuesday morning."

Chris shook his head. "He gave me a story about going for a walk. Then he said he was jogging. Then he got defensive."

"The timing isn't quite right for him as the murderer," Travis said.

"Unless we're off on the time of death for some reason," Chris said. "I think he could have done it if he had really raced the ATV down that path alongside the ditch. He ditches the ATV in the park, then runs home."

"We'll keep digging," Travis said. "When you get a chance, ask Willow to compile a list of things Von stole from her father or the ranch."

"Yes, sir."

On the drive to Idlewilde Estates, Chris's phone rang. The dashboard screen showed the call was from his father. He hesitated before answering, but if Dad suspected Chris was avoiding him, it would only increase the tension between them. "Hello," he answered.

"Hello, Chris," Ted said. "Your mother and I want you to come to dinner Wednesday evening."

"I'm working a case right now," Chris said. "I don't know if I can get away."

"You can find time for dinner. There's someone I want you to meet."

Chris's gut tightened. Those words from his father had never turned out well, from the colleague's daughter he had wanted Chris to date to another friend's business opportunity that had turned out to be a scam. "Who is it?" he asked.

"David Vandermeyer is with the state attorney general's office. They're looking for someone with a background in Colorado water law. I told him you'd be perfect for the position. He's very interested in meeting you."

"Dad, I already have a job."

"Vandermeyer was impressed with your on-the-ground experience, but it's time to move on from that. This is a terrific opportunity that could lead to even bigger things in the future. And I can guarantee it pays a lot more than you'll ever make working for the county."

As usual, his father was charging ahead with what he wanted for Chris, with no regard for what Chris wanted for himself. "I'm not interested," he said.

"How do you know if you don't even talk to this man?" Ted asked. "This isn't doing grunt work in some big firm, the way you were before. At least hear what he was to say."

It was impossible to fight his dad when he was being so reasonable. "I'll see if I can get the time off," Chris said.

"Do you need me to speak to the sheriff? I will."

"No. Don't do that." He wasn't a kid who needed an excused absence from class. "I'll take care of it."

"Good. Come at six thirty. We'll eat at seven."

Ted ended the call and Chris braked hard to allow a doe and twin fawns to cross the highway in front of him. As he watched the deer, he took several deep breaths, willing himself to calm down. His father loved him and wanted what was best for him, even if he never listened to what Chris thought was best for himself.

Fine. He could go to dinner and listen to the state lawyer, politely thank him for the opportunity and move on. Vandermeyer likely wouldn't understand. Maybe most people wouldn't. But this—spending his days behind the wheel of his cruiser, talking to people from all walks of life, doing everything from mediating a dispute between ranchers to writing a speeding ticket to investigating a murder—this was what made him want to get out of bed in the morning and mostly made him satisfied at the end of the day. All the money and prestige of a state job was never going to feel like that.

He found the address the ditch rider had given him, a sprawling gray stone house encircled by a black wrought-iron fence. Chris was halfway down the side of the fence when a muscular Doberman rushed at him, barking furiously.

A slender man who appeared to be in his seventies followed the dog to the fence. "Can I help you, Deputy?" he shouted over the dog's barking.

Chris eyed the dog and moved closer. "Could you put the dog inside so we can talk?"

The man nodded and dragged the still barking and lunging dog away. He returned a few minutes later. "Come around to the gate," he said, and gestured toward the front of the house.

At the gate, Chris showed his identification. The man introduced himself as Gerald Pierce. "We've had a report of an illegal ditch diverting water from the irrigation canal," Chris said.

Pierce frowned. "I'm not sure I understand," he said.

"I need to inspect the irrigation canal where it runs behind your property," Chris said.

Pierce's frown deepened, until his bushy eyebrows almost met in the middle. "There's no damage to the canal," he said.

"I need to inspect it," Chris said, keeping his voice and his expression firm.

Reluctantly, Pierce led him toward the back of the property. Chris had to admit what he found impressed him. He had expected a crude trench cutting into the Daimler Ditch to divert a stream of water. Instead, Pierce—or someone he had hired—had built a concrete-lined canal with a series of miniature locks to bring water up from the ditch to an area of the backyard enclosed by chain-link fencing. The fencing was lined with green shade cloth. Chris studied the structure. "This all must have taken you some time to build," he said.

Pierce straightened. "I was an engineer before I retired. I enjoy projects like this."

Chris nodded toward the enclosure. "What are you growing?" he asked, though he already had a good idea.

"It's all perfectly legal," Pierce said.

Chris walked over to the fence, which was only about five feet high, so he could clearly see inside. The roughly ten-square-feet space was crowded with a small forest of marijuana plants. Chris stopped counting when he reached twenty.

"It's not illegal to grow cannabis for personal use in this state," Pierce said.

"No, sir, but there is a limit of six plants per person or twelve per household."

"My son and his wife live with us, and we have medical licenses, which allow us to grow more. You'll see that the area is enclosed, not visible to neighbors or the street, and there's a lock on the gate."

Chris nodded. He'd taken required courses on the state's drug laws, and this was in line with what he remembered. He looked Pierce in the eye. "What do you need so much pot for?" he asked.

"My wife and I use it for medical purposes."

"There's enough here you could sell it."

"I don't. I might gift it to a friend occasionally, but we never sell it. That would be against the law."

Pierce might be worth taking a closer look at, but his pot crop wasn't why Chris was here, at least not directly. "You're going to have to find some other way to water your grow," he said. "The plants might not be illegal, but taking water from the irrigation ditch is." He delivered his routine lesson on why Pierce did not have rights to the water that ran by his house.

Pierce listened, growing more glum by the minute. "Is it possible for me to purchase a share of the water rights?" he asked.

"I'm afraid not," Chris said. "Most of them are passed down through families. Occasionally a share comes up for sale, but not often."

Pierce looked to his fancy system of locks and sighed. "I was really pleased with how the watering system turned out."

"You'll have to dismantle it," Chris said. "Right away. I'll come back tomorrow to check and if it's still operational, you can be fined seven hundred and fifty dollars a day."

Pierce nodded. "I understand."

Chris gave Pierce his card and let himself out the front gate. He was walking to his cruiser when his phone rang.

"Are you still out at Idlewilde?" Adelaide asked.

"Yes."

"We just got another Peeping Tom complaint from a woman there. Audrey Clements." Adelaide rattled off an address. "She says it happened earlier this morning and her husband finally convinced her she should call. You need to go by and take her statement."

Chapter Fifteen

The Clements residence was only a couple of streets over from the Pierces. Audrey Clements and her husband, Bruce, met Chris at the door of the Southwest-style adobe home. They were a trim, slight couple with matching short-cropped gray hair and the deep tans of people who had spent a lifetime outdoors. "I feel bad getting you all the way out here for what is probably nothing," Audrey said as she led the way into the living room.

"It's not nothing." Bruce put a hand on his wife's shoulder and addressed Chris. "Audrey is not the type of person who imagines things. She told me she saw a man looking in our bedroom window while she was undressing this morning and I believe her."

"Bruce ran outside but he didn't see anyone," Audrey said. "And it was very early. Still dark out. So maybe it was just a deer or some other animal."

"Some of Audrey's friends have been talking about a Peeping Tom in the neighborhood," Bruce said.

"Sally Coe said she heard a rumor that there was a man who was looking in windows," Audrey said. "But I just couldn't believe..." She spread her hands. "I'm sixty years old. What kind of thrill is someone getting looking at me?"

"Let's sit down and you can tell me what you saw." Chris motioned toward the sofa.

They sat, the Clementses side by side, his arm around her shoulder. "I had just pulled my nightshirt off, getting ready to take a shower," Audrey said. "I glanced toward the window. The weather is so nice, we've been sleeping with the window open. And there was, well, a shadow. A man-shaped shadow. I gasped and covered myself with the nightshirt and whoever it was ran away."

"Did you see his face?" Chris asked.

She shook her head. "He really did look like a shadow. I think he must have been wearing all black."

"How tall was he?"

She looked at her husband. "Not tall. Maybe Bruce's height."

"I'm five-eight," Bruce said.

"Was he fat or thin?" Chris asked.

"Just…average." She shrugged. "I'm sorry, but I really only caught a glimpse of him."

"Which direction did he head when he ran away?"

"West. Toward the backyard." She looked puzzled. "I would have thought he would head for the street."

"Have you had any other reports like this?" Bruce asked.

"We've had at least one other," Chris said. He stood. "If you think of anything else, call me." He handed Audrey his card. "And if the man comes back, call 911."

"Thank you." She shook her head. "I felt silly even calling you, but it is upsetting."

"I'm glad you called. The more information we have, the more likely we are to catch this person."

He returned to his cruiser, but didn't start it right away. He studied the Clements house, then pulled up a map of Idlewilde Estates on the computer unit in his cruiser. The Clementses lived on Lodgepole Lane. The woman who had made the previous complaint lived on Ash Drive. The park was flanked by Ash Drive and Cedar Court. Aspen Lane ran between Ash and Cedar.

And Adam Treadwell lived on Aspen. Adam Treadwell, who had been seen running from the park—running from the direction of Cedar—last Tuesday morning. The same morning the woman had called in a complaint about a Peeping Tom.

Chris started the cruiser. Time to have another conversation with Adam Treadwell.

WILLOW STOOD BACK, arms crossed as the locksmith finished installing the new lock on the office door. He inserted the key and turned it, tried the door, then opened it again and removed the key. "That should do you," he said, and handed Willow the key.

"Thank you." Willow pocketed the key and accepted his bill. She paid him and he left.

Darla entered as the locksmith left. "Who was that?" Darla asked. "What was he doing here?"

"That was a locksmith. I had him install locks on my bedroom door and on the door of my dad's office."

"Why did you do that?" Darla asked.

"To keep out people who don't have any business in those rooms."

Darla sniffed. "I hope you're not planning on continuing to live here after Sam's will is probated," she said.

"Why not?" Willow asked.

"Because half the ranch will belong to Emmet and he intends to sell. You'll have to sell, too. It's not as if you ever wanted to run the ranch, anyway. Your father knew that. It's one of the reasons he left half the property to Emmet."

"The ranch is in a conservation easement," Willow said.

Darla waved away this objection. "You can still sell it. Whoever buys it simply has to agree to keep it as a ranch. This place is a moneymaker, so it won't be hard to find a buyer."

"First, you have to prove your will is valid," Willow said.

"Are you accusing me of lying?" Darla asked.

"I guess the court will decide that."

"Your father would be very disappointed by your attitude," Darla said. "Then again, you often disappointed him. You could have been such a help to him. Instead, you insisted on moving away, only running home when you needed something from him." She sighed and shook her head. "Such a shame."

She left the room, leaving Willow to stare after her, angry tears stinging her eyes. Part of her realized Darla had been trying to make her angry. She told herself she shouldn't take the bait. But there was enough truth behind the words that they provoked real pain. Willow had disappointed her father—not because she'd wanted to hurt him, but because she could never be the person he'd wanted. The knowledge that he had never understood or accepted that had hurt, and now that he was gone, they would never have a chance to heal that old wound.

ADAM TREADWELL CLEARLY wasn't pleased to see Chris. "What do you want, Deputy?" Treadwell demanded when he answered Chris's knock on his door.

"I need to come in and ask you some more questions," Chris said.

"I'm busy right now."

Treadwell started to close the door, but Chris blocked the move. "If you don't want to talk to me now, we can go down to the station to do it."

Treadwell hesitated, then stepped back. "You can come in," he said. "But I can't give you much time."

They moved into the living room—aspen paneling, a large entertainment center, a bookcase with golf tournament trophies. "Is your wife home?" Chris asked.

"She's upstairs. There's no need to disturb her. What is this about?"

"We've had another report of a Peeping Tom in the neighborhood," Chris said.

Treadwell stiffened. "What does that have to do with me?"

"I thought as homeowners' association president, you'd want to know."

"There's nothing I can do about it," Treadwell said. "It's probably some kid playing a prank and the women are overreacting."

"I don't think this is a kid."

"It doesn't matter to me what you think. I really need to go. I'm going to be late for my appointment." He started to move toward the door again.

"What were you really doing in the park Tuesday morning?" Chris asked.

The question froze Treadwell in midstride. He turned to face Chris again. "I already told you—I was taking a walk."

"A walk past the Brecks' house on Ash Drive?"

Treadwell's face blanched. "I don't know what you're talking about."

"What about the Clementses' house on Lodgepole

Lane? The big adobe? Did you walk by there this morning? Did you stop and look in the window?"

"I don't like what you're implying," Treadwell said. "You need to leave now."

"Adam? Is something wrong?" A slight, blonde woman appeared in the doorway, concern edging her voice.

"It's nothing, Dot. Go back upstairs."

She turned to Chris. "What is it, Deputy?" Her face was pale, but her gaze was steady.

"It's nothing," Treadwell said again, more forcefully.

"Are you Mrs. Treadwell?" Chris asked.

"Yes."

"Were you aware there have been reports of a Peeping Tom in the area?" Chris asked.

She turned to her husband, expression stricken. "Adam, you promised!" she said. "You said it wouldn't happen again."

"Dot, I—" He reached for his wife, but she turned away.

"Mrs. Treadwell, has something like this happened before?" Chris asked.

She nodded. "In Ohio, where we used to live. The police promised not to press charges if Adam would go to counseling. And he did. I thought he had put that all behind him."

"I didn't do anything wrong!" Treadwell protested. "I was just out for a walk. I'm not responsible if people don't keep their shades drawn."

"Mr. Treadwell, I'm going to have to take you in for further questioning," Chris said.

"I'll contact our attorney," Dot said, and left the room without looking at her husband.

"Did you have to do that?" Adam asked, looking after her.

"A better question might be, did you have to?" Chris asked.

"I know your father," Treadwell said.

"A lot of people do."

"What would he think of you, harassing a respectable citizen?"

"I don't think peeping in windows is very respectable."

Treadwell swore at him. Chris moved away to call for backup, and an officer to take a statement from Mrs. Treadwell. They had one less suspect now for Sam Russell's murder, but Chris couldn't say he felt good about it.

"THAT DEPUTY IS BACK." Darla peered out the front window Tuesday afternoon, frowning. "Why does he keep hanging around here?"

"He's trying to find my father's murderer." Willow smoothed her hair and tried to ignore the flutter in her stomach at the thought of seeing Chris again.

"He hasn't found anything yet," Darla said. "And it's annoying having him around all the time."

"Then leave." She gave Darla a cool look.

"I need to get back to Albuquerque," Emmet said. "I'm running out of clothes."

"Hush," Darla said. "You can buy clothes in town."

Emmet rolled his eyes. "As if Eagle Mountain has anything resembling fashion."

There was a knock on the door and Willow hurried to answer it. "Hello, Deputy." She smiled at Chris. "What brings you here?"

"I wish I could say it's because I wanted to see

you—which is true—but I'm actually here on official business."

"Oh." Her smile faded and she stepped back. "Have you arrested someone?" she asked. "Did you find Von?"

"Not yet." He glanced toward the living room, where Darla and Emmet watched from the sofa. "Maybe we should talk in Sam's office."

"Don't keep secrets, Deputy," Darla said.

"Maybe you two should go into town and buy those clothes," Willow said. She led the way to her father's office and shut the door behind them.

"How's the search for help going?" Chris asked.

"I found someone," she said. "Or rather, a neighboring rancher, Darrell Williams, is loaning me one of his cowboys, for as long as I need him."

"That was good of him."

"Yes." She sank into the desk chair. "And it was a good reminder for me that my dad had more friends than he did enemies."

"I spoke to Bud Carstairs. He lives in Junction now, but he told me he didn't have any hard feelings about your dad, and I believe him."

She nodded. "Bud was always a good man. He was already having a hard time keeping up with the ranch work when his wife got sick. Dad hated that he sold the place to developers, but the sale gave Bud the money he needed to look after his wife before she died." She met his gaze. "Enough small talk. Why are you here?"

He unzipped his leather satchel and passed over a folded paper. "That's a warrant authorizing the sheriff's department to search all your father's papers and anything else in his office. We were waiting for someone from the Colorado Bureau of Investigation to help us with that, but they've been dragging their feet about sending someone, so the sheriff assigned me to do it."

"Oh." She unfolded the paper and stared at it, but the words there didn't really register. She wasn't surprised by the request, only by the enormity of the task. "There are reams of documents in here," she said. "It will take forever for you to go through them all."

"I'm hoping you'll volunteer to help me," he said. "You know what's here better than anyone, and you've already unearthed every break we've had so far. You found out about the feud your dad was having with Adam Treadwell, and that he had fired Von King."

"I don't know if those are breaks, or if they only muddy the waters," she said.

"Will you help?" he asked.

"Of course." She looked around. "Where do you want to start?"

"Do you have a copy of your dad's will?" he asked. "You've told me about it, but I'd like to see it."

"You could have asked your dad to show it to you."

"It's easier this way."

"All right." She opened the top left drawer and took out a legal-size envelope and passed it to him. "This is a copy of the will your father drew up for my father," she said. "I don't have a copy of the will Darla presented."

"Have you heard any more about that one?" He slid a sheaf of papers out of the envelope and scanned them.

"Ted says he's sent it to an expert who specializes in disputed documents."

"Hmm." Chris flipped through the pages of the will, briefly studying each one. After a few moments, he set the will aside. "I can't see how anyone but you benefits from this will," he said.

"Dad wasn't necessarily killed because of money,"

she said. "Maybe someone was angry with him. Von was angry because Dad fired him. Dad and Adam Treadwell argued about the irrigation ditch behind Idlewilde Estates."

"We don't think Treadwell killed your father," Chris said.

"Why not? Or are you allowed to say?"

"The story will probably be in the next issue of the paper. At the time your father was killed, Treadwell was skulking through the streets near his house, spying on women who were getting dressed."

She stared, mouth open. "He's a Peeping Tom?"

Chris nodded. "He confessed. He's been in trouble for this before, where he used to live. So that's one less suspect on our list."

"What about Von?" she asked.

"We've alerted every law enforcement office in the state and we're talking to everyone who had contact with him here, but no word yet."

"Who else is on your suspect list?" she asked.

"It's a long list," he said. "Other than Treadwell, we haven't ruled out anyone yet."

His words sent a shiver of fear through her. "Am I still a suspect?"

"You were closest to your father and you benefit from his will, so you're still on the list," he said. "But there are a lot of people ahead of you."

It wasn't exactly a declaration of his belief in her innocence, but for now it would have to do. She regarded the paper-strewn desk. "Where should we start?"

"Bank statements and the ledger," he said. "Let's see if Sam made any unusual payments in the weeks prior to his death."

"Do you think he was being blackmailed?"

"I'm not assuming anything," Chris said. "I'm just looking for anything that stands out as unusual."

For the next couple of hours, he sat on one side of the desk, she on the other, passing papers back and forth and discussing what they read. "I don't see anything unusual, financially." She sat back and stretched, arching her back to work out a cramp. "Just the usual receipts and payments."

Chris laid aside the ledger he'd been paging through. "Emmet said something when I was here yesterday. He said your dad didn't like banks and he kept most of his money hidden around the ranch."

She laughed. "Leave it to Emmet to latch onto that old rumor. But as you can see from all these bank statements, Dad had several accounts."

"Emmet was nosing around in the machine shed. He admitted he was looking for hidden cash."

"Do you think that's significant?" she asked.

He shrugged. "It might be a motive for someone to kill Sam—they heard he had a lot of money hidden and they decided to steal it."

"How horrible if that was what happened," she said. "It's terrible enough that he was murdered, but to have died because of a lie..." She stared past him, blinking back tears, weariness settling like a heavy cloak around her shoulders.

Chris's chair squeaked as he stood. "I could use some fresh air," he said. "How about you?"

She nodded, and stood and followed him out of the office, taking care to lock the door behind her. The hallway and living room was empty, though they could hear Darla's muffled voice somewhere in the back of the house. "Let's slip out before she sees us," Willow said.

"Do you want to talk a walk?" Chris asked.

"I've got a better idea," she said. "Do you ride?"

"I'm no expert, but I can stay in the saddle."

"Then let's go for a ride. It will give you a chance to see more of the ranch." And the opportunity for the two of them to do something together that didn't involve hunting a killer.

Chapter Sixteen

Chris managed to saddle and mount the horse Willow chose for him—a bay gelding named Paco—without embarrassing himself. Most of his previous experience with horses involved a few weeks at summer camp as a preteen. Willow, on a pinto named Pete, looked at home in the saddle. "I guess you grew up with horses," Chris said as she led the way up a hill behind the horse barns.

"Yes. Riding was definitely one of the things I missed when I moved away." They crested the hill and turned onto a well-worn path that cut across a stubbled field. "I had a crew in to cut hay here over the weekend," she said.

"So you're doing okay, running the ranch by yourself," he said.

"I wouldn't have remembered the hay if Von hadn't said something about it, but his comment is what prodded me to look at Dad's records. I'm getting a feel for what needs to be done."

"Are you still planning to hire someone to manage the ranch for you?"

"If Emmet inherits half, he wants to sell," she said. "I don't have the money to buy him out, so I'd have to sell, too. Which is probably for the best. As hard as my father tried to instill in me a love for the land and the work, it just didn't take. I loved him. I see the beauty of this place, but it's not how I want to spend my life."

"How do you want to spend your life?" It seemed an idle question, a way to keep the conversation going, but as he waited for her answer, he realized how much he cared about what she might say. Was she going to tell him that she longed to be far away from this place and this life—and him?

"I love teaching," she said. "I got into cultural anthropology because I thought I wanted to be a researcher, but I discovered what I really loved was sharing my knowledge with students and interacting with them."

"Could you teach another subject?" he asked. "If you couldn't find a position with a cultural anthropology department?"

"Sure. But I'm really overqualified for most teaching positions. I might look that direction if I keep getting turned down by the universities I've applied to. Maybe junior college, or even high school…" She shrugged. "I'm telling myself I don't have to worry about it until after the will is probated. Ted says with a contested estate, that could take months."

"As if you didn't have enough stress already," Chris said.

"This is how I de-stress," she said, and nudged her horse into a faster walk.

Paco followed Pete across the hayfield, and for the next ten minutes Chris focused on trailing Willow across the field, through a gate and around another rocky hill. He enjoyed the sight of her curvy figure in the saddle, her long braid flowing behind her. He felt free to admire her without being accused of staring.

They drew up short by a low log cabin, half the roof missing. The structure huddled against a rock outcropping, a short distance from a water tank where a windmill creaked in a faint breeze. "We'll water the horses here," Willow said, swinging out of the saddle.

"What is this place?" Chris asked as he led Paco to the tank.

"I think my great-uncle lived here for a while—my grandmother's younger brother, Ralph. After he died, my dad used it during roundups, sometimes. Then the roof caved in and now it's just another old building on the ranch. There are several—mostly built when my great-grandfather was first settling the place, some before that." She turned to study the cabin while the horses drank. "They're too primitive for anyone to live in—uninsulated, some with broken windows or gaps between logs, or even dirt floors. But they're part of the history of this place."

"I see places like this sometimes when I'm hiking in the mountains," Chris said. He moved to stand closer to her, their shoulders almost touching. The breeze blew the tendrils of hair that had escaped from her long braid, and he caught the floral scent of her shampoo, soft and feminine. "Places where people once lived, in such remote locations."

"It was a very different life," she said. "My great-grandmother talked about only going to town every six months. After she married my great-grandfather and moved here, she didn't see her mother for ten years."

"That would be hard," Chris said.

"Yes. Then again, when Dad and I couldn't see eye to eye about something, I would think maybe a few years apart might improve things between us." She glanced at him. "And you know I don't mean that, right? Especially now that he's gone. Now I'd give anything to argue with him again." She looked away, but not before he saw the glimmer of tears in her eyes.

"I know what you mean," he said. "Sometimes I feel that way about my dad, too."

"I keep forgetting that Ted is your father. The two of you don't seem that much alike."

"That's because we're not." He turned to watch the horses, who were cropping grass around the water tank. "I went to law school partly because I knew it was what he wanted. But when I discovered how much I hated working in a law office and went into law enforcement instead, he wouldn't even try to understand. He thinks I'm throwing my life away."

"My dad had a version of that song, too." Her hand rested on his back, warm and reassuring. Intimate.

"He's insisting I come to dinner Wednesday night," he said. "He's invited someone who works for the Colorado Attorney General's Office. Dad is hoping I'll make a good impression and this guy will hire me. It's as if he hasn't heard me the dozen times I've said I'm not interested."

"My dad used to fix me up with the sons of all his ranching friends," Willow said. "I was supposed to marry one of them, settle down and have a few children, who could then inherit both places and build a ranching empire. He accused me of deliberately being a snob when I couldn't manage to fall in love with any of them."

He turned toward her. "You win. Being fixed up with potential spouses is worse than being forced to interview over dinner for a job you don't want."

She laughed. "They were all perfectly nice young men, but they all saw me the way my dad saw me—a potential rancher's wife. The loyal helpmate with no ambitions of her own. Mind you, the rancher's wives I know aren't like that. But my dad and those young men thought they were. And that wasn't me."

"I get it," he said. "You want someone who sees you as you are and accepts that." He thought of Emmet and his complaint that Willow was too smart-mouthed. "Come to dinner with me Wednesday," he said. "Having you there will make it easier for me to avoid saying something to my dad that I shouldn't."

She laughed. "Now, that's an invitation I can hardly pass up."

He laughed, too. "Okay, not the suavest move on my part, but will you come to dinner, anyway? If you don't think it's too awkward, dining with your father's lawyer."

"I'd love to have dinner with you," she said. "And your father."

"You've made me so happy I could kiss you."

Her eyes met his, dark and mesmerizingly beautiful. "Then why don't you?" she asked.

He wasn't going to pass up an invitation like that, so he pulled her to him and kissed her, gently at first, then, when she curved her fingers around the back of his neck and arched her body to his, with more intensity. He had been wanting this almost from their first meeting, always holding himself back, unsure of her feelings for him.

But apparently, she had been wanting this, too. She kissed him with the ardor of a lover, her enjoyment of the interlude adding to his own pleasure. He reveled in the feel of her body against his, in the taste of her and the satin texture of her lips.

When at last they parted, a little breathless, she smiled. "That was nice," she said.

It had been much more than nice, but all he said—all he could manage, really—was a dazed smile of his own and "Yeah."

She smoothed her hand down his arm and twined her fingers with his. "We should get back to the house. Darla and Emmet are probably trying to pick the lock on the office door or climb in the window or something."

"Or Emmet will be pulling up floorboards, searching for Sam's hidden stash of cash." He went along with her teasing tone, though his mind was still partly on all the things he would like to do if only the two of them had the house to themselves.

"I didn't tell you, but I caught him in the barn loft this morning," she said. "He had actually pried up a loose board. I guess he was looking for Dad's hidden money, though I didn't realize it at the time."

Chris glanced over at the dilapidated cabin. "I guess if you want this place torn down, you could hint that the money is here and he'd take it apart for you."

"That's too much work for Emmet. He rarely does anything unless Darla prods him. I wouldn't be surprised to learn she's behind the money hunt, too."

"Does she have a job?" Chris asked.

"When she and Dad met, she was a receptionist for a truck dealership in Junction. I'm not sure what she's done since then, but I think she has plans to live off the proceeds from the sale of this ranch." She pulled herself up into the saddle and turned her horse to face him. "I guess that gives her a motive for killing Dad, but honestly, I can't see it. Darla is whiny and selfish, but she's not...brutal. And what happened to Dad was brutal."

"Yeah." Chris mounted and maneuvered alongside her. So much for thinking this murder wouldn't intrude on their moment of closeness. "I want to find Sam's killer," he said. "Because it's the right thing to do, and because I want you to have that peace."

"I wouldn't have kissed you if I didn't know that," she said. Then she turned her horse and rode away, leaving him to try to keep up.

WILLOW HAD TO suppress the impulse to gallop the horse all the way back to the house. For once she hadn't sabotaged herself with second-guessing and had been honest with a man about what she wanted—and it had felt so good.

That good feeling carried over as they unsaddled, groomed and fed the horses. But some of her exhilaration faded as they approached the house. "Darla's car is gone," she said, and hurried inside.

Chris caught up with her in the hallway. "Is something wrong?" he asked.

She didn't answer right away, having spotted a note tacked to the office door. "We've gone back to Albuquerque for a couple of days to attend to business," the note read in Darla's neat printing. "Back soon."

"You don't look very happy about this," Chris said, after reading the note over her shoulder.

"Oh, I'm thrilled they're gone." She moved past him toward the living room. "I'm just remembering what happened when she and my dad split up."

She stopped in the middle of the living room and looked around for anything out of place.

"What happened then?" Chris prompted.

"I was visiting at the time," she said. "I knew things were tense, but when I came down for breakfast that morning, my dad was in the kitchen by himself. He told me Darla and Emmet had left. I thought it was for the best, but of course I didn't say so. But then I noticed my mother's fruit bowl was gone." She turned to Chris, the pain of that memory still sharp. "It was a hand-painted pottery bowl my mother purchased on their honeymoon in San Francisco. She kept fruit in it, and Darla had always admired it. And then it was gone."

"You think she took it," Chris said.

"I'm sure she took it," Willow said. "Along with a blown-glass bluebird that always sat in the windowsill, and a crystal-and-gold anniversary clock that had belonged to my grandmother. All of my mother's most beautiful things were gone. My dad said it didn't matter, but it mattered to me." The sensation of being back in that moment three years ago, the hurt of having those treasured items—those memories—taken still stung.

Chris squeezed her shoulder. "I'm sorry you had to go through that," he said.

She nodded and pulled herself together to continue taking inventory of the items in the room. "Is anything missing?" Chris asked.

At that moment, she spotted the empty space on the table beside her father's chair. "There was a globe there," she said, pointing. "It was about the size of a cantaloupe and all the countries were cut from semi-precious stones." She cupped her hands, demonstrating. "I gave it to Dad for Father's Day last year. He really liked it."

"I remember seeing it," Chris said. "Do you think Darla took it?"

"Oh, I know she did. It's her way of asserting her claim."

"Will she bring it back?" he asked.

"No, but it doesn't matter." She shrugged. "The globe belonged to my dad, but I didn't associate it with him the way those other items she took represented my mom. It's not as if she took his watch or his rodeo belt buckle. Those are safe because they're locked in my room."

"You could press charges for the theft of the globe," he said. "And anything else you find missing."

"No. I'll wait and see what she has to say about it when she comes back."

"Do you really think they'll be back?"

"As long as she believes she has a chance at half the ranch, she'll be back."

He moved to stand facing her. "I don't think it's safe for you to stay here by yourself," he said.

"Until you find Dad's killer, I'm not crazy about the idea, either," she said. "But I don't have a choice. A ranch isn't something you can walk away from anytime you like."

"I think until we do find your father's murderer, I should stay here with you," he said. He moved closer, focusing her attention on his solid bulk, the reassuring breadth of his shoulders and the weapon at his side. Chris definitely made her feel safe.

"Are we talking in an official capacity?" she asked.

"Unofficial. Though I'll have to let the sheriff know. But he didn't object when I ran the idea past him."

"You actually talked to him about it?" She was torn between embarrassment and exhilaration.

"I'm determined to keep you safe."

She opened her mouth to tell him she was a strong, intelligent woman who was capable of looking after herself. But Chris had never suggested she wasn't those things. "Thank you," she said. "I would feel better having you here."

"I keep an overnight bag in the car in case of emergency," he said. "Just show me where to stash it."

She moved in. "I think you should put it in my room." Then she kissed him, and his response let her know he thought that was a very good idea indeed.

Chapter Seventeen

Chris followed Willow to her bedroom, moving by instinct, every sense focused on her: on the curve of her bottom in the faded blue jeans, the scent of her hair when he leaned closer, the softness of her hand in his.

She unlocked the door and led the way inside, and he glanced around, registering that the room was that of a teenager who had left home years before with no intention of remaining. There was a white iron double bed with a pale blue duvet, a single straight chair by the door, a student desk and a bulletin board, which was empty but bore the faint outlines of what must have been pictures and invitations and other souvenirs of high school.

Then Willow locked the door and moved into his arms, and their surroundings receded, no longer important. "Are you still on duty?" she asked, one hand resting just below his shoulder-mounted radio.

"Not for the last hour." He unclipped the radio, then unfastened the Sam Browne belt at his waist and laid them on the chair by the door.

"That's a good start." She undid the top button of his uniform shirt and brushed her fingers across the ballistics vest beneath. "So many layers," she said. "Like unwrapping a present."

He remained still as she unfastened each button, one by one, then pushed the shirt off his shoulders. She stood on tiptoe and kissed the top of his shoulder, then traced her tongue along the collarbone, sending shockwaves of sensation through him.

When she tilted her head and smiled up at him, a teasing light in her eyes, he could wait no longer, and ripped open the fastenings at the side of the vest, then tossed it aside.

"Yes, please," she said, and slid her hands up his chest. He pulled her close and kissed her hard, until they were both breathless. Then he walked her backward to the bed and they collapsed together on the soft duvet.

She traced the indentations the vest had made on his skin. "This doesn't look very comfortable," she said.

"You get used to it." He smoothed his hand down her hip. "And speaking of protection…do you have any?"

She laughed. "That was a smooth segue. And yes, I do."

This brought a host of other questions to mind—had she stocked up because of him, or was it her habit to always be prepared? But then she began unbuttoning her blouse and those thoughts fled.

They didn't say much after that, as they finished undressing and began the tantalizing pleasure of exploring each other's bodies. She communicated all he needed to know with a lifting of one eyebrow, a shift of her hips, a sigh or moan or shake of her head. He liked that she wasn't shy about letting him know what she liked and that she was bold in trying things he might like—which he did.

He reined in his own urgency, and let her set the pace, desire building. When at last he rolled on the condom and entered her, they were both trembling with need, and it took only a few seconds before they found a rhythm that satisfied them both.

She opened her eyes and held his gaze as they moved together, and he lost himself in that gaze, physical and emotional sensations melding. He felt closer to Willow in this moment than he ever had to any woman, vulnerable, but not afraid. He watched her climax overtake her and gave himself over to the pleasure that crashed through him, until at last they lay spent.

She moved to his side, her head nestled on his shoulder. He felt her lips curve against him. "Are you smiling?" he asked.

"I'm smiling," she said. "Aren't you?"

"I am." As long as he was with Willow, he might not stop, no matter what this case threw at them.

WILLOW WOKE WITH the pale light of dawn shining around the edges of the blinds, and the sensation she wasn't alone. She rolled over to look at Chris, who was asleep on his back, the sheet pushed down to his waist, and she allowed herself the luxury of straight-up ogling him. He was a gorgeous man and she was lucky enough to have him in her bed.

Of course, he was lucky, too, and she credited him as being smart enough to know it. Other men—usually ones she turned down when they propositioned her—had accused her of being too picky. But Willow didn't believe in settling. She wanted the best and Chris Delray was the best man she had met in a long time—maybe ever.

He opened his eyes, and the glint of amusement in them told her he had been awake for a while. "Are you just going to stare, or are you going to move a little closer?" he asked.

She moved closer. In fact, she slid on top of him, straddling his hips, his arousal firm against her.

"That's more like it," he said, and slid his hands up to cup her breasts, then stroked his thumbs across her nipples, sending sensation lancing through her. She pressed against him, rocking gently, unable to keep still as his mouth closed over one nipple. She felt the pull all the way to her toes, and closed her eyes to savor the sensation.

Then he flipped her over, rolling her to her side as if they were wrestling. She laughed and smiled up at him as he now loomed over her. "Is that all right?" he asked.

That he had asked made it more than all right. "It's perfect," she said, and wrapped her legs around his hips.

He blew out a breath. "Give me a second," he said, and leaned over to retrieve a condom from the nightstand.

She didn't think she would ever get tired of watching him—the play of muscle beneath his skin, the dimple that formed at one corner of his mouth when he grinned, the glazed look of his eyes as desire overtook him. He was gorgeous, and even better, he made her feel gorgeous.

They took their time, drawing out the moments, lingering over kisses and caresses. Laughter seasoned the lust, and the joy of being with him made every sensation more intense, until by the time her climax shuddered through her she wanted to shout with happiness—so she did. He followed with a roar of his own, and then they both dissolved in giggles, giddy with their delight in each other.

Afterward, they lay together, talking about getting up, but not actually moving. "What do you have to do today?" she asked, after his fourth declaration that he really should get up.

"Unless I get called away, I thought we should spend the day going over your father's paperwork."

"What a thrill," she said.

"It's boring, but necessary." He rose up on one elbow to look down at her. "Are you up for it?"

She nodded. "I want to find who did this—whether it's Von, or someone else."

"Me, too," he said. He caressed her cheek. "And this evening is dinner with my folks. Are you still up for that?"

"I am." Not that she wouldn't rather stay here with him—in this bed—all day and all night. But relationships were about more than sex—or at least, for her they were.

He kissed her. "Thanks," he said. "For everything."

"Oh, don't think I'm not going to make you pay." She snuggled closer, enjoying the sensation of skin on skin. "You might be losing a lot of sleep in the nights to come."

"Is that a promise?" He grinned, a wicked look that made her stomach somersault, and then his lips and hands were on her again, and she forgot all about who might be getting the better bargain.

CHRIS HAD TEXTED his mother early in the day to let her know he was bringing a friend to dinner, but her obvious pleasure at seeing Willow that evening made him cringe inwardly. "I'm so pleased to meet you," she said. "You must be very special, for Chris to bring you to meet us."

And what was Chris supposed to say to that? That

Willow wasn't special? Or that he'd mainly brought her to serve as a buffer against his father's demands?

Thankfully, Willow responded graciously. She complimented the house and remarked on the weather and steered his mom away from asking anything too personal.

Chris's mom took Willow's hand and pulled her into the family room, where Chris's dad stood with a stocky man with a thick head of white hair. A striking woman with a blond pageboy cut sat on the sofa.

"Chris, come meet David Vandermeyer," his father said. He turned to the white-haired man next to him. "David, this is my son, Chris. Top third of his class at University of Denver's law program."

Chris shook Vandermeyer's hand. "I'm a deputy with the Rayford County Sheriff's Department now," he said, pretending not to notice his father's frown.

"That must be interesting work," Vandermeyer said.

"I think so," Chris said.

"As I was telling you, Chris's specialty is Colorado water law," Ted said. "That's why the sheriff's department hired him and it's given him the kind of real-world experience that will be invaluable when he returns to law."

Time to change the subject, Chris thought. "What brings you to Rayford County?" he asked Vandermeyer.

For the next few minutes, they enjoyed a pleasant discussion about the Vandermeyers' second home in Idlewilde Estates, then Chris's mom summoned them all to dinner. Mrs. Vandermeyer—Marta—was seated next to Chris, while her husband sat across the table beside Willow.

"I wasn't aware you and Chris knew each other, Willow," Ted said after they had all helped themselves to roast pork.

"We met recently," Willow said.

Silence while everyone considered this. Chris had the feeling everyone was avoiding saying anything about Willow's murdered father.

Vandermeyer broke the awkwardness with what to Chris was an even more awkward topic. "Your father tells me you're interested in applying for an opening we have at the Colorado Attorney General's Office," Vandermeyer said. "I'd be happy to arrange an interview."

"Thank you," Chris said. "But Dad must have misunderstood. I'm very happy with the sheriff's department."

"I think you owe it to yourself to consider this new opportunity," Ted said. His tone was light, but the tight lines around his mouth betrayed his agitation. "You should be making better use of your degree and training."

Chris ignored his father. "I hope you find the right person for the job," he said.

"Did I overhear you say you have a home in Idlewilde Estates?" Willow asked.

"Yes," Vandermeyer said. "We purchased it about four months ago."

"We fell in love with the area," Marta said. "It's exactly the kind of neighborhood we were looking for."

"I know the family who used to own that land," Willow said. "I often played there as a child. You have some lovely views from there."

"That was one of the things that sold us on the place," Marta said.

The conversation segued to more mundane topics, and for the rest of the meal no one mentioned Chris's job prospects. After dessert and coffee the Vandermeyers said their goodbyes. David handed Chris a business card. "In case you change your mind about that interview," he said. "We could use someone like you."

When the Vandermeyers were gone, Ted turned to Chris, his jaw tight, shoulders stiff. "It wouldn't kill you to go to an interview," he said.

"An interview would be a waste of time for both of us," Chris said.

"This kind of opportunity doesn't come along every day," Ted said.

"I'm not looking for another opportunity," Chris said.

"Your education is wasted where you are now," Ted said.

"I don't agree," Chris said, his anger rising.

"I'm very disappointed in your attitude."

"Then you're going to have to learn from your disappointment. I intend to stay in law enforcement."

He was aware of Willow and his mother watching this exchange. Now his mother spoke up. "Maybe you'll be sheriff someday."

This wasn't about being sheriff or having a powerful position or making a great deal of money. But if he tried to point that out to his parents, would they believe him? Could they conceive of a success that had nothing to do with those things? "I'm doing work I find satisfying, that makes a difference, that I think is important," he said. "I'm sorry if that isn't enough for you."

His father's jaw tightened, as if he was clenching his teeth, but he said nothing. Chris turned to Willow. "I think we'd better go."

She thanked his parents for the meal and they said their goodbyes. They drove back to the ranch in silence, a full moon bathing the passing landscape in a silvery light. When he turned his truck onto the road to the ranch, Willow spoke. "When I told my father I was going away to school to study anthropology, he told me I was wasting my time," she said. "He wasn't a fan of higher education, but he said if I had to go to college, I should study something practical, like business."

"I guess parents have visions of what their children's lives should look like," Chris said. "When reality doesn't match that vision, they fight it."

"Dad never stopped fighting it," she said. "When I came home he offered to teach me to manage the ranch for him. I told him thank you but I wasn't interested. I know that hurt him." She sighed. "And then he was killed and I've had to learn, anyway."

"But it's not something you want to keep doing," he said, a knot in his stomach from the knowledge that went with it—that doing what she wanted, what she was trained for, meant leaving here. People had long-distance relationships all the time, he told himself. But the thought brought little comfort.

"I'll find something that fits," she said. "The way you've found your fit." She reached over and took his hand. They drove the rest of the way home like that, hands clasped, the silence between them warm and comforting, like a blanket wrapped around both of them. *I'm not going to let her get away*, he thought. No matter what happened, he was going to find a way to build on what had started between them.

Back at the ranch, he helped Willow make the rounds to check on the horses, then went around the house, making sure all the doors and windows were secure. "When I was growing up, we never locked the doors," she said. "But I guess even in the country, times change."

"I don't think anyone would try to break in, especially with my cruiser parked out front," he said. "But it's smart to be safe."

She moved into his arms and they began kissing, when hard pounding on the door startled them. "Open up!" a man's voice shouted. "I need help!"

Chapter Eighteen

Chris moved to the door and flipped the switch for the porch light, then checked the security peep and frowned. "It's Trey Allerton," he said.

The door vibrated with the force of Trey's knock. "Open up!" he shouted.

Chris unlocked the door and opened it a few inches. Willow moved in close to look around him. She remembered Trey as handsome and cocky, a man who coasted through life on charm and looks. Tonight, deep shadows beneath his eyes detracted from his looks, and his easygoing charm had vanished, replaced by edgy tension. "Where is Von?" he demanded.

Willow stepped up beside Chris. "Von is gone," she said. "I fired him."

Trey shook his head. "He didn't go far," he said. "He was at my place not half an hour ago. He took another shot at me and this time he almost got me."

"You'd better come in." Chris held the door open wider.

Trey hurried inside, and glanced around. "You're sure Von isn't here?"

"He isn't here." Willow felt sorry for Trey. He looked so shaken.

"Sit down and tell me everything that happened."

Chris led Trey into the living room and urged him to sit on the couch. Chris sat next to him and Willow moved into the chair opposite.

"I was in the trailer with Courtney and Ashlyn," Trey said. "We'd just had dinner when we heard a truck pull up in the driveway. I looked out and saw Von's truck. I told Courtney I didn't want to talk to him, that we would just ignore him. Then he laid on the horn. He yelled that he knew I was in there and if I didn't come out, he'd set the place on fire. I was worried he was wild enough to do it, so I went to the door. I had my phone in my hand and told him I was going to call the sheriff if he didn't leave. Von ought to know I don't have cell service out there, but he either forgot or he didn't care. He pulled out a pistol and would have killed me if I hadn't dived back into the house. Then he got back in his truck and peeled out of there. I thought for sure he was headed here."

"What were you going to do if you found him?" Chris asked.

Trey looked away, mute.

"Are you carrying a gun?" Chris asked.

"I've got a right to defend myself," Trey said.

"Von left here four days ago," Chris said. "If you have any idea where he might be living now, you need to tell us."

"The thing you need to know about Von is that he isn't right in the head," Trey said. "I mean, he believes things that aren't true, like conspiracy theories and stuff. And he lies about everything. Not to mention, he's mean as snakes. He told me stuff he learned how to do in prison—ways to kill people and stuff. I thought he was just trying to impress me, but maybe he really wanted to scare me."

"So where do you think he's hiding?" Chris asked. "Did he ever mention any place to you?"

Trey shook his head. "If I knew, I'd tell you. But I'm saying when you do find him, he's going to lie to you. He'll probably tell you I killed Sam Russell." He didn't look at Willow, but kept his eyes fixed on Chris.

"Why would he say that?" Chris asked.

"Because I think he killed Sam and he knows if you catch him, he'll have to go to prison for the rest of his life. So he wants to blame me."

"Did you kill Sam?" Chris asked. "Or did you help Von do it?"

"No! I liked Sam. He was helping me. I wouldn't kill him."

"Why do you think Von killed him?" Chris asked.

"He said Sam had a lot of cash hidden around the place," Trey said. "Like, hundreds of thousands of dollars. Von wanted that money."

"You could probably use that money, too," Chris said.

"Who couldn't? But I told him that idea was bananas. You don't get the kind of wealth Sam had by sticking your money in a hole in the ground."

"Did Von tell you he was going to kill Sam?" Chris asked.

"No. But he was talking about the money and it's the kind of thing I think he would do."

"Why do you think Von shot at you?" Chris asked.

"Because he's psycho. Or maybe because he knew I heard him talking about wanting to get his hands on the money Sam had hidden." His gaze darted around him, wary. "Which means I could be in even more danger if he finds out I spoke to you."

"You need to report this to the sheriff," Chris said.

"You're a sheriff's deputy, and I'm reporting it to you."

"I'll call this in, but you'll need to come into the station and make a formal statement."

"I'm making my statement to you. I just want you to find Von and stop him. And remember, he's dangerous, and he's definitely armed. That's against the law, isn't it? For a convicted felon to have a firearm?"

"If he has one, yes."

"I know he has one. He shot at me." Trey licked his lips. "When you do find him, you need to call in a SWAT team or something. Take him out before he kills you."

"Are you sure you don't know where Von might be?" Willow spoke up for the first time since Trey's arrival. "Maybe he mentioned a friend in the area?"

"I don't know anything, I swear." Trey took another step back. "I better go. I don't like leaving Courtney alone this long with a maniac like Von running loose." He turned and dashed out the door to his truck, then sped out of the drive.

Chris and Willow watched from the window until the plume of dust marking Trey's route disappeared. "I don't understand him," Willow said. "Whenever he would come here before, to talk to my dad, he always bragged about his time in the army, like he was trying to impress Dad with how tough he was. Now he's practically hysterical about Von."

"Having someone try to kill you would frighten most people," Chris said.

"Yes, but this goes beyond fear. He seemed almost as worried about what Von might say about him as he was about Von shooting him."

"Sometimes the people who talk the most about their bravery are the first to fall apart under pressure," Chris said.

"Maybe you're right." She turned from the window. "What are you going to do?"

"I need to call this in. I could use the radio, but I'd rather use your phone."

"Of course." She moved away and he went into the kitchen and dialed Travis's number.

Travis answered with his usual greeting. "What's happened?"

"I'm at the Russell ranch. Trey Allerton just showed up here practically hysterical. He claims Von King took another shot at him, and this time he almost didn't miss." He related all the details. "Allerton thinks we should bring in a SWAT team and stop Von before he kills one of us."

"Huh," Travis said. "Did Allerton have any idea of where to find Von?"

"He says no. And he refused to come into the station to give us a formal statement."

"Any sign of Von around the ranch?" Travis asked. "Any more trouble there?"

"No. Darla and Emmet went back to Albuquerque, so I'm sticking close to keep an eye on things."

"Uh-huh. Well, you look after Willow." He ended the call before Chris could say anything else. Chris replaced the phone receiver in the cradle. The sheriff was hard to read. He ran a tight department, with a culture of discipline and training. But he was also married to a woman he had once helped to convict—falsely, as it turned out—of murder. So the idea of one of his deputies being involved with someone close to a murder investigation wasn't foreign to him.

Willow entered the kitchen. "What did the sheriff say?" she asked.

"The sheriff is a man of few words," Chris said. "I

told him I was staying here to keep an eye on things, and he seemed to agree that was a good idea."

Willow looked amused. "Well, as long as he agrees." She filled a kettle. "I'm going to make a cup of cocoa. Do you want some?"

He moved in behind her and wrapped his arms around her. "That sounds good."

He set out cups while she heated milk and made the cocoa. Then they carried their mugs into the living room and curled up together on the sofa. It was a domestic, homey scene that filled him with contentment, in spite of his lingering concern over Allerton's visit.

"I'm still thinking about Trey's visit—and about Von," Willow said, as if channeling his thoughts.

"Me, too," Chris admitted.

She leaned her head back to look up at him. "What was Von in prison for? Can you tell me?"

"Burglary. Theft. Some assaults. He served five years of a seven-year sentence."

"Maybe someone with that kind of history would kill a man to get to a lot of money he thought the man had hidden," she said. "And since Von never found the money, will he come back to try to get it?"

"I thought you said there isn't any money," Chris said.

"There isn't. But apparently Von doesn't believe that. And I can't shake the image of all those things he'd taken from my dad piled up in his closet—little bits of my father's life that Von stole. Maybe that wasn't enough for him. Maybe he wanted it all."

"He might come back," Chris said. "Or he might never have left."

She looked startled. "What do you mean?"

He leaned forward to set his half-empty mug on the

coffee table. "I've been thinking about those old cabins you said were on the ranch. How many of them are there?"

"There's the one I showed you," she said. "And two others."

"Are any of them habitable?"

She frowned. "As in 'move in and spend the next few months'—no. But as a temporary hideout—maybe. You saw the one I showed you—it's pretty wrecked and clearly no one was there when we were. The second one is in even worse shape, more of a ruin than a cabin at this point. But the third…the third is fairly intact. But it's really remote. I mean, you couldn't get there in a vehicle. You'd have to ride a horse or walk."

"I think we need to check it out," he said.

"Now?" She looked alarmed.

"Not now. And not alone. We need backup." He stood and went to the phone. This time it took the sheriff longer to answer. "Willow and I have been talking," Chris said. "There are three abandoned cabins on the ranch. Two of them are in pretty bad shape, but she says the third one is solid. I think Von might be hiding out there. It's worth checking out."

"Good idea," Travis said. "Where is it?"

"Willow says it's pretty remote—not accessible in a vehicle. We'd need horses. And backup."

"Not something to do in the dark if we don't have to," Travis said. "We'll go in the morning. I'll meet you at five thirty. Does Willow have horses we can use or do I bring my own?" Travis's family owned a large ranch above town.

Chris looked at Willow. "Do you have horses the sheriff can use?"

"Of course."

"See you in the morning," Travis said, and hung up.

"What do we do now?" Willow asked.

He pulled her into his arms and kissed the side of her neck. "We'll just have to find some way to pass the time," he said.

She slid her arms around his neck and arched her body to his. "Maybe we can think of something," she said, and kissed him, long and deep, and he thought that waiting might never be easier.

WILLOW WOKE TO pitch dark and the smell of smoke. She fumbled one hand from beneath the covers and groped on the bedside table for the clock, turning it to face her. Twenty minutes after four in the morning.

She sat up, moving carefully to avoid waking Chris, and tiptoed to the bathroom. When she returned to her room, the smell of smoke hit her again, like wood and burning leaves. The odor penetrated the fog of sleep and sent a stab of fear through her. She hurried to the open window and peered out.

At first, she saw nothing, then a faint glow in the distance drew her attention.

"Chris!" she shouted.

He was out of bed and by her side faster than she would have thought possible. He grasped her arm. "What is it?"

Her throat closed around the horrible words, but she forced them out: "I think the barn is on fire."

Chapter Nineteen

Willow turned and began pulling on clothes, still buttoning her shirt as she ran from the room. She stopped in the kitchen to grab the phone and dial 911, but no one answered. The call didn't even go through. She started to try again, then realized the phone was dead.

Panic swelling to fill her chest and clog her throat, she ran toward the back door, where she shoved her feet into muck boots. She had her hand on the doorknob when Chris jerked her back. "Whoever set the fire and cut the phone lines might be out there," he said.

"I'm not going to let the horses burn," she said, and jerked away from him.

"Go out through the garage," he said. "If someone is watching the house, they might not expect that."

"By 'someone,' you mean Von." She turned toward the garage. "Can you call for help on your radio?" she asked.

He was already keying the microphone. "Dispatch, this is Deputy Chris Delray, reporting a fire in progress at the Russell ranch." He rattled off the address. A woman's voice answered, but it was so distorted by static Willow couldn't make out the words.

"Dispatch, do you copy?" Chris asked.

Another burst of static.

Chris released the mic. "I'll try again in a minute. I need to help you with the horses."

She wanted to race to the barn, to throw open the door and start driving the animals from their stalls, but Chris made her wait. He checked that the coast was clear, then persuaded her she needed to move slowly, sticking to the deepest shadows near outbuildings or trees.

When they reached the barn itself, however, she could hold back no longer. The far end—the section that held equipment and hay, but no animals, was already ablaze. She tried to shove open the big main door, but it refused to budge. Inside, one of the horses whinnied, and another kicked hard at the wall.

Chris helped her wrench open the smaller door on the side of the barn. Willow ran along the center aisle, opening each stall door as she went. Smoke swirled around her, making it difficult to see and more difficult to breathe. "You have to get the main door open!" she shouted over her shoulder.

Chris moved to the main door and shoved hard, but it refused to move, not even when Willow threw her weight behind his. "We'll have to take the horses out through the main door," he said.

She looked down the aisle between the horse stalls. The animals were already panicking, and they would fight going through the narrow entry. But they didn't have a choice. She rushed to the first stall and grabbed the halter of its occupant, Pete, and led him out of the stall. Eyes rolling, clearly frightened, he came with her to the door, where he balked.

"Come on, Pete," she pleaded, and reached to open the door, which had somehow closed behind them. The doorknob turned, but the door itself wouldn't budge.

She let go of the horse and threw herself at the door, but it remained fixed.

Then Chris was beside her, adding his strength to hers as they tried to force the door.

"I think it's barricaded from the outside," he said when they had exhausted themselves and leaned, panting, against the door. Smoke stung her eyes and nose and made breathing difficult. By now some of the horses had left their stalls and milled, anxious and whinnying, in the aisle, as the flames popped and crackled behind them.

"We're trapped," she said. Someone—Von King?—had set this fire and barricaded them inside, with no way out.

Chris squinted into the smoke and the mass of milling animals. There had to be another way out. He tried his radio again, but raised nothing but static. His gaze shifted upward. "The loft," he said. "Is there an opening there? We could jump."

Willow nodded, and stumbled toward the ladder to the hayloft. He followed, but before they reached it they saw the whole area was engulfed in flames. The heat, and a choking cloud of smoke, drove them back.

One of the horses began kicking violently at the side of the stall. "They're terrified," Willow said. Tears streaked her face, though Chris couldn't tell if she was crying from her own terror or from the stinging smoke.

"Wet down some horse blankets," he said. The thick wet wool would provide a little protection from the heat and flames, and buy them a few more precious minutes. He went in search of tools, and found a pitchfork and a shovel. He used them to batter at the main door, but it was made of heavy wood and refused to give way. He tried shoving at it with his body, throwing himself at it, but it resisted, as if something heavy blocked it on the other side. He moved down the wall ten feet and began striking there.

Willow joined him, battering at the wood with a shovel. The sound of the fire increased, flames crackling, wood popping, horses screaming and rafters groaning. It was very hard to breathe now, and he fought back panic at the thought of burning to death in here.

Then the wood splintered. Willow cried out and they attacked the weakened boards with more fury, until they gave way. Fresh air rushed to them. He forced his way out and pulled her after him.

Willow stumbled toward the front of the barn. "If we can get the main door open, we can save the horses," she cried.

He spotted the problem as soon as they reached the door—an iron bar wedged in the track the doors needed to slide in. "Willow, wait!" he shouted, intending to tell her he needed to remove the bar first.

A gunshot sounded, loud and distinctive. Willow screamed and dropped to her knees in front of the door.

Chris's vision blurred, even as he dove for cover, automatically reaching for his gun. He blinked to clear his eyes, and forced himself to look, not at Willow's crumpled figure, but in the direction the shots had come from. A shadow moved behind a woodpile opposite the barn.

"Von!" Chris shouted, and fired at the shadow.

"Don't worry, you're next," Von called. He raised a rifle to his shoulder, a weapon with a much greater range than Chris's pistol. Chris fired, anyway, his bullet striking a log in front of Von, sending wood chips flying. It was enough to throw off the other man's aim, the bullet harmlessly hitting the side of the burning barn.

Chris risked a glance at Willow. She lay so still. Too still.

Von raised the rifle again. "Why did you do it?" Chris called. If he could get Von talking, he could buy time. How long before the sheriff was due to arrive at the ranch?

Von lowered the weapon. "Why do you think? For the money."

"The money you thought Sam had hidden?"

"That. And the money Allerton promised me."

So Trey had been right that Von would try to throw the blame on him. "Allerton promised you money?"

"Money he never paid me. But don't worry, he's next."

"Von, we can talk about this," Chris said.

"I'm done talking."

Willow moaned and both men turned to look at her. She tried to sit up, and her lips moved, but Chris couldn't make out what she was saying. All that mattered was that she was alive.

Von raised his rifle again, aiming not for Chris, but for Willow. Chris stood, deliberately making himself a target. "Von!" he shouted, and when the other man turned his head, Chris fired.

Von dropped the rifle and slumped forward.

"Hold your fire!" someone shouted, and Travis stepped from the shadows in the rocks above and behind Von, a rifle cradled in his arms. "You're a good shot," he said to Chris. "But you didn't have the range with that pistol."

Chris ran to Willow. She tried to stand, but he pushed her back down. Blood ran from a wound in her shoulder. "The horses," she said.

Gage jogged up. "Ambulance and a fire crew are on the way," he said.

Travis joined them. "Get that bar out of the way," he said, indicating the length of metal that was blocking the door. "We have to get these doors open. Chris, get Willow out of the way."

Chris scooped up Willow and carried her away from the barn and the flames. Travis and Gage shoved the doors open and began driving out the horses, shouting and slapping at their rumps, and even prodding at them with the pitchfork to get them to move.

The ambulance arrived, followed by two fire trucks. Others arrived, too—neighbors with horse trailers, and at least one veterinarian, who loaded two animals who had been singed by the blaze and took them away for care.

The ambulance took Willow away and Chris found Travis and Gage among the crowd. "Why did you two show up so early this morning?" he asked.

"Only half an hour early," Gage said. He jerked his thumb toward Travis. "He wanted more time to go over everything before we headed out to arrest Von."

"I'm more than grateful you like to be thorough," Chris said.

Travis nodded, then turned to Gage. "You need to take my weapon," he said, and unfastened his holster. "Chris's, too. As of right now, we're both on mandatory leave while our use of force is investigated. I'm putting you in charge until I'm back on duty."

Gage took their guns. "You'll each need to come by the station and give a statement," he said. "But before then, I need some directions to this cabin where you think Von was hiding. I want to send a couple of deputies up there to collect evidence."

It was late afternoon before Chris made it to the hospital. Willow was out of surgery, awake, but a little groggy. Chris was startled to find his father seated in a chair beside the bed. Ted stood as Chris entered the room. "Willow has been telling me what happened," he said. "Are you all right, son?"

His father's gaze flitted over him, and for the first time Chris realized his hands and clothes were streaked with soot and he reeked of smoke. "I'm okay," he said. "What are you doing here, Dad?"

"I came to give Willow some good news." He looked at her.

Willow nodded. "Tell him."

Ted turned back to Chris. "A judge has ruled Darla's will is invalid. I hired an investigator in Albuquerque who tracked down the witnesses on that document. They both stated they witnessed that will in 2016, not 2019. Darla had carefully changed the date so that it appeared to have been executed after the will I drew up for Sam."

"Your father thinks one of the witnesses called Darla on Tuesday to let her know what was going on and that's the reason she and Emmet left so suddenly," Willow said.

"That is good news." Chris moved to the other side of the bed. "How are you feeling?"

"I'm going to be okay, thanks to you." She squeezed his hand weakly.

Ted stood, as if to leave, but just then a nurse came in. "I need to check the wound, if you would give us a moment, gentlemen," she said.

Ted and Chris moved into the hall. Ted looked at his son as if he had never seen him before. "Willow told me you saved her life," he said. "You killed Von King."

"The sheriff killed Von," Chris said. "I never could have made the shot with my pistol."

"You'd never be faced with something like that working for the state," Ted said.

"Dad..."

"I'm not saying I think that's what you should be doing," Ted said. "I may have believed that before, but I've been thinking a lot about what you said the other night, and about what happened today." He touched Chris's arm. "I don't understand what draws you to this work, but I'm impressed by your dedication. I know you resent the way you think I've tried to run your life, and maybe some of that resentment is justified. When you have children of your own you'll understand this instinct to keep your children safe. So I hope you'll forgive me for my ham-handed attempts to do that."

"I'm not a child for you to protect any longer," Chris said.

"You'll always be my child, but I understand what you're saying. And I didn't raise you to be foolhardy or take unnecessary risks, so there's some comfort in that." He glanced toward the closed door of Willow's hospital room. "Besides, I think now you might have another reason to be careful."

Chris nodded, but said nothing.

"I'll leave you with her," Ted said. "But call if you need anything, okay?"

"Okay, Dad. And...thanks." For helping Willow. For trying to understand his son's choices. For so much Chris couldn't put into words.

Ted clapped him on the shoulder, then left. The nurse emerged from the room and slipped down the corridor, and Chris went back inside, to the woman who did indeed make him want to be more careful. And more bold.

Epilogue

Two months after she was discharged from the hospital, Willow sat in Ted's office, signing the papers to lease the Double R Ranch to Micah Carstairs, son of her father's former friend Bud. She shook hands with the young rancher once the paperwork was done. "I know you'll do a great job with the place," she said.

Micah nodded. "Thanks for giving me the chance. Dad's excited about seeing the place again. He says it's been too long."

She was still humming with happiness at the rightness of that moment when she met Chris for lunch afterward. "How did it go?" he asked, taking her arm and walking with her toward a booth near the back of the café.

"It went great. I have to think Dad would be pleased. Micah is going to do a much better job with the place than I would have."

"Then I'm happy for you," he said, though she thought his smile didn't reach quite to his eyes.

"Is something wrong?" she asked. "What did you do this morning?"

"The DA had Courtney Baker in for questioning again today," he said. "She stands by her statement that Trey Allerton was with her the morning your father was killed."

"So Von was solely responsible for killing my father."

"We'll never know exactly what happened, but we found one of Von's drinking buddies who confirmed that Von had been talking about getting hold of Sam's hidden riches. After your father fired him, he must have decided to get what he wanted once and for all. We think he took the watch the same way he took the other things he stole—he saw it and wanted it, so he took it. But he threw it away after he realized it would tie him to the crime. Same with the ATV. He took it on impulse, then realized he couldn't keep it. Or maybe he thought ditching it would delay anyone finding Sam's body until he could establish an alibi."

"I hate I lost Dad that way," she said. "But I hope he'd be happy with me leasing the place to Micah. Bud Carstairs and Dad were friends for a long time. It feels good having the families connected again."

He laced his hands with hers. "Can you tell me yet what you've decided to do?"

He had asked her this question only once before. She had told him she had plans, but they weren't firm enough for her to share them. She admired his patience, since she had kept him waiting for weeks. "I'm happy to tell you," she said. She let the silence build, the tension growing, then she laughed. "I'm the new social studies teacher at the high school."

"You're going to teach high school?"

"Yes, and I can't wait. I'm really excited about it."

"It's very different from a full professorship at an eastern university. They didn't mind that you were overqualified?"

"I had to convince them that I didn't see this as a

demotion. I'm ready for different. And teaching high school students will be a great challenge for me."

"You'll have to find a new place to live."

"Yes," she said. "And that's going to be a problem. Apparently, there's a shortage of rentals in the area."

He looked down at the table, avoiding her eyes. "I have an idea."

"Oh?"

He shoved out of the booth. "This isn't how I planned to do this," he said.

"To do what?"

He dug into his pocket and pulled out a small box. "I've been carrying this around for a couple of weeks, searching for the right time. I wanted the moment to be special."

"Oh, Chris." She covered both his hands with hers. "It will be special because it's you."

He dropped to one knee beside her. "Willow Russell, will you marry me?"

She was dimly aware of murmurs of conversation around them, and of several people pulling out cell phones to record the moment. She forced her mind away from all of that and stared at the man in beside her. "Oh, Chris."

"Please say yes," he whispered.

"Yes!" She threw her arms around him, then pulled him to his feet. The crowd that had gathered around them broke into applause. He slipped the ring on her finger, then they kissed. "To think when I came home to the ranch, I thought it was the worst thing that could happen," she said. "I never would have believed it could lead to the best."

"You're the best," he said, and kissed her again.

Whatever happened to them now, they would face it together, and look forward to building something completely new.

* * * * *

LET'S TALK
Romance

JOIN US ON SOCIAL MEDIA!

Stay up to date with our latest releases, author news and gossip, special offers and discounts, and all the behind-the-scenes action from Mills & Boon...

millsandboon

millsandboonuk

millsandboon

It might just be true love...